THE HERO,
THE PROTECTOR,
THE HEALER,
AND
THE LOVER

CAROL BRANNIN

ISBN 978-1-0980-1892-4 (paperback)
ISBN 978-1-0980-1894-8 (hardcover)
ISBN 978-1-0980-1893-1 (digital)

Christian Faith Publishing, Inc.
832 Park Avenue
Meadville, PA 16335
www.christianfaithpublishing.com

Printed in the United States of America

DEDICATION

Dale H. Hunter
August 15, 1925–December 8, 2019

This book is dedicated to my dear friend, Dale Hunter. He is ninety-four years old and a World War II Army veteran. Dale was only a boy of eighteen when he was sent to Europe to fight in 1943. He would return home as a man and the recipient of a Purple Heart. He was wounded in the leg. He is also the recipient of France's highest honor which was presented to him in person in 2015.

It is ironic, but I began writing this book when Dale was in the hospital recovering from a broken leg a few months ago. Many times, I have almost stopped writing, but he has encouraged me to finish, and I have done so. I thank him for his patience and believing in me during what became a very emotional journey into the past.

Dale has dedicated his life to service and volunteer work. He taught many young men and women to fly and some were to follow with a career in aviation. He also taught safe boating classes for many years. Dale is an accomplished speaker and teacher. He has helped me tremendously during the thirteen years that we have been friends.

Also, Dale was recently chosen as one of the top 200 veterans in Illinois, and he was honored at an event in Chicago in December 2018. His service during World War II is documented in the Illinois Veterans History Project which can be viewed on YouTube.

ADDITIONAL DEDICATIONS

Gene (July 5, 1946–August 1, 1987)

Mike (August 17, 1946–May 13, 2011)

Without the inspiration, friendship, love, and memories of these two wonderful men, this book would not have been possible. Their hearts, souls, and kindness live within the pages.

Julie (Carol's daughter who gave technical support as well as love and understanding)

Chloe (Carol's granddaughter, the sweetest, kindest little girl in the world)

Linda Eaton (Carol's good friend and research assistant who gave encouragement as well as confidence during a difficult and emotional journey)

Carol's grandmother, who loved her from the beginning, and her mother (February 8, 1915–July 29, 1985), who learned to love her.

AUTHOR'S NOTE

Although this novel is fiction, 80 percent of it is based on actual events and happenings. There are some composite characters. The personalities and hearts of the main characters are true, whereas the events in their lives are not completely true. The resemblance to anyone dead or alive is coincidental. While many places, cities, names, and dates have been changed, some have not.

As you read this book, it is my sincere hope that you develop a love and understanding of *The Hero, the Protector, the Healer, and the Lover* because the many parts of their stories that are true deserve to be understood. Everyone will have a favorite character and the one they will be anxious to read about in the following chapters. Of course, my favorite is *the hero*.

It was an emotional journey to write this book. John's character, as *the lover*, was the most difficult to describe and establish in a clear, resolute manner because of his unpredictable personality. He was somewhat of a chameleon and complicated as well as deeply troubled, but what he did for his friends as well as what they did for him cannot be challenged. I hope I have done him justice.

This is a tragic epic love story, and the love and tragedies are true. Even though it is heartbreaking and at times devastating, it is also very tender and sensitive. I hope you love the main characters as I do. They lived in a different time than the world of today, and their dreams, personalities, and lifestyles exhibit the era in which they lived.

Carol Brannin
Kansas City, Kansas
Chicago, Illinois
Springfield, Illinois
May 2019

HOW THE BOOK GOT ITS NAME

Many years ago, as Gene, Mike, Carol, and John were walking along Lake Michigan in Chicago on a windy autumn day, there was a conversation between them that would never be forgotten by Carol. Although her wonderful friends, whom she had loved so much, are all gone now and all that is left of them are her treasured memories, this is that conversation:

"Someday, in the distant future, you are going to write a book about us, aren't you, Carol?" asked Gene.

"Possibly. Do you think I should?" asked Carol.

"I'm not sure, but I think you have it in you, and you are certainly capable of it," Gene paused. "But if you do, make us better than we were. I haven't been a very good man. I've messed up too much in my life."

"I don't agree with that. I think you are the best, kindest man I have ever known, but how do you want me to portray you?" asked Carol.

"As someone who helps people and does good deeds. Someone who has overcome adversity and will triumph and shine in the face of it. I don't want to be remembered as just a guy who goes to work every day and makes money, but make me a better man than I have been," said Gene.

"I suppose I could do that," said Carol. "And you, Mike, how do you want to be remembered?"

"I should have done more for disabled and homeless veterans and for you three. You are my best friends, and I should have done more to help all of you and taken better care of you. With all my money, I could have done almost anything," said Mike.

"That shouldn't be too difficult," said Carol. "That leaves you, John. What shall I write about you?"

"Make me happy, always smiling, and someone whom everyone will love, and portray me as loving everyone," said John. "I haven't always been very happy, and I always wanted to be dignified and charismatic. Describe me that way too, because I've never quite made it."

"That would work," said Carol. "You guys are good. Maybe you should write the book instead of me."

"No. It has to be you. You're the only one who can do it," said Gene. "You will know what to write and what to keep secret. You can write about bad things that have happened to us, but you will know when to stop. You won't cross the line. The book will be somewhat sad. But some truths can't be told, and those are the really bad things. You know what I mean, don't you, Carol? You are the only one who knows."

"I know exactly what you mean. It's what won't be told that is the really sad part," said Carol as she spoke to Gene in the kind, understanding voice that he had grown to love over the years. Gene and Carol hugged one another tightly. They knew the secrets they shared were safe forever.

"But what about me? How should I portray myself?" asked Carol.

"You taught me how to overcome many problems, both physical and mental," said Gene. "And you taught me how to handle abuse and bullying since I was eight years old."

"When I came home from Vietnam, you kept me from going down the wrong path, or I suppose I should say, going off the deep end," said Mike. "And you didn't even realize you were doing it."

"You taught me how to write with my left hand and how to speak clearly and remember words that were hard for me after the accident, and you made my head stop hurting," said John.

"You taught Terry to communicate, Cathy to eat, Rodger to be sober and drug-free, Nathan to want to live, Alan to love and be kind, and Ryan to forgive," said Gene. "It was you who did all that, not us."

"Don't forget that I wanted to give my heart to Gene. I really was serious about that," said John. "And also, I promised Gene that I would comb his hair when he dies so it won't look bad when he is in his casket. Can you remember all this?"

"I'll always remember everything," said Carol. "Just as I remember my little white toy kitten that Gene won for me so long ago at Fairyland Park, my blue bag that I always carried because I travel light and it was like an old friend, that Mike can never stand it when someone makes me cry, and my favorite spot nestled in the bend of Gene's arm with my head resting gently on his chest.

Thus the name of the book was born long ago as four friends walked along the shore of Lake Michigan. They each chose their own title and how they wished to be remembered, *The Hero, the Protector, the Healer, and the Lover.*

CONTENTS

INTRODUCTION

Several things happened during the childhoods and young lifetimes of the four friends Gene, Mike, Carol, and John from 1954 through 1987. They were all born in 1946. The first two to meet were Gene and Carol when they were eight. Carol and Mike met when they were twelve. John became part of their group at graduation rehearsal in 1964 when they were seventeen and eighteen.

When Gene was only eight, he was very sick and needed to have surgery. A group of firemen from a firehouse near his home would let him sit in the fire truck, have lunch with them, and watch them play basketball. They sent him on a trip to see old fire trucks in a museum. It didn't have a name then; now what they did for him would be called make-a-wish.

They tried to help fellow students being bullied as well as the bully. This is an honorable thing to do now, but not so much so in the 1960s. Carol and Mike were somewhat rebellious and thought school rules were to be challenged, and they were penalized for this, whereas Gene did many of the same things they did, but he followed the rules. Thus he graduated with honors and awards and no marks against him. Carol and Mike would learn a lot from Gene in their lives.

Gene, Mike, Carol, and John attended prom together in 1964. The prom they attended that year was not like the regular prom. Although it didn't have a name then, now it would be called an alternative prom. Gene and Carol were crowned prom king and queen, and Carol gave her crown to Bonnie, whom she had also given a dress and jewelry to wear that day in addition to fixing her hair, and then Bonnie got to dance with Gene, and she never stopped smiling.

When Mike returned home from Vietnam, he asked Gene and Carol to bring him a T-shirt and jeans to the airport so he could change from his uniform because people were screaming protests at the soldiers and throwing rocks and rotten food at them. There were no parades or cheers for the returning Vietnam veterans, even those who had been wounded.

Mike's older brother, Ryan, died when he was twenty-eight from a cancer that at the time was thought to be fatal and affected the gay community; later this would be known as AIDS.

There was severe abuse in the workplace of those who were handicapped, and other employees were not allowed to help them or stop the abuse. Today, because of laws that have been passed to protect them, this would not happen.

They spent their childhood and grew to adulthood in a world much different than the world we live in today. They all would have fit better and been happier and more content in today's world.

There were many who could never understand the close, ever-lasting relationships between the pretty, kind girl with the long red hair and the three handsome, gentle young men. It was hard to comprehend how four people could love one another so much. Mike's mother, Colleen, had understood them from the very beginning, but it took his father, Alan, much longer; but when he came around, what he did for them was incredible. They didn't pass judgment on the four friends. They loved, cared for, and helped each one individually.

Gene's parents, Carol's parents, and John's mother did not understand the scenario of three guys and one girl even though they loved them all very much. In the beginning, it was not the life Stella, Carol's mother, would have chosen for her daughter, but she realized early in their relationships that it was destined to be.

When John was asked to join them at graduation rehearsal, the dynamics of the group changed, and they all became determined to help John and make his life better. They were successful, but there was a price to pay, and it may have involved destroying the eternal happiness of at least one, and possibly more, of the group.

They were never concerned about themselves. Their relationship with John was totally unselfish, and they all loved him unconditionally. They were all supportive and protective of one another, especially of John in the beginning.

At the time they moved into the house on Lansing Street, it seemed to them to be the right thing to do. When they put their lives and jobs on hold to care for John after the horrific accident and later for Gene after his strokes, it also seemed to be the right thing to do. They never tried to impress or please others. They just wanted the four of them to be together as long as possible so they could be there for and help one another.

It was probably Mike's dad, Alan, who actually understood and loved them the most. He dedicated his life to helping John with operations, medical expenses, his job, his family, and anything else he could. Although somewhat hesitantly at first, John accepted his help and thrived on it. John needed what Alan had to give, and he was always grateful. Alan's main goal in later years was to be there for John whenever he was needed. John was quiet and a little shy, but his smile would melt your heart, and this was something Alan had missed from his own children. Alan enjoyed being needed.

Although Alan and Mike had their differences, if it wasn't for Mike's friendly, outgoing nature, the other three would not be with them. Mike was frequently a go-between, but Alan respected his opinions and suggestions. In the end, they were able to put their differences aside and accept one another's flaws.

Gene evoked great admiration from Alan. He didn't fight the system as Mike and Carol did. He was honest and genuinely good and kind to everyone. It was Gene who Alan wished he could have been more like. Gene was strong and a born leader, but when he desperately needed Alan's help as well as that of his other three friends; they were all there for him without question.

No words could describe Alan's feelings for Carol. She had stolen his heart the first time he met her when she was twelve. He admired the way she stood by and helped her friends through so much. She was vulnerable, sweet, kind, and grateful, always so grateful, and appreciative for all he did for them.

But what he loved best about her was that she was always first to answer or respond to questions. She never hesitated with her comments or opinions. She was smart and not the least bit shy.

Gene was the hero, Mike was the protector, Carol was the healer, and John was the lover, possessing so much love in his heart that there was enough love for everyone.

Avalon Manor

In the fall of 1958, Carol was twelve and her cousin Ethan was fourteen. It had been a warm fall, and they were still riding their bikes into early December. They were poor kids, and their junky bicycles were their main source of entertainment as well as transportation.

When their parents were working, Carol and Ethan stayed with their grandmother. She had raised seventeen children, and although she loved Carol and Ethan, their general whereabouts weren't of primary concern to her. They would leave early in the morning on their bicycles and not return until dark.

They would go to different schools and parks and play ball, they would go to the library, and sometimes they would go to the restaurant on Minnesota Avenue where Carol's mother worked. She would fix a corned beef sandwich for them, served with a dill pickle. If they had change in their pockets, they would see an afternoon movie at the Jayhawk theater or go roller-skating at the rink on Central Avenue or go to the dime store.

But when it got close to suppertime, they always did one thing before they went back to Grandma's house. They would ride their bikes through Avalon Manor and look at the nice, pretty homes and the people who lived there. The area was noted for homes that were beautifully decorated at Christmas. The decorations were always elaborate and tasteful.

Something that fascinated Carol more than Ethan were the beautiful chandeliers and the lovely tables and the happy families sitting around the tables having dinner. It just made Ethan hungry seeing all the food, but Carol liked seeing the families eating together. They never stopped or stared long because they didn't want to be noticed. There was one large three-story gray stone house that Carol was particularly drawn to. The curtains were always open wide in the dining room. The dad was at the head of the table. He had red hair, just like Carol's, as did two boys and a girl. The mother at the other end of the table had curly, blond hair, and she was very pretty. There was also a small blond boy.

As they passed the house one fateful night, there were several children in the driveway that circled around the side of the house. Two little girls walked by them with gingerbread cookies.

Carol asked one of the girls, "Are they having a party?"

"No, Mrs. McVary just decorated for Christmas, and she is giving cookies and hot chocolate to the neighborhood kids, and Santa is there, and he gave us a present. This is what he gave to me." The little girl held up a baby doll.

"Come on, Carol. We need to go home. It's getting late," said Ethan.

"Let's go see her decorations," said Carol as she threw her junky bike behind a bush.

"Look at our clothes. She'll know we are not neighborhood kids," said Ethan.

But it was too late. A handsome red-haired boy about her age was picking Carol's bike up out of the bushes.

"Mom has some great cookies. We don't want to leave your bike here. It might get stolen. My name is Mike. What's your name?"

"My name is Carol, and this is my cousin, Ethan."

Ethan waved from a distance. He was shy; Carol was not.

"Carol, that's a pretty name. I like that name, Carol, and you have the same color hair as mine," Mike smiled.

As they walked down the driveway, they saw a fireplace against the back wall with Santa and his sleigh and reindeer above. There was a manger and snowmen and a gigantic Christmas tree with elegantly wrapped presents under it. And the beautiful blond lady was there in a red dress with white fir trim. The small blond boy was standing beside her.

Mike was bold and eager to make introductions. "This is my mother, Mrs. McVary, and my little brother, Danny. Mom, these are my new friends, Carol and Ethan." They had only met a few minutes ago, and he already referred to them as friends.

Mrs. McVary graciously put her arms around both Carol and Ethan.

Danny was studying them both and then said, "Carol, you are really pretty, and, Ethan, you have blond hair like me and my mom."

They sat down to eat their cookies and drink their hot chocolate. It was getting dark, but the Christmas lights made it bright and beautiful. The neighborhood kids had all left by now. Then Santa appeared with another boy and girl. Again, Mike was quick to introduce them.

"That's my dad and Ryan and Cathy. These are my friends, Carol and Ethan."

"Well, let me see what's in my bag. If I give you each a present, will you put it under your tree and not open it until Christmas?" asked Santa.

Then Ethan, who had hardly said a word, spoke up, "We won't have a tree this year, probably no presents either."

Carol tried to think of something to cover up what Ethan had just said, but she couldn't. This was actually more embarrassing to her than Ethan eating twelve gingerbread cookies.

"We have some other trees. We will give you one." Mike's voice was very sincere, and as Carol and Mike's eyes met, she suddenly realized he was trying to protect her. No one had ever done anything like that for her before.

Mrs. McVary was trying to come up with the right words. She had known from the beginning when she saw their bikes and clothing that they weren't from the neighborhood. But Santa saved her.

He opened his bag of presents. "I need to know your ages so I can give you an appropriate gift."

Ethan answered, "I'm fourteen, and Carol is twelve."

Cathy responded quickly, "I'm fourteen too, like you, Ethan, and Mike is twelve, just like Carol. Ryan is sixteen, and Danny is ten."

Santa handed Ethan a nicely wrapped present, as he did Carol. "Thanks," said Ethan.

"Thank you, but you really didn't have to give us a present. The cookies and hot chocolate were enough."

Mrs. McVary put her arms around the pretty young girl who seemed mature beyond her years. "You know, it's getting late and it is almost dark. Why don't I put your bikes in the van, and I'll take you home," said Mrs. McVary.

"We'll be all right. It's not far," said Carol.

"Where do you live?" asked Mike.

"We're staying at our grandma's house," answered Carol.

"Grandma lives on South Baltimore. I live in Armourdale, but I'm staying at Grandma's too. My mom is working late at the dime store." Ethan had suddenly found his voice.

"That's too far. I'm taking you two home," said Mrs. McVary.

"Can we go too?" asked Cathy and Danny together.

"Danny, you need to get ready for bed, and, Cathy, I would appreciate it if you would help him," said Mrs. McVary.

"He doesn't need my help, Mom. He's ten," said Cathy.

"Please, Cathy," said Mrs. McVary.

Cathy smiled, "All right."

Mike put the bikes in the van. He sat in the front seat with his mom, and Carol and Ethan sat in the middle seat. Mike turned around and asked Carol, "Where do you live?"

"I live out by West Junior High," said Carol.

"That's where I go to school," said Mike enthusiastically. "I'm in the seventh grade."

"I am too," said Carol.

Mike was thrilled. "Isn't that cool, Mom? Same grade, same school."

"That's great," said Mrs. McVary.

Mike helped them get their bikes and presents to the door.

Carol went back to the car to thank Mrs. McVary. "Thanks for everything. You have been very kind to us."

"You will have to come back again soon," said Mrs. McVary.

Mike smiled and waved as they drove away.

Although they did not realize it at that time, Carol and Mike had begun a journey that would take them to many places together and through many years. They were to touch one another's life in a very special way and also the lives of many others.

THE LIBRARY

After meeting Carol, Mike couldn't wait to look her up at school. They didn't have any classes together, but he found her in the cafeteria eating lunch alone. Carol was never interested in the large groups of girls who formed cliques and were snobbish.

"Mind if I join you?" asked Mike.

"Sure, I would love your company. I don't really like to eat alone, but I can't stand some of those girls. All they do is talk about and make fun of other girls. That's not my character," Carol said as she thought how handsome Mike was and how kindly he spoke to her.

"I can tell you are not like them." Mike blushed slightly. "I mean, I think you are nice."

"Thank you. I think you are nice too," said Carol.

Mike and Carol were only twelve, but they were mature for their age, not only in appearance but in the manner in which they spoke and were able to convey their feelings and opinions.

"Would you and Ethan come to my house Saturday? My family would like to see you again. Come about ten o'clock. Mom would like for you to stay for lunch," said Mike.

"We'll be there. Thanks for asking us," said Carol.

They were excited about Saturday. It was still warm enough to ride their bikes. When Carol met Ethan at their grandmother's house that morning, he had on a nice red sweater, and he had combed his hair.

"You look nice today, Ethan," said Carol.

"You don't look so bad yourself," said Ethan.

Carol had on light-blue jeans and a pink sweater.

They arrived promptly at ten o'clock as Mike had requested. Mike came to the door before they even knocked. Danny, Cathy, and Ryan were with him. Mrs. McVary waved to them from the kitchen. The smell of freshly baked cookies filled the house. Carol saw the look on Ethan's face. He was hungry, but he was always hungry.

Mike, Ryan, Cathy, and Danny gave Carol and Ethan a tour of the house, and they even showed them the pool and grotto.

"When it's summer, you will both have to come and swim with us," said Cathy.

"That would be great. I love to swim," said Carol.

"I do too," said Ethan. "But I'm not as good as Carol. She can swim all the way across the lake really fast."

As they were walking toward the kitchen, Carol couldn't help but notice a beautiful library filled with books on all four walls from the floor to the ceiling. There was even a library ladder. Carol went into the room and took a book from a lower shelf. She sat down on the floor and started reading it.

A tall, red-haired man came into the library. She immediately recognized him as Santa from the party and knew it was Mr. McVary. She quickly got up and put the book back on the shelf.

"I'm sorry. I should have asked permission. Please forgive me," said Carol sincerely.

"Well, it's the pretty young lady from the Christmas party. Do you like to read?" asked Mr. McVary.

"Oh yes, very much so. Your books are so nice, and this is such a pretty library," said Carol.

"My children have a lot of books upstairs that might be more to your liking," said Mr. McVary.

"I've read all the children's books. I like to read books like yours. If you would allow me to borrow one, I'll bring it back as soon as I'm finished." Carol's eyes were filled with the wonder of a child, but he didn't feel like he was talking to a child.

"Go right ahead and pick one. I would be happy to see someone read them," said Mr. McVary.

Carol picked the book on the end of the lowest shelf near the door. "I'll read this one first."

He glanced at the title. "Are you sure you'll like that book?"

"I like all books. I want to be smart someday, and if I read all your books, I should be really smart. Besides, by taking them in order, I can keep track of what I have read," said Carol.

"My dear girl, something tells me you are already smart," said Mr. McVary.

At that moment, Ryan, the oldest son, came to the door. "Carol, Mother has lunch ready. Would you join us?"

As Carol left the library, she said, "Thank you, Mr. McVary. I'll return your book soon." She smiled slightly, and so did Santa.

As they walked to the kitchen, Ryan said, "Dad must really like you. He doesn't usually talk to our friends, or even to us for that matter."

"He seems very nice," said Carol.

"Mom has quite a feast prepared," said Ryan.

And indeed she did. Ethan was already there, and Cathy had chosen a seat for him right next to her. Mike stood up and pulled out a chair for Carol next to his seat. Carol just hoped Ethan wouldn't eat too much and embarrass them both, but he didn't. He was fascinated with Cathy, and he was actually acting like a gentleman.

A few days later, Mr. McVary picked up a bulletin from the school Mike and Carol attended. It listed students on the straight A honor roll. Mike McVary was listed first, and right below him was Carol Sullivan.

Over the next six years, Carol would read every book in Mr. McVary's library. Not one book was returned with a torn cover or stained. Once he asked her about her love of books. She told him that since she was small, she would go to the downtown library with Ethan in the summer to get cool and in the winter to get warm, and that was how she started reading.

He knew then that Mike had found a very good friend in Carol but never could he have imagined where the path would lead them and how much happiness and sorrow they would share along the way.

Carol had opened her present from the Christmas party the previous week even though it said "Don't open until Christmas." No one had ever given her a present before except her mom and dad. It was a white-and-gold jewelry box, and it was musical. It was the most beautiful thing she had ever seen. She had no jewelry, but that didn't matter because maybe someday she would. Carol would keep the jewelry box forever.

STELLA AND COLLEEN

Carol's mother, Stella, worked during the lunch hour at a small Jewish restaurant on Minnesota Avenue in the downtown area of Kansas City, Kansas. One day Colleen McVary, Mike's mother, went there for lunch with a group of her friends. They sat in Stella's section. Stella was a good waitress—polite, efficient, and friendly.

Stella was accustomed to getting big tips from the many Jewish men who ate lunch at the restaurant because of her dark hair, striking features, and friendly personality, but she wasn't used to getting big tips from the ladies. Colleen left a very big tip that day. Stella hadn't seen the tip on the table yet when Colleen stopped and talked to her as they were leaving.

"You have a daughter named Carol, don't you?" asked Colleen.

"Why yes, I do. How do you know her?" asked Stella.

"She is a friend of my son, Mike. She is a remarkable girl. I would like to know what your secret is to raising such an engaging and smart young woman," said Colleen.

"Carol is a very independent and strong-willed girl. I think she was born that way. I don't know where she gets it. Neither her dad nor I were particularly smart especially in school," said Stella.

"She talks so nice to everyone. We certainly enjoy her company. She is a delight, and I think she is really good for Mike," said Colleen. "You will have to come to my house for coffee someday. I would love to get to know you better."

"I would love to. Let me know when you would like for me to come," said Stella.

After Colleen left the restaurant, Stella found a fifty-dollar tip on the table.

This was the beginning of a friendship between the two women that would last for many years. Neither lady had a husband who liked to do things with her. The men didn't like to travel or go to the movies or the theater or shop. Stella and Colleen did all these things together. They made an interesting as well as intriguing pair—Stella with her straight dark hair and dark eyes, and Colleen with her curly blond hair and blue eyes.

CHAPTER

THE GROTTO

The summer of 1961 was the summer of love and happiness. Carol and Mike were fifteen. Cathy and Ethan were seventeen. It was a hot summer, and the McVary pool and grotto were the places to be.

Cathy and Ethan would fall in love that summer, and they would relinquish their virginity. Ethan told Carol with her promise that she would never tell anyone. She never did.

Carol and Mike had spent a lot of time together in junior high. Most of their so-called dates consisted of sock hops, a few parties, movies, and roller-skating. Mike was cute and really nice to her, and Carol liked that very much. He often said he fell in love with her the first time he saw her riding the broken-down bicycle.

Ryan was nineteen, and for no apparent reason, he had decided to postpone going to college for a year. He wanted to work a year and make a little money of his own. Mr. and Mrs. McVary thought this was a wise decision on Ryan's part. He had been a good student and had lettered in football and baseball. Ryan had a new friend, Richard Noland, who had just moved into the neighborhood. Richard, who was seventeen, and Ryan hung out around the pool that summer, especially when Carol was there.

Carol was fifteen but could easily have passed for seventeen. Mike had grown a lot that summer. He was already almost six feet tall, and before he stopped growing, he would be six feet four.

Richard had blond hair and blue eyes. He was tall and very muscular. Carol saw him watching her as she walked to the end of the diving board. One day she went into the grotto to cool off, and Richard followed her. They talked for a while, and suddenly, out of nowhere, he kissed her. She quickly left the grotto.

A little later, Ryan had a question for Mike. "Do you consider Carol your girlfriend? Richard wants to know."

Ryan had never had a girlfriend, and Mike didn't want to make him feel bad. Mike said, "We are really just good friends. We have been to a few things together and to a couple of birthday parties and movies, but that's all. We are too young."

"So you don't care if he asks her out?" asked Ryan.

Mike shrugged his shoulders. "I guess not."

That weekend Richard asked Carol to go to the movies with him. Before she gave him an answer, she went to see Mike and asked him, "Richard asked me out. Should I go?"

"That's up to you. We've only been out a few times. It's not like we are going together," said Mike.

Carol was a little hurt, and Mike felt bad about it. "All right, I guess I'll go out with him. I just thought we liked one another."

"We do, but I can't even drive yet," said Mike.

This was the first and only time that Mike would ever hurt Carol's feelings. One of Mike's main goals in life was to protect Carol, and he would do so to the best of his ability for many years to come.

And so as the summer progressed, Carol Sullivan and Richard Noland went on their first date. It was popular that year for younger girls to date older boys, much to the senior girls' disappointment. Carol and Richard were a striking couple, and everyone loved them.

GOOD TEACHERS AND ROLE MODELS

Carol, Gene, and Mike actually met for the first time together in their sophomore geometry class. They had all just turned fifteen. Carol and Mike were already friends. Gene and Mike had met at football practice. Carol and Gene had met when they were eight, and although they both remembered that meeting, it was a long time ago. Carol looked older than fifteen. Gene and Mike had not grown to their full heights of six feet five and six feet four yet, and they were both a little skinny, and the muscular arms and legs and athletic builds they would eventually have had not yet developed.

Richard Noland was a senior and on the football team. He was six feet six tall and extremely muscular. He was also a swimmer like Carol and Mike. But his greatest pride that year was that he was Carol's boyfriend. Richard was very handsome, and he was popular and friendly.

Mike knew Richard because they were neighbors, but Gene first saw Richard as he walked Carol to her geometry class. Gene remembered thinking how great it would be to have a pretty, smart, nice girlfriend like Carol, and he wondered if he would ever be as tall and muscular as Richard.

It was the day of the first geometry test of the year, and Gene and Mike had football practice that morning. In practice, Gene had an accident and broke his glasses. In geometry, Carol sat next to the back seat in the last row by the windows, and Gene sat behind her.

Mike sat next to Carol. Carol was already in her seat when Gene and Mike entered the classroom.

"The test is on the board. Are you going to be able to see it?" asked Mike.

"No, I can't see the board. I'll probably fail it," said Gene.

Gene had a cut over his eye. "Gene, that's a bad cut. Are you going to be all right?" asked Carol in a very concerned and kind voice.

"I fell in football practice this morning and broke my glasses. I can't see the board," said Gene.

As Gene sat down, sophomore bullies Barbara, Rex, Janelle, and Norman stopped by his desk. "You shouldn't be so clumsy, Gene. You are probably going to flunk the test," said Janelle.

"You shouldn't have been trying so hard this morning. You are not that good," said Norman.

"You're as blind as a bat without your glasses and probably dumb too," said Rex.

"Somebody said you were going to run for president of the class. You won't win the election. Your grades will be too bad. Besides, you went to Central Junior High," said Barbara.

Rex picked up a piece of Carol's hair. "Pretty hair, pretty girl. You went to West Junior High, not much better than Central, and so did your red-haired friend. You're hanging out with real losers."

"Leave them alone," said Gene as he started to get up. Mike also started to get up.

The bullies went back to their desks. They were laughing and making fun of Gene as they walked away.

Carol turned around and looked at Gene. He was looking down at his desk.

"What is their problem? They were incredibly mean to you. I hate to see that happen to someone as nice as you. I think you are very smart and a great football player. Gene, you would be a very good class president, and, Mike, you would be a good vice president."

As the bell rang, Mr. Kirkland began calling roll and started the test. Gene didn't really know what to do. He could not see the test since it was written on the board. He was afraid to say anything because of the four classmates who had made fun of him.

When the class ended, Gene, Mike, and Carol were the last three to leave. Out in the hall, Mike said to Gene, "You need to say something to Mr. Kirkland. Maybe he will let you retake the test."

"He is pretty intimidating. I'm afraid to say anything to him," said Gene.

"I'm not," said Carol. "You need to get the grade you deserve. May I tell him what happened?"

Gene looked at Mike.

"Let her do it. She wants to help you. She didn't like the way those four bullies were treating you."

"You aren't afraid of him?" asked Gene.

"No, I'm not afraid," said Carol.

"All right. We will wait out here for you," said Gene.

Carol went back into the classroom. "Mr. Kirkland, may I please talk to you for a minute?"

"Yes, Carol. Come in," said Mr. Kirkland. He knew Carol was probably one of the best students in the class, and he liked her.

"Gene Sandusky broke his glasses in football practice this morning, and he was unable to see the board to take the test. Would you allow him to take it tomorrow?" asked Carol.

"He should have said something. He could have moved closer to the board," said Mr. Kirkland.

"There were four bullies making fun of him before class. He didn't want to ask for anything," said Carol.

"Tell Gene he can take it tomorrow or the next day if he doesn't have his glasses tomorrow," said Mr. Kirkland.

"Thank you very much, Mr. Kirkland. You are very kind. I will tell him," said Carol. She left the classroom to go to her two friends who were waiting in the hall. "Gene, you can take the test tomorrow or the next day."

"Thank you for helping me, Carol," said Gene. Gene had his new glasses the next day. He took the test and received an A on it. Mike and Carol also received an A on the test.

When Gene went to take the test, Mr. Kirkland said to him, "Gene, you have a very good friend in Carol. She is an exceptional young lady, very sincere and caring."

"She is very nice, and she wanted to help me," said Gene.

A few weeks later, Gene was elected president of the sophomore class, and Mike was elected vice president. On Thursday after the elections, Richard and Carol invited Gene and Mike to go out to eat with them to celebrate their victories. Of course, Richard picked everyone up because the other three were only fifteen and they didn't have a driver's license yet.

Richard was a senior instructor in physical education class that year. He was assigned to the swimming section. When Mike and Carol were seniors, they would also be senior instructors. Richard was a really nice guy, and Gene was looking forward to talking to him, but Gene was very quiet that evening. Both Mike and Gene had just turned fifteen and felt very young around Richard and very envious of his relationship with Carol, although both Richard and Carol were very attentive to them. Richard was a senior instructor during the hour Mike and Gene had swimming.

"So how do you two like swimming?" asked Richard.

"You know me. I could swim all day," said Mike.

Gene started to say something, but he stopped.

"How about you, Gene? Are you doing all right?" asked Richard.

Carol noticed that Gene seemed a little embarrassed. He was sitting next to her. She put her hand on his. "What's the matter, Gene? Maybe Richard can help you."

This was the first time Carol had touched him since he was eight and talked to him so kindly and in the voice that he would grow to love. "I'm not a very strong swimmer. I never have been. I have to take my glasses off, and I don't see well at all without them."

Mike put his arm around Gene. "I told Richard that might be the problem."

Richard got up and went over and knelt down between Carol and Gene. He put his arm around Gene. "I'm going to help you, Gene. I know you want to make a good grade in this class just as Mike does. I'm always going to try to keep you in a group close to me that I am working with. If I can't, I'll be sure you are in a group with Mike. I know in the water it is sometimes hard to see. We don't have appropriate goggles, but I am going to try to see if I can get some. If you just try to focus on Mike's red hair or my blond hair, you'll be able to keep track of us."

"That's a good idea. I hadn't thought of that," said Gene. There was a little relief in his voice.

"Just don't ever lose sight of me or Mike. We won't let anything happen to you," said Richard. "I'm going to try to get about a dozen pairs of goggles. You're not alone with this problem, Gene."

"Thanks, I didn't know what I was going to do," said Gene.

"That's all right. You are Carol's friend as well as Mike's friend, and anyone who is their friend is a friend of mine. I'll be going to Vietnam as soon as I graduate, so I am going to need you both to take care of Carol for me until I get back," said Richard.

Mike was a lot like Richard—aggressive, outgoing, and friendly. Gene was basically the opposite—reserved, quiet, and even though he was class president and a very good, charismatic speaker, he seemed somewhat shy, especially around girls, except for Carol. He didn't want anything to do with the girls who followed him around and would do anything to get a date with him; he very seldom, if ever, dated. Carol was different, and she intrigued him. He liked the idea that Richard wanted him to help Mike take care of Carol while he was in Vietnam.

Richard and Mike smiled a lot that night. Gene never smiled, but Carol saw kindness in his eyes and heard it in his voice, and she liked him very much, as she did Richard and Mike.

In swimming class two days later, Richard said, "Gene, come over here. I have something for you."

Gene walked over to the desk in the locker room where Richard was sitting.

"I got you some new goggles." Richard handed them to Gene.

He put them on. They fit perfectly over his glasses.

"Thanks, Richard. These are great. What do I owe you for them?" asked Gene.

"Nothing. It is my gift to you. I got twelve pair of goggles. I think there are others who would benefit from using them," said Richard. "In this class alone, I think Terry and Nathan could use them."

"They both could definitely use them," said Gene.

"Gene, ask Terry and Nathan to come see me," said Richard.

When he gave Terry and Nathan the goggles, they were both very grateful for Richard's kindness.

Richard asked Terry, "Who is that over there on the bench that you were talking to just now? I don't remember seeing him before."

"That's John Kelley. This is his first day. He didn't think he could take physical education because he is handicapped, but they told him that he had to. He is really scared," said Terry. "He doesn't know what to do."

"I'm going to talk to him, Terry. Would you like to go with me?" said Richard.

"Sure, I'll go with you," said Terry.

John was small and very thin. Within the next three years, he would grow to six feet three inches and develop very muscular arms. Richard sat down by John.

"Hi, John, I'm Richard, your senior instructor. Here's a pair of goggles for you. They will fit over your glasses and help you to see better in the water."

"Thank you," said John quietly. "I don't think I can do this. I can't walk without the brace on my leg. It's paralyzed and shorter than my other leg, and I can't take my shirt off." John reached back and pulled up his shirt to show Richard the terrible scars on his back. Terry saw it too.

"What happened to you, John?" Richard's voice was kind and reassuring.

"My dad beat me and tried to starve me," said John.

"Stay with him, Terry. I'll be right back," said Richard.

In a few minutes, Richard returned with Mr. Dalton, the physical education teacher, swimming coach, and an exceptionally nice man.

"John, this is your teacher, Mr. Dalton. This is John's first day in class. He's handicapped. Do you mind showing Mr. Dalton your back?"

"I don't mind." John pulled his shirt up again. "I would like to know how to swim."

"I'm sorry that someone hurt you. It hurts me to know what you must have gone through. Come back after your last class, and Richard and I will teach you how to swim," said Mr. Dalton.

"I'll be here," said John through his tears.

Mr. Dalton and Richard went back to the office. Terry hugged John and went to the pool where the class was warming up. John dressed and went to his next class.

"The goggles were a good idea. I'm sure they were expensive. We will reimburse you for them," said Mr. Dalton.

"No. It is my gift to them. It just started that I wanted to get a pair for Gene, and then I realized that others needed them too," said Richard. "I don't need money. I'm going to Vietnam."

Mr. Dalton shook hands with Richard. "Thank you."

After school, John was sitting on the bench in the locker room. He had on his swim trunks, a T-shirt, and his new goggles over his glasses. They both walked with him to the pool. As he sat on a bench, Richard helped him take off his leg brace, his shoes, and his socks. They both very gently helped him into the water. Mr. Dalton started working with John. Richard watched closely to see what Mr. Dalton was doing. Richard had been a lifeguard, but he had never taught someone who was handicapped how to swim. By the end of the hour, he would be adept at teaching anyone how to swim.

Mr. Dalton was very tall and strong, and he carried John back to the locker room like he was a little boy so he could shower before putting his brace back on. "Now that wasn't so bad, was it?" asked Mr. Dalton.

"No, I enjoyed it. You are both very nice to me," said John.

"Well, we think you are nice too, John. We will do this every day, and then you will pass the course, and in all probability, you will receive a good grade in swimming," said Mr. Dalton.

"I would like that. Thank you, Mr. Dalton and Richard. I like my new goggles," said John.

"Don't forget to take them off before you go to your next class," said Richard.

"I won't," said John as he smiled and waved to Richard as he left the locker room.

"You treated him very good, Mr. Dalton," said Richard.

"I had a little brother who had polio. He didn't make it. That little guy reminds me of him, always smiling through his tears," said Mr. Dalton.

John did get an A in swimming, but Mr. Dalton and Richard weren't finished yet. The next six week's physical education class was tumbling. This was where Terry excelled. In fact, Terry made the tumbling team. There were actually several things John could do with the help of Mr. Dalton, Richard, and Terry. He did the parallel bars well. He loved the rings, and John's muscles were developing in his arms. There were even some tumbling exercises that he could do on the mats. He would also, with the help of his three friends, receive an A in tumbling. Some other things were not so easy for him, but they managed to help him to get him through. He also did well in archery.

One day as John was going to the field to meet Richard and Terry to practice shot put, he saw the most beautiful girl he had ever seen. Richard had his arm around her. She had long red hair and pretty green eyes.

"Hi, John, are you ready to practice some shot put exercises?" asked Richard. "Terry is going to practice the long jump. John, this my girlfriend, Carol. Carol, this is John."

"Hello, John. I'm pleased to meet you." Carol shook hands with him and smiled slightly.

"Hello, Carol. It's good to meet you," said John.

Carol waved to Terry, who was already out in the field. "Bye, Richard. Bye, John. I'll see you all later."

And with this she was gone. Although John would never forget the vision of the beautiful girl he had seen that day, he wouldn't see her again for a long time. But when he did see her again, he would remember her gentle touch and her kind voice.

During the six-week section in physical education when they played basketball, Gene, Terry, and Richard all worked with John. He couldn't run on the court, but with Gene's help, John became very good at making baskets. John was allowed to make a basket in an actual basketball game with Gene's assistance. It was an intramural game, but to John, it was a championship game.

Mr. Dalton said to Richard, "Gene and Terry have been excellent working with John. Let's make sure they both get extra credit. The other students seem to accept John more now. And by the way, Richard, you are doing an exceptionally good job as senior instructor this year. You are the best one I have, or possibly have ever had, since the program began."

"Thank you, Mr. Dalton. I enjoy working with the younger kids," Richard paused. "Have you talked much to Terry?"

"No. He seems very quiet and shy, but he is really good at a lot of different sports," said Mr. Dalton.

"He asked me today if I thought he could be a senior instructor," said Richard.

"What did you tell him?" asked Mr. Dalton.

"Terry has been bullied and made fun all his life. He stutters and speaks real quietly and slowly so he can pronounce the words right. As a senior instructor, I know you have to sometimes be loud and talk a lot. I'm not sure if he would be able to do that or not," said Richard. "I wasn't sure what to tell him."

They looked at Terry and Gene helping John play basketball. "I wonder if Gene is going to be a senior instructor. They work well together. If Terry was a senior instructor during the same hour as someone like Gene or Mike, it would probably work," said Mr. Dalton. "I'll make a note and see who signs up next spring."

"Thanks, Mr. Dalton. Thanks for taking care of my friends," said Richard.

Richard had a lot of respect for Mr. Dalton. He was a really good, caring teacher. Richard often thought that if for some reason he decided not to make the Army his career after his time in Vietnam, he might be a physical education teacher with Mr. Dalton as his role model.

Mr. Dalton was impressed not only with Richard's athletic abilities but also with his sincere dedication to the younger students he was working with. When they were seniors, both Mike and Terry wanted to be senior instructors. Gene was unable to fit it into his schedule. Mr. Dalton chose both Mike and Terry and assigned them to the same hour. They would work well together and form a lasting friendship.

Mr. Kirkland was one of the best math teachers at the high school. He taught college prep classes and the very best sophomore math students. He was very strict, and he seldom talked or joked with his students; thus he was not a particularly popular teacher. One day toward the beginning of the year, he began his sophomore geometry class a little differently.

"I would like to speak to you today before we begin our geometry studies." Mr. Kirkland's voice was not angry, but the students knew he was expecting their undivided attention. "There seems to be some bullying going on in this class this year, and I do not like it. It seems that the students from Northwest Junior High have some issues and feel they are better than the students who came from Central Junior High and West Junior High. In case you haven't noticed, you are not in junior high anymore. You are now students at Avalon High School, and you should act like it. I have heard some very unkind, if not heartbreaking, comments made to some students. To make an excellent student feel so intimidated that he will not ask to sit closer to the board so he can see the test and is able to take it is totally uncalled for as far as I am concerned. Also, I have heard many comments making fun of someone that were completely out of line. Last week two students from this class won an election. Gene from Central is your class president while Mike from West is your vice president. Evidently, they have quite a few friends out there. So are you all going to support them, or are you going to continue mistreating them? I am aware that Mike and Carol have been involved in some questionable activities lately, trying to stop bullying in the school. Some teachers and counselors have questioned their ability to do this. I do not question their ability or their desire to do this, and they have my full support. My daughter is an adult now, but she was bullied all through school. Would anyone like to make a comment?"

The room was extremely quiet, and then one hand slowly went up.

"Yes, Carol, I was hoping you would speak," said Mr. Kirkland.

"On the second day of school, my friend Paul Williams was pushed down as he got off the bus. His forehead was cut, his nose was bleeding, and his glasses were broken. Mike and I went to help him. I went all the way through elementary school with Paul. In the second grade he had polio. His father also had it, and he died. Paul has worked very hard to even get to high school, and he hopes to graduate. That someone could be so cruel to Paul is too difficult for me to comprehend and for someone to bully Gene and Mike because they are also exceptionally good people. I'm sorry, I can't speak anymore," said Carol through her tears.

"You've done fine. Thank you for speaking," said Mr. Kirkland.

Mike reached out and touched Carol's hand.

"Does anyone else have anything to say?" asked Mr. Kirkland. "No one wants to admit they were wrong and apologize to the class officers?" He paused for a minute, hoping someone would speak, but nobody did. "Then class is dismissed. Tomorrow when you come to class, I hope you will bring a better attitude." As everyone left the classroom, Mr. Kirkland asked, "Terry, may I see you for a moment?"

Terry picked up his books and walked to Mr. Kirkland's desk. Carol, Gene, and Mike were leaving as Terry got to the front of the room. He dropped his books. Carol helped him pick them up and smiled slightly at him.

Mr. Kirkland waited until everyone had left the room, and then he shut the door.

"Terry, you look a little afraid of me. Don't worry, you are one of the good ones. You are one of only four students in the class to receive an A on the test. I heard Rex call you stupid, which was totally uncalled for, especially in light of the grade you received."

"He is very mean to me. I don't like him," said Terry.

"I don't like him either, Terry," said Mr. Kirkland. "I know you have the answers to some of the questions that I ask in class, but you don't raise your hand."

"I'm very shy. I stutter, and I speak very slowly so I can pronounce the words right, and I have always been made fun of for that," said Terry with tears in his eyes.

44

"I'm so sorry about that, Terry," said Mr. Kirkland. "There is an empty seat next to Gene and behind Mike and near Carol. I would like for you to sit there tomorrow instead of between Rex and Norman. Would you mind doing that for me?"

"Yes, I will," said Terry. "Thank you for helping me."

"Carol will always help you if you need it, as will Gene and Mike. I assure you that those three will not bully you or make fun of you. Feel free to come to me if you need anything," said Mr. Kirkland.

By the end of the year, in Mr. Kirkland's geometry class, Gene was the number one student. He excelled far above everyone including Carol, Mike, and Terry. Mr. Kirkland was very fond of Gene. The ability that Gene possessed to endear himself to teachers and adults as well as his fellow students was mesmerizing. Carol, Mike, and Terry learned so much from Gene, but he was always humble and would say that he learned from them.

CHAPTER

Sophomore Year

Sophomore year was a busy year with everyone trying to become accustomed to high school. Mike had a lot of responsibility that year as vice president of the class.

Carol and Mike had a good friend from junior high named Paul Williams. Paul had polio when he was seven and had braces on his legs and used crutches. One day when he was getting off the bus, a bully named Tom Davis tripped him. Carol was behind him on the bus, and Mike was walking a few feet away. They both hurried to help him up. His glasses were broken, and his nose was bleeding. Carol helped clean him up as best she could.

Mike had seen Tom trip Paul, and Tom was still hanging out close by laughing with some other bullies. As Mike approached the group, they scattered, all except Tom, although he had no intention of fighting Mike because Mike was a lot bigger than he was.

As Mike spoke calmly and deliberately, Tom could sense his underlying anger.

"Tom, you know Paul is a good friend of mine. Things that we take for granted are hard for him. I don't understand why you would want to hurt him."

By this time, Carol and Paul had joined Mike.

"Paul is my friend too. He tells me that you knock his book and pencils off his desk in algebra class, and he has a really difficult time getting them." And then Carol did something that Tom had never before experienced. Carol reached her hand out to shake hands with Tom. "Would you be our friend, Tom, and then we can all work together to help Paul?"

Tom shook hands with Carol. He didn't really understand because pretty, classy girls didn't usually even talk to him. "I guess so," Tom said.

Then Mike reached out to shake hands with him. "Would you like to tell Paul you are sorry?"

Neither Mike nor Carol were smiling, but they were being nice to him.

Not quite sure how to handle the situation, Tom reached out to shake hands with Paul. "I'm sorry, Paul. I'll pay for your glasses. It will take me a few weeks, but I've got a job."

Paul smiled and said, "You're lucky. I wish I could get a job, but I'm having a hard time just going to school."

Four new and unlikely friends walked into the high school together that day, Tom holding the door open for them.

"Gosh, this place is so big. What if it gets to where I have classes on the third floor and I can't make it?" asked Paul.

"If that ever happens, I'll carry you," said Mike. And a little over a year later, he did just that.

Although they didn't know it at the time, that one statement was to be repeated many times over, heard by many, and remembered forever.

Paul was the first of many who would be helped by Carol and Mike that year. It was just the beginning of their efforts to eliminate bullying from the school by helping not only the one being bullied but the one doing the bullying. That's how it all began. They would reach out and expand over the next three years. They were called everything from rebellious and activists to ambitious and policy-changers. They were even told that they were trying to take over the counselors' jobs. But they worked with those who fell through the cracks or would not go to the counselors for help.

Early that sophomore year, Carol and Mike told Carol's mother what they were doing. Her comment to them was, "You two are out of bounds. You are too far ahead of your time. Maybe someday people will care about bullying but not today. You could be causing a lot of trouble for yourselves." In retrospect, she was right.

They told Mike's parents about what they were doing the same day. Their comment was, "That's wonderful. The two of you should definitely be commended and honored for this good work you are doing." They never were.

CHAPTER

Ms. Henderson's Favorite Student

With the start of the school year, there was the anticipation of home-coming and football games. Richard was a football player, as were Mike and Gene. Richard had a light load of classes for his senior year. He even had a study hall. Carol, Gene, and Mike were sophomores and not so lucky.

Carol had her second-year clothing class the same hour as Richard had his study hall. They would stand in the hall outside the clothing class and talk and hold hands after the first bell rang.

Ms. Henderson, the clothing teacher, was strict and close to retirement. She did not like to see "her girls" dating or walking with boys in the halls. Carol and Richard weren't the only ones talking in the hall the day she lost her temper and said, "Girls you must be at your desk with your material out and ready to work before the second bell rings."

Carol immediately went into the room.

"I'm sorry, Ms. Henderson," said Richard as he smiled and went to his study hall.

Ms. Henderson watched him walk down the hall. She thought what a handsome young man he was and so polite. Carol was a lucky girl.

The next day they were there again. Richard was sure to leave Carol before the first bell rang this time. He really liked Carol, and he didn't want her to get in trouble with Ms. Henderson.

One day after Carol went into class, Richard asked Ms. Henderson, "I have study hall this hour. I was wondering if I could sit in on your class and learn some basics of sewing. My mom died several years ago, and my dad, and I always seem to have something that needs to be sewed."

Even though he seemed sincere, Ms. Henderson wondered if this wasn't just to get the opportunity to spend more time with Carol.

"I'll sit in the back. I won't bother any of the girls," said Richard.

Ms. Henderson thought to herself that as cute as he was, he would definitely bother the girls. He was actually bothering her, and she felt as though she needed a fan. But she said to him, "I'll check with someone in authority," which was exactly what she did.

It was agreed that Richard Noland would be her first male student and sit in on the class during his study hall period, and so he did for the whole semester. He took in everything that she said and did the work quietly and efficiently. She actually gave him some personal help because she was really fond of him. Richard received no credit for the class. Ms. Henderson said that if he had been graded, he would have received the highest grade possible. She wished that her other students were as motivated as Richard.

Carol and Mike could have learned a very important lesson from Richard. This was the way to get on a teacher's good side and secure a vote for National Honor Society. Richard would make National Honor Society that year. When Carol and Mike were seniors, they did not.

CHAPTER

RICHARD

During Carol's sophomore year, she spent a lot of time with Richard. They went to many school events together. They double-dated with Cathy and Ethan to the Christmas dance. Mike didn't go, nor did Gene. Richard would join the Army right after graduation. He wanted to go to Vietnam. He talked about it a lot.

On a warm spring day, a few weeks before Richard's graduation, Carol, Mike, Gene, and Richard were lying by the pool in Mike's backyard. Richard, who was usually boisterous around the pool, was quiet and reflective. He was never one to say anything too profound, but he did that day.

"I'm really going to miss you three when I join the Army. Mike and Gene, I know you don't like all the girls chasing you, and I know you both just want to concentrate on sports and your studies. And, Carol, I know you don't want a lot of guys asking you out all the time. I know you guys don't want a serious relationship. You all might remember that we talked about this once when we went out at the beginning of the year to celebrate your victories in the class election. A good solution would be for you, Carol, to just say you have a boyfriend, me, who is away at war. But when there is something you don't want to miss out on like homecoming, the Christmas dance, or prom, you and Mike or Gene can go together. That way none of you will be missing out on anything, and you shouldn't be bothered with anyone asking you out, that is unless you want to go out with them." That was the most they had ever heard Richard say. "What do you think?"

"It makes sense," said Carol.

"That's a really good idea, Richard," said Gene.

"Sure. It sounds good to me too." Mike got up to leave. "I have to go pick up Danny. I'll be back soon."

Richard did not realize at that particular moment how seriously Gene and Mike would take his suggestion.

Carol, Richard, and Gene walked back to the grotto where it was shady and cool. And there in the cool water in the grotto, Richard put his arms around Carol and kissed her sweetly as he ran his fingers through her hair. The kiss lasted quite a while, and Gene shyly looked away. But Richard wasn't doing this to embarrass Gene. He took Carol's hand, and they walked across the pool where Gene was standing.

Richard asked Gene, "Have you ever kissed a girl?"

"No, I haven't," said Gene quietly.

"I'm going back out by the pool. Mike and Danny will be back soon." Richard took hold of Gene's arm and Carol's hand and walked with them to the waterfall at the back of the grotto, and then he left them alone.

Carol touched Gene's cheek tenderly. "You don't have to kiss me."

"I would like to," said Gene as their lips met.

It was the gentlest kiss Carol had ever received, and Gene was amazed at how wonderful his first kiss had been. They both felt something very special for one another that day. The beautiful girl with the long red hair and the kind, gentle young man held tightly to one another's hand as they walked out to the pool to join Richard.

As Richard looked at his two friends, he was very proud of the plan he had set in motion for Carol, Gene, and Mike. It was rather odd that Richard, who was not brilliant, had presented his three friends with a going-away present that would benefit all of them and prove to be one of the greatest gifts they were ever to receive.

GENE'S SADNESS

As school started in the fall of their junior year, Carol and Gene were pleased to have two classes together, history and speech. They could study and practice their speeches together. Gene always welcomed any excuse to be with Carol.

Gene called Carol, "It's Saturday morning, and our history report is due Monday. Why don't I come pick you up, and we can work on it at my house."

"Sounds great. I'll be ready," said Carol.

When Gene picked Carol up, she had denim shorts on and a white blouse with ruffles. She had curled her hair, and it fell in curls down her back and over her bare shoulders.

Soon they were alone at Gene's house. They were hardly ever alone. So many girls wanted to date Gene. He wasn't interested, but he liked Carol. She looked exceptionally pretty to Gene that day. Gene asked Carol, "Do you mind going to my room? The books are there, and it will be easier to work."

"That will be fine," said Carol.

Gene's room was decorated in shades of brown with a touch of red here and there. It was masculine, like him. There were a lot of books and some sports pictures and memorabilia.

They worked on their report for several hours that day. They were both hard workers and very conscientious and in some ways perfectionists. They both wanted good grades, and on this report they were to receive them.

When they finished, Gene said, "I have a headache. I'm going to lie down for a while. Will you lie by me?"

"Of course I will." Carol lay down beside Gene, being sure to not get too close. She had to be careful with Gene. He was very special to her. Carol gently massaged his neck, temples, and the back of his head. "Does that make you feel better?"

"Yes. I love your hands on my head. It always makes me feel better, and I love the way you talk to me. There is a kindness and understanding in your voice that no one else has."

Gene and Carol kissed, and they held one another tightly. Gene found Carol extremely inviting, but they would never compromise their relationship in any way. That wasn't what they were about, and Carol knew this. They had so much respect for one another, and Gene would never do anything to hurt Carol as she would never do anything to hurt him. No one else knew how they spent the afternoon. They kept their feelings private and showed no public affection for each other. Because of Mike and Richard, this was the way they wanted it, but they were so perfect together.

Gene held Carol close. "I love you. I've never said that to anyone before."

"And I love you. I've never said it to anyone either," said Carol. "You seem sad today, Gene."

"It's just that Mike is my best friend, and he loves you too," said Gene.

Carol didn't know it was possible to love someone as much as she did Gene that day, but she knew it was not to be. What he said was true. Mike was his best friend and also hers.

They fixed a snack. It provided a good excuse for Gene to not take Carol home just yet. They both wanted to hold on to this moment for as long as they could. They felt safe and secure. There was no one to hurt them or criticize them or bother them.

"Is you head better now?" asked Carol.

"My eyes hurt now. We did quite a bit of work today. I need to get my eyes checked. I think I may need stronger glasses. It worries me. I can't see anything without them," said Gene.

"If you want me to, I'll go with you," said Carol.

"You would really do that for me?" asked Gene.

"Of course, we can go Monday after school. I can't go today dressed like this," said Carol.

"I think you look pretty." Carol curled up beside Gene on the sofa. "Do you ever think about the future?" asked Gene.

"I'll be a secretary. I will live in another city, probably Chicago, and I'll be a mother," said Carol.

"What about a husband?" asked Gene.

"Sure. I suppose I'll marry someday," said Carol with a little sadness in her voice.

"I can't see my future. Everybody else always knows what they want to do, but I don't. I can't even imagine it," said Gene. "What do you think that means?"

Carol put her arms around him and hugged him. "I don't know, Gene. I really don't know."

She had seen this side of Gene before. It was as though he could only see to a certain point and then there was nothing. Mike knew he wanted to be a lawyer, and Richard had hopes of a career in the Army. Gene didn't know yet, but he was only sixteen. He had plenty of time, and Carol hoped to help him.

On Monday after school, as they were headed to the eye doctor, Mike joined them.

"Gene's been having some bad headaches, and he is not seeing well," said Carol.

"I'll go with you," said Mike. "They might dilate your eyes, and you won't be able to drive."

"I like that we are always here for one another. Thanks for going with us, Mike," said Carol.

At the eye doctor's office, Carol and Mike both stayed with Gene as they thoroughly checked and dilated his eyes. He had a hard time focusing on the eye chart, let alone reading it, and his peripheral vision was not good. He definitely needed stronger glasses. Walking to the car, Gene could hardly see so Carol took hold of his arm.

"It's good that you came with us, Mike," said Gene.

"That's what friends are for, to always be there for one another," said Mike.

And they would be there for one another. Unfortunately, not forever, but for a long time to come.

Carol's friend, Linda Conley, was in the same history class as Carol and Gene. Carol and Linda sat by the windows in their assigned seats, and Gene sat on the opposite side.

One day they were told to get in groups of four to do a project together. Immediately many students both boys and girls surrounded Gene, asking him to be in their group. Gene looked over at Carol and shrugged his shoulders.

Linda noticed this and said to Carol, "Why doesn't Gene just tell them all no and come over here and be in your group?"

"It's just a project, Linda. It doesn't matter," said Carol.

"You know I watch Gene a lot," said Linda. "He never smiles, and he doesn't seem particularly friendly. But everybody is drawn to him. He is so incredibly popular. He fascinates me. I have never seen anyone with so much charisma, except maybe President Kennedy." Linda paused. "He is not really my type, but you like him, don't you? There is a really strong chemistry between the two of you."

"Gene has always been very nice to me. But I am going with Richard even though he is in Vietnam," said Carol.

"It doesn't make you real popular that you are going with someone in Vietnam. Everybody hates that war so much," said Linda. "Well, would you look at that. Gene already has his group, so what should we do now?"

Kevin Golubski and Jimmy Franklin sat in front of Carol and Linda and heard the conversation.

Kevin asked Carol, "Would you and Linda be in a group with me and Jimmy?"

"Sure, that would be great," said Carol.

"Well, I guess so, since Gene is taken," said Linda.

Carol could tell right away that Gene didn't care for his group. The two happiest students in class were definitely Kevin and Jimmy. When the grades were posted for the groups the following week, only two groups received an A, one being Gene's group and the other was Carol's group.

There was a pep rally that afternoon. Mike asked Gene if he wanted to go out for pizza with him and Carol afterward.

Mike was on the football team but never received the attention that Gene did. As Carol and Mike were waiting for Gene, he was once again surrounded by lots of girls and guys.

Mike said, "We might as well go on. He's not going to be able to get away from them for a while."

Carol and Mike had ordered the pizza when Gene walked in and joined them. He said, "I don't blame you guys for leaving. I would have left too, but it took me awhile to get away."

"Are you all right, Gene? You don't look like you feel so good," asked Carol.

Gene was rubbing his forehead. "I've just got a headache. I can't stand it when they all converge on me like that. It's not normal."

"The girls all want to go out with you, and the boys all want to be your friend," said Mike.

"You two are the only friends I want," said Gene.

Carol noticed the sadness in his eyes. Carol put her hand on Gene's hand, "Linda and I wanted to be in your group in history today, but it happened there too, didn't it?"

"Yes, I didn't like that either," said Gene.

"I think it would be neat to be that popular," said Mike. "What don't you like about it?"

There was a tear in the sleeve of his shirt, and two buttons were missing. "They tear your clothes, and one girl hurt my shoulder. They are so loud, and they give me a headache. I don't even know most of them. I don't understand why they do it," said Gene.

"I'm sorry, Gene. I didn't realize it upset you so much," said Mike seriously.

Carol gently touched Gene's hand. "I wish I could make it better for you, Gene. I know you don't want all that attention. You've helped me so much. I wish I could help you. You are so good and kind. I hate to see them bothering and hurting you." Carol rubbed Gene's shoulder.

"I like the way you talk to me. No one else has ever talked to me like you do. It always makes me feel better." said Gene.

This was the first time Mike felt that Carol liked Gene better than she did him. But it was all right because he liked Gene too.

At the Friday night football game, Gene was injured. He had a concussion affecting his hearing, eyesight, and his leg was hurt. He also had a severe headache. Mike and Carol took Gene to the emergency room that night. Gene's family was away, so Mike and Carol took him to Mike's house when he was released. Colleen was very comforting and caring to Gene.

Colleen, Carol, and Mike stayed up with Gene all night. When Alan left the house the following morning, he looked at them but did not speak.

Gene felt bad that day. They tried to get him to eat. Colleen put her arms around him and loved him, as did Carol and Mike. That afternoon when Alan returned home, Colleen was in the family room alone with Gene. She was feeding him a bowl of soup.

Alan spoke in anger, "You are such a baby, Gene. Can't you even feed yourself? Stop spoiling him, Colleen. He is acting like a child and you, Colleen, are encouraging him."

Colleen continued to feed Gene the soup without a word.

Alan was sitting at his desk in the library when Colleen went to talk to him.

"Alan, I try to be your quiet, obedient wife and not speak or stand up for myself, but I can't do it this time. There is no excuse for the way you treated Gene or me. He is only sixteen. He is injured, alone, and scared. I'm trying to comfort and take care of him until his family returns home," said Colleen.

"And when will that be?" asked Alan.

"They will return tomorrow, but I'm not finished yet. Gene is a very sensitive, kind, sweet boy. You hurt his feelings, as you did mine. He needs our support and love, not your criticism," said Colleen.

"He needs to grow up and be a man. Mike and Carol are more mature than he is," said Alan.

"He has been president of the class for two years and probably will be next year. He's an excellent student and on the football and basketball teams. What more do you want from him? He is quieter and more sensitive than Mike and Carol as well as less rebellious, and he doesn't challenge the system. He has no marks against him," Colleen paused. "This is my house too, and he is welcome to stay here as long as he needs to."

"I'm sorry, Colleen. I'm going to the office," said Alan. "I will apologize to Gene."

Colleen didn't know whether to believe him or not. She followed him as he walked to the family room where Gene, Mike, and Carol were. As Alan stood in front of Gene, all eyes were on him.

"I'm sorry, Gene, please feel free to stay here as long as you wish."

"Thank you," said Gene.

When Mike and Carol took Gene home the following day, his parents were very grateful for the care they had given to Gene in their absence.

First-Year Teacher

Junior English was an interesting class mainly because Mrs. Anders was the teacher, and it was her first year of teaching. Every day at the end of the hour, she would call on three students to read. It could be a chapter from a book, poetry, or something they had studied in class that day.

Each day she called on the same three students to read at the end of the class. First was Leon, second was Gene, and third was Carol. She never varied from this routine.

One day as the three finished their readings, Gloria had a question for the new young teacher. "I would like to know why you call on the same three students to read every day. Some of the rest of us might like to read also." Her voice was shrill and loud.

"I happen to like the sound of their voices. I don't like the sound of some voices. Leon has a beautiful, poetic voice. It is very smooth and clear. Gene's voice is very deep and masculine. It is strong and yet gentle. Carol's voice is very kind and genuine and so sensitive and touching. All three are very mesmerizing and soothing to listen to. But I will call on you tomorrow," said Mrs. Anders.

The following day as promised, Mrs. Anders called on Gloria first to read from the same book they had read from yesterday. Her voice was loud and not pleasant to listen to. Next she called on Norma, who seemed shocked to hear her name called. Norma read as fast as she could just to get it over with as soon as possible. The third person she called on to read was Terry. His eyes met Carol's for a moment, and she saw panic in them.

"Just relax, Terry. You can do it," Carol encouraged him.

Terry stuttered and had a difficult time talking. He seldom talked to anyone except Carol, Leon, and Gene. He started reading in a very slow and quiet voice. He had a hard time getting many of the words out. It was a horrible experience for Terry, and Carol, Leon, and Gene felt his pain as others in the class were making fun of him as well as laughing at him.

Terry was a very shy, gentle boy. He sat next to Carol, and as she got up to leave class, she saw that he was crying. She put her arm around him. "I'm so sorry, Terry. You did fine. Those who made fun of you are just bullies. You are so much better than they are."

Her touch was so gentle, and her voice was so kind. He liked the fact that she took up for him.

As Carol, Terry, Leon, and Gene walked out of the classroom that day together, Mrs. Anders stopped them.

"Terry, I am sorry that they made fun of you. I didn't mean for that to happen. You are a very nice boy. I didn't know how shy you were."

The next day was poetry day in English class. "So who would like to be first to read their poem or recite it from memory if they can?" asked Mrs. Anders.

Carol raised her hand, and Mrs. Anders asked her to come to the front of the class. She did not take a book or paper with her.

"So, Carol, this will be recited from memory. Is that correct?" asked Mrs. Anders.

"Yes, Mrs. Anders," said Carol.

"You may continue," said Mrs. Anders.

"The name of my poem is 'The Unknown Soldier' by Billy Rose." Carol recited the poem flawlessly and with great expression and sincerity.

"That was exceptionally good. Could you recite another poem?" asked Mrs. Anders.

"Yes, I can. My next poem is 'Rags' by Edmund Cooke." Carol once again recited her poem without error.

"Would anyone else like to recite their poem today?" asked Mrs. Anders.

No one raised their hand.

As they were leaving class that day, Mrs. Anders said, "Carol, may I see you for a moment?"

Carol went to her desk.

"I'm curious. How many poems do you have memorized?" asked Mrs. Anders.

"I'm not exactly sure, but I would say around five hundred," said Carol.

"That's amazing. I think you will probably be getting an A in this class," said Mrs. Anders. "You are also a very nice girl. I like the way you take up for Terry. The other students are so mean to him except Gene and Leon. They are very nice. Why is there so much bullying and cruelty?"

"I don't know. Mike and I have tried to stop it, but some teachers and counselors don't like us doing that," said Carol.

"My first year of teaching has been made better because of you and your three good friends. I need to ask you a question. Both of your poems were military-related. Why did you choose those?" asked Mrs. Anders.

"My boyfriend is Richard Noland. He graduated last year. He is in the Army now, and he is in Vietnam. He is a really good man. He did a lot of great things for Gene, Terry, and John last year and many others. He was their senior instructor. John wouldn't have passed physical education without Richard's help. My poems were dedicated to Richard," said Carol. "Do you have John Kelley in one of your classes? He's handicapped."

"Yes, he is in fifth hour. He is very quiet, and no one talks to him," said Mrs. Anders.

"I don't know him well, but I met him once last year. He is a good friend of Terry. Gene and Terry also helped him with physical education last year. Gene even helped him make a basket in an actual basketball game. They also helped him learn how to swim," said Carol.

"Well, I'm going to talk to him today. I promise I'll take care of him for you and Richard and everyone else," said Mrs. Anders.

"Thank you. From what Richard told me, he is a really nice boy who has been through a lot," said Carol.

As promised, Mrs. Anders did talk to John that same day. She would help him whenever he needed it, and she stopped the students from bullying him as she also stopped those who had bullied Terry.

John was very grateful for the help of the kind young teacher. He would never know that the person who put those actions into motion was Carol.

THE SAFE PLACE

Everyone has dark places in their lives where they try to stay away from to protect their own peace of mind and their ultimate sanity.

Although Carol knew Gene when they were both just eight, they didn't meet again until their sophomore year and then again at a pool party at Mike's house in the summer of 1962 just before their junior year and right before Richard left for Vietnam. Gene and Mike were both already active in sports and popular. In addition to sports, they were both good students and not particularly interested in girls.

Carol was a good student, but not particularly popular, especially with girls. Since she had dated Richard as a sophomore, she was known as the girl who was going with the guy in Vietnam, so most boys ignored her, except Mike and Gene. Carol had two classes that year with Gene, none with Mike.

It was early one morning. Everyone was already in homeroom. Carol's locker was on the third floor. It was in a deserted area of the school in a corner where the botany lab was located. Carol was late that day, and she was crying as she dropped her books as she was getting them from her locker. Gene and Mike were walking through the hall at that time taking a shortcut to their first hour class. They saw Carol drop her books and went to help her.

When she turned to face them, her eyes were red and her cheeks were tear-stained. Mike put his arms around her. She was crying, and Mike hated to see Carol cry.

"What's the matter?" asked Mike very concerned.

Carol just shook her head no. She couldn't speak. When Mike pulled her hair back to keep it from getting wet, Gene saw blood on the back of her blouse.

"You're hurt and bleeding. What happened?" asked Gene.

"Oh no, please get it off." She tried, rubbing it off with her jacket. "It won't come off. I've got a red sweater somewhere in here." She found it and put it on quickly. "Please tell me the truth, does it still show?"

Gene very gently pulled the sweater up a little in the back. "It doesn't show, but what happened? Did someone hurt you?"

"You have to let us help you," said Mike.

"I have to get to class. Please don't tell anyone. I am so ashamed and embarrassed. I just want to die," said Carol. As she bent over to pick up her books, she almost felt as though she was going to pass out.

Gene spoke very quietly and calmly to Carol, "Whether you want us to be or not, we are now involved. Someone has hurt you, and we want to help you. I can assure you of one thing, we are not going to let you die."

"Oh, Gene, I don't care. I just can't do this anymore. I'm so scared," said Carol as Gene put his arms around her, being careful not to hurt her back.

"I don't think you can be in class today," said Mike. "Let us take you home."

"I can't go home. I don't have any place to go. No place is safe, not school or home. Just pretend like you don't even know me. Stay away from me. I don't want you guys to get involved. I have to get to class now," said Carol as she walked away from them.

Gene and Mike went to their first hour class not knowing what to do.

"Gene, we have to help her," said Mike.

"Don't worry, Mike. I'll think of something. We don't have practice tonight. I'll see her in sixth-hour speech class. Can we go to your house?" asked Gene.

"Sure, Danny will be with me. I have to pick him up at school," said Mike.

Carol made it through the day to sixth-hour speech class. She sat immediately in front of Gene in that class. "Hi, Gene," said Carol very quietly.

"Hi, Carol," said Gene.

Mr. Eliason, the speech teacher, said, "Today we are going to have impromptu speeches. As I call your name, you will pick a subject from the box and speak on that subject from three to five minutes."

Carol's name was the third one called to speak that day. Normally she would be happy, today not so much so. The subject she drew was "a place in the world you would like to visit." As Carol started to speak, Gene felt so concerned for her, and he was worried that she wouldn't be able to do it. Her hair was uncombed, her clothes were wrinkled, and she looked like she had been crying for a week. Her voice was quiet, and it lacked the enthusiasm and expression that her speeches usually showed.

"I would like to go to California. I think it would be a safe place, and it is far away from here. There are a lot of people there. Maybe some of them would be nice to me and be my friends." Carol couldn't continue. She was crying as she sat down.

Gene wanted so badly to put his arms around her and comfort her. Richard wanted him to take care of her, and today he didn't feel as though he was doing a good job.

There were a few more speeches, the bell rang, and everyone quickly left the room. As Carol was leaving, Mr. Eliason said, "Carol, may I see you for a moment? Sit down. You are one of the best speakers in the class, but today you don't seem to be yourself. Is there anything I can do?"

"No, I just don't feel good. I'll be better tomorrow," said Carol.

"You seem very weak. How are you getting home?" asked Mr. Eliason.

Gene had been waiting outside the door. He went back into the classroom. "Mike and I will be taking her home," said Gene.

"You and Mike don't need to do that. If anyone sees me with you, they will hate you too. Just stay away from me," said Carol as she stood up.

"Do you think I care about that? We're taking you home," said Gene.

Mr. Eliason put his arm around Carol. As he did so, she cringed in pain. The sweater had slipped down a little, and he noticed the blood on her blouse.

Gene was quick to answer. "Mike and I will make sure she is taken care of. We are going to meet him now."

Mr. Eliason was torn as to how to respond. "If it was anyone except Gene, I don't believe I would let you go. You know I should report this, but you don't want me to, do you?"

"It wouldn't matter. It's too late," said Carol sadly.

"Mike and I need to talk to Carol. Would you please not report this and wait until tomorrow, and we will talk to you then?"

Mr. Eliason paused. "All right. Go ahead."

Gene took Carol's hand, and they walked out of the room without a word.

Mr. Eliason sat down and put his head in his hands. He had been a teacher for over forty years and was almost ready to retire. This wasn't the first case of abuse he had seen. But Carol was a smart, kind, pretty young girl. She obviously felt that her home was not a safe place and that she had no friends at school. But she seemed to have one friend in Gene Sandusky, and he assumed that the Mike they mentioned was Mike McVary. The boys were both good students, very active in sports, class officers, and didn't seem to be that interested in girls, except Carol. But they were all only sixteen. Were they going to be able to handle this situation? He would wait and see what they had to say tomorrow.

Mike was waiting for them right where he said he would be. Danny was in the car with him. Carol started to get in the back seat, but Gene stopped her.

"Why don't you sit in the front with Mike."

Carol did so. Mike immediately put his hand on hers as Gene got into the back seat. "If it is all right with you, Carol, we are going to take you to my house. Dad is out of town. Mom will help us."

"I hate for her to see me like this. I wish she didn't have to know," said Carol.

And then Mike's little brother Danny spoke, "Mom loves you, Carol. I can tell. In fact, we all love you, Mike, Gene, and me too. We'll protect you. We won't let anybody hurt you." He gently touched her hair but not her back.

When they arrived at Mike's house, he said, "Let me go in first. I need to talk to Mom for a minute."

Colleen was in the kitchen. "Hello, Mike. Where's Danny?"

"He's in the car with Carol and Gene. Would it be all right if Carol and Gene stay here tonight? I don't want to say too much right now, but Carol had some problems this morning. She needs to stay with us," said Mike.

"It's fine, Mike. I won't ask questions. I trust your judgment, but if you do need my help, please let me know. Don't wait too long," said Colleen.

"Thanks, Mom." Mike hugged his mom and went to his friends.

Colleen saw Mike and Gene helping Carol out of the car, and they slowly walked up the steps. Danny was following them carrying Carol's books. Danny went upstairs to his room to do his homework. Carol, Gene, and Mike went to the family room.

Carol spoke first in a very soft, quiet voice, "You guys need to be at football practice. Please don't waste your time with me."

They were both sitting by her on the sofa. Gene touched her cheek gently.

"You just don't understand, do you? Mike and I are not going to let anyone hurt you again. Your safety and happiness are the only things that are important to us right now. Please let us help you." He smoothed her hair back. "We both love you very much. We want you to believe that. We are not going to leave you alone tonight."

That evening Colleen could hear a lot of walking back and forth and water running upstairs. She had wanted to leave them alone, but she had the feeling they needed her, so she went upstairs. Mike was sitting on the floor outside the bathroom with his head in his hands.

"We need your help, Mom. Carol needs you," said Mike.

The bathroom door was open a crack. Carol was sitting on the edge of the tub. Gene was sitting beside her, painstakingly trying to help her get the blood off her body. When he looked at Colleen, she could see the pain in his eyes, and she knew he was feeling Carol's pain.

Colleen touched Carol ever so gently as Gene was doing. They cleaned her, getting the blood off her back and arms. When they were finished, they dried her very gently. Colleen got a nightgown from Cathy's room and put it on her. Gene picked her up and took her to Mike's room. After Mike turned the bed down, Gene put her to bed and covered her up.

She seemed so weak as she said to him, "Don't leave me tonight. Please don't leave me alone."

Gene kissed her on the cheek. "Don't worry. We will never leave you."

Carol woke up at five o'clock the next morning. Gene was sitting in a chair by the bed as was Mike. They were both awake.

"Don't you guys ever sleep? You don't look comfortable, Gene."

"I don't require much sleep," said Gene.

"I guess you guys were worried that I might jump out the window or do something else stupid," said Carol.

"We just wanted to be with you," said Mike quietly.

"Thank you both for caring about me," said Carol. "Do you think Cathy would mind if I wear her clothes today?"

"Not at all," said Mike. "We'll help you find something."

Carol took hold of their hands, and the three of them went to Cathy's room.

Cathy's clothes were really nice. Some still had price tags on them. Carol glanced at a couple of the tags.

"She has expensive taste," said Mike.

"Help me find something that is worn out so I will look normal." Carol pulled out a black skirt and a gray sweater. "This suits my mood." She started to change.

"We will give you some privacy while you change," said Mike.

They went back to Mike's room to wait for Carol. In a few minutes she joined them. Her hair was combed, and she was dressed in Cathy's clothes.

Carol sat down by Gene, and he took hold of her hands.

"Are you doing all right this morning? You seem a little different," said Gene.

"Different, good or bad?" asked Carol.

"I don't know. Just different. Sort of like you are trying to forget yesterday. Does your back hurt?" asked Gene.

"It hurts a little, but it doesn't bother me. My mom used to always say that I don't feel pain like normal people," said Carol.

There was a knock at the door. It was Colleen and Danny.

"May we come in?" asked Colleen.

"Sure," said Mike.

"How are you feeling today, Carol?" asked Colleen.

Everyone was looking at Carol except Danny, who was looking at Mike's yearbook.

"I need to explain everything to all of you and to Mr. Eliason today, and I don't know what to say. I know you all want to know the truth, but the truth is very bad."

"Would you like for Danny to leave?" asked Colleen.

Carol went and sat by Danny and put her arm around him. "No, he can stay. He might as well know too."

Carol paused and took a deep breath and took hold of Gene's hand.

"There is a man, an old friend of my dad, who stays at our house when he has a job in the city. He pays my parents to stay with us. I was just in the third grade the first time he stayed with us. When I was little I thought he liked me when he touched me and kissed me, but then he started hurting me. He told me that he knew how to hurt me in ways that would leave scars no one could ever see. Recently, he would come into Grant's when I was working late at night and try to talk to me. I was so afraid he was going to make me lose my job. He got on the bus with me one night after work and sat by me. I had a long walk home on a dark road when I got off the bus. When I got off, he got off right behind me. I ran so fast that night. I ran all the way home. He didn't catch me or come to the house that night. But I was so scared."

Gene made a decision at that moment. "When you work late at night, you will never have to ride the bus home again. I'll be there to pick you up. If I can't be, Mike will be there. If he can't be there, my dad or Mrs. McVary will be. You have my promise." Gene would stand by his promise.

"Thank you, Gene. I would like that," said Carol. "Ever since the third grade, I have always thought people could tell what was happening to me. That is when girls started not being my friends." They all knew it had taken a lot out of Carol to talk about for the first time what had happened to her.

Colleen held Carol in her arms. "It's all right. Everything is going to be all right."

Danny took hold of Carol's hand. "You can stay here. No one would ever hurt you here. We love you, Carol."

"Now I'm afraid Gene and Mike won't like me anymore," said Carol very quietly.

"It doesn't change the way we feel about you. It's not your fault," said Gene.

"What's the matter, Mike? You are so quiet," asked Carol.

"I can't stand it that someone has been hurting you for such a long time," said Mike.

"He won't hurt her anymore. I'm going to see to that," said Colleen.

And so she did. The bad man never stayed at their house again during the time Carol lived there. She was never sure exactly what Colleen did, but her mother never mentioned anything to her. Carol sometimes wondered if she even knew. She did know that Colleen had told Alan, and she was fully aware of how powerful of a man he was.

Danny touched Carol's hair. "See, Carol, I told you, Mom loves you. Will you make everything all right for Carol, Mom?"

"I don't know if I can make everything all right, but I am going to try. I'm going to talk to Mr. Eliason for you today. I don't want you to have to go through it again. Your mother is my best friend. I feel that I need to tell her. I hope you understand that," said Colleen. "Always know that you are welcome to stay here whenever you need to. This will be your safe place. Now I think you all should go to school."

71

As Colleen watched them leave for school that morning, she couldn't help but be aware of how hard Mike was taking what had happened to Carol. He had been trying to protect Carol since he first met her when she was twelve, and now he was also trying to take care of her for Richard while he was in Vietnam. Colleen knew that he thought he had failed her, as did Gene.

They were so young to have to deal with all this. She would do all she could to help them, but she could only hope that it would be enough.

That afternoon Gene and Carol were the last to leave their sixth-hour speech class. As they walked by Mr. Eliason's desk, he said, "Carol, I changed your grade on your speech yesterday to an A. The fact that you could even stand up there and speak is more than I or possibly anyone else could do. Mrs. McVary talked to me this morning. She cares very much about you and is a very good friend to you, as are Gene and Mike. Gene, I have never seen anyone at the age of sixteen show as much care and concern for their classmate as you do for Carol. I commend and thank you for that. Always know that if either one of you ever need anything, I'll be here for you."

"Thank you. Mrs. McVary didn't want me to have to talk about it again," said Carol as she hugged Mr. Eliason.

Carol wished she felt strong, but at that moment, she didn't feel strong at all. Gene noticed and took hold of her arm. Just as Mike was protective of Carol, so was Gene.

PRESIDENT JOHN F. KENNEDY

On Friday, November 22, 1963, President John F. Kennedy was assassinated. Carol was working on the school newspaper that afternoon. She was a senior in high school. As they distributed the newspapers to the classrooms, many students as well as teachers were crying.

When Mike picked Danny, Carol, and Gene up after school that day, they were all visibly upset and confused and saddened by the happenings of the day. They went to Mike's house where his parents were already watching the events on the television. Danny sat by his mom, and she put her arms around him.

"Why would someone kill our president? He was such a nice man," asked Danny.

"I wish I could answer that for you, but I don't know, Danny. There are many bad people in the world. Why someone would take the life of our wonderful president, I have no explanation for," said Colleen.

Carol cried as she watched the television, as did Colleen. Gene put his arm around Carol and held her tight, as Mike did the same to his mother and Danny. Alan sat alone, staring at the television showing no emotion.

"Last year, his brother, Ted Kennedy, came here for a press conference with the journalism class. He was very kind to us, and we all liked him so much. I'm sorry, I can't seem to stop crying," said Carol.

Gene gently kissed Carol through her tears, and she rested her head on his shoulder.

"It's all right to cry. Sometimes I wish I could, but I have never been able to," said Gene.

Carol and Gene went to their individual homes that night, but they returned to Mike's house early the next morning. It was Saturday, but Alan went to work. It seemed as though he was uncomfortable with the emotions of Colleen, Danny, and Carol and the way Gene and Mike were comforting them. The five of them stayed close during that time and formed a bond that they would call upon to help them through rough times in the future.

In fact, three months from the date of President Kennedy's assassination, on February 22, 1964, they were to experience what was to be one of the greatest tragedies of their lives.

Alan was so hard on his children, and his wife also for that matter. He didn't know Gene too well yet, but he seemed too quiet and reserved for Alan's strict requirements. Carol came the closest to his desire for what he wanted his children to be, but today she seemed more sensitive than he liked.

Colleen, on the other hand, was kind and understanding with the four young people who watched the progression of that tragic event with her that weekend and into the following week. The five of them stayed close through that entire time. They felt secure and safe together.

Danny was so young, innocent, and confused about the horrible assassination. Carol was so heartbroken at the loss of the greatest president she had ever known, or for that matter ever would know in the future. Gene was so strong and dedicated to taking care of everyone, but he didn't really know what to do for them. And Mike, who was always so happy, now was sad and afraid for the future and of Vietnam where he would be in just ten short months. Colleen had so much love in her heart for the four young people and just wanted to help them through this rough time.

When they returned to school, the first thing Carol did was to begin writing an article for the school newspaper on the assassination of President Kennedy. It was a very well-written article, but when the newspaper was printed, a meeting was called by the journalism teacher and newspaper sponsor, Mr. Chambers. First, he wanted to know who wrote the article. Second, he wanted to know why an article on the assassination of the president was on page 3 and not page 1. Carol was page 3 editor, and she told him that since it was past news, it appeared on page 3, and because there was not room for it on page 1. He said that under no circumstances should it have been on any page except page 1, and it should have had a byline. Carol knew she had done something wrong regarding a subject she felt so strongly about. In essence, it was her fault, and she would suffer the consequences of that mistake.

She was only seventeen and had so much to learn, but she would not be able to further her journalism career as she had hoped to do. Carol would always wish she had done a better job regarding the article she wrote on President Kennedy's assassination, which was the most important event of her young life.

DANNY—LITTLE BOY LOST

As Danny entered his sophomore year in high school, he became overwhelmed with homework and difficult classes. He wasn't into sports and college prep classes like his older brothers and sister. He was an artist and musician, but his dad and the counselors at school didn't want him to take those classes.

In the fall of the school year, he started helping Mike and Carol with their unofficial club trying to help their fellow students with a primary focus on those being bullied. Every day after school, that is where Danny could be found. The students he met there seeking help were not necessarily those students who made good grades or were active in school activities. They were the students who fell through the cracks in the system. Danny liked helping these students as well as getting to know them. He took this after his big brother, Mike. Danny looked up to Mike, not just because he was small and Mike was tall, but because he worshipped Mike. And he loved Carol because she was so kind and patient with him and she never criticized him.

Danny had a nice girlfriend. She was small and blond like him. Her name was Maria. That fall Danny and Maria double-dated with Mike and Carol to the homecoming dance. The only reason Carol and Mike went to the dance was so they could take Danny and Maria.

Every day after school, Danny would go to the small office that Mike and Carol shared to see if there was anything he could do to help. Carol would work with him for a while until Mike finished football practice, and then he would take over and work with Danny. Mike and Danny were very close. They always had been.

One day Danny asked Carol, "Do you think Mike is disappointed in me because I am too skinny to play football and too short for basketball?"

"Not at all, Danny. He is so proud of your drawings and your music and everything you do," said Carol.

"Dad's not proud of me. He doesn't even like me," said Danny.

Carol put her arms around him. "I'm sure he loves you. You should talk to Mike. He loves you so much, Danny. Do you remember when your dad broke your Christmas village because he thought you were too old to be playing with it? That night Mike got every single piece out of the trash, and he stayed up all night putting it back together. He was so careful that you couldn't even tell it had been broken."

"I still have the village. I thought Mike did that for me," said Danny as Carol wiped a tear from his cheek. "I don't want to go to college. There are a lot of jobs you don't have to go to college to do."

"You're right. I'm just going to junior college for two years," said Carol.

Danny hardly ever missed a day to help them. And help he definitely did. He was very good with people.

One cold day, February 22, 1964, Danny didn't come. Carol was there that day a few minutes before Mike and found an envelope on their desk addressed to both of them. As she read the first line, she put her hand to her mouth and gasped. It was a suicide note from Danny. Just then Mike walked in, and she handed it to him. He read it quickly and told Carol to call 911 and tell them to go to the lake and give them the picnic area number. She did as he asked.

Mike and Carol immediately left and headed for the lake.

"Do you think we're going to be too late?" Mike asked Carol.

"I don't know, Mike. I really don't know." But in her heart, Carol felt that it was already too late and that it was already over.

In the car heading for the lake, they didn't speak again as Carol finished reading the letter.

They drove directly to the lake area where they had picnicked many times. Several police cars were already there, as was an ambulance. Danny's body was on the ground covered with a blanket. He was lying on a hill overlooking the lake in the secluded picnic area. His school jacket was folded neatly in his car several feet away. Danny had shot himself in the head with his father's gun.

Mike fell to his knees and cried. Carol embraced him. At that moment there was nothing she could do or say.

A policeman asked Mike, "Was there a suicide note?"

Mike handed him the paper he had crumpled in his hand.

"Do my parents have to see it?" asked Mike.

"They will want to see it." The policeman took the note. "We need a positive identification."

Mike couldn't seem to move. At that particular moment, he wasn't sure if he would ever move again. Carol walked to the stretcher where they had moved Danny. He was still covered up. A policeman pulled back the cover. Carol could hardly look at him, but she did because she had to.

"Yes, his name is Danny McVary. He's only sixteen."

Just then Gene pulled up and came running toward them. Carol had called him before they left the school. Gene went to where Carol was standing, and he also identified the body. Then they both went to Mike and helped him up.

"Carol, can you drive Mike back to his house?" asked Gene. "I'll follow in my car."

Gene's dad was on the police force, as was Carol's dad. There was a policeman at the scene that day who knew both of them.

"Gene, why don't you drive Mike's car? I'll follow in your car. I don't think she should be driving right now."

"Thank you," said Gene.

When they got back to the house, several police cars were already there. A policewoman was sitting by Colleen. She was crying as Carol sat by her and put her arm around her. Gene stayed with Mike. Alan was staring at the letter he was holding in his hands.

The police were asking many questions. Mike answered most of them. Gene helped him when he could. Alan couldn't, for the first time, seem to speak.

The letter was printed in Carol's memory forever.

Dear Mike and Carol,

By the time you read, this, I will have taken my life. I write to you because you two and Mom and Gene are the only people in the world who love and understand me. I can't do what they want me to do, Dad and the counselors. I can't make it. I just want to stay a little boy. Please don't hate me for what I have done. I love you, Mike, Carol, Gene, and Mom. Tell Maria how sorry I am and that I love her too. If I was just half as strong as you four are, I might be all right, but I'm not strong, so I'm going to go now.

Love,
Danny.

That day the secluded picnic area where Danny was found was closed, never to reopen, as was Carol and Mike's office at the high school.

REHEARSAL AND THE INVITATION

On the day of graduation rehearsal, Mr. Frank Grant, auto mechanics teacher, went to see Mr. Steve Chambers, senior class sponsor and journalism teacher.

"Hello, Steve. Do you have a few minutes?" asked Frank.

"Sure, I always have time for you," said Steve.

They had been roommates in college and remained good friends as well as colleagues.

"I have a student, John Kelley, who is concerned about all the steps in the auditorium and the long processional to the seats and, of course, about going up to the stage and more steps coming down. He is afraid he might fall and mess up graduation. He knows he won't be able to keep up with the processional. He is considering not attending," said Frank. "He had polio as a child and wears a brace on his leg."

Steve thumbed through the pages of the yearbook to John's picture.

"He is a really good young man. He is a straight A student in my class. He works nights and weekends as a mechanic. He has worked really hard in school to get to this point. I would like to see him have a memorable graduation experience. I thought you might know someone who wouldn't mind assisting him down the stairs and on the long walk," said Frank.

"I know the perfect person to assist him," said Steve.

He made the change at that very moment, and John Kelley and Carol Sullivan would be walking in the graduation processional together. He knew Carol well, and if there was ever anyone who needed help, Carol would be there and willing to help.

"Thanks, Steve. I'll make sure that he shows up for rehearsal," said Frank.

This one small change would change the lives and futures of many. Mr. Chambers didn't mention anything about this to Carol. He knew he didn't have to.

When rehearsal day arrived, John was there. He had convinced himself that it was only a rehearsal, even though Mr. Grant had said everything would be fine.

John struggled on the stairs going up upon entering the building, but at least there were handrails. David Adair, a nice boy and a friend of Carol's from elementary school, was a few people behind John in the lineup. He saw John stumble and went up to him immediately.

"If you have any problems, John, I'm just a little behind you," said David. They were now at the top of the stairs.

"Thanks, David. I'm a little worried," said John.

David looked across the aisle and saw that Carol was in the same position as John, which meant they would be walking together.

"You're a pretty lucky guy right now," said David.

"What do you mean?" asked John.

David had already gone back to his place in line. As John walked into the aisle, he understood what David was trying to tell him. He saw a beautiful girl with long red hair and green eyes coming toward him. He immediately remembered her as Richard's girlfriend, and she recognized him. She smiled slightly and extended her hand to him.

"Hello, John. I'm Carol."

John was tall. He had dark hair, light-blue eyes, and a very sweet smile. "I can't believe it. I'm walking in with Carol Sullivan, the prettiest, smartest, most popular girl in the class."

John was so happy and excited that he missed a step and almost fell. He was embarrassed, but Carol quickly calmed him and assured him that everything would be all right as David came hurrying forward.

"Can I help?" asked David.

"Thanks so much, David. We will be fine. Just don't let them come too fast behind us," said Carol. David nodded and went back to his place in line again. "John, just put your arm through mine. Hold on to me as tightly as you need to. We are going to take our time. Just relax, and I assure you everything will be all right."

He did just as she said, and it seemed to get easier. John walked tall beside Carol, and he held tightly to her. She put her other hand on his arm to steady it because he was trembling a little. He knew that he could now make it without falling.

"I'm surprised you knew my name. I don't even have anything listed by my name in the yearbook," said John.

"In journalism we get to know our classmates pretty well. I wrote an article on the automotive department, and you were in it," said Carol.

"I remember that. It was a great article, but I didn't know you wrote it," said John.

"I met you once when you were a sophomore. Richard Noland was your senior instructor in physical education. Do you remember?" asked Carol.

"Yes, you were nice to me like you are now. Richard helped me a lot in that class," said John.

The rest of the rehearsal went smoothly.

When it was over, Carol said, "Let's sit here until some of the crowd clears out."

"All right." John suddenly realized that he was still holding on to Carol's arm. He pulled his hand away. "I'm sorry."

"There is no need to be sorry," said Carol.

As they got up and slowly walked to the aisle, Mike joined them.

"Mike, I want you to meet my new friend, John Kelley."

"Nice to meet you, John. I'm Mike McVary." Mike shook hands with John. "Would you like to go out for pizza with us?"

"Sure, that sounds great." John was very happy. Two of the most popular students in the class just asked him to go out to eat with them.

"You two wait here. I'm parked far away. I'll pick you up. Do you have a car here, John?" asked Mike.

"No, I wasn't sure how long it would last, and I can't drive after dark. I have really bad eyesight," said John.

"We'll take you home after we eat," said Mike.

"Let's sit over here on the bench," said Carol.

John noticed he was doing it again, holding on to Carol's arm. "I'm sorry."

"It's all right. You never have to be sorry about anything. That's what brought us together. I feel like I've known you for more than just two hours," Carol smiled slightly.

John couldn't stop smiling. Even though Carol was very open and friendly and she smiled a little, John sensed a deep sadness in her eyes. Because of his own problems, he was always acutely aware of other people's problems.

When Mike picked them up, Gene Sandusky, the class president, was with him. Mike introduced them.

"Hi, John. I remember you, physical education sophomore year. I helped you with basketball," said Gene.

"Hi, Gene. You were really nice to me, and you helped me so much," said John. John was excited. And now the class president was joining them. John couldn't believe it.

When they were waiting for their pizza, Mike asked John a question. "With all the graduation events coming up and prom, and some at night, why don't you go with us so you don't have to drive."

"I don't want to interfere, and I wouldn't have a date," said John.

"You and Gene and I will all be Carol's date. It takes that many to protect her from all the guys who would like to date her," Mike smiled.

"I've never been to a school party or a game or a play. I've never even been on a date. I might not be much fun for you to be around," said John.

"I would love for you to be with us. We will all take care of one another," Carol spoke very quietly as a single tear ran down her cheek. Mike reached over and wiped it away. Carol got up from the table. "Please excuse me. I'll be back in a minute." She was crying as she walked away.

Mike tried to explain Carol's emotions to John as his eyes were filling with tears also. "You see, John, about three months ago, my little brother, Danny, committed suicide. We had a small office where we tried to help people, but we closed the doors that day never to reopen them. Since then we have all cried, but my poor, sweet Carol has cried more than anyone. Today as she was helping and talking with you, I saw a little light in her eyes again. She's a giver and a helper. She needs to be doing that."

Gene said, "She has been through a lot lately. We are trying to help her, but sometimes I feel she helps us more than we do her. She is such a kind, gentle girl."

"I really like her. She was so nice to me during the rehearsal. She seemed to really care about me," said John.

"She does care about you, John. I could tell from the short while I saw you together," said Gene.

Carol returned to the table. As she sat down, John noticed how fragile, delicate, and beautiful she looked.

Gene very gently touched Carol's cheek. "Are you all right?"

"I'll be fine. I just get a little emotional once in a while. I can't help it," Carol said quietly. "Please forgive me, John."

"You've made it possible for me to be at graduation. I'll be forever grateful to you for that," said John. "I don't have any friends, and now you are all being so nice to me."

"Well, John, I think you may be wrong about that. You have three really good, loyal friends now," said Mike.

John looked at Carol. She smiled slightly, but she still had tears in her eyes as she put her arms around him and said, "I want you to be our friend. You seem kind. I don't think you would ever hurt me."

Gene didn't smile, but he seemed very sincere as he reached out to shake John's hand. "We would be honored if you would be our friend."

And so it was at graduation rehearsal in 1964 that a true bond of friendship had been formed between three young men and one young woman who were heading in different directions after graduation: one to a four-year university, one to junior college, one directly to the workforce, and one to Vietnam. It didn't seem to matter that they were all following different paths, for their destiny was to be friends for a long time.

GRANDMA AND GENE

When Carol met Gene in sophomore geometry class, she immediately remembered him as the little boy she had first met when she was eight years old.

Ethan was ten then, and he was repeating the fourth grade. He was in a split class of third and fourth grades. Unfortunately for Ethan, he was actually working more on a third-grade level. He told Carol about a little third-grader who the teacher asked to help him sometimes with his studies. He told her that the little boy had a patch in his eye and wore thick glasses. He fell down a lot and was always getting hurt. The other kids were mean to him and no one played with him. Ethan had the same problem, so they became friends. Ethan was tall, and his little friend was very small. His name was Gene.

One Saturday when Ethan and Carol were at their grandmother's house, Ethan asked Carol if she would go with him to visit his new friend.

"Maybe he can come to Grandma's house, and we can play in the backyard," said Ethan.

"Shall we ride our bikes?" asked Carol.

"Yes, I guess so," said Ethan.

And so they started out up two steep hills to Gene's house on Strawberry Hill. Carol's bike was too big for her, but she was always far ahead of Ethan.

"That's his house, the one with the fence," said Ethan.

They left their bikes in the yard and walked up the steps to the porch. Carol knocked on the door as Ethan stood back. He was shy with adults. A nice lady answered the door, and there was a small boy holding her hand.

"Hello, I'm Carol. This is my cousin, Ethan. We are staying at our grandmother's house on Baltimore today, and we wanted to know if Gene could play with us."

"Gene, this is Carol and Ethan. Ethan is the boy who is so nice to you, and you help him with his arithmetic," said Gene's mommy. "Do you want to go play with them?"

"Yes, Mommy," said Gene very quietly.

"I see you have bikes. Gene can only ride his bike on the sidewalk because he doesn't see well," said Gene's mommy.

"We will leave our bikes here. We will ride them home when we bring Gene back," said Carol.

"Gene is very small and not very strong, and he falls down easily. Please take good care of him," said Gene's mommy.

"We won't let anything happen to him," said Carol.

As they walked down the stairs, Gene turned and waved to his mommy. She noticed that Carol took hold of Gene's hand and Ethan took hold of his other hand. She had a good feeling about them, and she was glad they were her little boy's friends.

When they got to their grandma's house, their Uncle Ray was sitting at the kitchen table.

"Hi, my name is Gene. Ethan and Carol are my friends."

"Well, it's nice to meet you, Gene. I'm Uncle Ray."

Gene hugged Uncle Ray.

Their grandmother was sitting in her rocking chair in the living room. Gene went to her.

"I'm Gene, and I am in Ethan's class at school. Ethan and Carol are very nice to me."

"Well, I can certainly see why. You are a very sweet little boy," said Grandma. He hugged her, and she lifted him onto her lap. He was so small and as light as a feather. "Are you tired, honey? Do you need to rest?"

"I'm fine. I just wanted to hug you," said Gene.

"Well, you can hug me anytime you want to," said Grandma.

"We have a swing in the backyard. Do you like to swing?" asked Carol.

"That would be fun," said Gene as he slowly climbed down off Grandma's lap.

Ethan took Gene's hand, and they headed toward the backyard.

"Carol, come here a minute please," said Grandma. "Be careful and gentle with him. He is so small and delicate. You are a foot taller than he is, and Ethan is two feet taller."

Carol took her Grandma's hand. "I know, Grandma. We will take good care of him. Ethan takes care of him on the playground at school. The other kids are very mean to him, and sometimes they push him down. They make fun of him."

"I'm sorry to hear that," said Grandma. "Why are some kids so mean?"

"I don't know, but Ethan and I will always take care of him and treat him good," said Carol.

When Carol went to the backyard, Ethan was pushing Gene very gently in the swing. Ethan helped Gene get into the wagon, and they took him for a ride around the yard. Then they went inside. They colored and played Chinese checkers. Grandma gave them some milk and cookies.

Gene was rubbing his head as he went to Grandma. "What's the matter, honey? Don't you feel well?" asked Grandma.

"I have a headache," said Gene.

"What does your mommy do when you have a headache?" asked Grandma.

"She takes my glasses off, and she holds me and rocks me," said Gene quietly.

"I can do that." Grandma held out her hands to the sweet little boy and lifted him to her lap. She took his glasses off. He put his head on her shoulder, and she rocked him to sleep.

Ethan and Carol sat on the floor by their grandma. "He gets a lot of headaches in school, and sometimes he gets really sick. The teacher asks me to take him to the nurse's office," said Ethan.

"Poor little guy. He has a rough time. I'm very proud of you for taking such good care of him," said Grandma as she kissed the sweet little boy on the forehead.

About forty-five minutes later, Gene woke up. He put his arms around Grandma and kissed her on the cheek. "Thank you. My headache is gone."

She put his glasses on him. She could tell he couldn't see well at all without them.

"It's almost four o'clock. I think your mommy wants you home by four thirty," said Carol.

"I'm sorry, I got a headache. Will you let me come back again?" asked Gene.

"Of course. We love you, Gene," Carol said as she put her arms around him.

"Will you be all right walking home?" asked Uncle Ray.

"I'm fine now, but thank you for asking," said Gene.

As Grandma and Uncle Ray waved to them, they watched the three good friends walk up the hill to Gene's house.

"Did you notice how good Carol and Ethan treated that sweet little boy?" said Grandma. "They know he is not very strong so they walk slowly so he can keep up with them and not fall. He is so much smaller than they are."

"They are good kids. Carol is really the good one, but she is rubbing off on Ethan," said Uncle Ray.

When they got to Gene's house, Gene's mommy greeted them warmly, "Did you have fun?"

"Yes, Mommy, they are very nice to me," said Gene.

Gene's mommy took hold of Carol's hand. "You are both welcome to come here and play with Gene anytime."

"Bye, Gene. I'll see you at school Monday," said Ethan.

"Bye, Ethan, bye, Carol," said Gene.

Carol hugged Gene, and they got on their bikes and rode down the steep hills.

Gene sat on his mommy's lap in the big rocking chair.

"You like your new friends, don't you?"

"Oh yes, very much. They always help me, and they are very nice to me. Carol talks so nice to me that she makes me feel good. I wish they lived closer. Carol lives on Garfield, and that is far west. Ethan lives in Armourdale," said Gene.

"But they stay at their grandma's house a lot, don't they?" asked Gene's mommy.

"Yes, she is nice too, and so is their Uncle Ray," said Gene.

Carol and Ethan were invited to come play with Gene the following Saturday. They played inside for a little while, and then Gene asked his mommy if he could ride his bike on the sidewalk with Carol and Ethan. He missed a turn and hit the edge of the fence. It was a bad fall for the little boy. His mommy was watching, and she picked him up quickly and took him inside. Carol knew he fell because he couldn't see the edge of the fence. His mommy washed his skinned legs and arms and put some medicine on the cuts. When she was finished, she sat him on the sofa by Carol. He didn't cry, but he was very close to it.

"Are you all right, Gene?" asked Carol.

Gene nodded his head yes. Carol put her arms around Gene. They were only eight, but Carol felt protective of the sweet, gentle little boy, and Gene already loved Carol as only a small child can.

Gene had a book on his lap. "Is your book good?" asked Carol.

"The print is too small. I can't see well enough to read it," said Gene.

"Would you like for me to read it to you?" asked Carol.

"I would love that," said Gene. "I like the sound of your voice."

And so she read to Gene and would in the future many, many times.

At recess the next week, a bully named Caleb pushed Gene down, and he broke his right arm. He wasn't at school the rest of the week. On Saturday, Carol and Ethan went to his house. His mommy was glad to see them.

"You have company, Gene. Your friends are here to see you."

"Hi, Carol and Ethan. Nobody ever comes to see me," said Gene.

"Well, we are here now just to see you because we missed you," said Carol.

He was on the sofa. He had a cover over him and a pillow behind his back. There was a cast and a sling on his tiny arm.

"That boy really hurt me this time. I don't know why he doesn't like me."

"I miss you at school," said Ethan.

"I'm afraid to go back. I'm afraid of those mean boys," said Gene.

"I'll try to protect you better. I should have been with you that day. But I was too slow, and I had to stay in class," said Ethan.

"I should have waited for you," said Gene.

"Grandma is worried about you," said Carol.

"I would like to see her," said Gene.

"I have an idea. Why don't we go visit Carol and Ethan's grandma. I would like very much to meet her. Gene loves her so much," said Gene's mommy.

"That would be good," said Gene.

Gene's mommy carried him to the car. Carol and Ethan got in the back seat. When they arrived at Grandma's house, Gene's mommy carried him in.

"Look who's here, Grandma. Gene and his mommy came to visit," said Ethan.

"Well, there's my sweet little boy," said Grandma.

Gene held out his hand to her.

"I think he wants to sit on your lap. He is not too heavy, is he?" asked Gene's mommy.

"He's as light as a feather. Put him on this side so I don't hurt his arm." She kissed him. "I'm so sorry that mean boy hurt you."

Gene's mommy sat on the sofa and put her arm around Carol. "He doesn't want to go back to school. He is so afraid."

"I just don't understand the bullying and all the mean kids," said Grandma.

"My little Gene is so kind and sweet. He has never hurt anyone," said Gene's mommy.

"When I'm older, I am going to stop bullying. I'm going to make everyone nice," said Carol very seriously.

"She could probably do it," said Ethan. "Carol can do anything."

"Uncle Ray made a new swing just for you, Gene. You can swing in it with your broken arm. You'll like it," said Carol.

Just then, Uncle Ray came into the room. "I'll take him out in the yard and show it to him." He gently took the little boy from Grandma, and Carol and Ethan went with them to the yard.

"You are all so nice. I can see where Carol and Ethan get their kindness. My name is Theresa," said Gene's mommy.

"My name is Alice," said Grandma. "Carol and Ethan have practically raised themselves. Ethan doesn't have the best parents. His dad hits him. His mother is my daughter, Ramona, and she doesn't try to stop him. If I was younger, I would take them both and raise them. I've raised seventeen kids, and I don't think I did such a bad job. Carol's mother, Stella, is my youngest daughter. She was my best daughter. She tries to be a good mother, but I think Carol is too much for her. Carol is very smart. I don't know where she gets it. Carol doesn't like to stay at her house. She calls this house a safe place. I'm not sure what is wrong. I've asked, but she won't tell me. I hate the thought that someone could hurt her."

"Do you think it's her parents?" asked Theresa.

"No. They rent a room to a man who comes to town occasionally to work. She doesn't like him. But she won't say any more than that. She knows that her parents need the money that he pays them," said Alice.

"She is so pretty and kind, and she seems so much older than eight," said Theresa.

"Ethan tries to be like Carol, but he is a slow learner. He has always had so much trouble in school. I think that both Gene and Carol can be good influences on him," said Alice.

"I am so glad Gene has Ethan at school. He needs him. He is just so tiny and weak. He needs help with almost everything," said Theresa.

Uncle Ray and the children came in the back door. He was still carrying Gene. He very gently set him on Grandma's lap.

"Thank you for the swing. It's like a chair. It has arms and a bar across it so I won't fall out," said Gene.

"Thank you for taking care of my little boy. It is so kind of you," said Theresa.

Grandma put her arms lovingly around the little boy, being careful not to hurt his broken arm. He touched her hair and cheek with his tiny hand.

"He likes to do that because it helps him to see you better. Gene is a very special little boy, and he loves us. And when someone like Gene loves you, it makes you a better person," said Carol.

Theresa hugged Carol. "Come here, Ethan. You need a hug too."

"I like the way Carol talks. She always makes me feel better," said Ethan.

"She makes me feel better too, Ethan," said Theresa.

"Carol, would you go to school with me Monday, and, Mommy, you too?" asked Gene.

Theresa and Carol looked at one another. "Well, I will take you to school, but Carol has to be at her school at that time."

"I thought she could talk to my classmates, and then they would be nice to me," said Gene.

"I'll go. My teacher would let me. She's very nice. She would understand. You could call her. My mom wouldn't want to," said Carol.

Grandma noticed that Gene was holding tightly to Carol's hand, and she knew how afraid he was of going back to school. "She wants to help. I would say let her do it."

"All right. I'll pick you both up here Monday morning," said Theresa.

On Monday morning, Theresa called Carol's teacher and explained the situation to her. The teacher, Mrs. Collins, was very kind and understanding. Both Carol and Ethan were waiting at the curb when Theresa and Gene arrived on Monday.

"Are you all right, Gene? You look a little sad," said Carol as she took hold of Gene's hand.

"I'm a little scared, and my leg hurts," said Gene.

"I'll carry him in. The cut on his leg is really deep, and I know it hurts," said Theresa.

In Gene's classroom, Theresa and Mrs. Willis, his teacher, sat behind the desk. Gene sat in front of the teacher's desk, and Carol was standing beside him, but she pulled a chair up beside Gene just in case he needed her to sit by him. When all the students were seated, Carol began speaking. Although her voice was soft and kind, it held an edge of determination unusual for someone so young.

"My name is Carol Sullivan. I am in the third grade at Roosevelt Elementary School. But I recognize several of you from my grandmother's neighborhood, Adam, Sally, Claude, Felicia, Casey, and Paula. We've all played together on South Baltimore. Do you remember me? And, of course, Ethan too. He's my cousin. I'm here today with my friend, Gene. It is his first day back after getting hurt on the playground a week ago. His right arm was broken, and his leg was cut badly. He's smaller than most of us, and his arms are very tiny, so he is easily hurt, and he doesn't see well. We need to protect him and take care of him. When Ethan and I play with Gene, we are very gentle with him. My uncle made a special swing for him so he can swing without falling and hurting his arm or leg. He likes it very much. I will be going back to my school, and his mommy will be going home. We would like for all of you to look out for him and take care of him. Please don't let anyone be mean to him or hurt him. He is a very sweet, nice boy. Talk to him, get to know him, and be his friend. I'm very glad he is my friend." Carol hugged Gene and sat down beside him.

There was a voice from the back of the room. It was Caleb. "I'm sorry. I didn't mean to hurt him." Caleb was crying.

Carol walked back to him, and she put her arms around him and said, "I didn't think you would hurt him on purpose. Now maybe you can help protect him, so he doesn't get hurt again."

"I will. I promise," said Caleb.

And that day a plan took form in the little girl's mind that in the future, she would not only help the one being bullied but also the one doing the bullying.

Theresa and Mrs. Willis were both wiping tears from their eyes, as were many students. Carol had touched them all deeply. She spoke very quietly and softly to her little friend Gene, "We have to leave now. Will you be all right?"

Gene shook his head yes, but as he looked at his classmates, they all looked so big to the tiny little boy. Carol and Theresa helped Gene to his desk in the front row so he could see the board. He hugged them both, and then they left.

"You did a fine job, Carol. I think they will be nice to him, but it is so difficult to leave him. He just looks so small and helpless," said Theresa.

Two months later, Gene slipped on a patch of ice on an outside flight of stairs at school. He didn't see the ice and was unable to catch himself on the railing with his left hand. He was just not strong enough. He hurt his leg, his back, and his head. An ambulance was called. Gene was admitted to the hospital. Two days later, Grandma, Carol, and Ethan went to visit him.

Carol's first thought was how small he looked under the white covers in the hospital bed. Then she realized that he looked smaller because they were getting so much taller. His mommy was with him.

Grandma sat close to him. "How's my sweet little boy?"

"I'll be all right," said Gene through his tears, but yet he wasn't really crying. He just had a few tears in his eyes.

"You're the bravest little boy I have ever known," said Grandma.

"Hi, Carol. Hi, Ethan," said Gene.

"I miss you in school, Gene," said Ethan.

"Is anyone helping you with your reading and arithmetic?" asked Gene.

"Sally and Claude help me sometimes. They are not as smart as you, but I like that they help me," said Ethan.

Carol kissed her sweet little friend on the cheek. "We all love you very much, Gene. We miss you so much."

"I'll be home soon. Will you come see me?" asked Gene.

"We'll come to see you," said Carol.

"Don't forget me," said Gene.

"I promise you, we will never forget you," said Carol.

And they never did. All through his recovery time, they visited him. Ethan even brought his homework to him so he didn't get too far behind.

In the spring, Gene went back to school. He was in a tiny wheelchair, and his mommy went with him to help him during the day.

There was a firehouse in Gene's neighborhood, next-door to his house. Gene would sit in his yard and wave to the firemen as they drove by. They always waved back. They noticed his broken arm and now that he was in a wheelchair. His two special firemen friends were Rusty and Clayton. They would pick Gene up and take him to the firehouse to sit in the fire truck, have lunch with them, or watch them play basketball. They asked him about his injuries and his eyes. He told them about the kids at school making fun of him and hurting him. The little boy's story touched the firemen deeply.

They got together and gave him an all-expense-paid trip to Chicago. They would see all the sights and old fire trucks in a museum that he was very excited about. They would stay three days. The trip was for Gene and four others. His family couldn't go because of work and school. Those who went with him were his mommy, Grandma, Carol, and Ethan. It was the first time any of them had ever been on an airplane. Carol got them through the Kansas City airport, checked their luggage, and boarded the plane without any trouble. It was as though she had done it many times before. They got to do everything that was scheduled in Chicago. Everyone enjoyed the trip. They were so grateful for the kindness of the firemen.

That summer, Gene would travel to Chicago again, but this would be a much different trip than the first trip. Gene would be having heart surgery. It was a very serious surgery, and Gene was so tiny and weak. It would be a very long time before Carol and Ethan would see Gene again.

Carol and Ethan would visit Rusty and Clayton at the firehouse many times. They would talk about their memories of their little friend Gene, and they would cry, and they would pray for him.

On that first trip, Gene and Carol more than the others were extremely fond of Chicago. Little did they know in 1954, when they were only eight years old, that more than thirty years later, Chicago would be a primary location and an integral part of both of their lives.

Ten years later, in 1964, when they were seventeen and eighteen, Carol, Gene, Mike, and John were going to Gene's house for pictures before they went to senior prom. But their first stop was at Grandma's house. She was sitting in the same chair where she used to rock Gene when he was a tiny little boy.

"Hello, Grandma. We wanted to come to see you before we go to prom," said Carol. "You remember my friend, Mike, don't you?"

"Oh yes. You both look so nice. You've grown since I last saw you, Mike. Carol, your dress is pretty, and your hair looks beautiful. You both have the same color of hair. You two almost look like sister and brother," said Grandma.

"Mike has always looked out for me ever since Richard went to Vietnam. Mike will be going to Vietnam soon too," said Carol.

"Come home safe, Mike. You are so young, and war is so brutal," said Grandma.

Mike smiled, "I'll be all right. I'll be back. Don't worry about me."

And then John stepped up. "Oh my. Another nice-looking young man," said Grandma.

"This is my friend, John. I'll be walking with him in the graduation processional," said Carol.

"If it wasn't for Carol, I wouldn't even be able to be in the graduation processional. I need to hold on to her arm. I had polio as a child," said John. "I have difficulty walking, and I walk slowly."

"Carol will help you. You never have to worry about that," said Grandma. "She is an exceptionally wonderful girl."

John kissed Grandma on the cheek. "Mike and I are going to step aside. Carol has someone very special to see you now."

And then Carol walked toward Grandma on the arm of the most handsome man she had ever seen. He was six feet five inches tall and had the build of a football quarterback and a basketball player that he was. He had dark hair, light-blue eyes, and wore glasses. Grandma saw a familiarity about him but wasn't quite sure until Carol spoke.

"Grandma, do you remember the sweet little boy who used to sit on your lap in that same rocking chair years ago? This is that little boy you loved so much all grown-up. Grandma, this is Gene."

She put her arms around him, and they hugged for a long time, and Grandma was crying.

"Thank you for being kind to me when I was a little boy. I have never forgotten you," said Gene.

"Nor I you," said Grandma.

Mike added, "Gene was the best quarterback ever, and he took the basketball team to a state championship."

"That is wonderful," said Grandma. "You've grown so strong and tall and handsome. I hope you all have a wonderful time tonight."

"We will. We will all take care of one another as we always have and just as you took care of me when I was a little boy," said Gene.

Grandma gently touched Gene's cheek. "How are your eyes, sweetie?"

"I still don't see well, but I get by all right," said Gene as he took off his glasses and rubbed his eyes. "I still get bad headaches. I've actually got one right now."

Grandma kissed him on the cheek. "Your eyes are so pretty and so light. I always remember how light they were. Is your headache bad?"

"No, I'll be fine. I just look at Carol's pretty red hair and green eyes. It always makes me better to look at her," said Gene.

"You are still that same sweet little boy, although you are not little anymore," said Grandma. "I'll never forget when the firemen sent you on that trip to Chicago, and you invited us to go with you. Do you remember who our guide was on that trip?"

"It was Carol, and she was only eight but somehow she knew where to go," said Gene. "I always wondered how you did that."

"The firemen gave me a book on Chicago and a map. Other than that, I don't actually know," said Carol.

"I was a little boy in a wheelchair, and I put all my trust in you. I never doubted you for a minute."

Carol and Gene hugged one another.

As the four fine young people left for prom that evening, Grandma wondered how things would all turn out for them. Mike and John seemed like nice young men, but her heart was with Gene. There had always been something very special about him. She had loved him since he sat on her lap and hugged her when he was only eight. She would love to see Carol and Gene together forever, but in her heart she knew that would never happen. They were two people who to her seemed so perfect for one another, and yet as we all know, it is not a perfect world, nor has it ever been.

There was one more stop before Gene's house, but it was right next-door at the firehouse. As the foursome walked into the firehouse, the first two firemen they saw were Rusty and Clayton. Many of the other men were new, but Gene and Carol would have known Rusty and Clayton anywhere.

All the greetings were heartfelt and genuine, and there were many tears. Rusty was the most emotional.

"You know, Gene, I've seen you many times through the years. I've even watched you play football and basketball. But I still remember that tiny little boy that I picked up and carried over here to sit in the fire truck and have lunch with us so long ago."

"I'll never forget that. I was a little boy with so many problems, and all of you were so kind to me," said Gene.

"Remember the trip we sent you on?" asked Clayton.

"That was a good trip. It was a really good trip," said Gene.

"And we trusted this young lady to get you all where you needed to be, and she did," said Rusty.

"I had a lot of people depending on me. I couldn't let them down," said Carol.

"Theresa told me you were like a seasoned traveler at the airport, and it was as though you had been to Chicago a hundred times," said Rusty. "But the strange thing is, you were only eight."

"I wanted it to be good for Gene," said Carol.

"And you did just that. It couldn't have been better." Gene hugged Carol and kissed her on the cheek. "These are our friends, Mike and John."

There were many more greetings and tears in the firehouse before they left. Carol, Mike, and John liked it very much that everyone loved Gene because they also loved him.

JOHN'S FAMILY

Three days after graduation rehearsal, Carol and Mike invited John to go out to eat with them. John had to go to work for a short while after school that day to do some finishing work on a car for one of his teachers. They were to meet John at his house. His mother came to the door. She was pretty and youthful-looking. Her name was Rose.

Carol and Mike were introduced to John's sisters—Charlene was twelve, Darla was eight, and little Meggie was four. They were all pleasant and friendly.

"You're the first friends of John's who have ever come by to pick him up," said Rose.

"We just met three days ago. John's a great guy. We've just seemed to click," said Mike.

Little Meggie walked over and stood in front of Carol. Carol reached her hands out to Meggie and picked her up and set her on her lap. Meggie had brain damage from an injury Rose had received when she was pregnant. Meggie was a very sweet, loving little girl.

There were tears in Rose's eyes as she said, "Meggie never goes to anyone. She sees something very special in you."

"She's very sweet," said Carol as she hugged Meggie and Meggie rested her head on Carol's shoulder.

Mike said, "Since Carol and I both have red hair and green eyes, we can never marry because that would mean all our children would have red hair and green eyes."

Mike laughed, and Charlene and Darla thought he was funny too.

Rose smiled. "Do you mind if I ask a personal question?"

Carol smiled slightly at Rose, "You can ask us anything."

"Are you boyfriend and girlfriend?" asked Rose.

"No, we're just friends. We have known one another since the seventh grade." Carol glanced at Mike, but he quickly looked down at Meggie. He didn't feel like commenting at that moment.

"I feel so good about you two being John's friends," said Rose.

"John will always be safe with us. We will always be kind to him. We love him and will help him all we can," said Carol sincerely. "Gene is also our friend. He thinks the world of John. He can't be here with us today."

"Yes, he told me about Gene," said Rose. "He has told me about all of you. He is very fortunate that such good people care about him. I know that you are all very good students. And, Mike, I know that you and Gene both are on the football and basketball teams. I know that Gene has been president of the class for three years. And, Mike, I know that you were also a class officer. As for you, Carol, John has told me that you will probably receive a scholarship to the University of Kansas for journalism. John is very proud of all of you."

"Well, I think we are the lucky ones. John is incredibly nice," said Carol.

They could hear the pride in her voice as Rose talked about John. "John was the sweetest, most beautiful little boy. He would always smile even when he would fall down. He would just get back up and try again. He would say, 'Look, Mommy, I can do it.' But my precious little boy could never run and play like the other kids. He would sit on the porch and play with his little cars while he would watch the other neighborhood children riding their bicycles and playing ball and tag. He had so many problems, and I only wanted things to be better for him." Rose's voice cracked.

Mike walked over to her and hugged her, and Carol held her hand.

A short while later, when John walked in, Carol was still holding Meggie. He looked at them and smiled and said, "Why does this not surprise me? Meggie will only go to good people. She can sense it." John sat by Carol on the sofa and took Meggie in his arms. Meggie looked up at John and smiled. "Mom, do you want me to put Meggie to bed?"

"No, I'll take care of her. You go with your friends. You deserve it," said Rose.

"I cleaned up down at the garage. I didn't want you guys to see me all dirty and greasy," said John.

"It was a pleasure to meet you and your family," Mike said to Rose as they got up to leave.

Carol hugged Rose, kissed Meggie, and said, "Say goodbye to the other girls for us. You have a wonderful family."

"Thank you," said Rose.

As Mike, Carol, and John left, Rose took Meggie into the bedroom and lay down on the bed beside her. She would lie there awake late into the night long after Meggie fell asleep. Her tears soaked the pillow because she knew from that brief encounter with Carol and Mike and then with John that her son was already in love with Carol. But she also knew that Mike was in love with Carol even though he didn't say it. She could tell. John had told her that Carol had dated Richard before he went to Vietnam and that Mike would be going there soon. She knew that Richard's father was a banker and that Mike's father was a lawyer and that Gene's father was chief of police, and she thought of her own little family that lived far beneath the poverty level. But she also knew there was something special about the way Carol looked at John. Carol was such a pretty sweet girl, and she seemed so kind. It was early in the game. No one could know how it would all play out. After all, Carol and John had only known one another for a short while.

But there was one thing that Rose could not get out of her mind that night. She had once asked John to promise her that after she was gone, he would always care for Meggie. That evening she saw clearly that Carol cared for Meggie, and Meggie had already chosen Carol.

Rose wanted so much for her son. He had worked so hard to make it to his high school graduation day. Nothing had ever been easy for John. He needed an eye operation, but it was very expensive, and they had no insurance. Rose felt somewhat overwhelmed knowing that she still had three more children to raise. She only hoped that her health would hold out so she would be able to raise her children. It would be too much to expect John to raise the three girls with all his own problems. Rose had no other family. It was just her and her four children.

But in a few short years, Rose would receive help from a very unlikely source. Because of the relationship that had just developed between John and his three new friends, their lives were destined to be changed for the better.

CHAPTER

17

SENIOR PROM

They were a very impressive group of four who went to senior prom together. They were meeting at Gene's house before the prom for pictures. Carol's mother and John's mother were meeting them there. Mike's parents were unable to be there that evening.

All the guys were tall and dressed very well that evening, as was Carol. Mike was six feet four inches tall. With his wavy red hair and green eyes and youthful, pleasant appearance, he was very attractive in his light-gray suit, white shirt, and black tie.

Gene was six feet five inches tall. He had brown hair and light-blue eyes and wore glasses. He had a very athletic and muscular build. Gene was charismatic and very kind and gentle. He was popular and well-liked, but he never smiled. He was very handsome in a dark-gray suit, white shirt, and red tie.

John was six feet three inches and slimmer than the other two, but his arms were muscular. With John's dark brown hair and blue eyes, his navy-blue suit, light-blue shirt and tie, he was very striking. John wore glasses, but he was not wearing them tonight because they didn't help him much anymore. John had a beautiful smile, and he was always happy.

And then there was Carol. Her dress was knee-length because she didn't like long dresses. The skirt was tiered with different pastel colors. The bodice was light-blue princess style with a sweetheart neckline. Her dress was from a secondhand store, but it fit her personality as well as her budget, and it was also the prettiest dress at prom. Carol was five feet six inches and had the type of figure many girls envied. She had long, thick red hair that fell in waves and curls over her shoulders and down her back. She had green eyes and pretty, full lips. She wore very little, if any, makeup. She was a pretty, sweet, kind girl.

The parents sat on the porch and watched as the group of fine young people left. Mr. Sandusky was first to speak.

"Which handsome prince will end up with the beautiful princess?"

The ladies said nothing, but they were thinking.

John's mother, Rose, was first to speak, "John has never been to a prom before or even on a date. Carol is so kind to him. But Gene and Mike are kind to him too."

Mrs. Sandusky was a quiet lady, but tonight she had an opinion. "I have not seen the four of them together before. There is definitely a chemistry between Carol and John. It is electrifying."

Carol's mother, Stella, said, "Rose, don't worry about John tonight. Carol cares for him very much. She will always be kind to him. They will all take good care of him."

Rose replied, "Thank you. He is such a dear, sweet boy. I've always been so protective of him."

Mrs. Sandusky said, "You have some help now."

When the group of four arrived at the prom venue, they noticed how pretty it was decorated. All eyes were on them, and many greeted them. They found a table close to the door. Carol noticed that John was already having some trouble walking, so she held tightly to his arm. They sat down, and Gene and Mike went to get punch for everyone.

Janice and Roy were the first to stop by their table. Janice was visibly upset.

"Roy is going to Stanford and not to KU with me. We've been going together for four years."

Roy said, "What about Mike and Carol? Mike's going to Vietnam. That's a lot further than Stanford."

Carol took hold of Janice's hand. "You two will be fine. You'll probably both be back here next summer."

Janice smiled as Roy said, "Sure, we'll have next summer." Roy put his arm around Janice as they went to the dance floor.

"You made her happy. Now she has hope for their relationship," said John.

"This is a happy night. Besides, it is what she wanted to hear," said Carol.

"I'm sorry that I can't dance with you," said John.

"That's all right. I'm content to just be here with you. Mike doesn't like to dance. Neither does Gene, but he is a little more willing than Mike," said Carol.

Mike and Gene returned with the punch. As soon as they sat down, Denise Gardner asked Gene to dance. He hesitantly went to the dance floor with her.

Mike said, "Gene doesn't care for her. She is always bothering him."

After Gene danced with Denise, he sat back down. "I wish they would just leave me alone."

"The girls all like you, Gene," said Mike.

"You're lucky, Mike. They always consider you as being Carol's date, not me," said Gene.

Mr. Chambers, the class sponsor, walked to the microphone. "Excuse me, but could I have everyone's attention for a moment. It is time to announce the senior prom king and queen. The prom king is Gene Sandusky."

"I don't believe this is happening to me," said Gene as he got up and went to the stage.

"Poor Gene, I don't think he is very comfortable with that honor," said Carol very quietly as they all gave him a round of applause.

Mr. Chambers crowned Gene and said, "And the prom queen, I am very proud to say, is…"—he paused slightly—"Carol Sullivan."

Carol had a look of disbelief on her face as she hugged both John and Mike before walking to the stage. Mr. Chambers hugged Carol and crowned her.

"Now would the king and queen begin the next dance."

Gene took Carol's hand. "I guess we are going to have to dance together after all."

"I don't mind," said Carol.

It was a slow dance, and he held her close. Mike and John watched them.

"I'm glad they won. I thought they might," said Mike.

"I thought you would win," said John. "He loves her too, doesn't he?"

"He always has since sophomore geometry class. Gene is one of my best friends, but I think he always seems kind of sad. Even dancing with Carol, he doesn't seem really happy. Just like everyone else, he thinks Carol belongs to me, but she doesn't. I'm just her protector," said Mike.

"But you love her, don't you?" asked John.

Mike didn't answer, but he didn't have to. John knew. When the dance ended, Gene and Carol returned to the table.

"Sorry to take her away from you guys," said Gene.

"Congratulations," said Mike. "This couldn't have happened to two better people."

"You two looked good out there dancing," said John.

"Thanks. It felt pretty good to be dancing with the only girl in the room that I wanted to dance with," said Gene.

"Excuse me, there is something I need to do."

Carol got up and walked to the other side of the room where a group of about twelve girls were standing. They didn't have dates. One of the girls in the group was a small girl with curly blond hair named Bonnie. Carol had helped Bonnie with her hair that afternoon, and she had given her a dress and a necklace to wear. Bonnie was a very quiet girl and a slow learner. She didn't have any friends until one day she came up to Carol in the hall and asked her if she would be her friend. Of course, Carol said yes, and she helped Bonnie make some more friends, and she helped her with some of her classes. Carol took her crown off and put it on Bonnie's head. It looked pretty with her blond curls. Carol hugged Bonnie, and the shy little girl was smiling from ear to ear. Everyone clapped as Carol went back to her table and sat down. Mike and John were both smiling at the beautiful act of kindness their girl had bestowed upon her shy little friend. Gene got up and walked to Carol's side of the table and kissed her on the cheek.

"Well, I think I am going to have to dance one more time with our new queen," said Gene.

As Gene and Bonnie danced, she never once stopped smiling.

Others stopped by their table that night, but the four of them felt like they were the only ones in the room. Mike seemed so happy that evening, and he smiled a lot. Gene was somewhat subdued and quiet, never smiling, but he seemed happy enough, and he never took his eyes off Carol; she did look exceptionally pretty that night. John was just happy to be there with his new friends. As for Carol, she felt safe and loved with the three young men.

As Carol put her hand on John's arm to help him up, he was so happy to feel her touch again.

They were all quiet in the car until John said, "I thank all of you for inviting me to go with you tonight. This has been the best night of my life."

"We loved having you," said Mike and Gene almost simultaneously.

Carol didn't say anything, but she moved closer to John and kissed him on the cheek and then on the lips. John returned the kiss. She sat very close to him and put her head on his shoulder. John thought he had died and gone to heaven.

Many students in the class of 1964 couldn't afford to go to prom. Some students didn't have dates or the appropriate clothes; others were misfits, outcasts, handicapped, or had no friends. Others would not be graduating with their class. There was a separate prom that year where the venue, refreshments, and entertainment was free. In 1964, this happened to be the most popular prom. At that time, it didn't have a name. Years later, it would be referred to as alternative senior prom. This was the prom that Carol, Gene, Mike, and John chose to attend.

THE AWARDS ASSEMBLY

There was an awards assembly held in the auditorium at the high school in May of 1964. Only the students nominated in the various categories were invited to attend, as were their parents. It was held in the afternoon. Carol's parents were at work and couldn't attend. Mike's parents were there, as were Gene's parents. Mike and Gene were sitting behind Carol and her friend, Gary, from the journalism class and the newspaper staff. Gene immediately received several awards for sports, debate, and math. Carol, Gary, and Mike congratulated him.

At the awards assembly, Mike was nominated for several awards, but he didn't win in any of the categories. Carol was also nominated for several awards, but she also did not win. Mr. Chambers walked to the stage to present the journalism scholarship. This was a great honor and a big award because it involved a sizeable scholarship to the University of Kansas.

Mr. Chambers began speaking, "The student who is the recipient of the KU journalism scholarship is a young lady who has been a great asset to the newspaper staff. She is a hard worker and has written some excellent articles this year, several of which were sent to KU journalism contests." Mr. Chambers paused.

Gary nudged Carol. "This is yours, everything fits. I know you've got this one."

Gene and Mike heard Gary and agreed with him.

Then Mr. Chambers made his announcement. "The nominees are Gretchen Armstrong, Marilyn Gordon, and Carol Sullivan." When Carol's name was mentioned, there was an exceptionally large round of applause. He hesitated before announcing the winner. "And the winner of the scholarship is Gretchen Armstrong."

"Wow, that caught me off guard. I thought that was yours." Gary was surprised, as was Carol.

"I was almost ready to get up," said Carol. Gene and Mike were also surprised.

Carol, Gene, and Mike walked out of the auditorium together.

Gene said, "I didn't deserve all those awards. You guys were the top two students."

"Not for long. My secretarial practice teacher has lowered my grade," said Carol. "We are happy for you, Gene. Let's go out and celebrate your honors."

"I second that," said Mike.

Carol's friend Janice caught up with them. "That was so unfair. I can't believe what just happened in there."

"Don't take up for us, or they might take your award away," said Mike.

Mike and Carol got on opposite sides of Gene and put their arms around him.

Carol said, "We are so proud of you, Gene." Carol paused for a moment. "One thing I have learned from this experience is that you should never start to get up until your name is actually called."

But they were to learn many other lessons from the awards presented that spring. The only honor that Carol would receive in her senior year was Quill and Scroll Honor Society, which was automatic membership to the newspaper staff. She was nominated for the KU journalism scholarship, but she did not receive it even though she had done excellent work and had won outside contests. And so as it all ended, Carol's greatest victory was also her greatest defeat. She had been nominated for excellence that year in fifteen academic and sports categories but had not received a single award.

Mike was nominated in eleven academic and sports categories. He also did not receive any awards, but he did receive a letter in basketball and football.

In addition to the three awards that Gene won at the awards assembly, he was nominated in fourteen more academic and sports categories. He won everything he was nominated for, including a sizeable football scholarship, even though he had received a serious neck injury and concussion in a football game during his senior year. He also received an academic scholarship and one in leadership and debate. In addition, he received the basketball award, general physical education, good sportsmanship, speech, debate, mathematics, two more leadership awards, world history, business law and economics, National Honor Society, letters in football and basketball, and he was a graduation speaker. While Gene's ranking in the class was seventeen, because of the offices he had held and the magnitude of work he had done for the class, he was allowed to give a graduation speech.

At one time in their junior year, Carol and Mike had been ranked one and two in the class, which would have allowed them to be valedictorian and salutatorian respectively. Mike's final class ranking was twelve; Carol's was fourteen. They were not graduation speakers. There were 750 graduates in the class of 1964.

Gene would have gladly given all his awards to Mike and Carol. He was not comfortable with winning so much and all the attention he received. Gene felt that Carol and Mike were more deserving of awards than he was, but that was not true. Where Carol and Mike had broken rules, Gene had not. There was not a single mark against him on his record.

THE MEETING AND ONE SMALL VICTORY

There was a meeting called a few days after the graduation rehearsal. Those who would be in attendance at the meeting were the principal; several teachers; Mr. Chambers, class sponsor; three administrators; the guidance counselors; Gene Sandusky, president of the senior class; Janice Morgan, secretary of the senior class; and Carol Sullivan.

No one really knew why the meeting was being called. Mr. Chambers sat on one side of Carol, and Gene sat on the other side. Gene had a bad feeling, and he was worried for Carol, and she shared his feeling.

After opening formalities, the meeting began. Ms. Reynolds, Carol's secretarial practice teacher, was first to speak.

"There was a rule broken in the graduation rehearsal. Students are not to walk arm in arm down the aisle of the auditorium. It was Carol Sullivan, who did so with a boy whose name I do not know. Carol is the same student who did not put articles in the school newspaper on her own class and major, secretarial practice, after I had worked very hard to give her the information. She breaks rules and is rebellious and inconsiderate."

Gene felt so bad for Carol at that moment. He just wanted to put his arms around her and protect her from the impending harm. It bothered him so much to have to sit silently and watch her be hurt. But there were startled looks on many faces in the room that day. Mr.

Chambers was first to speak. Even though his voice was calm, his anger was obvious.

"For your information, the young man's name whom Carol escorted in the graduation processional rehearsal is John Kelley, who is an automotive mechanics major. The day before the rehearsal, John's teacher, Mr. Grant, came to me and told me that John was worried about being in the graduation exercises because he has trouble going downstairs and walking long distances, and he walks slowly. He didn't want to fall and disrupt the processional. He asked if I knew of anyone who would be willing to walk with him to give him some support as well as encouragement. I told him that I knew the perfect person to do this. I knew Carol would help him without even being asked. I was the one who put their names together, but I didn't know that by doing so, I was breaking a rule."

At this point, the principal started to speak, but Mr. Chambers continued speaking.

"I'm not finished yet. Carol wrote many articles on your department, Ms. Reynolds. They were all well written, as were all her articles, but there were other departments that also needed publicity. Carol's job was to write the articles, not to have the final say as to what was actually printed in the newspaper. I also believe that you gave Carol a lower grade than she deserved to keep her from making National Honor Society. And it worked. You and the counselors and others managed to punish both Carol and Mike McVary for trying to help their fellow classmates. You have succeeded, so what I would like to know is, when are you going to stop and leave her alone?"

There was silence in the room. Mr. Chambers broke it by saying in a much quieter voice, "I needed to get this all out in the open and off my chest. I'm retiring at the end of this school year, which is in a few days." He paused. "I didn't know that by helping John, I would be causing trouble for Carol."

Carol was on the verge of tears. Gene put his hand on hers. He knew, in Ms. Reynolds's opinion, this was probably breaking a rule too, but at that moment he didn't really care. He just felt so bad for what Carol was going through.

Mr. Olson, football coach and social studies teacher, spoke first, "Phoebe Mills was a girl in my class on the brink of failing. She was always late for class or not there at all. On the day of the final exam, Carol and Mike saw her running down the hill toward the school. They stopped me in the hall and asked if I would wait for her before I started the test. I told them that I couldn't hold up the test for one student. Carol told me that Phoebe needed my class to graduate. They had been helping her study, and Carol was confident she would pass the test. I waited for her. Carol thanked me and told me not to worry, there wouldn't be anyone like her or Mike in my class next year. I told her that was exactly what I was worried about. Phoebe passed the test."

Mr. Eliason, speech teacher, then spoke, "Carol has been through a lot during her school years that no young girl or boy should ever have to go through. Many of us don't realize what some students have to deal with just to be in school every day. Carol has made excellent grades in my class, and she is a very good speaker. It is unfortunate that she won't be a graduation speaker."

Mrs. Dombrowski, physical education teacher, spoke, "Carol has been very helpful to me as a senior instructor. There wasn't anything she couldn't do. She was always particularly helpful to students with special needs or those having trouble with a specific sport. I will miss her greatly."

Mrs. Jenkins, typing teacher spoke next, as she wiped away a tear, "Carol was my best student. She always wanted to help others." She was crying, and she couldn't speak any more, so she sat down.

And then Mr. Kirkland, geometry teacher, spoke, "It has been awhile, but in sophomore geometry I had four excellent students, two are in this room today, Carol and Gene. The other two were Mike and Terry. All were being bullied, especially Gene and Terry. Now, it is difficult to imagine Gene being bullied, but it happened. Carol took up for both Gene and Terry. Because of her, the bullying of two very nice, smart boys stopped. I know that both Carol and Mike are being punished and criticized for helping their classmates. It isn't fair, and I am sorry that this school has not treated them better."

Several other teachers spoke favorably of Carol and Mike that day.

Then Mr. Grant, auto mechanics teacher, spoke, "When I asked Mr. Chambers if anyone could help John at graduation, I had no idea that it would be breaking rules and the trouble it would cause. I would like to ask John Kelly to come in and speak to you now." Mr. Grant didn't wait for an answer or sign of approval from anyone. He went out into the hall and brought John back in with him. Mike also came into the room with John. They had been waiting in the hall for Carol and Gene.

John was a little scared, but he began speaking in a shy, nervous voice, "My name is John Kelley. I will be forever grateful for Carol's help so I can be at graduation with everyone else. If it wasn't for her, I would not be able to make it. I want very badly to be in the graduation exercises because I was once told that I would never graduate from high school or have a job or have any friends. Now I am graduating, I have a job, and I have the three best friends in the world, Carol, Mike, and Gene. All three of them helped me that rehearsal night, and I want to publicly thank them now, because without them I couldn't do it."

As John started to leave the room, Gene got up and gave him his seat. Gene stood behind John with his hand on his shoulder.

And then Carol took the one and only opportunity she would ever have to speak to this group on this subject. "I am so very sorry, Ms. Reynolds. In no way was it ever my intention to be disrespectful to you or anyone else. I know that other teachers and counselors agree with you, but Mike and I only wanted to help people. That was our only agenda. We didn't feel we were being rebellious or breaking rules. I hope that we did help some of our classmates over the past three years because that was our only intention. You all have my sincerest apologies." At this point, Carol had nothing else to say.

Principal Morton then spoke, "Carol Sullivan and John Kelley will walk in the graduation processional together, as they did in the rehearsal. Mr. Chambers, we are sorry to lose you. You're a great, caring teacher. You will be greatly missed. This meeting is adjourned."

Ms. Reynolds, the counselors, and a few teachers left right away.

Mr. Chambers hugged Carol.

She quietly spoke to him, "I wanted so badly to speak. I hope I did all right. Thank you for being on my side and taking up for me."

Gene and Mr. Chambers shook hands.

"Take care of her, Gene. She deserves so much more than this school has given her.

They walked out into the hall where Janice was waiting. Mike and John were with her. The other teachers followed.

Gene spoke to the group, "I want to thank you all for Carol and John. They are both very genuinely good, caring people. It's a small victory but a very important one for two people who are very special to me."

As Gene went to get the car, Mike asked Janice, "Would you like to go out to eat with us?"

"Thanks for asking, but no. I just need to go home." Janice hugged Carol. "I'm sorry this happened to you. You should be a graduation speaker."

In Gene's car, Carol rode in the back seat with Mike. She hesitated before letting go of John's arm, but he assured her it was all right.

Mike pulled a handkerchief out of his pocket and spoke in a quiet, gentle voice to Carol, "My sweet girl, let me wipe your cheeks and eyes, and I'll comb your hair a little."

"Thank you, Mike." Carol's voice was quiet as she choked back tears.

In the front seat, John and Gene were also quiet.

At the restaurant, Carol only ordered a salad. She ate very little. Mike fed her a few bites of his meal. She laid her head on Mike's shoulder and said as she felt her hair, "My hair is wet. Why is my hair wet?"

Mike took some napkins and ran them across her hair. "It's your tears, sweetie. It has been a very difficult and bad night."

Carol started crying again. "Don't leave me tonight, Mike. I don't want to be alone."

And he didn't leave her alone that night. He laid her in her bed that she had slept in since she was a little girl. He sat in a chair by her bed all night, and he was there when she awoke in the morning.

Gene took John home that night, and something he said would never be forgotten by John.

"You know, John, when Mike goes to Vietnam and I go away to college, Carol will really need you. Love her, hold her, and take care of her because she loves you, and when Carol loves you, it changes your life completely. No other girl is ever quite good enough again. You always compare them to her. She is a very special person, and it hurts me to see her so sad. Hopefully, she will be better before we leave."

"I'll take care of her the best I can, but I'm not nearly the man you are or Mike," said John.

"I think you are better than we are."

Gene walked to the door with John that night as Carol would have done. John thought it was a little strange, but it was obvious a bond had developed among the three young men and the sweet, kind girl that nothing would ever change.

The Day after the Meeting

The day after the meeting, Carol did not attend her first class, which was her two-hour secretarial practice class. She didn't want to see Ms. Reynolds.

Mike wanted to talk to John. He went to the auto mechanics shop. John was putting tools away. John and Mr. Grant were the only people there. Mr. Grant spoke to Mike and then told John he was leaving for the day.

"I'm used to closing up," said John. "I'm not as fast as the other guys." Mike was holding his head in his hands. John put his hand on Mike's shoulder. "How is Carol doing today?"

"I took her to her home and put her to bed. She didn't wake up, but it was like she was still crying. Her mother asked me to stay so I watched her all night. When she woke up, I held her in my arms for a while, and she told me she would come to school later, so I left. She has always been a really strong girl, but lately she seems so fragile. When I think about leaving for the Army and Gene leaving for college, I feel a little sick. I don't want her to ever be hurt. Don't let anyone hurt her, John."

As Mike looked at John, he once again saw tears welling up in the eyes of the strong six-foot-four football player. John knew that Mike was basically asking him the same thing that Gene had asked him the previous night.

"I'll always take care of her. I'm honored that you think I can," said John.

"I have no doubt about that. You love her, and that is all that matters. With you, I think she will get better. Sometimes I think that every time she looks at me, she sees what happened to Danny all over again. Maybe it's a good thing that I'm going to Vietnam," said Mike.

"I wouldn't go so far as to say that. She will miss you. It's like you two belong together," said John.

Mike thought for a moment. "That's what everybody thinks. Even my parents think we will get married someday. But I don't think so. We are just really good friends. I think that is all we are destined to be." But Mike knew he was saying this just for John's benefit because he did love Carol and always would.

GRADUATION

It is a fairly common consensus that graduations are usually boring with the processional, the speeches, and the long list of graduates being called. But the speech given by Gene Sandusky, class president, of the 1964 graduating class of Avalon High School, in Kansas City, Kansas, was like no graduation speech that had ever been given before or would probably ever be given again.

Gene was an excellent, charismatic speaker, and he won many awards in his senior year in both speech and debate. He would never give another speech that was to equal in presentation or content the speech he gave that fateful night in 1964. In fact, that night he felt that he would never speak publicly again, but many years later, he would be called upon to do so. Gene was accustomed to speaking in front of large groups and seldom showed any signs of nervousness, but that night was different. He spoke slowly and deliberately, never missing a beat, but for the first time in his life, he was nervous.

"Good evening, everyone. I'm Gene Sandusky, president of the senior class of 1964," said Gene as he stepped to the podium as the first speaker that night. "I had a speech all planned until a few days ago, but it seems irrelevant now. It was a typical upbeat graduation speech even with a bit of humor. But this has been a very intense, serious year with President Kennedy being assassinated, deaths of classmates, and Vietnam always looming in the background. The speech I have chosen to give tonight was written by one of our classmates. It is more timely and appropriate than mine was or ever could be. There is a quote that says, 'There are thousands of stories within each of us, most of which would break your heart.' This is one such story. This is John Kelley's speech.

Probably most of my fellow graduates don't even know me. I lived in the West Bottoms until the flood of 1951 when we lost our home and moved to a little house in Armourdale where I still live today. I went to John Fiske Elementary School and Central Junior High. I know many of you from those schools. One friend I met in first grade is Tom Davis. Another friend that I made at the same time was Paul Williams. Paul and I met at Bethany Hospital where we were both polio patients in 1951. Paul lived in another part of the city, but we met again as sophomores here at Avalon High. Paul passed away last summer. We always wondered if we would ever be able to graduate from high school. I guess now I am doing it for both of us. Paul and I had very different lives. Although we were both never able to run and play like other kids, Paul was bullied all throughout school, and I was not. Tom Davis was my friend all throughout childhood. Probably because of Tom, I was never subjected to bullying. Everyone was afraid of him. He was a tough guy, and everyone thought he was mean, and since I was his friend, they didn't make fun of me. I also have a degenerative eye disease. An operation when I was thirteen improved my eyesight, and my grades also improved. Until this point, my grades were very bad. I fell down a lot, but I would just smile and get up and try again. When we got to high school, Tom's tough guy image escalated. He was very mean to Paul. He would knock his books and pencils off his desk and make it difficult for him to get them. One day he tripped Paul as he was getting off the bus. This was witnessed by Carol Sullivan and Mike McVary. They went to Paul's assistance. This single event was to change the lives of many students. Carol and Mike would be with Paul, helping and encouraging him through the rest of his life. I had one class with Paul in sophomore year. He told me how Carol and Mike were helping others who were being bullied, but that wasn't where they stopped. They were also helping people like Tom who were doing the bullying. Paul told me that he asked Mike what he should do if he could no longer make it up the stairs to his third-floor classes. Mike told him if that day ever came that he would carry him, and he did just that. One thing that no one knew about me, except Tom, was that during my sophomore year, I was as close to committing suicide as anyone could be and lived to tell about it. I was having trouble walking, my eyesight was getting worse, and I was not doing well in my classes. I was not mature enough to figure out what to do. Tom encouraged me to talk to Carol and Mike, but their office was down a steep stairway in a far-away wing of the school, and I was unable to get there. So Tom would ask them for advice if someone was considering suicide and relay it to me. Paul also shared some of the advice they gave to him with me. Soon I made a connection with Mr. Grant, the auto mechanics teacher, which was one of the suggestions they had made. I was interested in auto mechanics and could actually do it because of my knowledge of cars. My eyesight wasn't a problem when I was working with cars. I would soon get a job with a mechanic near my home and was able to help my mother and three little sisters financially. This was a turning point for me. Without the help of Paul, Tom, Carol, Mike, and Mr. Grant, I would not be graduating today and most probably would not even be alive. I know that administrators, counselors, and some teachers have attempted during the last three years to stop Carol and Mike from helping the students, and I suppose they have to a degree finally succeeded. I want everyone to know that although I am not a high-profile student and have never been open and vocal about the problems and difficulties I have faced, I am truly a success story. My life matters, and without them, I wouldn't have a life. Thank you for saving me."

Gene paused before asking a monumental question.

"Would all the graduates, juniors, sophomores, and former graduates who have been helped by Carol and Mike during the past three years please stand."

Gene thought back to sophomore geometry class when Carol had helped him with the bullies who were making his life miserable, and since he was already standing, he raised his hand. Over two hundred people stood up. There was not a dry eye in the auditorium that evening. Gene sat down without speaking another word. Everyone was in some way moved and even changed by the speech, some probably going so far as to become better people because of it.

Next to approach the podium was Robert Anderson, the valedictorian. He had his speech in hand as he approached the podium, and then he tore it in half.

"I'm Robert Anderson, valedictorian of the class, but I can't follow that. I don't know you, John, but I wish I did. I do know Carol and Mike. In a perfect world where people always get what they deserve, Carol would be your valedictorian speaker and not me, but as we all know so well, it is not a perfect world. I had speech class with Carol last year. She is a very elegant, beautiful speaker. I'm sorry you won't have the opportunity to hear her speak today."

As Robert sat down, Charlotte Payton approached the podium.

"I'm Charlotte Payton, the salutatorian of the class. My prepared speech sounds very trite, and I cannot give it either. Carol is a good friend of mine, and she is a kind person with a heart of gold. As for Mike, I have gone to school with him since second grade. He is the gentlest, sweetest boy I have ever known. I know he is going to Vietnam soon, and I will worry about him until I know he is home safe."

As Gene, Robert, and Charlotte finished their speeches, before they took their seats on the stage, they each went to the graduates section. They hugged Carol and shook hands with John, Mike, and Tom.

Mr. Chambers approached the podium next.

"I am Mr. Chambers, senior class sponsor and a journalism teacher here for twenty-five years. At this point, usually the principal speaks. He will not speak today. He has relinquished his place to me. I am honored to have been the sponsor of this class. It has been a remarkable class with brilliant, spirited students, many of whom will certainly make a difference in the world. God speed to those of you going to war. Come back to us soon and safely. We have lost several students this year, Paul Williams, Donna Edwards, Jane Mitchell, and Danny McVary. Danny would have been in the graduating class of 1966, but he had extremely close ties to this class as we all know. We remember them fondly. I have not always agreed with decisions made by other teachers and administrators. This year I tried to the best of my ability to get justice for two very good students. I failed miserably until two weeks ago when I did win a small victory for one of them. I am retiring at the end of this school year, which is right now. Before I go, I want to thank one student, Carol Sullivan, for being the most exceptional student I have ever had the privilege of teaching in my career. With her prize-winning article on the assassination of President John Kennedy and several other articles, she has put our newspaper in the limelight. Thank you, Carol. It has been a pleasure working with you. It has been an extremely emotional night, but I think we have all learned some valuable lessons. John's speech that Gene gave tonight was possibly the best graduation speech that I have ever heard. And, Gene, your presentation was very good, and I respect your decision to give it. Goodbye and good luck to each and every one of you."

Mr. Thompson, superintendent of schools, approached the podium.

"There is not much I can add to what has been said tonight. I don't exactly know what all has transpired this year to bring such strong reactions from so many people. I hope to correct any mistakes or wrong actions that have been committed by my staff if it is not too late. Diplomas will now be presented."

As Carol walked across the stage to accept her diploma, everyone stood and cheered and applauded. John walked across the stage right after Carol alone and received the same reception. She waited for him at the top of the stairs and walked down with him. A few minutes later, Mike received a like reception as did Tom.

All the teachers and administrators left the auditorium first. Carol and John were sitting on the aisle. When Mr. Chambers walked by them, he stopped and hugged Carol and shook John's hand, and then he was gone. Carol never saw Mr. Chambers again. Three months after graduation, he passed away.

In 1964, the school had such strict rules. It was short of a miracle that Gene hadn't been stopped shortly after he began speaking, but for whatever reason, he was not. He was allowed to finish his and John's speech, as was everyone else who spoke that night.

MOTHER'S OPINION

Carol's mother prepared breakfast for her the day after graduation. This was something she seldom did. Carol sat down, wondering what her mother's agenda was for this unexpected treat.

"So how did you like graduation?" asked Carol.

"It will probably go down in the record books as the greatest and yet most unusual graduation ever," said Stella. "I do want you to know that I am very proud of you. What you, Gene, and Mike have done for John is remarkable and heart-wrenching. He was a boy who had so little, and now the three of you are on his side and helping him. I talked with Colleen and Alan McVary last night, and they give you the majority of the credit for helping John."

"Mike should get the credit. He is the one who invited John into our group," said Carol. "But John was easy to help. He is really nice."

"Don't hurt him," said Stella.

"I have no intention of ever hurting him. I thought for a minute you were actually trying to say something nice to me, but you aren't, are you?"

"I just feel that John is falling in love with you. He hung on every word you said. He can't take his eyes or hands off you. Gene's a football quarterback and very popular, and Mike is rich and sophisticated," said Stella.

"John holds on to my arm because it helps him with his balance and helps him to walk. As far as him not taking his eyes off me, I don't think you know, but he can't see for a very far distance. He listens closely to what I say because he doesn't hear well. As far as Gene and Mike are concerned, I like them because they are kind, and they have good hearts and not for the reasons you said." Carol got up to leave. "If all you see when you look at Gene is a quarterback and when you look at Mike is a rich boy, then I would like for you to take a closer look. They have both been very kind to me and taken care of me ever since Richard left for Vietnam."

"You are taking this wrong. All I am saying is, don't hurt John. Don't compound all he has been through in his life," Stella paused. "I know you love Gene. I can tell, and I can't say I blame you. He's a fine boy, but just be careful, that's all I ask. A girl like you could destroy someone like John."

Carol didn't respond. She didn't know what else to say. She just wanted to get away from her mother. Carol went to Mike's house. He lived the closest, and she knew Colleen would be there. Colleen met Carol at the door, and as she took Carol in her arms, Mike came running down the stairs. They walked with her into the family room and sat by her on the sofa. Colleen still had her arms around her as Mike took her hand.

"What happened?" said Mike. "I can't stand it when someone hurts you and makes you cry."

"Her mother just called me. She said some things to Carol that she shouldn't have said, and she wanted me to tell you that she is sorry," said Colleen.

"She's not sorry. She knew exactly what she was saying," said Carol. "You, Mike, or Gene would never say anything like that to me."

"I don't know all she said. All she told me is that she is worried about John getting hurt because he is so fond of you," said Colleen in a very kind, understanding voice. "None of us want to see John hurt. We are all going to help him. Isn't that right, Mike?"

"Sure, you don't have to do it alone. He is my friend also as well as Gene's friend. We won't let anything happen to him. I promise you that," said Mike.

"Mike, would you call Gene? I want him to be here too," asked Carol.

"Sure, Carol," said Mike as he kissed Carol and went to make the phone call.

Colleen spoke very calmly and kindly to Carol, "You know something, Carol, I wish you were my daughter. Your mother is my friend, but she doesn't understand you like I do. I think you are the nicest, sweetest girl I have ever known, and I love you very much, as do Mike and Alan. Your mother is entitled to her opinion, but that doesn't mean that she is right. You see, I know how kind you are and that you would never hurt anyone, especially John."

"Gene will be here soon," said Mike as he pushed Carol's hair back.

"Thanks, Mike. You and Gene and your mom are always there for me. I thank you all so much for that." Carol put her arms around Mike.

Colleen noticed the tears in Mike's eyes, and she knew that it wasn't John she was worried about being hurt as much as it was Mike. Unlike Stella, Colleen would keep her feelings as well as her opinions to herself.

Gene arrived in a few minutes, and he immediately took Carol in his arms. They didn't say a word. They didn't have to. Their kindness in their touch and their eyes as they looked at one another told it all. By not saying a word, they were saying more than anyone could ever say. They all sat quietly together for a long time that morning talking about nondescript subjects and about nothing. It really didn't matter because they all loved and understood one another. Gene never left Carol's side. She seemed so vulnerable that day, and she was so fragile and endearing. Gene just wanted to leave with Carol that day and take her away from everything and be with her and protect her forever, but it was not to happen then or at any other time.

Mike had been protecting Carol since they were twelve, and now he would soon be going to Vietnam, but he knew that even though Gene was going away to college, he would still protect her along with John. He was content with this knowledge, but he knew it wouldn't be an easy job.

GRANDVIEW BEACH

Two days after graduation, Carol, Gene, Mike, and John went to Grandview Beach. It was a pretty lake south of Kansas City with a sandy beach surrounding the lake. It was quiet and peaceful.

Mike, who always thought of everything, spread out some blankets on the sand and got four folding chairs out of the car. Mike wanted to make sure that if John wasn't comfortable on the blanket, there would be chairs available.

As Gene went to get drinks from the concession stand, Mike took a dip in the water. Carol stayed by John. They never wanted him to feel left out, so without even saying anything, they never left him alone. Carol was a little worried because she knew John wouldn't take his slacks off. When Gene came back with the drinks, Carol took her blouse and shorts off, revealing a light-blue two-piece bathing suit. John couldn't take his eyes off Carol as she put her long hair on top of her head and jumped in the water. She swam across the lake and back.

As she sat in a chair beside John, he said, "You swam really fast, and you are not even out of breath."

"I used to be on the swim team. I have always enjoyed swimming. Do you like to swim, John?" asked Carol.

John looked out across the lake. "Richard taught me how to swim when I was a sophomore. I liked it, and I was a pretty good swimmer. Richard was really nice to me. Does he write to you?"

"Not real often, but he does write. He tells me a lot about what's happening in Vietnam. It is really bad. I hope he will be all right because he is a really good man."

"If you want us to, John, we'll go out in the water with you," said Mike.

"Maybe later," said John quietly. John had on a T-shirt, and in the back it had come out of his slacks.

Carol put her hand under his shirt to rub his back. She had never done this before, and she wished she hadn't done it at that time. Their eyes met, and Carol pulled her hand away and immediately put her blouse on.

Gene and Mike both knew something had happened, but they didn't know exactly what. In that brief moment when Carol had rubbed John's bare back, she had felt the puffy scar tissue and deep scars.

John spoke quietly, "I've never had friends like you three before. We're here at this beautiful beach to have fun. I don't want to mess it up."

"If there is something you want to talk about, it's all right. We are here for one another," said Mike.

"John, you don't have to say or explain anything if you don't want to." Carol already knew from that brief touch, she more than anyone knew it would be painful to talk about.

John slowly pulled his shirt up and showed them his back. It was covered with some of the most brutal-looking scars any of them had ever seen. Gene and Mike stood in front of John so no one else on the beach could see.

"Who did this to you?" asked Gene.

"My dad. He hated me because I was crippled. It always happened when my mother was at work. She didn't know," said John.

"How old were you?" asked Mike.

"I was thirteen. I wasn't very big. He wouldn't let me have much food," answered John. He was shaking as Carol took hold of his hand. "He called me a stupid cripple and said I would be blind soon. He called me every bad name you could imagine. He threw my glasses away and told my mom that I lost them. He didn't want me to see him, but even though my eyesight was bad, I always saw him every time he came to beat me. I still see his face sometimes when I'm in bed and it scares me. I think he is back. He said I was useless and would never amount to anything and that I would never graduate from high school, have friends, or have a job. Do you remember, Gene, I put some of that in the graduation speech, but not all of it."

"I remember," said Gene. "Did he hurt your mother and sisters too?"

"He would hit my mother but not my sisters. He never touched them," said John.

"Where is he now?" asked Carol.

"One night I could hear him hitting my mom, calling her names, and throwing her around. She was pregnant with Meggie. He was drunk, and he had beat me earlier before my mom got home from work. He threw me against the wall, and it cut my head and ear open. I was still bleeding." John had to stop for a minute.

Carol didn't know what to say except to encourage him to keep talking. "You're doing fine, John. Get it all out. We're here for you. We're not leaving."

John continued, "I went to Charlene and Darla's room. I opened the window and told them to run to the neighbor's house and ask them to call the police. They were crying. They thought I was going to die that night, and I thought so too. I went into the room where he was beating my mom. I pulled him off her. There was so much blood. I thought she was dead, but when he was hitting me, she hit him on the head. The police came quick that night. They broke in the door, he fought them, and then he ran. I heard them telling him to stop, and then there was one gunshot. Two policemen were standing over us, my poor bleeding pregnant mother and the little bleeding boy. I remember the policeman telling me I was a brave little boy and that I had saved my mother's life. He picked me up and put me in the ambulance with my mom. I asked him about my dad, and he said he would never hurt me or anyone else again. I knew then that he was dead. Meggie was born several months later with brain damage from the beating my mom received that night." John had always managed to smile, but at that moment he couldn't, and he cried like the little boy in the ambulance that horrible night.

Carol took him in her arms. "I'm so, so sorry that you had to go through something like that."

Mike and Gene pulled the other two chairs close to John. The four friends who were only seventeen and eighteen stayed close together on the pretty beach. For three of them, it was the most horrific story they had ever heard, and the other one had lived it.

John opened his slacks and showed them his lower stomach and groin area covered with the same horrible scars as his back.

Mike looked away and said, "Your dad was a monster. What did he beat you with?"

"He had a belt with a heavy buckle on one end. He used that end. Sometimes he used a board. But it was when I saw him coming toward me with the knife that I would try to run. But I couldn't run, so I could never get away from him," said John.

A peaceful day at the beach had turned into something dark and sinister. Carol and John were eighteen. Mike and Gene were still seventeen. For a while no one could move. Carol had her arms around John. It had taken a toll on him, and he was trembling. Gene got a blanket and wrapped it around John, and he sat beside him and hugged him as Carol was doing.

"That had to be so difficult for you to talk about. You're the bravest person I've ever known," said Gene.

Mike was still sitting in front of John. He couldn't seem to move or speak.

Carol gently kissed the scar by John's ear. "What happened to you should never happen to anyone. Always know how much we love you, John. We will help and protect you all we can. I only wish we could take your pain away."

They sat there for a long time that afternoon. John didn't speak. It had taken everything out of him to tell his story. As they got up to leave, John looked up at Gene and Mike, who were towering over him.

"I can't get up. Will you guys please help me?"

Gene and Mike put their arms around John and practically carried him to the car. "We're going to be here for you, John. Whenever you need us, we'll be here," said Gene.

They helped John into the back seat, and Carol got in beside him. Gene got the blanket and covered him because he was still trembling.

As they were driving, Gene said, "I think we should keep him with us tonight."

"I agree," said Carol.

Reminiscent of what Gene and Mike had done for Carol long before they knew John, Mike said, "Let's go to my house. We'll stay there tonight."

When they arrived at Mike's house, Alan and Colleen saw them helping John and asked what they could do. Mike and Gene went to the family room to fix a place for John to lie down. Carol and John sat on the sofa. She still had her arm around him.

Carol spoke quietly to Alan and Colleen, "John's had a hard time today. He told us something that he has been holding back for a long time. We need to keep him with us tonight. We can't leave him."

"If you need anything, just let us know," said Alan.

They both knew not to say too much or ask too many questions.

Gene and Mike came back for them. John still couldn't walk on his own. The sofa made into a bed. They put John on the bed and covered him up. Mike sat by John on the bed and soon fell asleep, as did John. Gene and Carol sat on the love seat. Neither one of them slept that night. They were worried and afraid for John.

Carol had asked Colleen to call her mother, John's mother, and Gene's parents and tell them where they were and that they would be home in the morning.

Gene and Carol went to the kitchen early the next morning. Alan and Colleen were already there having coffee. "Did you two get any sleep?" asked Colleen.

"We got enough. We'll be fine," said Gene.

Alan reached out and touched Carol's hand. "It looks as though you've been crying in the night."

"I'm not so sure I'll ever be able to stop," said Carol.

"I don't want to ask what happened because I know that it is something bad," said Colleen.

"Yes, it was bad. It seemed to hit Mike particularly hard. It got to us all but him especially. If he doesn't tell you, in time, I will," said Gene. "I need to go back to them now."

"I'll be there in a minute," said Carol. "If any of us had any innocence left, it's gone after yesterday. I'll be all right, but I am worried about them, all three of them." Carol left the kitchen to go be with her friends.

John was awake. Mike and Gene were sitting beside him on the bed. Carol gently kissed John on the cheek.

"Are you better this morning, John?"

"Yes, thanks to all of you. You've saved me again," said John.

They never returned to Grandview Beach, although the previous summer it had been one of their favorite spots. It closed forever the following year when on the last day of school, two little boys climbed over the fence and drowned.

BEFORE PARTING

Before their paths took different directions, Mike, Gene, and Carol had discussed taking a road trip together. They were at their favorite pizza place a few days after Grandview Beach to ask John to go with them.

"John, we have been talking for some time about a road trip to California. We would drive down Big Sur from San Francisco to San Diego. Would you go with us?" asked Mike.

"I've never been anywhere. I've always wanted to go to California, and I would love to see Big Sur before my eyesight gets worse, but I couldn't afford it," said John.

"It's free. My dad thinks we deserve a trip. He's paying for everything," said Mike.

"But you would all have more fun without me. There are so many things, I can't do," said John.

"If you can't do it, we won't do it. We will be with you all the time. We'll never leave you," said Carol.

"All right, but, Mike, I need to talk to your dad and thank him," said John.

"We can stop by as soon as we finish eating," said Mike.

"Shall I bring a sleeping bag?" asked John.

Mike couldn't help but smiling. "If you want to, you can. We will probably usually have a room with two full beds. Of course, that would mean someone would have to sleep with Carol. Would you mind doing that, John?"

"I wouldn't mind at all," smiled John. That was the first time they had seen John smile since Grandview Beach, so Carol didn't mind that it was at her expense.

All of them except Gene felt excited and happy as they left for Mike's house. Gene always worried about the car breaking down, that they would get lost, or that he wouldn't be able to see well enough to drive, especially at night. Carol knew this. She could see the concern in his eyes. Carol took hold of his hand as they walked to the car.

"We'll have fun, Gene. Don't worry. Remember, I found my way around Chicago when we were only eight."

"You know I've always felt like that whenever you are with me, everything will be all right," said Gene. "It seems like it should be the other way around, me taking care of you."

"You know, Gene, there has always been something very special about you. You are not like other guys. I have to be really careful with you," said Carol.

"I'm not sure if that's good or bad," said Gene.

"I assure you it's good. You make me a better person," said Carol.

John had no idea Mike lived in a mansion. Mike was so unpretentious no one would ever guess he was rich. John didn't remember that night after Grandview Beach. He didn't remember the house, Alan and Colleen, or anything else after he poured his heart out to his friends. It was as though this was the first time he was ever in Mike's house.

Alan and Colleen were both in the living room when they arrived.

"Well, hello, Carol and Gene, and this must be John. Come in and sit down," said Colleen kindly.

"Dad, John wanted to thank you for offering us the trip to California," said Mike.

"I've always wanted to go to California. I've never been anywhere," said John.

Colleen and Alan were both studying this handsome new boy who had entered their son's little group of friends. Just as Gene had told his parents about John's revelations at Grandview Beach that fateful day, Mike had also told Alan and Colleen. It had been too much for the two young boys to hold in and handle on their own. Carol had told no one, and she never would.

"We would like for you all to enjoy Big Sur," said Colleen as she reached out and took John's hand. "Mike has such good friends. We were, of course, at graduation, and we were both very moved by your speech that Gene gave. I knew then that you would all be friends."

"Thank you. You are both very kind," said John.

Colleen and Alan knew that John had grown up in poverty and that he had been raised by a single mother and that he had three younger sisters. They knew that he was a hard worker and a good student. They knew about the severe abuse he had suffered at the hand of his father. They knew about his failing eyesight and about his leg so damaged by polio. They knew that Mike and Gene liked their new friend very much. But what they hadn't known until tonight was that he was in love with their precious Carol. They could tell by the way he looked at her. As Gene's parents hoped for him, they had also hoped that someday Carol and Mike would be together. But they both felt love for this young man who had every reason to be broken but yet at that moment seemed to be the strongest one in the group.

They were exceptionally young to be taking this trip alone, but Alan had made arrangements for their lodging along the way. Even though they had just graduated from high school and were only seventeen and eighteen, they were mature beyond their years.

"We do have one request. We want you to spend a couple nights with our oldest son, Ryan. He lives in Carmel now, and we haven't seen him for a while," said Alan.

Mike knew his parents wanted this to happen, and he wasn't sure how his friends would feel about it. He waited for someone to speak, but he didn't have to wait long.

Carol said, "I would love to see Ryan. He was always so nice to me from the very beginning. I was just a little girl."

Then Colleen said something that she never would have been able to admit a few years ago. "Carol knew Ryan was gay long before he told us. In fact, I think she knew before he was sure himself."

Alan didn't say anything, but he felt bad for his actions when he first found out. He hoped that Ryan would come visit them someday for Colleen's sake.

As they got up to leave, Colleen hugged John and said to him quietly, "I want this to be a wonderful trip for all of you because you have all worked so hard, but I want it most for you."

John was overwhelmed by these two kind people. "Thank you," he said. He couldn't seem to say anything else.

In the car, as Mike was taking everyone home that night, John said, "Your parents were very nice to me."

"They aren't always that nice. The family is fractured," said Mike. "They haven't talked to Ryan for several years until now. Danny's gone forever. Cathy is so strung out on drugs she doesn't even know where she is or what she is doing most of the time, and now I'm going to Vietnam. You've made an impression on them, John. They were moved by Gene's presentation of your graduation speech. And, Carol, they love you and always have. Thanks, everyone, for making my family come around."

John went to talk to Max, his boss at the garage, the following day. He offered John the two weeks off with pay. John was a little surprised but thrilled. Max would not tell John then, nor would he ever, that Alan McVary was paying for John's time off and had given him funds to give John a raise. If John had known this, he would not have approved. He had a little pride left when it came to his job. Alan was rich and manipulative and was trying to buy back the love of his son Ryan mainly for Colleen. He had enjoyed seeing her happy when talking to John. It had been a long time since he had seen her happy.

CALIFORNIA

Alan bought Mike a new van for the trip to California. It was actually a graduation present. It was light blue, Carol's favorite color. They left for California in the early morning hours two weeks after graduation. Mike, Gene, and Carol would share in the driving.

On their first night on the road, they stayed at a resort in Colorado where Alan knew the owner. Mike remembered going there when he was a child. They stayed for two days. The mountains were beautiful. At the higher altitudes, they saw snow and had a snowball fight, but it was June, and it was warm. Gene was uncomfortable driving in the mountains, so Carol took his turn.

They stayed in Reno, Nevada, before heading for San Francisco where they went to Chinatown, had dinner on Fisherman's Wharf, rode a trolley car, and drove across the Golden Gate Bridge.

Their next stop was Carmel and Ryan's house. Ryan lived with his boyfriend, Jeremy. As they pulled in the driveway, they were amazed at the magnitude of the house. It was two stories and overlooking the ocean with balconies running the whole length of the house along the front. There was a private beach with a boat dock and a pier.

Ryan and Jeremy met them at the door, and they looked as spectacular as their house. Ryan was a smaller version of Mike. He was thinner and not as muscular. His hair was a bit darker red than Mike's, but his smile and eyes were Mike all over again.

Jeremy, on the other hand, was tall and thin with fairly long blond hair. He was very attractive. Both Ryan and Jeremy seemed genuinely happy to see them.

"Well, everyone, this is my boyfriend, Jeremy," said Ryan. Jeremy smiled, showing movie-star teeth. "Of course, I'm sure you can tell this is my brother, Mike. This lovely young lady is Carol. And I know you must be Gene since you're taller than Mike, and you would be John. Come in and make yourself at home. I know you must be tired after such a long trip." They went into a beautiful room with views of the beach and ocean.

Jeremy sat by Carol and John on a rounded sofa.

"I've never seen a house this gorgeous before. I've never even seen the ocean before," said John. John had just gotten new glasses. They were very strong, but he could now see everything on this wonderful trip better.

"That makes me even happier that you can spend some time here with us." Jeremy was well-spoken, and he seemed very considerate of John.

A young Mexican man brought in a tray of fancy drinks for them. "The drinks are very good, but they are all nonalcoholic. I know you are all young," said Ryan.

Carol took the first drink. "This drink is delicious."

"Carlos will give you the recipe if you like," said Ryan.

Carlos then brought in a large tray of fruit. Carlos was very attentive and nice to Carol especially. She was the first girl he had seen in the house in a long time. The conversation was easy and friendly. They all seemed happy to be together.

Ryan and Mike walked out on the balcony. "How are Mom and Dad doing? I know how hard Danny's death was, especially on Mom," asked Ryan.

"There are good days and bad days. Mom enjoyed helping us plan this trip. I really think she planned it as much for John as for anyone else. She has grown very fond of him," said Mike.

"Jeremy and I listened to the tape you sent us from the graduation three times. Gene's speech, or I guess it was actually John's, was very powerful. The video was great too," said Ryan.

"I guess it was a night to remember, or maybe to forget. I'm not sure which," said Mike.

For no apparent reason, Ryan hugged Mike. Then they went back inside. Jeremy and John were still talking. Jeremy seemed to really like John.

Carol and Gene went to see the pool. Gene looked out at the expansive indoor pool.

"That's the nicest pool I have ever seen. Pinch me to make sure I'm not dreaming."

Carol playfully and gently pinched Gene's arm. He pulled her close to him, and they kissed.

"I couldn't help that," said Gene.

"I know. It felt good," said Carol.

The moment they touched, excitement and anticipation raced through their bodies and enveloped their hearts.

It was just the two of them, the way they liked it. Gene hugged Carol, and they kissed passionately and made love in the elegant house by the most beautiful pool they had ever seen. They both would have liked for it to last longer, but it was wonderful and satisfying. They lived for their stolen moments of bliss. It was what seemed to excite them most. They seemed to always be in a hurry, and they didn't know why. It was as though Gene thought there wasn't much time left, and he had to live fast and with passion, and he did just that. No one else was even near the pool side of the house. They could have stayed there all day, but they went back to where the others were.

That evening Carlos prepared a delicious Mexican meal, probably the best Mexican food any of them had ever tasted. The conversation at dinner was easy and carefree, but as they were having dessert, Ryan announced, "Jeremy and I hope to get married someday."

For a moment there was an awkward silence, and then Carol lifted her glass and spoke, "Congratulations, let's drink to Ryan and Jeremy's happiness. I'm so glad you two have found one another."

Everyone else joined in with their congratulations. "We've even discussed adopting a couple of kids someday," said Ryan.

"That would certainly make Mom and Dad happy," said Mike. They have always wanted grandchildren. Since I'm going to Vietnam and then college, it's going to be awhile before I'm at that point."

"But you do want kids someday, don't you?" asked Ryan.

"I guess if I'm married to the right woman."

Carol and Mike's eyes met briefly, and then they both looked away. Gene noticed the look between them, but before he could digest what it meant, Ryan asked him, "How about you, Gene? Do you want to have children?"

"I would love to have children. But I'm not sure I'll ever find a girl who would be willing to marry me," Gene seemed a little embarrassed at being the center of attention and also with the nature of the question.

"And you, John, what about you?" asked Jeremy.

John looked at Carol. Carol spoke to John in the kind gentle voice that the guys always loved, "It's all right, John. You can tell Jeremy."

"I love children. I have three younger sisters. I'll never be able to father a child. I've had a lot of injuries," said John with tears in his eyes.

Carol put her arm around John. "Some things are hard for John to talk about, but he will be fine."

Jeremy put his hand on John's. "I'm sorry, John. I can see it is painful for you."

"It's all right," said John as he turned and looked at Carol. "How many children would you like?"

"One or two if I ever get married," said Carol quietly.

Ryan sensed there were slightly uncomfortable feelings in the room, so he changed the subject. "You know something, Carol, I think you are the only girl who ever actually made me question my sexual preference. I have always had an extreme fondness for you."

Gene, who seldom spoke on such subjects, said, "I think we all share that fondness."

Mike joined in, "I second that."

John didn't speak. He didn't have to. He just hugged Carol.

"I imagine you are all exhausted. We have guest bedrooms upstairs, and there is one on the main floor to the right. It has a king-sized bed and a daybed. Our master suite is in the south wing," said Ryan.

As everyone began milling about, John hesitated for a moment before approaching Ryan.

"Do you mind if Carol and I stay together in the main floor suite? I don't do stairs well, and I think I may need some help with a shower tonight. And maybe Gene and Mike could stay with us too. Sometimes I need help." For the first time since meeting Ryan, John felt shy and awkward.

Ryan put his hands on John's arms. "Please be comfortable here. We care very much about all four of you, especially you. My mom is extremely fond of you. She talked to me for a long time about you. Please know that you never need to be nervous around me or Jeremy. And we want the four of you to have whatever sleeping arrangements make you comfortable and happy."

"Thanks, Ryan. You and Jeremy are really nice," said John.

After Ryan and Jeremy left to go to their suite, the four friends didn't know exactly what to do. John had opened the door for them, but they couldn't seem to go through it.

Mike finally said, "I guess I feel kind of strange since Ryan is my brother. I'm really tired after all the driving today. I'm going to go upstairs and go to bed. Gene and Carol will help you, John. Is that all right?"

John hugged Mike. "That's all right, Mike. We'll see you in the morning."

Carol took hold of John's arm and Gene's hand, and they walked toward their suite. When they opened the door, it was the most beautiful room they had ever seen. From the window they could see the lights on the boats at sea.

Without words, Carol and Gene helped John to the shower. There was a seat in the shower. Carol removed his leg brace. Gene washed his scarred body, being particularly careful. Gene dried him gently, and Carol brought him a clean T-shirt and shorts.

"I'm sorry, I'm not pretty to look at," said John.

"It's all part of you, John. It makes you the person you are today," said Carol.

They helped him to bed. She turned out some of the lights and lay down beside him.

Gene covered John and said to him quietly, "I'm going to sleep on the daybed tonight. I'll be close if you need anything."

"Thanks, Gene. Good night," said John.

Carol kissed John gently and sweetly. She massaged his back, shoulders, and legs. He was totally relaxed.

"Are you all right?"

"I've never been better," said John. "Where did Gene go?"

"He's taking a shower," said Carol.

John started to wipe the tears from the corners of his eyes, but he was too weak. Carol did it for him. She lay close to him with her arms around him. She kissed him, and he returned the kiss. It was a beautiful moment, and John fell asleep.

When Gene came out of the shower, he quietly found his place beside Carol. She nestled in the bend of his arm with her head resting on his chest. It was her favorite spot.

Carlos prepared a great breakfast for them the next morning, and then they headed to the boat. They had to walk across the beach to the boat dock. John didn't know if he could make it. But before that thought could bother his mind, Gene was on one side of him and Mike on the other. The sand was soft and very difficult to walk on. The boat was big, and the seats were comfortable. Ryan, Mike, and Carol were diving and swimming in the ocean. They swam fast and far. Gene and Jeremy both stayed on the boat with John. When Ryan and Mike returned to the boat, Carol wasn't with them.

"Where's Carol?" asked Gene.

"She swam down to the cliffs. She wants to dive off them," said Mike.

"You should have stopped her. That's so dangerous," said Gene.

"She likes to do things like that. I can't stop her," said Mike.

A short while later, they saw Carol swimming toward the boat. She climbed up the ladder and wasn't even out of breath as Ryan and Mike had been.

"That was fun. The water is really rough. I love swimming in the ocean," said Carol as she sat down by Gene. "What's the matter, Gene?"

"You scared me diving off that cliff. I don't want you to get hurt," said Gene.

"I'm sorry. I won't do it again," said Carol. She hugged Gene, and he kissed her on the cheek.

That afternoon, they swam in the pool. Jeremy gave John a wet suit. It was a tank top with leggings. Carol and Jeremy helped him put it on, and he swam with them for the first time. Jeremy gave John the wet suit as a gift.

The next morning Ryan asked Carol to walk with him on the beach. "Are you having fun?

"I've never had so much fun. You have both been so kind to us. You have treated John so well. He was so nervous about meeting you and Jeremy, and now he loves you both," said Carol.

"Jeremy and I were talking about you last night. It is almost like you have three guys in love with you. We are in disagreement on who we think you love," said Ryan.

"That's interesting. What are your opinions?" asked Carol.

"Jeremy doesn't want me to tell you what he thinks, but I probably will. He doesn't think he knows you well enough. I think he knows you about as well as I do," said Ryan. "Maybe I'm prejudice, but I think you love Mike. You two have known one another for so long. I think he would protect you with his life. His smile when he looks at you is undeniable love at its grandest. You have to see that."

The four guys in the house could see them walking on the beach. Ryan took his jacket off and put it around Carol's shoulders and held her close to him. The guys could tell she was crying.

"What do you think they are talking about? He's making her cry. I hate it when someone makes her cry," said Mike concerned.

"They are probably talking about us," said Gene.

Jeremy and John looked at one another. They knew that was probably true.

"And Jeremy, what does he think?" asked Carol.

"Jeremy didn't hesitate for a minute. He thinks you love John," said Ryan.

Carol paused before answering, "Mike is gentle and tender with me. He has seen me through some bad times. He treats me as though I am so fragile that I might break. I'm not that fragile. John always smiles and never gives up. He has so little to smile about and every reason to give up. He says I make him happy. Gene doesn't smile, and sometimes I don't think he is particularly happy, but when he touches me, it is with passion, and my heart feels like it could explode. He is a risk-taker, and he is so strong. There is something very special about Gene, and there always has been."

"Oh my god, we really missed it. You're in love with Gene." Ryan was surprised.

"But you know something, I don't think we will ever be together," said Carol.

"Why, what would hold you back?" asked Ryan.

"John and Mike. John needs me so much right now, but I don't think he will ever marry me or anyone else. As for Mike, I think we are destined to be just friends."

Carol and Ryan turned to go back to the house. He still had his arm around her. They knew they were still being watched, but they didn't care.

When they went back into the house, everyone was abnormally quiet. Carol sat down by John with Ryan's jacket still wrapped around her.

Carol finally broke the silence and spoke in a very serious voice, "Ryan and Jeremy, I've made a decision. I want to just stay here with you. I'll be your surrogate and conceive and have your babies, as many as you want."

There was an awkward moment of silence, then Ryan laughed. Soon Mike and Jeremy joined in, and then John reluctantly, as though he had missed the joke. Gene didn't laugh. He turned and looked out the window at the ocean. Carol went to him and put her arms around him.

"Oh, Gene, I'm just kidding. It was a sick attempt at being funny. You know I don't do it well."

Gene turned around. There were tears in his eyes. She had never before seen him cry. He hugged her and held her close to him. No one in the room was laughing now.

They would leave soon after this. They all thanked Ryan and Jeremy profusely for their hospitality.

As they were getting in the van, Ryan could be heard saying to Carol, "Go with your heart, always go with your heart."

As they turned onto Highway 1, Mike turned to Gene and asked, "What the hell just happened back there?"

Gene said, "I have no idea."

But he did know, and although John had sat quietly through everything, he also knew.

They would return to the beautiful house on the beach two more times. On the second trip, Mike would not be with them. He would be in Vietnam. Ryan and Jeremy lived there for many years. They never married or adopted children. Over twenty years later, the four friends would return to California accompanied by Alan and Terry. It would be bittersweet and their final journey together.

THE SAILORS

As they were driving down Big Sur toward Los Angeles, they stopped at a diner overlooking the ocean for lunch. John was having a hard time reading the menu with his new glasses, so Carol was reading it for him. There were two young men at the next table in Navy uniforms. They couldn't help but hear what was being said.

"Are you sure you're up to going to Disneyland, John? It is a lot of walking," asked Carol.

"I don't want you guys to miss it because of me," said John.

"Jeremy didn't want me to tell you right away because he didn't want to embarrass you, but he gave me a wheelchair that he used a couple of years ago when he broke his leg. He thought you might be able to use it today," said Mike.

"All right, I'll use it. I just hate holding you guys back," said John.

"We just want you with us," said Carol. She turned away as her eyes welled up with tears. She was facing the two sailors, and they could see she was crying.

"Excuse me," said one of the sailors. "I couldn't help but hear that you are going to Disneyland." He handed Mike a stack of tickets. "We went yesterday. We didn't get to use all our tickets. We were told to report back to our ship."

Mike graciously took the tickets. "Thanks, we'll use them. Where are you from?"

"We're both from Oklahoma," said one of the sailors.

Mike smiled at the sailors. "We're from Kansas. This is our last trip before we all go different ways. We've all just graduated from high school. I'm going into the Army, probably Vietnam."

As the sailors got up to leave, they shook hands with everyone at the table. "Godspeed. Enjoy today," said the sailors.

When Mike went to pay the bill, he was told the sailors had already paid it for them.

At Disneyland, they only did things that John could do with them. They enjoyed it, but they lacked the youthful innocence they would have had a few months earlier.

As they sat in a small patio restaurant having lunch, Mike said, "I can only imagine how much Danny would have enjoyed this. He would have loved Tomorrowland and Fantasyland. They say this is the happiest place on earth. What do you guys think?"

"It's fun, but maybe we are just too old," said John.

"I don't feel particularly happy. I hope there is someplace happier in the world. Maybe it is just that our trip is almost over, and I don't want it to be," said Carol.

"Our memories of it will be good, but I agree with John, we are just too old. And I agree with Carol, that it doesn't make me particularly happy," said Gene. "But I'm rather difficult to make happy."

They left shortly after this. It was time to go home.

During the rest of the trip, they seemed to grow even closer, if that was possible. They were even kinder and more considerate of one another than ever before. They stayed close to each other and held on to every word and action. They knew their time together was running out. They knew that once they parted, things would never be quite the same again, and they would probably all four never be together again, at least as they were at that moment.

CHAPTER

27

MIKE'S GIFT TO JOHN

When they returned from California, Colleen and Alan wanted to know all about the trip. Mike told them everything and how wonderful Ryan and Jeremy had treated them.

Mike was cleaning out the van the day after they got home. Alan came out to help him. He noticed the wheelchair in the back.

"Jeremy gave the wheelchair to John. It was good he did because it was just too much walking for John," said Mike. Mike sat down and wiped sweat from his forehead. "I was thinking about giving the van to John. I don't know how much longer John will be able to see to drive or able to walk for that matter. Being with him twenty-four hours a day, I saw his problems more clearly."

"Give it to him. When you come home from Vietnam, we will get you another one," said Alan. This was not the same dad Mike had memories of from just a short while back.

"You know, Dad, John needs to be able to support his three little sisters and his mom. I don't know how he is going to be able to do it." Mike put his head in his hands. "I'm leaving soon to go fight in a war that I'm not even sure I believe in. I'm leaving behind people who need me, John, Carol, and Mom."

Alan put his arm around his son. "You don't think I need you?"

"You're stronger than they are," said Mike.

"I have an old friend who is a doctor in Dallas. If anyone would know whether John's problems could be helped, it would be him," said Alan.

"He doesn't have anything to lose, but I won't be here," said Mike. "Maybe Carol and Gene could go with you."

"I'll call Dr. Wilson. Bring John by tomorrow, Carol and Gene too," said Alan.

"I'll have them here," said Mike.

And so here they were again meeting at the McVary house. Mike didn't tell them much, just that his dad wanted to see everyone.

After the usual formalities, Alan said, "John, if you would allow me to, I would like to see if my friend, Dr. Brett Wilson, in Dallas, can help you."

"You have already done too much for me, the van, the vacation," said John.

"This is different. Colleen and I are worried about your overall health and your eyesight and your legs. He wants to talk with you," said Alan.

"All right, but how do I get there?" asked John.

"I'll take you," said Alan. "I would like for Carol and Gene to also accompany us." He looked at Carol.

"Yes, a thousand times yes." Carol didn't hesitate.

Nor did Gene. "I'm honored that you would ask me. I think I can speak for both of us. We would do anything for John."

Thus the small group of friends, minus one, would begin their longest journey together. But this time the journey would be different. There wouldn't be any fun and pleasure, and there could be pain and failure for John. But there was a chance that there could be an improvement in John's overall condition, and that was worth the risk.

FAIRYLAND PARK

There was a large amusement park in south Kansas City that Carol, Gene, Mike, and Danny had gone to the previous year and had a really good time. As they were sitting around the pool at the McVary house one evening, Mike mentioned the park.

"How would you guys like to go to Fairyland Park before I leave?" asked Mike.

"I love that place. I'm ready to go," said Carol.

"Fine with me," said Gene.

"How about you, John?" asked Mike.

"I've never been there before," said John. "But I'll go if you think I can."

"Of course you can," said Mike. "And I have a great idea. Let's take your three little sisters."

Carol and Gene were both aware of the worried look on John's face. "I think it might be too expensive," said John.

"It's my treat for all of you and the girls. It would be fun to see their faces and watch them have a really good time," said Mike.

Colleen had heard the conversation and said, "I'll fix a picnic lunch for you."

"That would be great, Mom. Thank you," said Mike.

They went to the park on a weekday knowing it wouldn't be too crowded. They took Meggie's stroller. She was four but small for her age, and she couldn't walk very fast. The first ride was a train that went all around the park. They all went on it. Meggie sat between John and Carol and held tightly to their hands. Carol and Gene took Meggie on the merry-go-round. Carol was acutely aware that John was already tiring. Gene noticed this too. All the walking was too much for him, but she knew he wouldn't say anything because the girls were having so much fun. John had declined Mike's offer to bring the wheelchair. He didn't want to worry the girls.

Mike took Charlene and Darla on several of the smaller rides, and then they headed for the big rides. Mike and Carol went with Charlene on the Trip to Mars. No one else wanted to go on it. It was the only ride Gene didn't like because it made him dizzy. Charlene backed out at the last minute at the Boomerang. It was definitely the wildest ride in the park, so, of course, Gene and Carol went on it together and loved it.

There was an old wooden roller coaster at the park. It was very high with large drops, and it was really fast.

"Who is brave enough to go on the roller coaster with me?" asked Gene.

"I'll go with you," said Carol. "It's my favorite ride."

As Carol and Gene went on the roller coaster, Charlene and Darla went on the octopus. Mike and John sat on a bench with Meggie to wait for them.

"You wanted to go on the roller coaster with Carol, didn't you?" asked John.

"Not really. I like to see Carol and Gene do things together," said Mike. "I like to see her do things with you too, John. I've been close to Carol since we were twelve. She is such a good person that I want my two best friends to do things with her too. Besides, Gene doesn't usually like places like this, but he seems to be having a good time today."

As they started walking toward the car to get their picnic lunch, Charlene said, "Carol, why don't you go through the Tunnel of Love. I know there is someone who would like to go with you."

They didn't expect this from Charlene; after all she was only twelve, and it caught them without words.

"I think it is John's turn," said Mike.

John looked at Carol and then Gene. It only took a second for him to make a decision.

"You have all helped me so much today. Carol and Gene, I want you two to go through the Tunnel of Love. I'm not up to it right now."

Carol hugged John and took hold of Gene's hand, and together they entered the dark, cool tunnel. Gene immediately put his arm around Carol. They kissed and hugged in the tunnel. It was one of those private, stolen moments that they treasured so much. It always seemed as though that was when they felt the closest.

Charlene was a little disappointed. She had really wanted John and Carol to go through the tunnel together. But it was all right because she liked Gene too, as she did Mike.

Mike and Gene got the chairs and blanket from the van and the picnic lunch Colleen had packed for them. They found a shady spot near a playground. Mike sat on the blanket with the girls to eat. Carol and Gene sat in the chairs by John. After eating, Charlene and Darla went to the playground, and Meggie had fallen asleep.

"This was a good idea. Thanks, Mike. My sisters have never done anything like this before. They are having so much fun. Carol and Gene, thank you for helping me. The three of you are always so good to me." John was on the verge of tears as Carol put her arms around him.

When Darla and Charlene came back from the playground, Mike said, "I've got an idea. Let's go to the midway and win some stuffed animals." The girls were thrilled, and they jumped for joy.

They loaded up the van and parked as close to the midway as they could. Meggie was awake, and they put her in the stroller. The other two little girls were pulling at Mike trying to hurry him. Mike bent down and talked to them quietly.

"Let's slow down just a little so we can all stay together. Now I'm going to push Meggie, and, Charlene, will you take Darla's hand, and I'll take her other hand."

Charlene was only twelve, but she understood exactly what Mike was doing. Carol and Gene were both helping John out of the van. She saw the trouble he was having walking. She went over to

John and put her arms around him. Darla followed her big sister and did the same thing.

Charlene said, "We love you so much, John."

"I know, honey, I know you do," said John quietly.

Little Darla just patted him on the back.

They didn't play that many games, but every game Gene and Mike played that night, they won at least one stuffed animal, sometimes two. The girls had kittens, dogs, bears, and tigers, and they were excited. The girls each had five prizes, so it was a good time to quit, but Gene threw one more basketball and chose a little white kitten and handed it to Carol.

She kissed Gene on the cheek. "Thank you, Gene. I love it."

As they were leaving the park, they walked by the Ferris wheel. Mike stopped and bought two tickets. "Carol and John, you two are going on the Ferris wheel."

"I don't think I can get up in the seat," said John.

"Sure you can, with our help," said Mike.

When the wheel stopped, Mike and Gene made sure John was secure in the seat, and Carol sat beside him. Then Mike and Gene went with the girls to sit on a nearby bench.

On the Ferris wheel, John had his arm around Carol, and she rested her head on his shoulder. Carol was still holding her little white kitten that Gene had won for her.

Charlene was sitting between Mike and Gene on the bench.

"I'll tell you a secret if you promise not to tell anyone. John really likes Carol. He might even be in love with her," said Charlene quietly.

"We know, Charlene. We already know," said Gene.

"But I think you and Mike are in love with her too," said Charlene.

"Yes, we are in love with her too," said Gene.

"I think you and Mike are both very nice, but John is my brother, so I like him the best," said Charlene. "What's wrong, Mike? You are so quiet."

"Oh, I was just thinking how great this day has been," said Mike.

"We have had so much fun today. We don't normally get to do things like this. Thank you, Mike and Gene, for everything." Charlene kissed both of them on the cheek. Darla followed and did the same thing.

As they drove away from the park, the lights were just coming on. A few years later, Fairyland Park would close forever. All the rides would be removed and weeds would grow where there had once been so much pleasure.

They never regretted going to the park that day. Carol would never forget the kindness Gene, Mike, and John had shown that day to the three girls as well as to her. But that was what they were all about, kindness, understanding, and caring. Others didn't always understand their relationships, but it didn't really matter. They knew what they felt for one another. They also knew that in the end, the consequences of their attachments to and genuine love for one another would probably not be favorable, but that beautiful day in the summer of 1964, when they were all so young and free, had been a really good day.

FAREWELL PARTY

There would be a party before the journey began for John, Carol, Gene, and Alan to Dallas and the other much further journey for Mike to Vietnam.

The party was at Jeff Moore's home. It was for Jeff, Mike, Vito Sorrentino, and Jerry Watson. They were enlisting in the Army and hoped to stay together, but that was not to be.

Carol and Mike both remembered the first party they ever went to together was in the seventh grade, and it was Jeff Moore's birthday party. They all turned thirteen that year. Now they were eighteen, and they were going to Vietnam.

Jeff was very close to his older sister, Connie.

She asked Carol, "So what can we do to keep these guys from enlisting?"

"I don't think we can stop them," said Carol.

The four friends stayed close that night, but the party was too crowded and loud. They left early and went to a drive-in movie. Sitting in the dark, watching some nondescript movie, they felt closer than at the party.

"That party was one of the saddest things I have ever been to. No one really wanted to be there." Mike tried to joke about it, but it wasn't working.

Then Gene, who never joked, said, "Please don't ever have a party like that for me."

Carol smiled, "I promise I won't." Then she turned to John, "You're awfully quiet tonight. Are you all right?"

"It's just that my two friends are going away. I'm going to miss them and worry about them," said John.

Gene spoke without turning around, "I'll be close. If you or Carol ever need anything, all you have to do is call me. I'll probably come home a lot of weekends, and you can both come up to school to see me. I'd like that."

"Thanks, Gene. I guess you won't be too far away," said John.

Carol put her hand on Gene's shoulder and kissed his cheek. It was wet and salty, but she knew he didn't want anyone to know he was crying, especially John, so she didn't say anything. He was the strongest of all of them. Mike and John always thought Gene had the best chance to be successful and happy in life. Carol wasn't so sure. He was always so good to them, and he helped John so much.

Mike, who was also visibly emotional that night, said, "I'll be far away and gone for a long time, but all three of you will always be with me. This turned out to be a pretty good summer after all."

Mike took John home first and then Gene. Carol moved up to the front seat with Mike. On the way to Carol's house, Mike pulled into the parking lot by the football field. It was deserted and strangely quiet.

"We had some good football games here this year. Gene was a great quarterback. I'm glad he is going to play in college." Mike's voice was quiet and reflective.

"When you come back and go to college, will you play football?" asked Carol.

"I don't know. I'll probably be all out of shape or maybe I'll be in better shape. I don't know anything for sure. I wish I had a better feeling about leaving tomorrow. I just don't know what to expect." Mike hugged Carol tightly to him.

She kissed him, and he returned the kiss a thousand times over.

"My god, you are so beautiful tonight."

Their feelings were so gentle and kind to one another. They didn't want that night to ever end. At that moment, if they had a choice, they would have stayed together forever. He held her so close.

He had to remember every curve of her body and every second of this night. It had to last him a long time.

"I don't want to go to war without ever having made love to a girl, and I want that girl to be you," said Mike.

And so on the night before Mike left for Vietnam, Carol and Mike made love, as she had done with Richard two years earlier. She was surprised that Mike was still a virgin. He was not surprised that she wasn't.

The sunset was breathtaking over the deserted football field.

"It actually looks kind of pretty here, doesn't it?" Carol's voice was quiet and soft.

"It's nothing compared to you," said Mike.

Even though they felt it, neither one of them had said the word *love* that night.

Mike drove Carol home and walked her to the door. And with one more kiss, he was gone and would be for a very long time.

As Carol watched him drive away, she thought, *Please, dear God, let him come home safely.*

The handsome, gentle young man and the beautiful, kind girl had finally made it out of the friend zone and into another place that they liked much better.

THE GOOD DOCTOR

It was raining the day they left for Dallas. They were taking the big blue van. Alan and Gene would share the driving. It was a Sunday. They stayed that night at a hotel near the hospital in some ways reminiscent of the California trip, yet so different, knowing the grueling tests John would be going through in the morning.

At the hospital the next morning, Carol and Gene helped John into a hospital gown, and then they were ushered into a large office where they waited for Dr. Brett Wilson.

Dr. Wilson arrived soon. He was a fairly young man. Since he was Alan's friend, they were expecting an older man. After initial greetings, he pulled a chair up close to John.

"John, right now I just need to look you over and talk to you. Would you like for your friends to leave?" Dr. Wilson's voice was kind and reassuring.

"No, I need them to stay with me. I'm a little scared," said John.

"No need to be scared. I Just want to see if I can help you." Dr. Wilson's assistant wrote down everything he was saying. "You have beautiful eyes, extremely light blue, which is where the problem lies. We will check them thoroughly with the hope that we can keep your eyesight from deteriorating more." He looked at John's legs and gently removed the brace. "Once again, I will need to examine your legs more thoroughly."

At this point, he needed to examine John's back, so he pulled the gown down, and for the first time the horrific scars were revealed to Dr. Wilson as well as to Alan. Before Dr. Wilson could say anything, John showed him the scars on his stomach and groin area. Alan did not look away, but he reached out and took Carol's hand.

Dr. Wilson spoke to John quietly and compassionately. "What monster did this to you?"

"My dad did it," said John.

"How old were you?" asked Dr. Wilson.

"It first started when I was about six. It got really bad when I was between ten and thirteen. One night he threw me against the wall and busted my head open by my ear. My mother was pregnant, and he wouldn't stop hitting her. My little sister was born with brain damage from that beating. There was blood everywhere. The police came, and my dad fought them and ran, and they shot him, and he died. And it was all over forever. I've left out a lot, but I get nervous when I talk about it," said John.

"You've done fine, John." Dr. Wilson's voice was very consoling. "I've seen scars on POWs. I've seen people from prison camps in World War II. I've seen former slaves who were subjected to terrible beatings, but never have I seen anything to equal this. They are so extensive and were done with a heavy object."

"Sometimes a board, a belt with a heavy buckle, or a knife. The knife hurt the worst," said John.

Dr. Wilson gently covered John's back with the gown and also covered his stomach. "You were small. You have grown considerably since this happened."

"Yes, I was little. He didn't let me have much food. He was very big," said John.

"Did you ever tell anyone, a teacher, a friend?" asked Dr. Wilson.

"No. He only did it to me when my mother was at work. When my mom saw blood, I just told her I fell. I had polio when I was five, and I did fall a lot." John suddenly felt very tired.

Unlike Alan, Carol and Gene knew most of what John had revealed.

Dr. Wilson took hold of John's hand.

John smiled and asked, "Will you help me, Dr, Wilson?"

"I will certainly try. I will do anything I can to help you. You have a beautiful smile, John. Most people who have gone through what you have become bitter and unhappy. But you're not, are you?" asked Dr. Wilson.

"It always made my mom happy when I would get up smiling when I fell down. Carol likes my smile too, and she is really nice to me. I wouldn't have been able to be in the graduation exercises without Carol. And Alan, Gene, and Mike are good to me too." There were tears running down John's cheeks, but he was still smiling.

"The first time I saw you, I noticed your wonderful smile." Carol turned and put her face against Gene's chest to muffle her sobs.

Dr. Wilson couldn't help but notice Carol's beauty and her kindness, and he thought how lucky the three men were to have her with them.

"Well, John, we will do all the tests we can today if you feel up to it," said Dr. Wilson.

"I'll be fine," said John.

"I hope we can slow down the deterioration of your eyesight. Have you ever been diagnosed with retinitis pigmentosa?" asked Dr. Wilson.

"I've never heard that before," said John.

"I've read about it. I thought that might be what John has," said Carol. "I've read about it in one of your books, Alan, just a few months ago. I didn't know for sure."

"I'm curious. I imagine you know about polio also," said Dr. Wilson.

"I know that sometimes in later life, a person who had polio as a child can have recurrent or residual pain that affects other limbs or parts of their body not originally affected by the onset of polio," said Carol.

"And the scar tissue. What do you know about that?" asked Dr. Wilson.

"I think that some of the puffy regions can be smoothed and flattened and some of the deep scars can be closed up with skin grafts since John was so small when it happened," said Carol

They were all looking at Carol in disbelief. John, Alan, and Dr. Wilson were not only astounded by Carol's knowledge but in her ability to state her opinions so clearly and precisely. Of course, nothing Carol ever did or said surprised Gene.

"I may ask your opinions again. You are extremely smart," said Dr. Wilson. Dr. Wilson put his hand on John's shoulder. "You have a lot of people who care very much about you, John. The tests will be grueling, but I will be with you through it all," said Dr. Wilson. "Do you want anyone else with you?"

"Carol always stays with me through rough times," said John.

Dr. Wilson looked at Carol, and for a moment she could see tears in his eyes. "Will you be all right with that Carol?"

"Yes, I'll do all I can." Carol walked over to John and gently put her arm around him.

"Would you like something to drink?" asked Dr. Wilson.

"No, we're fine," said Alan.

Gene and Alan walked to a waiting room down the hall.

"Thank you, Gene, for being such a good friend to John, Carol, and Mike," said Alan.

"They are the best friends I have ever had," said Gene.

"Carol loves you very much," said Alan.

"When we were in California, Ryan thought she loved Mike and Jeremy thought she loved John. I really think she loves all three of us. She has trouble leaving John's side, and I'm having a hard time thinking about leaving her when I go away to college. Mike had trouble leaving too," said Gene.

"I know," said Alan.

"I hope Dr. Wilson can help John," said Gene.

"He will. I don't know how much, but he will be able to do something," said Alan. "And it appears as though Carol is going to help."

In another part of the hospital, Dr. Wilson and Carol had stepped out of the room while John was getting x-rays.

"You are a very good friend to John," said Dr. Wilson.

"John is a really kind person. I want to do all for him that I can," said Carol.

"He is a wonderful young man. When Alan called me, I didn't realize the extent of his injuries. I hope we can help him." Dr. Wilson's voice was full of concern for the fine young man who had just become his patient as well as for his friends, particularly the pretty girl sitting by him.

All tests were complete in the late afternoon. John was asleep when they went to his room. Dr. Wilson was at his bedside as was Carol.

"I want to keep him overnight. One of the tests was a little hard on him. I'm sorry. I didn't want anything to hurt him."

"You two need to go get some rest. I'll stay with him," said Alan.

Gene put his arm around Carol, and they walked back to the hotel room together. Carol was very tired, and she quickly found her favorite spot nestled in the bend of his arm with her head resting on his chest. Gene held Carol close to him all night. He didn't sleep. He watched her even breathing and her eyelids occasionally open a little and then close again. He smoothed her hair and wiped away a tear that escaped from the corner of her eye. Gene loved Carol so much. He always had, and he always would. He knew as Carol did that they would not be together forever. He wondered why things were so hard for them. If Carol's mother could have chosen someone for her daughter to marry, it would have been Gene.

When they got back to the hospital in the morning, Alan was helping John dress as though he was a little boy. Carol helped with his brace, and Gene combed his hair and put his glasses on him. When Dr. Wilson came into the room, John was sitting on the side of the bed. Dr. Wilson sat down next to him.

"We have all the results of your tests. I wanted to make sure we had everything before you left for home. There are several things we can do for you that are very minor surgeries. An operation on your good leg will relieve some of the pain you have been having. An operation on your bad eye should stabilize the deterioration. Also, we can improve the condition of some of the scar tissue. That was actually Carol's idea. Everything should be successful. Does that sound all right to you?" asked Dr. Wilson.

"Yes, thank you, Dr. Wilson," John smiled and shook his hand.

"John, you are basically in very good health. Your heart is excellent, and your vitals and blood work are good. When can you all come back? Would next week be too soon?" asked Dr. Wilson.

"That will be fine," said Alan.

"I know you are going away to college soon, Gene. We want to be sure you and Carol can be here too," said Dr. Wilson.

"We will both be here," assured Gene.

Dr. Wilson pushed John's wheelchair to the front door of the hospital and helped him into the van. He shook John's hand one last time and said, "I'll see you soon."

John smiled a confident smile and said, "We wouldn't miss it for the world."

An Unexpected Visit

When John, Carol, and Gene arrived at the McVary house the day before John's surgeries, they had a pleasant surprise. Mike was there.

He said, "I'm still going to Vietnam, but I'm on leave for two weeks."

John said quietly, "Mike, you should be doing something more fun than being here for me."

"This is where I want and need to be right now. I wouldn't have it any other way," said Mike as he hugged John. They were both suddenly overcome with emotion.

"I'm still going with you," said Alan. "So you'll have four people helping you."

"I'll need all the help I can get." John hugged Alan and kissed him on the cheek.

Alan suddenly realized that none of his children had ever hugged him that genuinely, or at all for that matter.

The trip to Dallas seemed longer than usual. The following day, John's surgery was also long. Alan and Mike were nervous. Carol was worried. Gene was the rock for all of them that day.

Dr. Wilson would spend a considerable amount of time with John and his friends over the next three days. Alan and Mike prepared the van so John would have a place to lie down on the way home. Dr. Wilson spoke very kindly to John in Carol and Gene's presence.

"John, you are the bravest young man I have ever met. I only wish that I could do more for you, but the risk is too high. I'm honored and privileged to have met you."

John smiled. He didn't really feel like it, but he knew his smile made Dr. Wilson feel good as it always did his mother.

"Thank you for everything you have done for me."

Once again, Dr. Wilson pushed John's wheelchair to the hospital entrance where Alan and Mike were waiting in the van.

And so the long ride home began. John was uncomfortable and in a little pain, but he was going to be all right and somewhat better than before, and that was all his friends cared about. They had convinced him to stay at the McVary house in their first floor guest room for a while so there would always be someone with him.

Mike left for Vietnam a few days later with no fanfare. He liked the fact that John was staying with his parents. His mom and dad both loved caring for John, and in turn, John was so grateful for their care. His mom had seemed to come to life a little, but he knew the day John left, she would have a hard time.

As the summer came to an end, John was well, and he went home; Gene left for college; and Carol prepared for junior college. The times were changing.

GONE TOO SOON

In the fall of 1965, Carol's cousin Ethan was killed in a tragic hunting accident. He was hunting with his best friend. As they climbed through a fence, his friend's gun fell over, went off, and shot him through the heart. Even though he was smaller than Ethan, his friend picked him up and carried him to the nearest house. But it was too late. He was already dead. He had been married for a year and was the father of a small baby boy.

Gene came home from college for the wake and funeral. He had known Ethan since he was eight, the same time he had met Carol. Gene, Carol, and John went to the funeral together. Colleen and Alan were there. Cathy was not. Ethan broke Cathy's heart twice, once when he got married, and now when he was tragically killed long before his time. Ethan was only twenty-one years old, and Carol was nineteen, and she had loved Ethan like a brother.

Carol didn't sit with family members at the funeral that day. There was a lot of arguing, and some people were accusing Ethan's friend of killing him. Carol and Gene knew his best friend, and they knew the gun went off accidentally. They couldn't understand all the fighting because Ethan had always been such a gentle, good man. Gene, Carol, and John went out into the hallway. Carol's Uncle Ray was sitting in the hall with his face in his hands crying.

He looked up at Carol and asked her quietly, "Did he know how much I loved him?"

"He knew you loved him. He always knew," said Carol through her tears. Carol hugged him, and then Carol, Gene, and John left.

They got in Gene's car, and Carol said, "Please just drive far away from here. Just keep driving, I can't stand it here."

At the wake the night before, it had also been bad. Ethan hadn't changed the beneficiary on his life insurance policy at work from his parents to his wife and baby. Carol had expressed that she didn't think that was right in front of family members. Carol, Gene, and John had left early then too.

As Gene drove toward Missouri, Carol couldn't stop crying. "My own mother thinks it is right for his parents to have the money. And my poor uncle that was crying in the hallway has a horrible secret that he will carry with him to his grave. Ethan and I knew, but we could never prove anything because no one would talk to us about it."

Gene pulled into a park and stopped the car. He held Carol in his arms as she cried uncontrollably, and then she got out of the car and stopped several feet away and threw up. Gene went to her and held her hair back, and John took a towel to her. They walked back to the car with her and sat quietly for a moment.

"I can never understand why people are so mean to one another. It is as though they are trying to destroy each other. Ethan would hate what happened at his funeral. It just makes me sick."

Gene smoothed her hair. "We'll always be kind to you. It hurts me to see you like this."

"I'm so afraid right now," said Carol.

John put his hand on her shoulder. "What are you afraid of? You have always comforted me when I was afraid."

"I'm afraid for us. I'm afraid we are going to be separated and none of us will be able to survive on our own," said Carol.

"I'm not going anywhere," said John.

"You know I don't date anyone at college," said Gene.

"I wouldn't blame you if you did. In fact, I wish you would. You need to find happiness, Gene. It's not with me. I'm too messed up," said Carol.

"Nobody I meet can ever measure up to you," said Gene.

"I almost threw up in your car a while ago. Would that have made you hate me?" asked Carol.

"No, I could never hate you," said Gene.

"I just want to go away with you two, somewhere far away," said Carol.

"We will. We will very soon. I promise," said Gene.

Carol was still broken from Danny's tragic death. She hadn't healed yet, and maybe she never would. Now, with Ethan's death, she was broken even more. All John could think of was that they needed Mike back with them. He always knew what to do and say.

CALIFORNIA AGAIN

Gene had promised Carol that the three of them would take a trip soon, but they all agreed that they could wait until the school year ended. Carol would be graduating from junior college, and Gene would have his sophomore year behind him.

But the spring of 1966 did not pass smoothly. In April, two friends who had enlisted with Mike were killed in Vietnam, Jeff Moore (Connie's brother) and Vito Sorrentino. Mike had never met up with them again. He would always say that taking the leave for John's surgery saved his life.

In June 1966, Carol received an associate in arts degree from junior college. It had been hard for her because her heart just wasn't in it, but she made it anyway. Carol did love the professors and lectures at junior college, and she knew that continuing at a four-year college would be beneficial. Alan had even offered to pay for her college education, but this was all she had planned for. Her schooling was now over. She needed a permanent full-time job and some stability in her life. She needed to somehow come to terms with all that had happened.

John had visited Alan and Colleen many times since his surgery, but the visit today, the day after Carol's graduation, was different. They were always glad to see John, but today he noticed that Colleen looked tired and worried.

"Is something wrong, John? You look a little nervous," asked Alan.

"After Ethan's funeral, Gene and I promised Carol we would take her on a trip. I think she needs it now more than ever," said John.

"That would be great. Go wherever you want. I'll pay for it," said Alan.

"No. I want to pay this time. But we want the two of you to go with us," said John.

"And where do you want to go?" asked Colleen.

"We were all happy with Ryan and Jeremy in California. They would love for the two of you to visit them," said John. "I love Ryan and Jeremy very much, but this is for Carol, not me. She needs all of us right now. She is not very happy."

Alan looked at Colleen. "Let's go see our son and help our dear Carol."

"All right," replied Colleen as she looked at John. "I'm having some heart problems. We will need to fly. Let us know when you've set a date."

"I will." As John drove home, he was wondering if he was doing the right thing. John had to be the go-between for Ryan and Jeremy and the parents. This was an unfamiliar role for him, and it would prove to be the most difficult yet.

When Gene and John picked Carol up the day of the trip, she only had a small blue bag over her shoulder.

"Is that all you are taking?" asked John.

"I travel light. Remember, I'm low maintenance," said Carol.

They were going to stay a week, so everyone except Carol had to check in luggage. They sat close to the front of the plane, Alan and Colleen with Gene, Carol, and John behind them. John had never flown before, so he sat by the window. Several times the stewardess asked Carol if she was all right and if she needed anything.

Carol asked Gene, "Do I look that bad?"

"No, you just look a little tired." Gene smoothed her hair back. Gene was usually bluntly honest, but he lied a little today. Carol looked weak and pale. He had noticed this when he came home from college.

When the plane landed, the stewardess said to Gene, "I've asked the passengers in front to let your group off first."

Gene didn't argue, and suddenly he realized that Carol wasn't the only one who was pale. Colleen was as white as a sheet, she was extremely thin, and she looked ten years older than she had looked before Danny died. The group of five departed the plane.

Ryan and his chauffeur were waiting in the terminal. Ryan greeted his parents both with a handshake. He greeted John the same way and said, "Jeremy is waiting at home for us." Then he put his hand on Gene's shoulder. "Thanks for bringing her." He hugged Carol tight and kissed her on the forehead, and she hugged him.

As they went to get their luggage, Alan said quietly to Colleen regarding Ryan's welcome to Carol, "That's the most affection I've ever seen him show to anyone."

Colleen didn't respond. They were here to try to win the affection of their son back and also to get to know Jeremy. But they were also here for Carol. She just hoped Alan could keep it together.

As they drove up Big Sur, toward the house, everyone was impressed with the beauty of the coastline. When they arrived at the house, Jeremy met them at the door. The greetings between Jeremy, and Alan and Colleen were stiff and somewhat cold. John was happy to see Jeremy again as was Carol because they both really liked him. Gene was nice but a little tense as he had been on the previous visit.

A beautiful dinner was served, but Carol couldn't eat much. Carlos was always very attentive to Carol, and she was very nice to him. Carlos stopped by her chair and quietly asked, "Can I get you something else?"

"No, I'm just not very hungry." Carol kissed Carlos's hand.

After dinner, they sat in the living room looking at the view and tried to make small talk, but conversation didn't flow freely. Ryan wasn't sure about sleeping arrangements. He explained the layout of the rooms.

Alan said, "Colleen and I will go upstairs. I bet the balcony view is even better there. John should have the downstairs suite."

"There's a daybed in that room. Carol and I will stay with him," said Gene.

Ryan kissed Carol on the head. "Get some rest, my sweet girl. We'll talk in the morning."

Carol nodded her head yes.

In their room, Carol curled up in a fetal position on the daybed. She went to sleep right away.

Gene and John lay down on the king-size bed. They didn't say anything, but in a few minutes, Gene gently picked Carol up and laid her between them in the big bed. John took hold of her hand. Gene again smoothed her hair back and said, "I didn't want her to get cold, and she looked lonely over there."

When Carol woke up in the morning, both Gene and John were still by her. They were awake but being quiet.

Carol asked, "How did I get here?"

Gene put his arm around her and said, "Well, I picked you up and brought you over here with us. I wanted you to be closer to us."

"Thanks." She kissed them both on the cheek. She liked it this way, in the big bed with both of them.

After breakfast, of which Carol was able to eat some, Ryan asked her to go out on the balcony with him. He sat on the glider. Carol sat beside him and put her head on his shoulder. He put his arm around her.

"You seem a little better this morning. But you seem so delicate and fragile, and you have lost weight, and you are a little pale. Do you have any idea how much I care about you and want to see you well and happy?"

"I know you care about me. You always have," said Carol.

"Would you like to see a good doctor while you are out here?" asked Ryan.

"If you think I should," said Carol.

"My parents and John think you are broken, and they are very worried about you. Gene hasn't said anything, but I think he is worried too. He is just trying to protect you," said Ryan.

"Why don't you be my doctor," said Carol.

Ryan smiled, "I'm not qualified."

"I don't want to see the doctor alone," said Carol.

"I'll arrange for Gene and John to stay with you," said Ryan.

That afternoon Carol, Gene, and John met with the doctor.

Dr. Rhodes said, "You seem very nervous and afraid, Carol. You're not afraid of me, are you?"

"No. I'm all right as long as they are here with me," said Carol. "These two guys are my good friends, Gene and John, and I need them."

"Tell me what you are afraid of," asked Dr. Rhodes.

Carol hesitated and then quietly spoke, "I'm afraid Mike is going to be killed in Vietnam. I'm afraid John's eyesight and legs are going to get worse someday. I'm afraid Gene is never going to find happiness."

"And what about you, Carol? What are you afraid of for yourself?" asked Dr. Rhodes.

"Nothing. There is nothing I'm afraid of for me personally. I'm just afraid for others because I love them so much," said Carol.

"You are a very sweet, kind girl and very sensitive. These two guys are lucky to have such a caring friend," said Dr. Rhodes.

"I think I'm lucky to have them," said Carol.

"Ryan gave me the tape of graduation. It was very powerful," said Dr. Rhodes. "You have lost a lot of people close to you, haven't you?"

"Yes. Danny and Ethan and Vito and Jeff. The last two were killed in Vietnam. Mike and Richard are in Vietnam now," said Carol.

"And you loved or love all of them, right?" asked Dr. Rhodes.

"Yes, very much," said Carol.

"Carol, that graduation tape made me cry, and I don't cry easily. By listening to it, I know how close you four friends are. Mike will come home from Vietnam, John will be well and fine, and as for Gene, I think he is happy right now here with you two," said Dr. Rhodes.

"You've been very nice to us. I can see why Ryan and Jeremy like you," said Carol.

"You're not broken, Carol. You may be a little tattered around the edges, but you'll be all right," said Dr. Rhodes. "If you want, you can come back and talk to me again before you leave."

"Thank you." Carol hugged the pretty doctor, and they all said goodbye.

Dr. Rhodes sat quietly for a while. Then she felt a single tear run down her cheek. She was a doctor. She wasn't supposed to cry, but they were so young and they seemed so good and pure. She knew that three young men were in love with the beautiful, kind girl who had just left her office. As Gene had said in his graduation speech, 'There are thousands of stories within each of us, most of which would break your heart.' And this was one of them.

During their visit, Ryan and Jeremy took them out in the boat four times. They drove along Big Sur, saw Carmel and all its beauty, walked along the beach, and had many delicious meals prepared by Carlos. Jeremy was the driver on most of the excursions.

Toward the end of their stay, Jeremy asked Alan and Colleen if he could talk to them out on the patio. Alan was somewhat surprised since Jeremy had said very little to them since their arrival. Jeremy seemed nervous, and they didn't know what to expect.

When he began speaking, his voice was a little shaky, "I just want you to know that your coming here means a lot to Ryan and to me. Ryan has told me so much about you. He is so proud of his family. He has told me all about your beautiful home and the pool with the grotto. He told me about how Carol and Ethan first came into your life with their rusty bicycles and tattered clothing, but because Mike, Cathy, and Danny liked them so well, you embraced them. He told me about Colleen's beautiful friendship with Carol's mom, Stella, and how you decorate for the holidays, especially Christmas. He even told me about Danny's dog, Goldie. I hung on every word because I have no life stories of my own to tell. I grew up in an orphanage in the Bronx in New York. Two years ago, when Carol, Gene, Mike, and John came here to visit, I liked them so much that I felt like they were my family. John and I hit it off, and we could talk about anything. And Mike, the way he takes care of Carol, made me realize what a good person he is. Carol is so sweet and beautiful inside and out. Ryan told me once that when he was young, if he had ever thought a girl like Carol could love him, he would have been straight. Gene is a strong, athletic man. He is very intense and has a dark sense of humor. It took awhile for him to warm up to us, but he loves Carol so much like Mike and John, although I think he may love her the most. I know all the things you have done for John. I respect you so much and thank you for that. I know how much Ryan loves you both. I also love you. We are not bad people. We are just different. Mike gave us a tape of the graduation. We have watched it many times, and it always makes us cry. I always think of all the people Carol and Mike helped, and then they were punished for it. And John's speech and Gene's presentation of it was so powerful." At this point, Jeremy became a little emotional.

Colleen walked to him and hugged him. "Our son loves you, and we love you. Take care of him for us."

"I will. I promise you that I always will," said Jeremy.

"I'm sorry if I ever doubted you and if I didn't seem friendly. Thank you for talking with us," said Alan.

They walked back inside with Colleen holding Jeremy's arm. Ryan was watching, and he knew that everything was all right.

Carol, Gene, and John didn't return to Dr. Rhodes's office. She felt better now, and Carol loved being between Gene and John in the big bed every night. It had been a good trip, and they all felt very close and happy as they prepared to return home.

CATHY

In the summer of 1966, Cathy came home. She had dropped out of college and gone to Southern California where she had been living in a hippie commune in the desert for over two years.

Alan called Carol at work one afternoon. "Carol, we need your help. A strange man just brought Cathy home. She doesn't want to see a doctor, but she doesn't look well."

"I'll be there as soon as I get off work." Carol was very concerned about what she would be able to do. "Should Gene and John come with me?"

"It might be a good idea." Alan sounded very upset.

A short while later, the three friends arrived at the McVary house. They noticed a dilapidated brown van parked in front. Alan came to the door, and Carol and Gene went upstairs with him. John didn't know Cathy, so he waited downstairs with Colleen.

Alan knocked on her bedroom door. "Cathy, someone is here to see you."

Cathy was sitting on the floor. Carol sat by her and hugged her.

"I'm glad you're home, Cathy."

Cathy started crying, and she couldn't speak. Carol motioned for Alan to leave and for Gene to stay. Cathy was skin and bones. Her hair was matted, and her clothes and body were filthy.

As Carol wiped some dirt from Cathy's face, she said, "We are going to give you a bath and some clean clothes. Gene is going to help me. Do you remember Gene?"

"Yes, I remember Gene." Cathy's voice was barely audible.

Gene gently picked Cathy up and took her to the bathroom. Carol removed her dirty clothing. She made the bath water warm, and Gene put Cathy in the tub. Carol washed and dried her, talking to her quietly all the while. Gene started to lay Cathy on the bed, but she said, "I have to sleep on the floor. I can't sleep in a bed."

He put her on the floor and covered her with a fluffy, pink blanket.

Alan knocked on the door. He asked Carol, "Would you talk to her friend? He's on the porch."

Carol and Gene went downstairs. The man on the front porch was as dirty as Cathy had been. He had long black hair and a beard.

"You must be Carol. I'm Charlie."

He held out his hand to Carol. She shook his hand and greeted him with a hug as though he was someone important.

"These are my friends, Gene and John. They will help me with Cathy."

He looked at them and said quietly, "All the way home Cathy talked about Carol and Mike. Is Mike here?"

"No, he is in Vietnam now." He looked down, and Carol put her hand on his shoulder. "Mike would be so grateful to you for bringing his sister home."

Charlie studied the three of them. "When she was talking more, she told me about the four friends that would be you three and Mike, right? She didn't belong out there. When I first found her, she was starving and already strung out on drugs. She said if she could get back here, you would all help her."

"We will. We'll all help her," said Carol sincerely and kindly.

"I don't think her parents want me in the house, but I would like to say goodbye to her," said Charlie.

Carol put her arm around him and said, "Come with me." She took him upstairs.

When Cathy saw Charlie, she said, "Thank you, Charlie, for bringing me home. I love you."

"Get well, my pretty little girl. I'm going to leave now," said Charlie.

Cathy seemed to relax, and she closed her eyes. She would never see or ask about Charlie again. Charlie left then, and Carol walked him out to his van. Gene and John thanked him and said goodbye; Alan and Colleen said nothing. Carol talked to him for several minutes before he pulled away.

John sat down by Colleen. "Carol never ceases to amaze me. She sees no difference in him from anyone else."

"And that is why Carol and Mike were able to help so many in high school. Everyone was equal in their eyes," said Gene. "I was never as good as they were at that. I always envied them."

"But you have sure stood by me through a lot. I thank you for that," said John sincerely.

Carol would stay by Cathy all night, and she would be there when Cathy awoke in the morning just as Mike had done with her many times. Carol would take her vacation time and more time off to stay with Cathy.

They all knew from past experience that rehab didn't work for Cathy, and she didn't want to see a doctor. Within the next few weeks, it wasn't so much what Carol did but it was the love with which she did it that made Cathy improve. Carol counted the bites of food she gave Cathy, making sure she ate one or two more bites each day.

One day Carol left the room for a few minutes, and when she returned, Cathy was standing by the window looking out at the pool.

"Does no one swim anymore?" she asked Carol.

Carol put her arms around Cathy. "Not since Mike left."

Cathy went back to her bed on the floor and cuddled up in her blanket. Carol knew at that time that Cathy would be all right.

When September came, Cathy returned to college as a junior. It would not be easy to catch up, but she knew that this time she would make it.

Gene—Four Years Later

Gene graduated from college in 1968. Gene's parents and brother were there, as were Carol, Mike, and John. Gene received a scholarship to play football in college, and he was as popular in college as he had been in high school. He had graduated maxima cum laude. There were two other students who had tied with him. He was asked to give a graduation speech, but he declined.

He had not spoken in front of a group since their graduation in 1964. He had once told Carol that he could never give a speech equal to John's speech he gave that night. Carol knew it had torn him to pieces, and he felt he could never speak publicly again. But many years later, Gene would speak again for a subject and a cause that he would feel very strongly about.

Carol was happy that Gene had finally dated in college. She had wanted so much for him to have a good college experience, and she felt he had. He had never become involved in the party and drinking scene at college. But Gene seemed deeply troubled, and on his graduation day, he was very uncomfortable with all the attention he was receiving. He had studied and worked very hard in college. Now he was just really tired of school. Even though he wanted to go to graduate school, he was seriously thinking of taking off a year first.

As a business major in college, Gene began working at TWA in Kansas City, Missouri, shortly after graduation. Carol was working at an insurance company in Kansas City, Missouri. Carol and three girls she worked with had rented a large two-story house on Lansing Street close to downtown. Mike had made it back from Vietnam and was now trying to become a college student. John was working as a mechanic.

Gene's love for Carol had not changed. He knew she loved him too, but there were still two others in the picture. He often thought that if there was ever any sign that Carol and John could end up together, he would not stand in their way.

And then there was Mike, his best friend. Mike had changed, but then everyone changed after going to war. They were still young. There was plenty of time. Maybe things would all work out, but he knew that would probably never happen.

But there was a strange scenario that Gene couldn't get past. He couldn't think of one of them without thinking of all of them. If he thought of planning a trip, he thought of it for all of them together. It was as though they were bound together for eternity.

THE HOUSE ON LANSING STREET

After Carol and her three friends from work had lived in the house on Lansing Street for about a year, things began to change. Donna married her high school sweetheart and moved out; Jackie was the victim of workplace cutbacks, so she moved back with her parents; and Rosalind, afraid the rent would be increasing, also moved back home.

One evening, knowing Mike was home from college for the weekend, Carol invited her three friends over for dinner. All still lived on the Kansas side. They arrived together in Mike's car. After dinner, as they were sitting in the living room, Mike had an unusual proposition.

"You know, I've been thinking a lot since I got home from Vietnam."

The other three looked at one another smiling slightly because they knew since his return home, he had been reflective, if not somewhat cynical, but they were all anxious to hear what he had to say.

"In fact, Gene is the one who first gave me this idea. He said he can't think of one of us without thinking of all three."

When Mike said this, Gene immediately looked at Carol.

"I think you're taking what I said a little out of context," Gene said quietly. "I would never put Carol in the same category as I do us."

Carol reached out and took Gene's hand. "It's all right, Gene. Don't worry, we can say anything to one another." It was as though roles had changed in the last four years, and the once-strong quarterback was now the most sensitive one in their group.

"I'll get right to the point. Since the four of us like being together, and you have this really cool house, instead of girls, why don't we move in with you and share all expenses?" Mike's bluntness took them all by surprise, and they were without words for a moment.

John took the reins and spoke first, "Personally, I think it is a good idea, but you know where I go, Meggie will eventually go."

"There is an extra bedroom on each floor. They have been using them as offices." Mike had thought things through.

Their eyes went to Gene. As usual, they were all particularly interested in his opinion. "It would buy us another year or two to decide where our lives are going. I wouldn't mind being with you guys a little while longer."

"If we have three yes votes, then I guess it's settled," said Carol.

Gene quickly responded, "No, your vote is the only one that counts."

"Then I guess it is a yes. But, Mike, you'll be away at college and then law school. That's several years," said Carol.

"But I won't be far away. We'll have weekends, holidays, and breaks," replied Mike.

For whatever reason, no one said anything for a while. All during this conversation, Carol had been sitting by John on the sofa, gently rubbing his leg. She continued to do so.

Hesitantly, the three guys prepared to leave. Carol hugged them all and said, "I love you, guys. Come back soon?"

"Don't worry, we will," said Mike.

They sat quietly in the car for a while before Mike drove away.

Then Gene said, "When you were in Vietnam, Carol was really down and sad. When we went to California, the three of us took the downstairs bedroom with the king-size bed. Carol was going to sleep on the daybed. But after she went to sleep, I picked her up and put her in the big bed between me and John, and she was better in the morning."

Gene looked back at John, and John knew exactly what he was trying to tell him.

"I should go back. I don't want her to be alone," said John.

Mike circled around and drove back to the house. John got out of the car, and Gene asked him if he needed any help. Without waiting for an answer, Gene got out of the car and walked to the door with John. He quickly went back to the car. As he got to the car, he turned to see Carol embracing John.

"Why did you do that? You love her, and yet you always want her to be with John," asked Mike.

"I think you've done the same thing," replied Gene.

"Sure, I have, before I went to Vietnam. Vietnam changed me," said Mike.

"No kidding," said Gene. "You know in high school, some people thought I was just a dumb jock, but in college I studied really hard. That's all I did. I didn't like being away from you three."

"It was just the opposite for me. I did all right in high school, but now in college, it's like I forgot how to study," said Mike.

Gene changed the subject, "We are for the first time in really different places in our lives. How do you feel when you see Carol and John together like we just did?"

"I don't really know anymore. I'll always love her, but I have always liked the two of them together too. But another part of me feels that she really belongs with you. I just hope you realize how much she loves you," said Mike.

"I could never take her away from John, or you for that matter. It's tearing me apart," said Gene.

"You know, I'm the one who invited John to join us in the beginning. I'm afraid by doing so, I really screwed you, my best friend," said Mike.

"I wouldn't change anything. I'm the one who gave John's speech at graduation. I haven't given a speech since." Gene took off his glasses and rubbed his eyes.

"You know, I want to say that things will all work out, but I don't really believe that," said Mike.

Within the next week, all three guys would move into Carol's house. They were happy to be close, and they felt secure and content.

LETTERS FROM VIETNAM

In the summer of 1968, Richard Noland was killed in Vietnam. In one of the last letters Carol received from Richard, he told her that he didn't think he would be coming home from the brutal war. And he was right. He was buried at Fort Leavenworth National Cemetery in Kansas. He received a Purple Heart and many other medals for his service to his country. He had been a young man of nineteen when he went to war, but he was there for over six years. He was twenty-five when he was killed.

Carol heard two contradicting stories regarding how Richard was killed. One was that Richard was a passenger in a jeep with three other soldiers on a blistering hot day in Vietnam. They passed a small boy and an old woman walking along a deserted road. Richard threw a candy bar to the boy. The woman had on a heavy cape abnormal for a hot day. Richard noticed this just after they had passed them. A heavy cape on a hot day made no sense. Richard tried to tell them to speed up, but it never came out. The jeep blew up. Two of the soldiers were killed, Richard being one of them. The little boy and the old woman continued walking down the road.

This was told to Carol by one of Richard's friends who was in Vietnam. She also heard that Richard had been killed in a helicopter crash. She would never know which story was true. For whatever reason, she had the feeling that the first story wasn't actually the way Richard had died.

Carol received many letters from Richard while he was in Vietnam. In the beginning they were basically love letters. Richard loved Carol very much, and he was looking forward to coming home to her. But as the years passed, the letters became dark in nature. He was very descriptive about the injuries he had seen and also about the things he had done. It was all so tragic.

Richard had been such a good man. She remembered that night when they were sophomores when Richard took Carol, Gene, and Mike out for pizza to celebrate their victories in the sophomore class officer election. That was the night he had first asked Gene and Mike to take care of her until he returned from Vietnam, and she would never forget how seriously they had taken his request. He had helped Gene, John, and Terry so much in sophomore physical education as their senior instructor. They all remembered him and loved him as much as Carol loved him.

In the end, if it hadn't been for Richard, Carol might not have known Gene, Mike, and John to the degree that she did. It was rather sad, but what had brought Gene and Carol together would also prove to be what was to keep them apart.

LOSS OF INNOCENCE

When Carol first met Greg Martin at work, they were immediately attracted to one another. Their relationship moved very quickly to the point where Greg talked about marriage. Carol knew that Sam, who was their boss at the insurance company, did not think Greg was the right man for her. A little over a year after they met, Carol was pregnant with Greg's baby. Carol wanted a baby, and they had talked about marriage, so she was happy, but the happiness was short-lived.

Greg had two sons by his first marriage, and when he found out that the baby would be a boy, he insisted that Carol have an abortion. Carol was definitely against abortion, and she wanted the little baby so very much. Greg made an appointment with a doctor in Topeka, Kansas, and he had his way as he always did. Carol was almost past the point when a baby could be aborted.

They stayed at a motel in Topeka that night. Carol was bleeding a lot and passing blood clots. Greg told her this was normal.

Greg was hungry, and he asked Carol if she wanted anything to eat. She didn't, and at that moment she wasn't sure if she would ever be able to eat again. Carol would never forget or forgive herself for what she had done that day.

When they got back to Kansas City, Greg let Carol out at her house on Lansing Street and drove away quickly. It was Saturday morning, and everyone was home. Greg knew this, and he didn't want to chance a confrontation, especially with Mike.

Mike met Carol at the door. "What's wrong? You've been crying."

"I need to lie down." Carol stumbled slightly and put her hand to her head.

Gene caught her and gently picked her up and took her to her bedroom.

"What's wrong? Carol's never sick," said John. "She looks so pale and weak."

Gene held Carol in his arms. Mike and John sat close by. "You need to tell us what happened. Did Greg hurt you?" asked Gene.

"Please don't hate me," said Carol through her tears. "Greg made me have an abortion. I didn't want to. I was almost past the point for it to be safe. It was a little boy, and I just killed him, and now I won't stop bleeding."

Mike beat his fist against the wall. "I knew something bad was going to happen. I hate him so much for doing this to you. I could kill him."

"We just have to help Carol now. Forget about him," said John as he put his arm around Mike.

Gene lifted the covers. He saw the blood coming through her clothing. "We need to take you to the emergency room."

"I don't want to go there. Please don't make me," said Carol as she put her hand on Gene's arm.

As Gene smoothed her hair back, he spoke very quietly and gently, "I don't want anything to happen to you. Let us help you. Is it all right if we call Mike's mom?"

"I guess so, but I don't deserve to be helped. I just killed my baby," said Carol.

"I'm going to call Mom now. You haven't hurt anyone. It was all Greg's fault," said Mike as he left the room to call his mom.

"You'll be fine, Carol. Colleen will help you," said John.

As Carol reached out to touch John's hand, she noticed there was blood on her hand.

"John, would you please get me a damp cloth?" asked Gene.

John did so. Gene cleaned the blood off her hand very gently. Gene held Carol close to him. He had never, in all the years he had known her, seen her so vulnerable and fragile. He knew that they would in all probability be able to save her life, but would they be able to save her from the feelings she had about herself?

Colleen walked into the room within a short time.

Mike said to John, "We should step out and let them be alone."

"Colleen, would you like for me to leave too?" asked Gene.

"Oh no. She needs you by her," said Colleen. "Mike told me what happened. I'm so sorry. We need to have a doctor check you out. You've lost a lot of blood. Gene and I are going to take you to the emergency room. We all care very much about you."

"If you and Gene think it is necessary, I'll go," said Carol.

"We do," said Gene. Let us help you."

Gene picked Carol up and carried her to the van.

She held tightly to his hand. "Please don't leave me, Gene, not right now anyway."

"I won't leave you," said Gene.

"You are all going to hate me for what I've done," said Carol.

"We will never hate you. It wasn't your fault," said Gene.

"It's Greg that Mike is so angry with, not you," said Colleen.

When they arrived at the emergency room, Gene very gently picked Carol up and carried her into the hospital. Colleen answered all the questions at the reception desk and nurses' check-in area. Then Carol was taken to a room. Dr. Mink and Lisa, the nurse who cared for Carol that day, were both very kind and caring. Carol knew it was because both Colleen and Gene were being so kind to them and showing so much concern and love for her.

Gene did not leave Carol's side when they took her for x-rays. When they were back in the room, Carol was resting peacefully. They had given her something to help her relax.

Colleen put her arms around Gene. "I told them that you were not the father and not responsible for what has happened."

"I wouldn't mind them thinking I was the father, but if I was, this wouldn't have happened to her," said Gene quietly.

"You handle situations so well, Gene. That is one of the reasons I wanted you with us. And you love and care about her so much as John and Mike do, but Mike is so full of anger right now that I don't think he would be of much help. And as far as John is concerned, he just isn't strong enough to handle a situation like this," said Colleen.

"Colleen and Gene, I appreciate all you have done for me," said Carol.

"I thought you were sleeping," said Colleen.

"No, I'm just resting my eyes," said Carol as she reached out for Gene's hand. "Are you all right, Gene?"

"I'm fine. I am just so sorry this happened to you. You are the sweetest, kindest girl I have ever known, and you should be treated better," said Gene as he picked her hand up and kissed it.

"Carol, would you like for me to call your mom or dad?" asked Colleen.

"No. You and Gene are all I need. I'll be fine now," said Carol.

When Dr. Mink returned to the room, he spoke kindly to Carol, "We are going to keep you here for about three hours just to make sure everything is all right. Will you both be staying with her?"

"Yes, we will be with her," said Colleen.

"We won't leave her alone," said Gene.

"Will I be able to have a baby someday?" said Carol through her tears.

"Yes, there should be no problem. It's good that your friends brought you in when they did because the potential was there to develop a serious problem," said Dr. Mink.

"I wanted the baby so much, but he wouldn't let me have it," said Carol.

"I know you did. Just stay strong. You'll be fine. Try to get some rest," said Dr. Mink.

Carol dozed off and on. When she became restless, Gene held her hand tighter and talked to her in the kindest voice and words that Colleen had ever heard.

"Gene, do you mind if I ask you a personal question?" asked Colleen.

"You can ask me anything. I just hope I have an answer for you," said Gene.

"There is no right or wrong answer. I just worry about you, Gene, because I love and care for you so much," said Colleen. "I've seen Mike, John, and Carol show happiness and anger, actually very little anger with John and Carol, but occasionally they do show it. But with you, Gene, I never see real happiness, and you never seem to be angry."

"Right now, I am happy that Carol is going to be all right, and I'm angry at Greg for what he made her do. I just don't smile or get mad," said Gene.

Colleen hugged Gene and kissed him on the cheek. "My dear, sweet Gene, please don't think I am being critical. I love you so much. I think you are the kindest best man I have ever known, and so does Alan."

"I feel different emotions. I just don't show my feelings," said Gene.

"Oh, Gene, I love your quiet, strong personality. Alan has told me more than once that he wishes he could be more like you. I just hope that someday you can be genuinely happy. Please allow yourself that luxury," said Colleen.

"Once years ago, I told Carol that I couldn't see far into my future like others can. I was only sixteen then, but I still don't see my future today. I don't see everlasting happiness or success. I don't know what it means. Neither does Carol, and she can usually think of an explanation for everything," said Gene quietly.

"Because you are such a good person, I just hope you have a good life. We don't always know what our futures hold, but that doesn't mean we don't have a future," said Colleen. "What do you want to do with your life?"

"If I even had a clue, I would at least be more content. But between you and me, I just don't have any idea," said Gene.

"You, John, and Carol are all like family to Alan and me. Never forget how much we love and respect you. We would do anything to help the three of you as well as Mike," said Colleen.

"You're a nice lady, Colleen. Carol always feels you understand her better than her own mother. I tend to agree with her," said Gene.

"Carol's mother is my best friend, but Carol is too much for her, and she always has been. Carol is so spirited and strong and yet tender and delicate, and she is adventuresome and likes to take risks.

In some ways she is a lot like you. Do you remember how Carol used to like to jump off the cliffs at the lake and swim where she wasn't supposed to swim?" asked Colleen.

"Yes, I remember that quite well. She did that in California too. She can be a little reckless. In fact, sometimes she scares me. But she also shares qualities with Mike. They can both be rebellious and challenge the system. I've always envied them that quality. Also, they both have the ability to be friends with anyone and help people," said Gene.

"And then there is John, sweet, kind John. Both Carol and John are so generous. Once John had a piece of cheesecake, which you know is his favorite. He cut it in seven pieces because there were seven of us. Carol would do the same thing. That was in California. You took care of all of us on that trip. Do you remember?" asked Colleen.

"I'll always remember everything about those California trips. Carol was so happy there. You know, she wanted to stay," said Gene.

"I know, but she didn't want to leave you guys," said Colleen.

"Did I hear someone say California?" asked Carol very quietly. "I was having a dream about California."

"Well, look who's awake. I just mentioned that you liked it there. We all did," said Gene. "I hope it was a good dream."

"Not really good or bad, just strange. Did I ever tell you that I went to California once with my mother and Aunt Martha? They wanted to see California, so we drove there in an old, beat-up car. I'm surprised we made it," said Carol.

"Did they enjoy the trip?" asked Colleen.

"Yes, we drove along Big Sur from San Francisco to Los Angeles," said Carol. "Something strange happened on that trip. I haven't thought about it for a long time, but I used to have dreams about it. I guess it's on my mind because of what just happened to me."

"What happened?" asked Gene as he took Carol's hand.

"We were in a deserted area north of Los Angeles. My mom stopped on a cliff overlooking the ocean and walked down a hill to take a picture. Martha was in the back seat of the car lying down. It appeared that I was alone. I was on the edge of the cliff looking out over the ocean. A van pulled up and a man with long black hair and a beard and three girls about my age got out of the van and started walking toward me. They were smiling and talking to me. Then another van pulled up with two men and several Boy Scouts. The man and three girls left right away. My mom was back then, and she asked me what they said to me. I told her I couldn't understand them. After we got home, we were watching the news one night, and they were talking about the Sharon Tate murders, and it showed Charlie Manson and three girls. We both recognized them, especially Charlie and Susan Atkins. I talked too much. That made me really tired," said Carol.

"Were you afraid?" asked Colleen.

"No. Not at all," said Carol quietly. "Susan Atkins cut Sharon Tate's baby out of her stomach. That's what happened to me yesterday."

Gene put his arms around Carol. "You are going to a really dark place right now. Try not to think about it," said Gene.

"I won't think about it anymore. I'm sorry, Gene," said Carol.

"You don't have to be sorry. I just want you to think about something good," said Gene.

"I'll think about you when you were a little boy. Colleen, did you know Gene was a really cute little boy? He had a little curl on his forehead, and he wore the cutest overalls. He was so tiny and sweet, and I was a head taller than he was," said Carol.

"Well, Carol, if you ask me, I think he is still pretty cute," said Colleen.

"You went from Charlie Manson to me pretty quickly," said Gene.

"But remember, you told me to think about something good, so I thought about you because you are a really good man," said Carol.

Gene kissed Carol on the cheek as Dr. Mink came into the room with a nurse.

"Lisa will take your vitals, and you can probably go home. Are you all right? It looks like you've been crying."

"I'm not sure I'll ever stop crying," said Carol.

"She'll be fine. She just needs to go home," said Colleen. "Gene and I will take good care of her."

In the van on the way home, Gene held Carol close to him in the back seat as Colleen drove. Colleen was so proud of Gene that day. He was so mature and able to keep it together for everyone. When they got home, Mike met them at the front door. He hugged Carol and kissed her on the cheek.

"I'm sorry for the way I acted earlier. Please forgive me," said Mike.

"It's all right, Mike," said Carol.

"You need to talk to John. He's in a bad way. He is confused and worried and crying," said Mike.

John was sitting on the sofa in the living room. Carol went to him and put her arms around him.

"I'm so sorry, John," said Carol. "I want to talk to you. I want Colleen, Gene, and Mike to be here too because we both need them right now."

"I was so worried about you. I didn't know what was going to happen to you," said John.

"I'm sorry, John, that I worried you and made you cry," said Carol. "You are very special to me, and I've hurt you."

Gene handed John a handkerchief from his pocket. "I think you might need this, John. I'm going to sit here by you in my usual seat if that's all right with you." Gene helped him wipe the tears from his cheeks.

"I want you to stay by me, Gene. I need you." John paused for a moment and then looked at Carol. "You didn't have to do what you did, Carol. I know I'm not very smart, and I don't think well anymore, but I love you, and I would have married you and been a good daddy to your little boy. I would have been the best daddy ever and a good husband." John put his arms around Carol and his head on her shoulder.

As Carol spoke, she held John tightly to her. "John, I know you would have been a wonderful daddy and husband, and I wanted my little baby so much. But Greg had some say since he was the father, and he didn't want a child now. I tried to convince him to let me have the baby, but I didn't succeed. I had even named him."

"What was his name?" asked John.

"David. I thought that would be a nice name," said Carol.

"I like that name," said John

John was crying so much that Carol could feel his tears soaking through her blouse.

"John, I will think about little David every single day as long as I live. And the day I die, he will be first and foremost on my mind because I'll be seeing him soon. Always know, John, that this was not my choice."

"Gene or Mike would have married you, and Colleen would have helped you with little David. Everything would have been fine," said John.

"That is all true, and, John, you would have been the best daddy ever because you are the smartest, nicest person I know. And I love the way you think because you think with your heart, and I know you love me. I hope this doesn't make you stop loving me because your love is very precious to me, and if you stopped loving me, I'm not sure what I would do," Carol paused. "I'll pay a big price for what I have done. My life will never be quite the same again. I need your love right now, John. I won't ask you to forgive me, just love me if you can."

"I love you, Carol. I'm so sorry this happened to you," said John.

Gene got up and went to the kitchen. Colleen followed him and put her arms around him.

"I may not show happiness and anger, but I certainly show sadness. This is only the third time in my life that I have cried. My dad never wanted to see me cry. It was Carol who made me cry the other times also. For some reason, I feel I'll cry a lot more in the future," said Gene.

"Always know that I love you, Gene. You are such a good man," said Colleen.

Mike joined them in the kitchen. He was also crying. "I thought maybe we should let them be alone for a while. Do you think they will be all right?"

"It may take some time, but hopefully they will be fine. Everyone is just hurt right now, but time will heal some of the hurt," said Colleen.

"But time will never heal it all," said Gene. "Carol will never forget that little baby boy. She is such a truly good person. She never hurts anyone. She only wants to help everyone."

"No, she will never forget him, but that's all right. She must remember him. She is the only one who will remember him forever," said Colleen.

"I'll always remember him and this day. I couldn't forget it if I tried," said Gene. "Is there anything we can do to help her?"

"I would say just be kind and gentle with her, but you are always that way," said Colleen. "I'm going to stay here with you tonight. Mike, are you all right? You are so quiet."

"I don't know what to say or do or feel. I wanted Carol to have a good life. That's all I ever wanted," said Mike.

Colleen held Mike in her arms. "I know, Mike. I know."

They all silently went to their individual rooms that night, and Colleen went to the guest room. Within a short while, Gene got up and went to Carol's room. She was soon beside him nestled in the bend of his arm with her head resting gently on his chest. There was no conversation. They were just two people trying to figure out what their futures would be. That night they couldn't imagine anything being worse than what had just happened. But their lives would not be easy or free from tragedy, and they were to experience many things worse than this day had been. They were two really good people but bad things do happen to good people.

For two weeks, Carol did not want to leave the house, let alone go back to work. She didn't even answer phone calls. Gene never left her side. He took off time from work to stay with her. He held her close to him and spoke to her kindly and tried to convince her that things would get better. Colleen stayed with them also during this time. Gene was the only one who could encourage Carol to eat. Although Mike went back to school and John went back to work, they were there every evening, night, and morning.

Alan was the only visitor Carol wanted. When he came to visit, he held Carol in his arms for a while and told her how much he loved her and how sorry he was for what had happened. He hugged her and kissed her gently, but she returned to Gene's arms as she always did.

Carol was so grateful for the love, care, and kindness Gene as well as everyone else showed her during this time. But she credited Gene with saving her, and she so much wanted to repay him for his kindness to her. Within too short a time, Carol would return Gene's love and care a thousand times over. It would be the most devastating and worst time of their lives. Unfortunately, they could not change or know what the future held for them. To a degree, their destinies were already determined and carved in stone.

THE LONGEST JOURNEY

In January, 1969, the four friends would begin their longest journey together. It would take them to places in their hearts and souls that they had not visited before.

Because of the ice and heavy snow, Carol was late getting to work. Her boss, Sam Hagan, called her into his office to take dictation shortly after she arrived. A few minutes later, the receptionist knocked on Sam's door. She told Carol that she had a phone call.

Before anyone could ask her to take a message, she said, "You probably should take the call. It's Memorial Hospital."

Carol took the call and then returned to Sam's office. "I need to leave. There has been an accident. John's hurt."

"Let me take you," said Sam.

"No, I have my car," Carol hesitated. "I don't know when I'll be back."

"Stay as long as you need to. I hope he's all right," said Sam.

As Carol went out into the snowstorm, the snowflakes stung her already damp cheeks. A few minutes later, she arrived at the hospital right behind Gene who was just parking his car. Gene held her hand, and without a word, they walked into the hospital through the emergency room doors.

They were told that John had already been taken to the ICU. His mother was with him, and the emergency room doctor wanted to speak to Gene and Carol. Everything was moving so fast. They were taken to a private room, where the doctor was waiting for them.

The doctor spoke rapidly, "I'm Dr. Ross. I assume you're Gene and Carol. The other name listed is Mike. Is he with you?"

"No, he's away at school," replied Carol.

Dr. Ross spoke very honestly and calmly to them, "John's mother asked that we call and speak with you. She is having a hard time right now. John was working on a car at the garage. A portion of the roof collapsed from the heavy ice and snow. It fell on John. He has severe traumatic head injuries plus multiple other injuries. His right arm and hand are crushed. He is in a coma."

Carol's heart felt as though it could jump out of her chest, but she was the first to speak, "Is he going to make it?"

"Right now, I don't know. We will do all we possibly can. Go to him now. Talk to him. Let him know you are with him," said Dr. Ross.

In John's room, they both embraced his mother, Rose. She looked so alone and frightened.

"I need to pick the girls up at school."

"Would you like for me to pick them up, or would you rather I took you?" asked Gene.

"Could you please take me. My car wouldn't start, so I came here in a cab," said Rose.

Gene looked at Carol. "Will you be all right? I'll be back soon."

"Yes, be careful out there," said Carol as she pulled a chair close to John's bed.

There was a nurse on the other side of the bed carefully watching his vitals and the many tubes inserted into his body. "I'm Monica, I'll be with him at least today and tonight."

"He's been through so much. I don't know how much more he can take," said Carol.

Carol was glad as well as relieved when Gene returned. As afternoon turned into evening, Carol left the room to make three phone calls: one to Mike, one to Alan McVary, and one to Jeremy in California. John and Jeremy had remained very close, and they talked on the phone often.

When she returned, Gene asked Carol, "Don't you want to get some rest?"

"I can't leave right now," said Carol.

It would be a long time before either Gene or Carol left John's bedside.

In the quiet hours of the night, they would talk to him. It was mostly Carol at first, but when Gene realized what she was doing, he did the same. They talked to him about California and the house in Carmel, about his sisters and mother, about senior prom, about graduation, and about Fairyland Park and anything else they could think of. When Carol ran out of words, she would quietly sing to him, and when she didn't know the words to the songs, she would just hum. Mike and Alan were there early the next morning, as was Jeremy, who had taken a red-eye flight from California. Even Cathy came. She would stay with Rose and help her all she could.

"Thank you for coming, Cathy." Carol was surprised to see her.

"I will never forget how long you and Gene stayed with me when I was curled up in my blanket on the floor," said Cathy.

"I didn't think you knew I was even there," said Carol.

"I knew. I always knew. Just as John knows you are all here with him now. He knows how much you all love him. Don't ever stop talking to him," said Cathy.

Alan left with Cathy to take her to Rose's house.

Gene and Mike went to the garage where the accident happened. It, of course, was closed. Together they cleaned up every bit of debris and hauled it away. Then they chopped at the snow and ice until every speck of blood was gone. It had been Gene's idea to do this. He didn't want John's mother and sisters to see all the blood.

As the days turned into weeks, they all stayed with him—Carol, Gene, Mike, Alan, and Jeremy. Someone was with him all the time. Then one day he woke up. Carol and Gene were there. His first words formed perfect sentences.

"You have a nice voice, Carol, you can really sing. Hi, Gene. Where's Mike?"

Gene touched John's trembling hand. "Mike will be here soon."

"We're so glad you are awake," said Carol.

Although John didn't say anything more that evening, the doctors said this was a good sign. The next day when he opened his eyes, Carol was the first person he saw.

"You're really pretty. Has anyone ever told you that before?"

"You have my dear, sweet John, many times over," said Carol. "Do you remember what happened?"

John had a frightened look on his face. "I was conscious for a while. I saw all the blood."

"Don't try to talk too much," said Gene.

John could hardly move his head as he tried to look at both of them.

Gene moved to the other side of the bed by Carol. "Is that better?"

"Yes, thank you. That's where you should always be anyway, Gene. Right next to Carol," said John quietly. "Am I going to make it?"

"You're going to make it, John," said Gene.

"Alan and Jeremy have been here too. They will be up later. And Cathy has been helping your mom and sisters," said Carol.

"I thought I heard their voices," said John.

As several doctors came into John's room to examine him, Carol and Gene stepped out. They sat on a sofa in the ICU waiting room. Gene put his arm around Carol, and she leaned against his chest. After they examined John, two of the doctors came into the waiting room to talk to Carol and Gene. The doctors were not smiling, but their voices were somewhat encouraging.

"He has come out of the coma fine. He is going to live, but it will be a long struggle for him. For as badly as his head was hurt, he is talking really well. We don't know yet about his movements. He needs to heal a little more," said Dr. Adams.

"He's strong. He will never stop fighting," said Carol. She hadn't moved. Her head was still on Gene's chest.

Before they left, Dr. Matthews said, "You two are very good friends to John. That alone will help him get better."

"Thank you." Gene spoke for both of them. Carol had fallen asleep. Gene didn't want to move for fear of waking her.

Five weeks after the accident, Jeremy went back to California. He had been staying with Alan and Colleen. Jeremy thought so much of John, as did Alan. This was one thing they had in common. They spent hours by his side in the hospital room. Colleen wasn't feeling well, and Ryan had come to visit her as well as John for the last two weeks of Jeremy's stay.

Mike never missed a weekend. Sometimes he even came to be by John's side when he should have been in class. Mike had decided that John's life and well-being was much more important than college and rightly so.

Sam, Carol's boss, had been very kind, and he had approved her indefinite leave from work to care for her friend. She was even being paid for the time off. Gene wasn't so fortunate. He lost his job at TWA, but he got another job fairly quickly.

John's shoulder, arm, wrist, and hand had been broken and basically crushed, and his back was severely injured. His legs had suffered superficial cuts and bruises. His head was hurt badly, but it seemed to be healing well. Therapy was a long process, but each day he seemed to get stronger. John had a large room in the hospital. Many therapy sessions were given in his room. The equipment was brought to him. If he happened to mention that a milkshake or fried chicken sounded good, he would have it at his next meal. Because there were still some lingering effects from his head injuries, for months there were nurses with him around the clock. There were a whole group of doctors caring for him, a specialist for each part of his injured body. Even Dr. Wilson, who did his surgeries years ago in Dallas, came to visit and be a consultant on his care and treatment.

One day, close to the end of John's hospital stay, Carol and Gene were helping him learn to write with his left hand since his right arm and hand were almost completely useless.

"You would think I was someone important, the way they treat me here," said John.

"You are important, John. Do you have any idea how much I admire you? All the grueling therapy and operations and treatments you've been through and you've never given up or complained once," said Carol.

"I've been here for a long time. I don't have health insurance. How can I ever pay for all this?" asked John.

Carol looked at Gene. Neither one wanted to tell him, but he should know. Gene took hold of John's good hand. "You don't need to worry about that, John. Alan and Jeremy are paying every cent of your bill."

"I don't believe it. Why would they do that?" asked John.

"It's for all you've done for us. It's been you all the way, John. You've kept us together. You've saved us from ourselves. You're the one who made it come together between Alan and Colleen with Ryan and Jeremy. You've helped me, Mike, and Carol." Gene spoke quietly, but his words were clear and honest.

"But I think you all have helped me," said John.

"John, my dear John, you are the one who helped me recover from Danny's death, and you didn't even realize what was happening. You began the day of graduation rehearsal and continued until I was well. And then when I was, well, I was able to save Cathy. Alan will never forget that." Carol spoke as Gene did, quietly and yet distinctly. The three friends held on to one another for a long time that night. They were afraid to let go.

On a bitterly cold winter day, John had entered the hospital. On a pleasant, warm summer day, he went home. He had been in the hospital for over six months. All the nurses and doctors were there as were his friends. It had been a long journey for John, and for his friends for that matter. John had proved time and again that he was a survivor. They went to a dark place with John, and they all returned.

Although John was doing well and much better than originally expected, he still had a long road to recovery ahead of him. He was still weak and needed therapy. Carol, Gene, and Mike made sure he was never alone. They helped him, not by doing everything for him, but by helping him to do things for himself. When they were at work, John's mother or Carol's mother would stay with him. Alan would also help. Sometimes he needed help with his food or something as simple as brushing his teeth or putting on his socks. Occasionally he couldn't get the words out that he wanted to say, but they helped him with that also.

What John looked forward to most during that time were the evenings when the four of them would sit in the living room after supper and watch TV or just talk. Carol would sit by John on the sofa. Sometimes she would put a pillow on her lap and gently lay his head on it. Other times they would just hold hands.

Gene would help him shave, dress, and comb his hair. Gradually, he was learning how to do everything again.

But what impressed everyone about John was his smile. It was still there. He had never lost it. He was not angry, bitter, or depressed. He was just happy to simply be alive.

THE BEGINNING OF THE END

In future years, Carol, Gene, Mike, and John would all remember the house on Lansing Street fondly. They would all agree those years were some of the best years of their lives. The house sheltered some tragedy and heartbreak, but then everything does. As Carol always felt, you can't have happiness without some sadness. Carol was still working at the insurance company; Gene had returned to TWA at their request; Mike was struggling through college; and John was back working at the garage.

Their lives had settled into complacent routine and mediocrity. Occasionally, one of them would meet someone outside their little group and actually go out on a date, that is, except John. They were his only friends. Carol was, to everyone's disappointment, still seeing Greg Martin from work. Carol's boss, as well as Greg's, was still Sam Hagan. He liked Carol very much, as she did him—just as an employee and boss, nothing else.

Sam invited the four friends to meet him at a downtown restaurant for dinner one Saturday evening. Carol knew what he wanted to talk about, but against her better judgement, she agreed to the meeting.

At first, conversation seemed to flow easily, and the food was good. Sam was a very attractive man of forty-five. He was a kind, friendly, smart man and a very good boss.

"You might wonder why I wanted to meet you, guys. I've heard so much about you all that I feel like I already know you," said Sam.

"I hope what you've heard is good. Carol thinks a lot of you. You have been very kind to her," said Mike.

"It has all been remarkably good. And I would have known each one of you without introductions," said Sam. "I want to talk to you like I am one of your group. I'll be number 5. Carol is very special to me as I know she is to all of you. She is like a fragile butterfly that could be so easily broken. I don't want to see her hurt," said Sam.

"I've been trying to protect Carol since we were twelve years old. Sometimes I haven't done such a good job," said Mike.

"You have always been wonderful, Mike," said Carol.

"I'm going to get right to the point," Sam paused. "I'm afraid Carol is going to marry Greg Martin from our office. He is fifteen years older than she is, and I don't think he is the man for her."

Mike hated Greg for what he had done to Carol, but he doubted that Sam knew, and he didn't think this was the time to bring it up.

"We like our living arrangements, but we know that eventually somebody will probably get married," said Mike.

"How did you all meet Carol?" asked Sam.

"We were both twelve. Carol and her cousin, Ethan, came to my mom's Christmas party," said Mike.

"We met at graduation rehearsal. She helped me so I could be in the graduation exercises. I couldn't have done it without her," said John.

"We first met when we were eight and then in our sophomore geometry class. Some kids were bullying me, and she took up for me and helped me. We were just fifteen. The following summer we got to know one another better at a pool party at Mike's house." Gene turned to Carol. "Do you love Greg?"

Carol put her hand on Gene's arm. "I don't know, Gene. Sometimes I just don't know what to do."

Gene put his arm around her and kissed her on the cheek.

"It is so important to all of us that Carol is never hurt. She has done so much for me. I would like to take care of her, but sometimes I can't even take care of myself," said John.

"I had a head injury in Vietnam. I can't stand to talk about it or think about it. Sometimes in college, I don't think well. I come home on weekends, and Carol can always help me get my studies straightened out, no matter how difficult," said Mike.

"Since I first met Carol, I have never met anyone who could equal her. I think the world of her," said Gene quietly.

"You are a lucky girl, Carol. These three guys really do love you the way you should be loved," said Sam.

On the way home that night, Gene sat in the back seat with Carol. When they got home, they all went to their individual bedrooms. A few minutes later, Gene left his bedroom and went to Carol's. She was already in bed, but she welcomed him with open arms. That night Gene and Carol kissed and held one another tight and had the most fantastic sex imaginable. But sex was always good between them. They not only felt the pleasure for themselves, but she could feel his pleasure as he could feel hers. Gene was so big and strong, and Carol was so soft, warm, and inviting. The chemistry between them was undeniable. They needed to be close. They said very little, but they didn't have to say anything. Gene and Carol had always been able to talk for hours about everything and about nothing. They were perfect for one another. They always had been, but that night was very special.

They knew they didn't have much time left together in their house on Lansing Street. That night, for the first time, Gene realized that Carol was ready to move forward into a new life scenario. Mike had already moved on, although no one, not even him, knew exactly where he was going. John would never move on, and Gene wondered exactly where that left him.

The following Monday, Sam called Carol into his office and shut the door. He sat in a chair across from her and held her hands in his.

"Thank you for letting me meet three of the nicest guys I have ever met. You know they all love you, especially Gene. I think I like him the best. He is quiet and solemn, but he treats you so kindly and gently, and I have no doubt that he always would. It was beautiful to watch."

"You're a good man, Sam. Thank you for caring about me," said Carol. She kissed Sam on the cheek and left his office.

Their love was true and real, but deep in her heart, Carol could never understand why her wonderful Gene was always so sad. It was as though there was some underlying hurt that he carried with him always. Once in a while, when they were close, he would let his guard down and relax just a little. Those were the moments when she felt as though he totally belonged to her.

FAREWELL, COLLEEN

Colleen McVary died of congestive heart failure on a warm summer day in 1969. She was forty-eight years old. Her heart started to fail shortly after Danny's death, and she only lived for five more years. Now she would be with her sweet little boy in heaven for eternity.

Her funeral was private. That was the way she wanted it. Ryan and Jeremy came from California. Mike and Cathy were there, as were Stella, Carol, Gene, and John. Alan was the only one who seemed to be holding up well. Colleen was loved so much by those present, and her death had come as a shock to all of them.

Stella missed her terribly. They had been friends for eleven years. Stella was crying inconsolably as Carol got up to read Colleen's farewell. In her will, she had requested that Carol read the farewell she had prepared, and if she was unable to do so, she wanted Gene to read it.

Colleen's farewell was read by Carol:

"As the flowers of summer bloom and the warm winds blow, I will leave you, my loved ones, to join my sweet little Danny, my dear Ethan, and brave Richard, Jeff, and Vito whom we lost in Vietnam. They were all so young and left us way to soon. For those I leave behind, I want them to know how much I have always loved them—my wonderful Alan, whom I have been married to since I was eighteen; my sweet Cathy whom Carol and Gene brought back to us; my son Ryan and his friend Jeremy, whom John helped us to love and reconcile with; my best friend, Stella, who has shared her heart and her daughter with me."

Carol was crying, and she could not continue. Gene went to her side and took the paper from her hand and continued to read:

"And the four friends Carol, Mike, Gene, and John, who have given so much to so many and have shared their hearts, souls, and lives with me. I want to stay, but I must go now. Care for and love one another as though I am still with you. My spirit watches over you always, and I will be there with you in the flowers that grow and the winds that blow. Until we meet again. Colleen."

As Carol and Gene sat down, they felt that they had done justice to Colleen's farewell. Even though Carol had been unable to finish, Gene had helped her, so it had happened the way Colleen had requested. Everyone except Alan was either crying or obviously moved by the farewell speech.

Before they left for home on the day after the funeral, Ryan and Jeremy had requested that everyone join them for lunch. Stella had to be at work, so she couldn't be there, and Alan said that he wasn't feeling well, which was to be expected since he had just lost his wife. They all met at the Savoy, which was Ryan's favorite Kansas City restaurant. The food was good, but no one seemed to be particularly hungry.

Neither Ryan nor Jeremy had seemed happy since their arrival, but they were there for a funeral, so that could be expected. As they finished their meal, Ryan said he had an announcement to make. Mike and John who were always optimistic thought they might be going to announce that they were planning to someday get married or adopt a baby, but as Carol and Gene, who were extremely sensitive to the feelings of others, looked into Ryan's eyes, they knew that would not be the announcement.

Ryan spoke slowly and calmly, "This is not what I want to be saying so soon after Mom's death, but since we are all together, I suppose it is as good a time as any. I have cancer. It is some strange type that they don't know much about yet. It seems to affect the gay population, and they say it is quite brutal and fatal."

Everyone was shocked and totally without words.

Carol was usually able to break the silence, but this time it was particularly hard for her. Carol was sitting next to Ryan. She put her arm around him. "Is there a treatment for it yet?"

"No, there may be soon, but it probably won't be in time to help me," said Ryan.

"How long do you have?" asked Carol.

"Six months at the most." Ryan hugged Cathy, who was sitting on the other side of him.

"I've only just found you again, and now I'm going to lose you. Why do I lose everyone I love?" sobbed Cathy.

John, who was sitting next to Jeremy, said, "I am so sorry. During those two trips we made to California, I developed a fondness for both of you. You both treated me, as well as everyone else, so well. I felt as though I had known you forever." John hugged Jeremy.

And then very uncharacteristic for Gene, he got up and went to the other side of the table and hugged both Ryan and Jeremy. "Thank you for letting me get to know you. I love both of you. And thank you for all you have done for Carol and John."

"On our second trip to California, you healed me when I was broken," said Carol quietly. "I love you, and thank you for that. If there is anything we can do, please let us know."

Mike was obviously shocked and completely without words. Carol put her hand on his as he tried to speak. "I love you, guys. You are my big brother, and you were always the healthiest one in the family."

"Not anymore. I'm not healthy anymore," said Ryan. "I can't tell Dad right now. It is just too soon after losing Mom."

Later that day, they took Ryan and Jeremy to the airport. Goodbyes were difficult. Ryan said goodbye to Carol last.

He hugged her and said, "And you, my dear Carol, I always have the hardest time saying goodbye to you. I remember the little twelve-year-old girl on the rusty bicycle who came to Mom's Christmas party. Do you remember how you asked Ethan how many cookies he ate and he said twelve?"

"I remember, Ethan was always hungry." Carol's voice broke. "I didn't want to cry today, but I can't help it." Gene put his arms around Carol.

"You four take care of one another and Cathy too," said Ryan. "And, Carol, remember to go with your heart. Always go with your heart."

They nodded, waved, and Jeremy gave John one last hug, and then they were gone. Ryan died in January 1970. He never returned home again. He was cremated, and his ashes were scattered along Big Sur and the Pacific Ocean. Ryan was only twenty-eight years old.

THE CONVENTION

Carol and Greg Martin attended an insurance convention in San Diego. When they returned, Greg was bragging about what a good time they had at the convention. But Sam Hagan, who was Greg's boss as well as Carol's, had heard differently from the home office in Hartford. He had received a call telling him that Greg had gotten drunk at the final night banquet and proceeded to dance with the wife of the company's vice president, touching her inappropriately and stepping on her toes. He was loud and obnoxious and using very bad language in the wrong company.

Sam called Greg into his office. "I've had some reports about the convention from the home office."

Greg was apologetic. "I had a couple of drinks. I'm sorry."

"You know, Greg, I like you. You're a good salesman. But in all honesty, I don't think you are the right man to be dating, let alone talking about marrying, Carol," said Sam.

"She loves me," said Greg.

"Really. Do you love her?" asked Sam.

"I'm getting there. I know she has a bunch of strange room-mates," said Greg.

"Does she say they are strange?" asked Sam.

"No, but I've met two of them. Mike, the redhead, doesn't like me at all. He hardly spoke to me. And I met the cripple, and I didn't like him very well," said Greg.

"I would like to suggest that you don't refer to him as a cripple in front of Carol, or anyone else for that matter. His name is John. He was recently in a very bad accident and in a coma for a long time." Sam was so angry that he could hardly keep a tremor from his voice.

"Why are you so concerned about this?" asked Greg.

"I happen to think a lot of Carol. She is a very special person," said Sam. "Have you met the other guy, Gene?"

"No, I haven't, should I?" asked Greg.

"Suit yourself. I like him, but then I like all of them," said Sam. "You'll have to admit that you didn't use very good judgment at the convention."

"I will admit that," said Greg.

"Try to be kind, Greg. It is a trait that becomes most people." Sam shook hands with Greg.

After Greg left his office, Sam sat alone with his thoughts for a while. That evening, for some reason that he wasn't even sure of himself, he stopped by Carol's house on Lansing Street. He didn't tell them he was coming.

Mike came to the door. "Hi, Sam. Come in."

Gene and Carol were at the dining room table with John. They were painstakingly trying to teach him to write with his left hand so it would be legible. They all greeted Sam warmly.

John said, "Sam, look at my writing. I'm improving."

Sam looked at the paper John handed him with his trembling left hand. "That's really good, John. I can read every word you've written."

"Thanks," said John. "The only thing is, I can't stop shaking."

"You've worked hard enough for today. Let's go into the living room," said Carol.

Carol sat on the sofa, John beside her. John was rubbing his eyes.

"Your head hurts, doesn't it?"

John nodded yes.

Carol put a small pillow on her lap. "Lay your head on my lap. It always makes you feel better."

"But we've got company. Sam's here to visit us," said John.

"Sam doesn't care if I rub your head," said Carol.

John rested his head on the pillow, and Carol massaged carefully chosen areas of his head.

Sam pulled his chair up a little closer to where John could see him better. "I'm right here by you, John. Do whatever makes you feel good." Sam reached out and touched John's hand. "I just wanted to see you guys tonight for no particular reason."

"It's always good to see you," said Gene.

"I like you, Sam. You seem like a really nice guy. And you're a good boss for Carol," said Mike.

"Thanks, guys. She is an excellent employee," said Sam. "You know, the four of you have a slightly unusual relationship, but it is also extremely beautiful. I envy what you all have together. It is as though you are always thinking of one another. I have never known anyone as unselfish and as truly good as the four of you.

John still had his head resting on Carol's lap. "They have been really good to me. I wouldn't have made it without them."

"And, my dear John, I think you are a big part of what makes them good," said Sam.

Gene was always quiet, but he had been unusually so this evening. He went to sit by Carol on the sofa and touched John's head as she was doing. "These are the three best friends I have ever had. I would give my life for any one of them."

Mike pulled his chair closer to the group and shook hands with Sam. "You seem to understand us better than most people. That's important to us. We're just four people who happen to love one another."

Sam was intrigued with the relationship of the four interesting young people with him that night. He was rather envious. Mike was so protective of everyone. John was so thankful for their help, and all they had done for him, and he openly showed so much love for his friends. Carol was so caring and nurturing and had helped them through so much. And Gene was the one they all looked up to, and even though he kept a low profile, it was obvious he was the leader of the small group. Sam knew that what the four of them had, few others would ever attain in their lifetimes. Sam didn't want to leave that night. He wanted to hold on as long as he could just as they did.

"Do you remember once I said I would be your fifth friend. Maybe I should say, I would like to be an honorary member of your group."

"You already are and have been for a long time," assured Carol. "You gave me a leave from work to care for both John and Cathy. None of us will ever forget that."

"I've never regretted doing it for you. The four of you are not your average people that we meet daily. Carol, I knew you were very special the day I hired you. You have never disappointed me." Sam glanced down at John. "Poor guy, he has fallen asleep."

Carol spoke quietly so as not to wake him. "John works so hard to get better. He knows how we worry about him."

That evening the four friends plus one were together in the house on Lansing Street. They felt safe and close. Sam felt sick when he thought of gentle, kind Carol marrying Greg Martin. He wondered why it is that we open our hearts and let bad people in.

The Dark Place

After the accident, John had tried working in an office behind a desk for a while, but it hadn't worked out. He was back at the garage, but he couldn't do all the things there that he used to do. He had never regained the use of his right hand and arm, and he never would.

Gene got a job at a large advertising agency in Chicago. He would be moving there soon. Gene was pleased to get the job since that was what he had studied in graduate school. His office would be in a very impressive building high above the majestic city below. He was anxious about the move but also worried.

Mike had graduated from college and was now contemplating either going to graduate school or law school. He really didn't care anymore. He was tired of school and studying.

And there would be a marriage. Carol would be marrying Greg Martin. There would be no wedding. They would just elope.

They had decided to go to the restaurant where they had gone with Sam, Carol's boss, a year earlier. This would be their last evening together. They had all been to dark places during the years since they had graduated from high school. They were no longer innocent and carefree.

Mike had been to Vietnam. Nothing could be darker than that. He never talked about Vietnam or the wounds he received there. It was as though he wanted to erase that part of his life entirely from his mind.

John had suffered a horrific accident and was in a coma and was hospitalized for six months. He would never regain the use of his right arm and hand, and because of the accident and the traumatic head injuries, he had suffered his life would never be the same again.

Carol had never been able to come to terms with the deaths of Danny, Ethan, Richard, Colleen, and Ryan. In addition to her own personal tragedy that she never spoke of, everything at times seemed almost unbearable to her, but she had always tried to stay strong for her friends.

As for Gene, no one ever knew, or for that matter ever would know, what his dark place was, but something held him back from allowing himself to be truly happy. He would carry it with him forever.

Their meals were good that evening, but no one seemed to be very hungry except John. He still had trouble doing everything with his left hand. That evening Carol did as she always did and would occasionally cut a piece of food for him or wipe a spot off his shirt. He always liked it when she took care of him. John so much wanted to ask Carol who would take care of him when she was gone, but he didn't have to. They all knew this is what he was thinking.

They were, of course, giving up the house on Lansing Street. Carol and Gene would be moving. John would move back to the house where he grew up. As for Mike, he would still live at school, but he would just as soon live in his van or in a tent somewhere. He was friendly with a lot of homeless veterans. He seemed to feel comfortable with them. In just a few years, Mike would help many veterans find housing, and he would also help them get VA benefits and monetary settlements for their injuries and illnesses that plagued them from their time spent in Vietnam or elsewhere.

Conversation had always flowed so free among the four of them, but tonight not so much so. In some ways they just wanted it to all be over, but the truth was that they didn't want this night to ever end. They wanted to hold on to it for as long as they could.

Carol finally spoke. "Well, guys, if no one else is going to speak, I guess I will. I don't know how we will each remember all that has happened over the last years, but I hope it is with fondness and not regret. I don't regret anything as far as it concerns the four of us, but I do wish we were all happier right now. Mike, you have protected me and taken care of me since the day we first met when we were twelve. You have wiped my tears and dried my hair. You have fed me when I was too weak to lift my hand to eat, and you have sat up with me all night when I was afraid to be alone or you were afraid to leave me alone. You've always been there for me. We have never doubted our feelings for one another."

"No matter how many miles are between us, I will never forget you, and a part of me will always be with you," said Mike.

"And, John, my dear sweet John, I have told you before that I have loved you since the day you took hold of my arm and we walked down the aisle at the graduation rehearsal. Your smile and the love you gave me that night touched my heart. I think you, more than anyone, have kept us together this long. I'm grateful for that and to you for being such an inspiration to us all," said Carol.

"I'll always love you, and I will miss you so much," said John.

Carol reached out and put her hand on Gene's hand. "I always leave you for last, Gene, because words can never do justice for what I feel for you. Wherever you may go, my heart goes with you. You will always be in my prayers. I wish the best for you, always the very best. I fell in love with you when I was fifteen, or maybe I should say eight. You have a very special place in my life. What you have done for me is beyond words. I would never have made it without you. You are the best man I have ever known, and that will never change. I will never forget any of you. In many ways we are bound together forever."

"You know, Carol, we have all learned a lot from you, especially me. You taught me how to take care of Cathy and John. I watched you and learned from you. For that and many other reasons you are very special to me," said Gene.

No one said anything else. They were just trying to remember and digest all that had been said.

Mike finally spoke, "Maybe that was your graduation speech that you were never allowed to give. It was really good. I wish I had a copy of it."

"It came from my heart. I don't think I could recreate it," said Carol.

"Thanks for giving my speech at graduation, Gene. You did a really good job. I'm not sure I ever told you that," said John.

"You thanked me in many ways and many times over," said Gene. "That seems like a lifetime ago. You saved me that night. My speech wasn't very good."

ROSE

In 1972, John's beautiful mother, Rose, was diagnosed with brain cancer which was metastatic from the breast cancer she had years ago. They had recently moved her to the hospice area of the hospital. Everyone knew she wouldn't be going home. She didn't always recognize people, and her speech was very difficult to hear and understand.

Every evening John and Carol went to see her. Either Charlene, Darla, or Meggie would go with them. John was the one person that Rose always recognized. She would smile when he came to see her. He made her happy just as he had when he was a little boy when he would fall down and smile and get up and try again.

Rose tried so hard to talk. It was as though she had a lot to say, and she knew she didn't have much time left. One day she told John and Carol about a nice white-haired man who came to see her many times. She said at first she thought he was Santa Claus, but then she thought it might be God. She said he told her that he was going to pay all her hospital bills. John asked her if she knew his name, but she didn't answer.

After that time, she was usually sleeping, and she was someplace between life and death. She never got a chance to tell John who she thought it was.

In the spring of 1972, Rose died. John had, of course, already moved home to help care for Meggie. Darla was still in high school, and Charlene was going to junior college.

When Rose died, even though she had no health insurance, there were no hospital bills just as there had been no hospital or doctor bills after John's accident. John was so overwhelmed with all that had to be done that at the time he didn't give it much thought, but Carol thought about it a lot, and in her heart she knew.

John missed his mother very much as did his sisters. He also missed the house on Lansing Street. One day he called Carol and asked her if she would take him by the house on Lansing Street just once more before the new tenants moved in. She picked him up, and they drove to the house.

As they pulled up in front, Carol asked John, "Would you like to get out of the car?"

"No, I just wanted to see it again, because I can. I want to see my mother again too, but I can't," said John.

"She loved you so much, John. Always remember that," said Carol.

"I will, and I'll always remember this house too," said John.

"It was a good house, John. It was a really good house. The four of us had some wonderful years there. A lot happened to us during those years, some bad things, but many good things. It was our haven from the storm," said Carol as they drove away.

Goodbye, Avalon Manor

Carol Sullivan and Greg Martin eloped and were married in Las Vegas at the Little Chapel on the Strip. They still worked together at the insurance company in the Commerce Tower in Kansas City, Missouri. Greg was fifteen years older than Carol. He was divorced and had two young sons.

On October 29, 1975, Carol and Greg's daughter Julie was born. When Julie was just two months old, Greg received a promotion and was transferred several hundred miles away. Greg had already left to look for a new home. Carol stayed behind in Kansas City with Julie. Carol's mother, Stella, came by to help her pack one afternoon, and she had a message from Alan McVary, Mike's dad.

"Alan would like for you to come by his house," said Stella.

"Did he say what he wants?" asked Carol.

"No, he probably just wants to say goodbye," said Stella. "I told him that it would be quite a while before you leave. He has called me several times since Colleen died just to talk about her. I think he is lonesome without her. They had a strange relationship, but then I guess most relationships are strange."

"I'll go now. Sometimes that big house in Avalon Manor comes to me in a dream, the way it looked when Colleen decorated it, especially at Christmas," said Carol.

Twenty minutes later, she pulled into the driveway. It didn't really look that much different, but it was. When Carol rang the doorbell, she expected the maid to answer, but Alan himself answered the door.

"Hello, Carol. Motherhood becomes you."

They hugged and walked into the living room.

Carol looked for Goldie, but she didn't see her. Goldie was Danny's big Golden Lab that Alan never liked. Alan never wanted her in the house, but Danny would sneak her into his room on the third floor. The day Danny died, Goldie came into Alan's study and never left his side again.

"Where's Goldie?" asked Carol.

"She died a few weeks ago. She was sixteen years old, the same age as Danny was when he died," replied Alan. "Mike helped me bury Goldie behind the grotto. He thought it was strange to bury her there, but it seemed appropriate to me. She always liked to lie in the shade. It was as though she was guarding the pool waiting for all of you to return, but no one ever came back."

Carol couldn't speak, but somehow she knew that it was all right and that he had invited her to his house just to listen.

Alan spoke slowly and quietly, "You know it is really strange, but I never cried or showed any emotion when Danny died. People thought I didn't love him, but I did. He was the sweetest, best little boy in the whole world. I had to stay strong for the family and you. When Ethan was killed, I didn't cry either. Cathy loved him so much. Everyone had expected them to get married, but he married someone else. He was more like a brother to you than a cousin. I had to be strong for you and Cathy. When Richard was killed in Vietnam, I didn't cry. His father was my neighbor and best friend, and he was your boyfriend. Once again, I needed to stay strong for Richard's father and for you. Even when my beautiful Colleen died, I didn't cry. She was so young, and everyone loved her. She was your mother's best friend. I had to stay strong for everyone, so I didn't shed a tear. When Ryan died, I didn't cry. Jeremy and John were both so distraught. They both loved him so much, and I had treated him so badly years ago. I had to stay strong for Jeremy and John. But the strange part is that when Danny's dog died a few weeks ago, I cried a river. I couldn't stop, and memories of everyone came back to me and flooded me with sadness. I never even told any of them how much I loved them."

Carol smiled through her own tears. "They knew. They all knew you loved them."

"The first memory I have of you is when you were looking at my books. You asked if you could read one, and I told you the children's books were upstairs, but you didn't want to read children's books. You wanted to read my books, and so you did," said Alan.

"I think I read almost all of them." Carol picked a couple of books off the shelf and thumbed through them.

"You and Mike were the top two students in your class and had been many times throughout the years. You were both robbed of that honor, and no one can ever make it up to you," said Alan.

"It still hurts and always will that we were penalized for doing good deeds," said Carol.

"You know, Colleen and I were at graduation. We were sitting along the aisle not too far back. I remember a lot about that graduation. John's speech that Gene gave that night was very powerful. It brought everyone to tears. It wasn't only the words that John had written, but it was the way Gene presented it entirely from his heart. It was so emotional that he had to pause a couple of times. I thought that any minute someone would stop him from speaking but they didn't, and he was allowed to finish. John and Gene both became like sons to me and Colleen that very night. Most graduations are boring, but the class of 1964 was anything but boring. Everyone was rooting for John to make it down the long stairs and aisle. About halfway there he tripped slightly. Mike was already seated but walked back to you, and John and helped the rest of the way. I was so proud of the way you and Mike treated and took care of John that night, but I never told you so. I remember when Gene asked everyone to stand who had been helped by Carol and Mike. Gene was already standing, so he simply raised his hand. It was difficult to imagine the six-foot-five-football quarterback being bullied, but he was, as you so well know, in his sophomore year. They said about two hundred stood up. I think it was a lot more. How many did you help?" asked Alan.

"Over the three years, it was about 675," said Carol.

"You two were quite a team." Alan walked over to his desk. "I have many pictures on the walls, but these two are my favorites."

Alan picked up two framed pictures from his desk and handed them to Carol. One was a picture taken in the backyard by the big tree they used to climb. Carol was in the middle. Ethan was behind her with his hand on her shoulder, and Mike was on the other side with his arm around her. Danny, Cathy, and Goldie were sitting on the ground in front. Ryan and Richard were sitting on a branch to the side.

Carol remembered the picture well. "I was thirteen. I remember that dress. We were all young and innocent. Most of them are gone now. They died so young."

As Carol looked at the other picture, she remembered that night well. It was the one taken before senior prom of Carol, Gene, Mike, and John.

"Did you ever think it was strange, the four of us doing everything together?" asked Carol.

"Not really strange. I always wanted you and Mike to end up together, but that was not meant to be," said Alan. "I knew all about Richard asking Mike and Gene to take care of you until he got back from war. I know they both took that responsibility very seriously, and you all kept any feelings you had for one another quiet and secret."

"I didn't know Mike told you about that," said Carol.

"He didn't tell me. Mike and I didn't talk much then. Richard told me right before he left for Vietnam. He was a good man," said Alan.

"You know what I would like to do? I would like to see their rooms one more time," asked Carol.

"All right. They haven't changed. Colleen wanted to leave them the way they were. She always thought about having grandchildren someday," said Alan. Alan and Carol walked upstairs and stopped first at Cathy's bedroom. There were still dolls and stuffed animals on the shelf.

"I stayed overnight with Cathy here." Carol touched a fluffy pink blanket on the chair. "Remember when she came back from

California with Charlie so thin and wasting away and on drugs, she slept on the floor with that blanket for weeks. I would bring her food and something to drink. I tried to get her to eat a little more each day, and she did. How is she now?" asked Carol.

"She's trying to get her degree in business. Since the drugs, she has been having so much trouble," said Alan.

They closed the door quietly and went to Ryan's room. "Ryan's room was always so impersonal. He was into sports, but he never had any pictures or memorabilia. There is nothing to show that Ryan ever lived here," said Alan.

"That's the way he wanted it. Ryan didn't even know who he was yet when he lived here. He didn't want anyone to know who he was," said Carol.

Mike's room was next. It was red, white, and blue and filled with baseballs, footballs, pictures and more pictures. "This room looks like Mike, happy and smiling. I used to think I knew Mike the best of all my children, but sometimes I don't think I ever really knew him at all except when it came to you," said Alan. "Did you ever realize how much he loved you?"

"Yes, I knew. I loved him too," said Carol. "He took care of me when I was having a hard time, always so kind and gentle."

"Let's go up to Danny's room. I haven't been there for a long time," said Alan.

There were still odds and ends of toys in his room, boats and cars, his drawings and musical instruments, and then Carol saw Danny's village. Alan picked up the snowman.

"I broke this village once. I thought Danny was too old to be playing with it. Mike got every single little piece out of the trash that night and painstakingly glued it back together piece by piece. That's not one of my prouder moments."

"One thing that I have learned, basically since Danny's death, is that we really have no control over things that happen. There was nothing that anyone could have done or said to keep Danny from leaving us the way he did," said Carol.

Alan and Carol went back downstairs.

"I often wonder who loves or loved you most, Mike, Gene, Richard, John, or your husband. I would like for you to say Mike, but it wasn't Mike, was it? I know who it was, Carol. I saw it in your eyes on graduation night. Colleen and I both knew that night that you and Mike were not destined to be together," said Alan.

"John captured my heart that night. I loved him unconditionally, but he would never marry me or probably anyone else. John would never be able to father a child. He knew I someday wanted to be a mother. I told him we could adopt, but because of his physical problems, he didn't think they would give us a child. I loved him then, now, and always. I know he feels the same about me. It hurts my heart. But of all of them, I loved Gene the most. I loved his spirit, and he lived as though there was no tomorrow. He wasn't afraid of a challenge, and he had a dark sense of humor just like me. He always thought that I loved Mike and John more than him, but that wasn't true. I told him so, but I don't think he believed him." Carol wiped a single tear from her cheek.

"Colleen knew that you loved Gene and he loved you long before I did," said Alan.

Carol hesitated for a moment. "Before I leave, there is something I want to say, and I don't want you to say yes or no. When John's mother, Rose, was dying in the hospice, a very nice gentleman came to see her. She had no insurance and massive hospital bills as John had once had after his accident. He paid off all her hospital bills and put a considerable amount of money in the bank for her children. She told John this, but she died before she could tell him everything. I think the nice gentleman was you." Carol kissed Alan on the head. "Goodbye, Alan. Take care of Mike. Love him with every ounce of love within you. He always needed you the most of all of your children."

"I will, I promise. Goodbye, my dear girl." Alan walked her to the door and watched her drive away.

At that moment, she wasn't sure if she would ever see Alan again. But within a short while, both Alan and Carol would be called upon to help their best friend in one of the most devastating events of his as well as their lives.

Alan had changed considerably over the years. Carol knew he felt responsible for Danny's death, and he would spend the rest of his life trying to do good deeds to make up for his shortcomings. He had been unkind to Danny when he was just a little boy, and he was not proud of his actions. Colleen, Mike, and Carol had been most affected by Danny's death. He had tried to be kind to them, and he hoped he had succeeded. He had tried to help John all he could and would continue to do so.

He also loved and respected Gene. Alan realized how cruel and mean he had once been to Gene. He would have liked to see Gene and Carol together, but it was not to be. This was something his money could not buy.

GOODBYE, STRAWBERRY HILL

On the way home, Carol went by her grandma's house on South Baltimore. It looked old and unkempt. The pretty flowers and bushes that her grandma had taken such pride in were gone. As a child, she had always loved that house. It represented a safe place.

She was close to Strawberry Hill where so many of her aunts and uncles and childhood friends used to live. It also looked different as her grandma's street had looked. Then she went by Gene's house on Twelfth Street where his parents still lived. She almost didn't stop, but for whatever reason she did, and she would be forever glad for the time she spent with them that day. Gene was their youngest son. His older brother now lived and worked in Chicago, as did Gene.

Mrs. Sandusky opened the door and greeted Carol warmly. "Come in, Carol. It is so nice of you to come by to see us. Tony, come see who is here." She hugged Carol.

"It's the beautiful queen. It is good to see you." Mr. Sandusky had always called her the queen since Gene and Carol were chosen prom king and queen.

"You both look good," said Carol. "How is the family?"

"They are all fine," replied Mrs. Sandusky.

Carol knew that for the moment they were all avoiding the one subject that they all wanted to talk about, and that was, of course, Gene.

Mrs. Sandusky said, "Gene loves his job, and he has many friends in Chicago. He has a nice wife, and his son is only two months older than your daughter."

"There were always so many girls who liked Gene. He is such a good person. He is the most genuinely kind man I have ever known," said Carol.

"Gene was always so shy with girls until he met you. Remember prom night when the four of you came by for pictures, I honestly wanted it to last forever. You were all so good together. Those pictures we took that night are some of our most prized possessions. That is our favorite one." Mrs. Sandusky nodded toward the mantle where there was an eight-by-ten picture of Gene and Carol on prom night. I wanted so much for Gene. He was my sweet little baby boy. You know what I wanted for him, don't you?"

"Yes, you wanted us to be together," said Carol.

Mrs. Sandusky was crying, not for herself, but for their dear Gene and what could have been but now never would be.

"After the four of you left for prom that evening, we talked about how much those three guys loved you and how much you cared for and probably loved them," said Mr. Sandusky. "That night I thought you liked John the best. Theresa thought you liked Mike. But we both agreed on one thing, that Gene loved you the most."

"It was probably foolish of us, but we didn't want things to change. We wanted everything to always be like it was that night," said Mrs. Sandusky.

"I think I did too, except that I was still tormented by Danny's death," Carol paused. "They were all three such good guys. Mike had been in my life since seventh grade. We were best friends. We had been through a lot together. He was so gentle with me. I think he knew how close I was to breaking. John was such a happy, truly good person. His life hadn't been easy, but he never gave up. I wanted to make things easier for him and help him. With Gene I felt an extremely strong connection. I loved Gene so much. I don't think I'll ever stop loving him."

"That you came to see us makes me realize how much you really did love Gene," said Mrs. Sandusky. "When he was younger, I don't think Gene knew how to show his true feelings. He still may not know how."

"Gene was with me through so much. Together we helped Cathy through her ordeal, and we worked together to help John after that terrible accident," said Carol.

"My Gene had no medical training, yet the two of you worked so well together," said Mrs. Sandusky.

"That was the key, we were working together. We wouldn't have been able to do it alone," said Carol.

"I often think of John and how well he is doing now. That was such a terrible accident. I still take my car to him to work on. Thank you for giving John his life back," said Mr. Sandusky.

"That prom night, I just wanted time to stand still as you did. I knew that within two months, Mike would be in the Army and probably in Vietnam, and Gene would be away at college. John had so many hardships he was facing. I only knew some of his problems that night. I wanted to help him, but I didn't know if I would be able to," said Carol. "Did Gene ever tell you about the day we went to Grandview Beach right after graduation?"

Mrs. Sandusky shook her head yes and put her hands to her mouth. "Gene was visibly upset. He had to talk to someone, and we were here. John is a survivor."

Carol hugged both of them. "I will never be able to explain or understand all that happened especially that spring and summer of 1964. We were four kids who became adults somewhat before our time. Our innocence was gone. Mine left the day Danny died. I used to think if I could just forget about Danny, everything would be all right, but I can never forget him. If I forgot Danny, I would be forgetting Gene, Mike, and John also, and I don't ever want to do that. Goodbye now. I love you both, and I love Gene. I always have and always will." With this Carol left. She was glad she had stopped to see them. She would never see them again.

CHAPTER

47

1975 AT STELLA'S HOUSE

She was still the same Carol they had loved so much, only now she was holding her small baby girl in her arms. Carol was sitting on her mother's front porch when John and Mike arrived. Carol looked exceptionally beautiful. Her hair was full and almost to her waist. She had on a light-blue peasant-type dress, very feminine and typical Carol style. Mike hadn't been able to feel much since before he went to Vietnam. Today he realized that he wasn't dead after all because his feelings had returned as he looked at Carol.

Mike and John had come to say goodbye. Carol was leaving soon to join her husband in their new home and city. John kissed her on the cheek and sat next to her on the glider. John had on a light-blue shirt and gray slacks. He looked healthy and stronger than he had the last time she saw him.

"Your baby is beautiful. What's her name?" asked John.

"This is Julie," replied Carol.

Mike also kissed Carol and sat in a chair across from her. "She looks like her mommy." Mike was wearing fatigues, his red hair was shoulder-length, and he had a beard. He looked skinner than she had ever seen him.

"How's school?" asked Carol.

"I hate it. I don't think I'll ever get out of school. I'm not very smart anymore. I get bored, so I go protest," said Mike.

"What do you protest?" asked Carol.

233

"Usually the war, but it can be anything. We don't care," said Mike.

"And you, John, how are you doing?" asked Carol.

"I'm all right, but I still miss you and Gene," said John.

She turned away and shrugged her shoulders. They both knew she was fighting back tears. She touched her little baby lovingly. "I love my little girl, and I love being a mother."

Just then Stella came out on the porch. "Hi, Mike and John." She reached out and took the baby from Carol. "Let me take little Julie so you three can talk." She went back inside.

When Carol looked at John, he saw the sadness in her eyes. Her eyes were empty like all the life had been drained out of her.

"Have you talked to Gene lately?" asked Mike.

"He calls me once in a while. You know, his little boy is just two months older than Julie," said Carol.

"We don't talk much anymore. I guess I'm losing all my friends," said Mike.

"Carol, you know Gene loved you so much, more than life itself, I think," said John.

"We're both married now, and we have children." Carol buried her face in John's chest and cried.

Mike looked out toward the street. "We've really messed up. We couldn't go on any longer the way we were, but we didn't know how to end it. Would you like for us to leave, Carol?"

"No, please don't leave yet. I miss what we had. I miss it so much." She paused to regain her composure. "Always know, John, how much I love you. I will never forget you. And, Mike, I've loved you since we were just kids. I hope someday you both find love. Please take care of one another."

"Who's the love of your life, Carol? Is it your husband, me, John, Richard, or Gene?" asked Mike. "I'm sorry, I shouldn't have asked that question."

With the mention of Gene's name, she looked into John's eyes, and then she looked at Mike. "I love Gene with all my heart, but I always knew we would never be together forever. I don't really know why, and I don't think he does either, but it just wasn't meant to be.

It hurts my heart. I hope that we will all be together again someday, but if we are it will never again be as it was when we lived in that wonderful house on Lansing Street."

"We had a good run. We had good times and bad times. That will have to sustain us forever," said Mike.

"I'll never forget you and all you have done for me. Nothing will ever take my memories of you away." John couldn't say anything else.

They hugged for what seemed like an eternity, then they went to Mike's car and they were gone. Carol couldn't move. She stood in the same spot until the car was out of sight.

Stella was watching out the window. She had always known that this day would come. And now it was all over. There's a saying that love conquers all, but that didn't happen for the four of them.

Carol stood on the porch for a long time, remembering the good times and the bad times. The first memory that came to her was walking with John down the aisle on graduation night, and she could hear John's speech and Gene's presentation of the speech on that fateful night.

At that moment, Carol didn't think that the four of them would ever see one another or all be together again, but she was wrong. They would all be together several more times, the first being in 1984.

TREASURED MEMORY

Less than two weeks later, Gene called Carol at her mother's house. He wanted to come by and see her and her baby.

Carol told her mother, "Gene will be here this afternoon. Is that all right? He is here in Kansas City visiting his family."

"Of course, Gene is welcome in my home anytime," said Stella.

"You've always liked Gene, haven't you?" asked Carol.

"He's the kindest young man I have ever met," said Stella. "Does he have a happy marriage?"

"Not really, but he doesn't talk much about it," said Carol. "But then we don't talk much about anything lately. He doesn't want to interfere with my life."

Carol and Stella sat in silence, thinking and remembering. Carol's baby daughter, Julie, woke up in a smiling happy mood as always. Carol dressed her in a pretty pink dress and sat down and waited for Gene.

When Gene arrived, Carol went to the door with Julie in her arms. He immediately put his arms around both of them. "It's good to see you, Carol. May I hold Julie?" asked Gene.

He gently took Julie from Carol. "I can't help but notice the way she looks at you. She already loves you," said Carol. "She doesn't go to just anyone."

Carol and Gene went into the living room where her mother was waiting.

Stella greeted Gene warmly with a hug and kiss. "It's so good to see you, Gene. Please sit down." Carol and Gene sat on the sofa as he still held Julie. "It's so sweet, the way she looks at you."

"You can tell Gene has had practice. His son is just two months older than Julie," said Carol.

"Congratulations, Gene. I'm sure you are a wonderful father," said Stella.

"I hope so. There is a tremendous amount to learn," said Gene.

Stella noticed how gently and sweetly Gene touched and played with Julie. Then she thought of Greg and how critical and mean he was with his older children and how he basically ignored Julie. He was definitely not gentle and kind with Julie, those words never being used to describe Greg.

"I'm going to leave you two alone. I know you have a lot to talk about. Would you like for me to take Julie?" asked Stella.

"She's fine. She seems to really like Gene," said Carol. "But then everyone has always liked Gene."

"Not so much anymore," said Gene.

"I'll talk with you two later. Can you stay for dinner?" asked Stella.

"Sure. Would you like for me to stay, Carol?" asked Gene.

"Of course, I would love for you to stay," Carol hugged Gene. He put his arms around her, but he still held little Julie.

As Stella was in the kitchen preparing dinner, she couldn't help but think about the changes she noticed in Gene. He looked much older than twenty-eight, and he had gained a considerable amount of weight. He didn't look well, and she noticed that he moved slowly. He didn't really seem happy, although he did seem happy to see Carol and Julie. She was worried about him. She wondered if Carol would even notice any of the changes because she loved him so much. And if she did notice, she wouldn't say anything.

"Look how tightly Julie holds your finger, and she doesn't take her eyes off you," said Carol.

"She probably sees the way you look at me and talk to me. Even though she is only a baby, she can feel the love between us," said Gene.

"It never changes. What I feel for you. Do you realize that?" said Carol.

"I know. It doesn't change for me either." Gene pulled Carol close to him and kissed her as she rested her head on his shoulder.

"Are you all right, Gene? Please tell me you are," asked Carol.

"I'm fine. I have problems with my neck from that football injury. I just can't turn it too far to the right. My knees and back hurt from football too, but that's all. I'm just getting old," said Gene.

"We're only twenty-eight, that's not old," said Carol.

"I wish I could be sure that Greg will never hurt this precious little girl or you. How can I be sure of that?" asked Gene.

"Please don't worry. I'll protect her with my life," said Carol.

"But who will protect you?" asked Gene.

"I'll be fine," said Carol. "But what about you, Gene, what about your marriage?"

Gene ran his fingers through her long hair. "I'm just not sure it is going to work. I'm trying, but sometimes I don't know what to do. Maybe I just don't know how to be happy."

They held one another and talked quietly until Stella called them for dinner. Gene was still holding Julie. She was still awake and extremely content.

Carol and Stella both wanted to take Julie so Gene could eat, but neither one of them said anything. Somehow they both knew that he wanted to hold the sweet little baby. Stella had fixed sloppy joes, french fries, and salad which were easy enough to eat so he continued to hold Julie.

"How about dessert? I have chocolate pie," said Stella.

"That sounds good. I can't turn it down," said Gene.

"How long will you be in Kansas City, Gene?" asked Stella.

"I'm going home tomorrow, but I'll be back soon," said Gene.

For a moment Stella could see tears in Carol's eyes, but she quickly looked away. She knew that Carol was thinking that when he came back, she would be gone.

"Gene's going on a trip to Canada with some men he works with. They are going white-water rafting. That sounds exciting," said Carol.

"It will be my first time on a trip like that. You know, I have never been fond of water sports, but they make you feel like you have to go to be successful," said Gene.

"Are you a strong-enough swimmer?" asked Carol.

"Not really, especially for that type of water, but I am hoping I won't have to swim," said Gene.

"I hope you have a good time. You could probably use some relaxation," said Stella.

"Most of the time my job is pretty intense and stressful. I think this afternoon is the most I've relaxed in a long time," said Gene. "I've always loved the way you talked to me, Carol. The sound of your voice has always helped me no matter how bad I was feeling. You never criticize me or ridicule me. You only love me, and you always have. I don't think there is anyone else quite like you in the world."

Carol kissed Gene on the cheek. She took Julie from him. "I need to feed Julie. Will you come with me?" asked Carol.

Gene followed Carol to the living room, and they sat on the sofa as Carol opened her blouse and proceeded to feed her daughter.

Gene rubbed little Julie's back and said, "This is the most beautiful thing I have ever seen. Thank you for sharing this moment with me. When I think of you, this is how I will always remember you."

It was time for Gene to leave. Stella and Gene said goodbye. He carried Julie to the door. As Carol took her from him, Julie held tight to his finger until he took his other hand and gently released her grip. Carol and Gene kissed one final time. And as he walked away, the tiny baby girl who was only two months old appeared to raise her hand and wave goodbye. Carol buried her face in Julie's blanket and cried. There was so much that was left unsaid that day. But maybe that was the way it was supposed to be.

Stella was watching as she had been several days earlier when Mike and John left, but this time it was different, so very different. Stella so much wanted to talk to Carol. She had so many questions for her. In the past Stella would have simply blurted out her questions and feelings, but not tonight. It had been such a beautiful and peaceful day and evening. She couldn't chance ruining it.

She was just going to treasure the memory of the tiny baby girl waving to the wonderful, loving man as he walked away.

Her kind, pretty daughter with the long red hair that he loved so much and the handsome, gentle young man were parting again, possibly forever but maybe not. They never knew for sure. They were both married to others and the parents of tiny babies. In all reality, their story could have ended that night, but their lives were not that simple. In all probability, they were only able to thrive if things were complicated and difficult.

THE VISIT

Cathy moved back home to the big house in Avalon Manor for a short while in the summer of 1978. One afternoon as Cathy and Alan were sitting by the pool, Cathy had a suggestion for a vacation with her dad.

"You know something, Dad. I would like to visit Carol and her husband and children. I have never really thanked her for all she did for me. It would be a good chance to break in the new car you gave me. Would you go with me?" asked Cathy.

"I'd love to," said Alan. "I miss Carol."

"What about Mike? Would he go with us?" asked Cathy.

Just then Mike came outside and jumped in the pool. "Did I hear my name mentioned?"

"We are taking a road trip to visit Carol and her family. Would you like to go with us?" asked Cathy.

"No. I would love to see Carol and the children, but not Greg. We have a history. He doesn't like me, and I don't like him. But I know someone who would like to go, definitely John," said Mike.

"Great. I'll call him," said Cathy. "Do you think Gene would meet us there?"

"He's having some problems right now, and besides, he doesn't like Greg either," said Mike.

"Does John like Greg?" asked Cathy.

"John loves everyone. Unlike me, he never holds a grudge," said Mike.

When Cathy called, Carol sounded excited about their visit, but not nearly as excited as John. He was thrilled that Cathy and Alan would invite him to take a trip with them but excited even more that he would be seeing Carol. And so the journey began for Cathy, Alan, and John.

They arrived at Carol's house on a Saturday in the early afternoon. Greg was washing the car in the driveway. The boys, Scott and Wayne, were playing catch. Carol's little girl, Julie, was three, and she was playing with her dolls on the sidewalk. Her mother was with her. They all greeted one another warmly. John hugged Carol. As he did so, he was the only one who noticed how stiff her body became.

Cordial introductions were made.

Greg said, "Why don't you sit over in the shade. I'll get something to drink."

Alan offered to play catch with the boys.

Scott, the youngest, asked John, "Would you play with us too?"

"Well, Scott, I can't. I have an injured arm and bad leg, but thank you for asking me," said John.

Scott smiled and went to play with Alan and Wayne. Greg had heard this exchange as he was sitting the drinks on the table.

"John, Cathy, and Alan, I want to thank you for all you have done for Carol over the years," said Greg.

"I think we are the ones who should thank Carol. Carol and Gene saved my life once. There are really no words to express gratitude to someone who has saved your life, but just know that I will never forget what you and Gene did for me," said Cathy. Carol hugged Cathy, and there were a few tears from two old friends.

Carol's little girl, Julie, had been sitting on her mommy's lap. She climbed down and walked over to the other side of the table where John was sitting. She was a beautiful child with long red hair with highlights of gold just like her mommy. She touched John's right hand that hung limp at his side. Julie rubbed her small hand across the scars, and then she bent over and kissed the back of his hand.

"You are a very sweet little girl. Would you like to sit on my lap?" asked John.

She reached out her hands to John, and he picked her up and set her on his good leg. She lay back in the bend of his arm. She reached down and picked up his bad hand and held it in her tiny hand. She looked up into his pale-blue eyes and said, "You have pretty blue eyes."

"Thank you, Julie," said John.

She put her small finger under his eye. "You have a tear, and now there is another one. Are you sad?" asked Julie.

"I'm not sad, honey. I just have something in my eye," said John.

Carol's little girl sat on John's lap holding his hand the remainder of the time they were there that afternoon. Carol tried to avoid making eye contact with John. She knew if she did that, Julie would notice her tears also. Carol couldn't help but remember that day at her mother's house in Kansas City more than three years ago when Gene came to say goodbye and how he had held Julie that whole afternoon and how much she had seemed to love him. Gene had actually seen Julie another time in Kansas City when she was one and once in Springfield when she was two, and each time she seemed to remember him and love him.

Greg and Carol were taking their visitors out to eat that night. They knew they wouldn't be seeing the children in the morning, so when the babysitter arrived, they all said goodbye to the children. John gently lifted Julie off his lap. She handed him his cane.

"Julie, will you do me a favor and take good care of your mommy."

"I will," said Julie.

Scott said, "We'll take good care of her too."

John hugged Scott and Wayne. Julie kissed his hand, and he kissed the top of her head.

They took separate cars to the restaurant. Cathy, John, and Alan left first. As they drove away, Carol noticed that Julie's eyes stayed fixed on John. She waved until the car was out of sight.

It was as though the little girl knew all about John and loved him as her mother did. Carol had always said that John was one of the most genuine truly good people she had ever known. Could her small child see that? In her heart she hoped she could, just as Meggie had seen it in her so many years ago. Small children, even infants, seemed to sense the good in people as they had in Carol, Gene, and John.

As a small child in elementary school, Carol had always had empathy for anyone who was in any way different. Sometimes she would help students or even adults who were complete strangers. When Carol was in the third grade, there was a new boy in her class named David. He was older and taller than his classmates, he wore glasses, and he was very shy, and when he did speak, he spoke very slowly and had a difficult time finding the right words. The kids didn't like him, and they made fun of him. Carol became his best and only friend. They lived a block from one another. They walked to school and home from school every day together for four years. He was the same David who had helped John up the stairs at the graduation rehearsal a few minutes before Carol took hold of John's arm.

Carol had met and helped David in 1954. This was the same year Carol and Gene had met in her grandmother's neighborhood when they were eight years old.

GREG

Somehow Greg had managed to put on a good face in front of Carol's friends, but it wouldn't last.

"Thank you for being nice to my friends, especially John," said Carol.

"He seems like a nice-enough guy," said Greg.

"But you don't like Mike, do you? Why not?" asked Carol.

"I don't know. There is just something about him. I only met him once when he came into the office. I can tell he doesn't like me. I think he is a little too protective of you," said Greg. "Cathy and Alan seem nice."

"They are nice, but so is Mike. And Gene, what about him?" asked Carol.

Greg was slow in answering. "You know Sam, our old boss in Kansas City, was pretty fond of you and your group of friends. I respected Sam. I referred to John once as a cripple, and Sam told me in no uncertain terms that I should never do that again. I think it is strange that you all still hang out after all these years, and it is odd that two of them are not married, and the other one didn't marry until after you did."

"Would you like for me to respond to that?" asked Carol.

"I frankly don't care what you do," said Greg.

"I choose to respond. This is the first time I've seen John in three years. John is one of the strongest, most determined people I have ever known and should never be referred to as a cripple. As far as Mike being protective of me, he has been that way since we were twelve. We were just kids. As to why they aren't married, I guess they just haven't found the right person yet," responded Carol.

"Or is it just that they haven't found anyone to equal you," said Greg.

"I can't answer that, but you've said nothing about Gene. You totally ignored me when I mentioned his name," said Carol.

"I may have seen Gene once, but I don't know him. I would like to meet him someday," said Greg. "You know, before we were married, Sam tried to talk me out of marrying you. He basically said I wasn't the right man for you. He told me that Gene was the one who loved you and that you loved him."

"That was a long time ago. I would like for you to meet him someday. But would you promise me one thing?" asked Carol.

"And what might that be?" asked Greg.

"If and when you do meet him, be kind. Please be kind to him," said Carol.

"I will," said Greg.

Julie knocked on the door. "I can't sleep. Can I get in bed with you?"

"Sure. Come here." Carol helped Julie up on to the bed with them.

Both Greg and Carol kissed their little girl as she did them. She snuggled between them in the big king-sized bed. She felt safe, secure, and loved. For a brief moment, Carol thought of many years ago as she lay between Gene and John in the big bed in California overlooking the ocean and how safe, secure, and loved she felt that night. She could feel the tears run down her cheeks and land on her little girl's nightgown.

"Mommy, you have tears just like John. Do you have something in your eye too?" asked Julie.

"I think so, but I'll be all right," said Carol.

Greg didn't say anything. He just turned to face the wall.

They were still married, but basically it was in name only. Carol knew that their days as husband and wife were numbered. The marriage had been destined to fail from the beginning. She would continue to try, but there was only so much that she could do.

THE REUNION (TWENTY YEARS)

In the spring of 1984, there was a twenty-year class reunion of the 1964 graduating class of Avalon High School. Carol was still living in Springfield, Illinois, with her husband, Greg Martin, their daughter, and his two sons.

In the large realm, Springfield is not that far from Chicago where Gene lived, but the two of them did not keep in touch. Gene often thought about calling Carol, but he hadn't for some time primarily because of her husband. Among the four of them, the only two who kept in contact were Mike and John, partly because they both still lived in Kansas City but mostly because of Alan's fondness for John.

When Mike found out about the reunion, he called John and asked him if he wanted to go. They both agreed they would go, not knowing whether Carol and Gene would be there.

A few days before the reunion, Mike called Janice, Carol's friend from high school. She was head of the reunion committee.

"Hello, Janice. This is Mike McVary."

"Hi, Mike. Carol is coming to the reunion," said Janice.

Mike laughed. "I didn't even have to ask."

"I received your reservation and John's. I thought you would be calling," said Janice.

"Have you heard from Gene?" asked Mike.

"Not yet, but a lot of people wait until the last minute. I'll let you know if I hear from him," replied Janice.

Mike paused and then asked, "How many reservations did Carol make?"

"Just one. She's coming alone. She's flying in on April 2, United flight 319 from Chicago, arriving in Kansas City at eight forty-five," answered Janice.

Mike thanked Janice again. She had known what he wanted before he even said it. He was very anxious to see Carol. In his heart he hoped she was still the same, but he knew that was highly unlikely. She was a married woman raising three children. Suddenly, he was really nervous and scared.

The day before the reunion, Carol boarded her connecting flight out of Chicago to Kansas City. She took a window seat close to the front. As the plane quickly filled, soon there were only center seats left. And then Carol saw the tall man entering the plane. It had been almost seven years since she had seen him, but Carol immediately knew it was Gene. Carol noticed the white cane and that his glasses were much thicker than before. A stewardess was walking with him.

As he passed the seat in front of her, Carol said, "Hello, Gene."

Their eyes met. He thanked the stewardess for helping him and said "Excuse me" to the man in the aisle seat and sat in the middle seat. "Hello, Carol. They don't make these seats for football players, do they?" Without hesitation, he kissed her on the cheek.

"The seats are tight, but with you next to me, I don't mind. How have you been, Gene?" asked Carol.

"Better since I'm sitting by you," Gene replied. As Carol noticed he was struggling with the seat belt, she quickly helped him. "I'm sorry. Thank you for helping me. I couldn't see it."

"It's all right, Gene. I'm with you now. Everything will be fine," said Carol.

"No matter how bad my eyesight gets, it is strange, but I can always see you fairly clear," said Gene. He hesitated and seemed somewhat embarrassed. "I've been using the white cane for about three months now. It is hard to get used to, and I don't like it, but I bump into things and miss steps without it. And the headaches are much worse."

There was a deep sadness in his voice, but Carol had heard it before, and she hoped she could help him as she had done many times in the past, but she had a feeling that this time things would be different.

"As long as I am beside you, there is nothing for you to worry about. I'll take care of you, Gene. I won't let anything happen to you," said Carol in the kindest, most reassuring voice he had ever heard.

"I know, and that is why I have always loved you. Suddenly, it is as though all the cares and troubles in the world have been lifted off my shoulders just by being next to you. I'm so glad that you are here and that you accept me as I am," said Gene.

"I love you, Gene, and I'll treasure the time we have together. I'll protect you, and I won't leave your side. It seems so natural for us to be together like this." Carol took hold of Gene's hand.

He put his arm around her, and she rested her head against his broad shoulder. They would hold tight to one another until the plane landed, and even then they wouldn't really let go.

Carol had always worried about Gene's worsening eyesight, and she wondered how bad it was now. She could tell that he was very sensitive about using the white cane, and she would try to make him feel as comfortable as possible. Seeing Gene so vulnerable and dependent was difficult for Carol as she was certain it was for him. He had always been a born leader and so strong and independent, but now everything had changed. She knew how hard the reunion would be for him, and she just hoped that she would be able to help him.

It was as though they were the only two people on the plane.

"I'm so glad you're going to the reunion," said Carol.

"I almost backed out at the last minute," said Gene. "I wanted to see you, Mike, and John, but I just can't give a speech."

"My sweet Gene, I hope they don't ask you to speak. I know it would be hard for you." Carol spoke to him with so much understanding and kindness.

He realized no one had spoken to him that way since the last time he had seen her.

"Do you remember the last time we were on a plane together?" asked Gene.

"The second trip to California. I wasn't doing so good. You know it wasn't the doctor or anyone else who made me better then. It was you, it was all you. When you put me in that big king-size bed between you and John, I felt so loved and secure. You took such good care of me, of all of us for that matter." Carol's voice was quiet and reflective.

"I always wanted you to find happiness. If it couldn't be with me, then with someone else. Are you happy, Carol? Please tell me you are happy." The once-infallible Gene had tears in his eyes. She had only seen this two other times.

"My daughter is wonderful, and I love her very much as I do Greg's boys," said Carol.

Gene could hardly look at Carol, but yet he couldn't take his eyes off of her. "He's not kind to you, is he? Has he hurt you?"

"Not the way you think. It's mostly just verbal and mental abuse, not physical anymore. He can be very cruel," said Carol.

"Take your little girl and get away from him. Come to me or John or Mike. You know how the three of us would treat you. I can't stand to think of someone hurting you," Gene spoke with compassion and sincerity.

"My dear, sweet Gene, let's not talk about me anymore. I want to know about you. Are you happy? How are your children?" asked Carol.

"I love my children very much. I miss them. They are far away, and I don't get to see them as often as I would like. I don't like being divorced. I don't think I can ever be really happy. I don't know how to be." Gene was always so honest and real.

"I've always been so proud of you, Gene. All the awards you got in high school, the graduation speech, being class president for three years, not to mention you were the best football and basketball player the school ever had. And then graduating at the top of your college class. But now all I want is for you to be happy," said Carol.

"I'll tell you one thing that would have made me happy. I was so embarrassed to get all those awards, and you and Mike, who should have won in every category you were nominated in, won nothing. To make it worse, Mike and I were nominated in the same category several times. I was praying he would win, and he didn't. That was twenty years ago, and I still can't get over it." Gene took his glasses off and rubbed his eyes.

"You know, I think one is as bad as the other. You felt you got more than you deserved, and Mike and I were just the opposite. But, Gene, you were spectacular. You have to know that. You deserved everything you won. We were all so proud of you and happy for you. You had no marks against you on your record. Mike and I had a lot against us," said Carol.

"I wanted so much for you to win that Kansas University journalism scholarship." Gene put his glasses back on. He couldn't see without them anymore, and he wanted to see and remember everything about this wonderful woman sitting beside him. "You deserved that scholarship. That you didn't get it was the greatest injustice of all."

They couldn't seem to stop talking on that plane ride. They wanted it to last forever when in all reality it was almost over.

"I gave Janice my flight information so Mike and John might be there to meet us. Do they know you are coming?" asked Carol.

"I haven't talked to them, but I just made my decision to go to the reunion yesterday. I called Janice. I'm sure she told them," said Gene. "I was so afraid to fly alone, and then I found you."

"You have nothing to be afraid of now. I'll stay close to you and protect you as you have me so many times," Carol paused. "It has been seven years since I've seen them. I'm a little afraid."

"Why are you afraid?" asked Gene.

"I always worry about John. I want to see him well and happy, but I'm always afraid he will be worse. And I hope Mike has found some peace. The war took a lot out of him. He wasn't the same when he came back," said Carol.

"Were you afraid to see me?" asked Gene.

251

"No. I feel differently about you. With you, the thought of even possibly seeing you again made me feel alive and happy. There is no fear," said Carol.

After a very smooth landing, the plane was on the ground.

The stewardess who had helped Gene board the plane quietly asked him, "Would you like to get off first? I could get you a wheelchair if it would be helpful to you."

"No, I'll be fine," said Gene.

Gene was having a hard time getting up. The man sitting by Gene in the aisle seat said, "I'll help you if you need it." He stood back to let Carol and Gene get off first.

As Gene moved to the aisle seat, he tried to get up but felt very weak and almost fell as the man caught him. Two rows back, a tall man was getting up and preparing to leave the plane and noticed the problems Gene was having. He said excuse me to those in front of him and came to Gene's assistance.

"My name is Reggie. Can I help you?"

"I can't seem to get up. I don't know what's wrong," said Gene.

Reggie very gently and with ease helped Gene up. "You're taller than me. I bet you played basketball. What's your name? You look familiar."

"I'm Gene Sandusky. I just played at Avalon High School about twenty years ago," said Gene.

"I remember you. I was in the class of 1966," said Reggie. "You played football too. Were you a quarterback?"

"Yes, I was for three years," said Gene.

"So was I. I always recognize another quarterback," said Reggie. "Now we need to get you off this plane."

Gene had his arm around Carol. She held him closely and tightly as they exited the plane. Reggie held on to him on the other side.

"Can I help you down to baggage claim?"

"Thank you, but I'll be fine now, or at least I think I will be. I'm just going to sit down and rest for a minute," said Gene.

Carol took Reggie's hands in hers. "Thank you so much for helping him."

"I wish I could do more for him. Good luck and God bless you," said Reggie as he hugged Gene and then walked away.

With Carol's help, Gene got up, and they started walking, but they only got to the next gate when Gene had to sit down. Carol put her arms around him.

"Gene, we need to get you some help."

At that moment a small lady escort pushing an empty wheelchair approached Gene and Carol. She put her arm around Gene and said, "My chariot is here just for a handsome man like you. It has been awaiting a prince, and I believe you are him. My name is Millie. May I be your driver?"

"I'm all right. I think I can make it, but thank you," said Gene.

"You know, it takes a very big man to sit in this chair and let a little old lady like me push him. And I have a feeling that you are that big a man," said Millie.

Gene hesitated and then said, "I'm an awfully big man for you to push."

"But I've been waiting just for you," said Millie. "I can tell that you are a very kind man."

Carol and Millie gently helped him to the wheelchair. "You are such a tall man and so proud and brave. What's your name?" asked Millie.

"I'm Gene, and this is my good friend Carol."

"I'm pleased to meet you both, and now we will slowly make or way to the baggage claim area," said Millie as she looked at Carol. "You hold his hand so sweetly. You must care very much about him."

"Gene is the kindest, best man I have ever known," said Carol.

Millie noticed the tears in Carol's eyes, and she quietly hugged her.

When they got to their destination, Gene gave Millie a generous tip. She wished them well, and as they helped him to a nearby bench, he held tight to Carol's hand. He couldn't risk being separated from her, not yet anyway. They both knew that they would have very little time together, but it didn't really matter.

And then they saw Mike and John. The greetings were genuine and full of love. The four of them were so glad to be together that they could barely speak. They sat on the bench to wait for their luggage to arrive. In the past, Gene would relinquish his place next to Carol to his two friends, but not today. He did not let go of her hand, and he stayed as close to her as he could.

As the luggage started arriving, Mike asked, "How many suitcases do you have?"

"I just have one," said Gene.

"I don't have any. This is it," said Carol as she pointed to her small blue carry-on.

John said, "I remember that bag. It's the one you took to California. You said you travel light."

Mike went with Gene to get his bag. Gene was able to get up, and he was walking a little better.

"Is she all right?" asked Mike.

Gene was always so honest. "Not really. Her marriage is not what we would have wanted for her. She deserves so much more."

Mike patted his old friend on the back. "And you, Gene, how are you? I can't help but notice the white cane."

"I'm all right, Mike. My eyesight has just gotten worse recently," said Gene.

They stood in silence by the baggage claim area. John and Carol waited together just outside the area.

"You look good, John. Are you doing well?"

"My head still bothers me, and my arm and hand haven't improved. I remember how I used to lay my head on your lap when we lived in the house on Lansing Street, and you knew exactly where to rub my head to make it stop hurting. I miss you so much," said John. "But I'm worried about Gene. Is he all right? Is his eyesight a lot worse?"

"He will be all right, or at least I hope so. He is with us now. We won't let anything happen to him," Carol paused. "I miss you, John."

Carol seemed glad to see them, but he saw the emptiness in her eyes. He had seen it in her eyes before when he and Mike had gone to her mother's house to say goodbye right before she left Kanas City.

Mike went to get the car. John was still using the cane and walking slowly. Carol was acutely aware of how much more difficult things were for him now than they had been when she last saw him. Gene was watching closely, and he noticed too. When Mike returned with the car, even though with all his heart Gene wanted to sit in the back with Carol, without hesitation he helped John into the back seat. Carol followed, but not before squeezing Gene's hand in a thank-you gesture.

"It's good to be next to you again," said John.

Carol touched his cheek and moved closer to him.

As Mike drove across the Intercity Viaduct, he said, "I just realized, I don't know where I'm taking you two."

"I'm staying with my mom and dad out on State Avenue tonight," said Carol.

"I'll be staying on Twelfth Street," said Gene.

"Would you all like to have pizza at our favorite pizza place?" asked Mike.

They all said yes.

As they walked into the Pizza Inn, John said, "Do you guys remember this is the first place we ever went together after graduation rehearsal?"

They all remembered. Mike and Gene both assisted John up the steps, but Carol still stayed close to Gene and held his arm. They all felt safe and happy to be together if only for a little while.

As they waited for their pizza, Carol asked Mike, "So how's your life, Mike?"

"Well, I finally became a lawyer. It makes my dad happy," said Mike.

"But what about you, Mike? Does it make you happy?" asked Carol.

"I suppose it does. I'm finally doing what was expected of me," Mike paused. "But there is one other thing. I met a girl in law school. She's several years younger than me, but we've been seeing one another for about a year now."

Carol took his hands in hers. "That's great, Mike. I'm so happy for you. Are you bringing her to the reunion tomorrow?"

Mike reluctantly continued. "I asked her, but she said no. I've told her about the four of us."

"That may not have been such a good idea," said John.

"I haven't told her everything. It's just that sometimes I like to talk about us, and she seems to understand. She wanted us to have this time together. Her name is Carol, and she has long red hair," said Mike. "But that is where the similarities end. Sometimes I wish she was more like you."

Carol hugged Mike. There was nothing she could say.

"When I first met her, you wouldn't believe what I said. She told me her name, and I said, 'Carol, that's a pretty name. I like that name, Carol,'" Mike looked at Carol. "Do you remember when I said that to you?"

"You said that to me the very first time we ever met," said Carol. She smiled slightly at Mike. It was kind of funny but also a little sad.

Then to change the subject from himself, Mike asked Gene, "Since your divorce, Gene, have you been dating anyone?"

"No. There's no one out there for me," said Gene.

"There will be a lot of single girls at the reunion tomorrow. Maybe you can rekindle an old flame or meet someone new," said Mike.

Carol and John knew immediately Mike had just made a mistake and probably for the first time really stepped out of bounds with Gene as he responded quickly to Mike's comment, "You just don't get it, nobody ever gets it. I don't want anyone. Carol is the only girl I have ever loved or ever will love. How many times have I heard, 'Oh, she likes Mike the best' or 'She likes John the best.' Even my own family, my mom picked Mike, my dad picked John. No one ever picked me, yet I was always the one who loved Carol the most." They were seeing a side of Gene they had never seen before.

"I knew, Gene. I always knew," said Carol. She hugged him and kissed him gently on the cheek.

"Wow, some best friend I've been," said Mike.

"I knew too," said John.

"John, if it had seemed like you and Carol would be together, I would never have stood in the way, but that didn't happen either, and now she is in an unhappy marriage. It's all our fault, and it's killing me. How could seemingly somewhat intelligent people screw things up so badly?" said Gene.

No one had anything to say. Gene had said it all in a few words. Someone had to say something, but for a few minutes no one could.

And then John spoke quietly and truthfully, "I loved Carol too, probably as much as you did, Gene. But I knew Carol wanted to have a baby, and I knew I couldn't father a baby, so I never would have married Carol or anyone else."

Maybe they weren't meant to have relationships within their small group. And quite possibly, they weren't strong enough to have relationships outside their group. It was as though they depended too much on one another. Both Carol and Gene had always felt that the four of them together could accomplish anything, whereas apart they could do nothing.

The next day they went to lunch together at the hotel where the reunion would be that evening. Mike picked everyone up. Carol helped Gene with ordering since he was having trouble reading the menu. He could only eat a little of his sandwich and soup. His hands were shaking.

"Gene, could we order something else for you? You haven't eaten much," said Mike with concern.

"I'm not hungry. I just want you all to stay with me. Will you promise not to leave me alone?" asked Gene.

"Gene, we are not going to leave you for any reason," said Carol. "I have an idea. Let's go to the room and rest for a while."

"That would be good," said Gene.

When they got to the room, Gene sat on the sofa, Carol sat on one side of him, and John sat on the other side.

"I called last night to see if we could have adjoining rooms. John and I will be right next door to you and Carol," said Mike.

"Thank you, Mike," said Gene.

As Mike got up to take his bag into the adjoining room, Carol got up to follow him. She spoke quietly to Gene, "I'll be back in just a minute. I need to ask Mike something. John will be here with you."

Gene nodded his head yes.

When they were in the adjoining room, Carol said to Mike, "I'm worried about Gene. He wasn't like this on the plane. He seemed to start feeling bad as we got off the plane."

"That's why I thought we should have adjoining rooms. You know how Gene is. He won't say anything," said Mike.

"I know," said Carol.

As they walked back into the room, John was holding Gene in his arms as Gene had held him many times. Gene was crying.

Carol sat by Gene and took him from John and held him tightly. "What's wrong Gene? It's something more than a headache, isn't it? Please tell us."

"I told my doctor in Chicago that I could barely see and that the headaches were worse, but he said I have always had bad eyesight and bad headaches. He wasn't concerned. I just don't want you three to hate me and leave me," said Gene.

"Gene, I have loved you since we were eight, and I love you now, and I'll love you forever, and we are not going to leave you. You are the kindest, best man I have ever known." Carol held her dear friend in her arms for a long while that day as John and Mike stayed close to them.

Carol knew as did everyone else that their time together would be short, or so they thought at that moment, but things had a way of changing into something totally unexpected and altering the lives and futures of those involved.

Both Gene and John had experienced a lot of heartache in their lives, but the next six months would test their endurance and strengths beyond anything they could ever imagine, and Carol and Mike would have their abilities to help them stretched to the limit and beyond.

Carol and Mike had tried to help those being bullied in school when they were only fifteen. They were thirty-seven now, but the old lessons they had learned so well would come back to them many times over. They had not backed away from the challenges in the past, and they would not back away now, but the challenges ahead would be more difficult, serious, and life-threatening than anything they had ever experienced in the past.

At the reunion that night, the four friends walked in together. Gene didn't want to use the white cane. Carol stayed close to him on one side and Mike on the other. She held his arm tightly and kept him as close to her as she possibly could. Carol held John's left arm as he walked on the other side of her.

There were many enlarged pictures from 1964 decorating the banquet room. There was a picture of Gene as quarterback on the football team, as class president, and Gene passing the robe to the junior class president. There was a picture of Gene and Carol as prom king and queen and one of the four of them on prom night. There was a picture of Gene and Mike on the basketball court and of Gene giving the graduation speech.

Gene stumbled and almost fell, but he caught hold of Mike's arm. He held on to Carol's hand as he said, "I just have a really bad headache."

Mike asked Gene, "Would you like to leave?"

"No, I'll be all right," said Gene.

Everyone was looking at them, especially at Gene. They looked at the rest of the pictures. Although there were pictures of others from the 1964 class, it was obvious that Gene was the most popular in 1964, and he was still loved by everyone. Carol held Gene's hand to try to stop it from trembling. They found a table and sat down. Friends stopped by their table all evening. Everyone was being very kind, but sometimes Gene could hardly speak. Carol spoke for him when she could. Mike and John also tried to help.

Later in the evening, Janice and Roy came to their table and sat down by Gene. Janice asked, "Is there anything we can do for you?"

"No, I'll be all right," Gene answered in a voice that was barely audible.

"I know you guys are staying here at the hotel tonight. So are we," said Roy as he hugged Gene. "I love you, Gene. If there is anything we can do, let us know." As Janice and Roy got up to go back to their table, they noticed the tears in Gene's eyes.

When they got up to leave the party, a strange silence came over the entire room.

Gene spoke quietly to Carol, but Mike and John also heard, "Please stay close to me. I can't see, and I feel like I could pass out."

People stood back and parted and let them go through. When they got to the room, Gene sat down on the bed. Without a word,

Mike helped him take off his shoes, jacket, shirt, and pants. He helped him lie back and covered him up.

"We'll be right next door if you need us."

Carol got a cool washcloth. She gently removed his glasses and wiped his face with it. Mike and John went to their room without saying anything else.

Later, John said reflectively, "You know, whenever Carol has been there for me, so has Gene right by her side. He helped me learn to write with my left hand, he bathed me, shaved me, and fed me. After the accident, he never left my side. He talked to me when I was in the coma just like Carol did. And on the second trip to California when you were in Vietnam, he took care of Carol, your parents, and me."

"You know, John, right after your accident, Gene and I cleaned up all the debris at the garage and hauled it away, and we chopped at the ice and snow until all the blood was gone. Gene didn't want your mom and sisters to see it. Did you know that?" asked Mike.

"No, I didn't know," replied John. "I've never done one thing for Gene, not one single thing,"

"You wrote a pretty good graduation speech for him," said Mike.

"That was more for me. I wanted Gene to give it, but I didn't think it would ever happen," said John.

Carol did not leave Gene's side that night. At one time he was cold, and she lay close beside him to warm him.

Toward morning he woke up. "Where's John and Mike?"

"They are in a room right next door to us. Would you like them here with us?" asked Carol.

Gene shook his head yes. "I can't see you very well. Where are my glasses?"

Carol picked up his glasses from the nightstand and put them on him. She kissed him gently on the cheek. "Is that better?"

"Yes. Thank you. You look really pretty." Gene's voice was very weak.

John and Mike came into their room.

John took hold of Gene's hand. "I never thanked you for saving my life. I just need for you to know how much I owe you. I'm forever grateful to you, Gene, and I love you."

Mike said, "Thanks for all you did for my parents, Cathy, Carol, and John. You've been more than my best friend, you're my hero."

Gene closed his eyes as John still held his hand.

Mike asked Carol, "Don't you think you should try to get a little rest?"

"I can't. I'm so worried about Gene," said Carol. "I really think he should see a doctor."

"Dad could probably get him in to see his doctor this morning," said Mike. "Do you think he will agree to go?"

"I think he will go," said Carol.

Mike hugged Carol and went back to his room and called his dad.

AFTER THE REUNION

When Gene woke up the morning after the reunion, he was still weak and shaky, but he seemed somewhat better, and he was very content to allow his friends to help him. Carol and John gently gave him a sponge bath in bed. Then John shaved him, the same way Gene had shaved him many years ago. Mike helped Gene dress, and he told him that he had an appointment with his dad's doctor at ten o'clock.

They ordered breakfast, but Gene couldn't eat anything, which was best because he would be taking many tests that morning. When they left for the appointment, Carol and Mike helped Gene. Walking was difficult for him.

As they walked toward the lobby where Mike was picking them up, Gene said, "I forgot the cane. Would you get it for me, John?"

"It's all right. You won't need it. I'll be right by your side. I won't leave you," said Carol.

Alan met them at the doctor's office. They got a wheelchair for Gene. They were taken to a private conference room where Carol and Mike filled out a lot of forms and other paperwork.

Dr. Shannon was a highly respected physician with a very gentle, caring bedside manner. He addressed his comments directly to Gene.

"I'm going to send you for several tests: MRI, Cat scan, EKG, blood work, eye tests, and some memory tests. It shouldn't take more than three hours, and then I will meet you all back here for the results.

Gene didn't say anything, but Dr. Shannon could see fear and worry in his eyes. "What's wrong, Gene?"

"Can someone stay with me?" asked Gene hesitantly.

"Sure. Who do you want to be with you?" asked Dr. Shannon.

"Carol," said Gene.

"Is that all right with you, Carol?" asked Dr. Shannon.

"I'll stay with him," said Carol as she took hold of Gene's hand.

And so the testing began. Carol helped him into a hospital gown and held his glasses for him. She tried to stay close to him so he could see her, and she held his hand whenever she could. When all the tests were over, they went back to the conference room. It was the first time Gene had ever had the type of tests he did that day, and he was very tired.

As Carol put his glasses back on him, he said, "Thank you for staying with me and helping me."

"This is where I need to be right now, right by your side as you have been by me so many times," said Carol.

When Dr. Shannon entered the room, he had the test results. "Well, Gene, you held up well during all the tests. There were quite a few of them. I hope they weren't too hard on you."

"I'm just worried. I don't know what's happening to me," said Gene.

Carol held tightly to his hand.

"Well, Gene, it appears you have had a TIA. Do you know what that is?" asked Dr. Shannon.

"I don't know," said Gene.

"A TIA is a transient ischemic attack, which is a mini stroke." Carol spoke quietly, but Gene hung on every word she said.

"Very good, Carol. Are you a nurse?" said Dr. Shannon.

"No. I've just read a lot of medical books," said Carol.

Dr. Shannon continued, "TIAs are fairly common. Sometimes they are not even noticed, other times they can be significantly more serious. You fall somewhere in the middle. You are experiencing some weakness, hand tremors, headaches, trouble eating and digesting food, and trouble with your eyesight. These should all clear up fairly soon, hopefully completely. You probably had it the night of the reunion. The good news is that you are young, and the bad news is that you are young. This is not real common in a man your age. I'm giving you a prescription, but it is very important that you see a doctor as soon as you get home." Dr. Shannon looked at Carol. "Are you two a couple?"

"No. We live in different cities," replied Carol.

"I live alone," said Gene. "I ride to work with a friend who lives in the same apartment complex where I live. I haven't been seeing well for a few months, so I haven't been driving."

"That's good. The decline in your eyesight could possibly be related to the TIA, but it is too soon to tell," said Dr. Shannon. "I know you flew here. It would be good if you didn't fly alone."

"I took the liberty of changing your flight, Gene. You and Carol will be flying back to Chicago on the same flight," said Mike.

"Thanks, Mike," said Gene.

"And how will you get home from the airport?" asked Dr. Shannon.

"I'll take a cab," said Gene.

Dr. Shannon put his arm around Gene. "I know you are feeling bad right now and you are worried, but you're going to be fine. It will just take a little while. You have a good group of friends with you. I've known Alan and Mike for a long time." Dr. Shannon paused. "I'm sorry that I assumed you and Carol were a couple, but it just seemed that way to me."

"That's all right," said Gene. "Thank you for everything."

"You're welcome. You are a very nice young man, and I've enjoyed meeting you," said Dr. Shannon.

On the drive back to the hotel, Alan asked Gene a question. There was no answer. Gene had fallen asleep. His head was on Carol's shoulder.

"He's exhausted. The tests were hard on him." Carol gently stroked his cheek.

Carol was sitting between Gene and John in the back seat. Mike was in the front with his dad, who was driving. Mike looked back at his friends and his eyes connected with John. They both noticed as Carol ever so gently kissed Gene on the cheek. They both could tell how much Carol loved Gene and how concerned she was for him and how much he loved and needed her. But they both knew that soon she would be going home to her children and husband, and that alone was heartbreaking.

Mike and John knew how hard it would be when they took Carol and Gene to the airport the next day. Their goodbyes were always difficult, but this one would be exceptionally so.

Alan would have asked them to come to the house in Avalon Manor, but somehow he knew the hotel was where they wanted and needed to be that night.

"If you need me to take you to the airport tomorrow, let me know," said Alan.

"We will, Dad. Thanks for everything," said Mike.

Alan hugged Mike and John. Then he hugged Gene, which was something he had never done before.

"Goodbye, Gene. I hope you are better soon. Don't ever give up. If you need anything, please call me."

"I will. Thank you for getting me into the doctor." Gene's speech was still hesitant and somewhat slurred.

Then Alan turned to Carol. "And you, my precious girl. I shall never forget you. I'll always remember the little twelve-year-old girl who read all my books. I don't exactly know what to say to you. I wish you could be with Gene. He needs you so much, but I know you can't be with him because of your small children. Always know that he loves you. He always has and always will. Do what you can for him."

"Goodbye, Alan. You are tearing my heart out. I have to go now," said Carol. She kissed him on the cheek and left to catch up with her friends.

Alan looked at them one last time as they walked away, then he got in his car and drove home. The thought went through his mind that he would never see the four of them together again as they were that night, and in essence, he never did.

They ordered room service that night for dinner. John and Mike were hungry. Carol and Gene were not. That night they talked and reminisced into the wee hours of the morning. Gene tried to stay up as long as he could. He was so weak and shaky, and he still couldn't see clearly. He hoped the doctor was right and it wouldn't last long, but something told him it wasn't going to be that easy. It seemed as though things were never that easy for Gene.

They helped Gene undress and get into bed just as they had the previous night. There were a few tears running down his cheeks. He couldn't seem to control it. Carol held him in her arms, and they all comforted him. They understood what he was going through. He had always been so strong and confident, and now he couldn't seem to do anything.

They all stayed close to him that night. John and Mike eventually fell asleep as did Gene a short while later. Carol lay awake with only her thoughts to keep her company. Just as Gene was worried about his condition and his future, so was Carol.

Miracle on Flight 721

As they arrived at the Kansas City Airport the following day, a foreboding sense of dread and concern was predominant in Carol's heart, probably in all of them. The terminal was already crowded as usual. Mike stood in line to check Gene's bag. As they approached the check-in lanes, Gene was having a hard time walking. Security immediately requested a wheelchair for him. They also offered to get one for John. The plan was for Mike and John to accompany Gene and Carol to the gate and wait with them until they boarded the plane, primarily so Mike could help Gene. It was a long distance to the gate, so John accepted the wheelchair.

After Gene went through check-in, he sat down on a bench. His nose was bleeding, and his hands were trembling. Security seemed very concerned about his condition.

"Are you sure your friend is going to be all right?" A security woman directed her question to Carol.

"He had a TIA two days ago. The doctor said it would be safe for him to travel. I am definitely worried, but he really wants to get home." The deep concern in Carol's voice was evident.

Gene got up and moved to the wheelchair with Mike's help. He used the white cane for support. In a halting speech, he thanked the security guards for their help.

As they walked away, one of the security guards called gate 24, where they would board Flight 721 to Chicago, and told them that a man with some worrisome to severe health problems would be on their flight. She gave them his name and the name of the young woman who would be flying with him.

They stopped in the terminal at a small café to get something to drink, and Mike and John wanted lunch. Carol ordered something to share with Gene. A group of young people at the next table pulled out chairs so they could push the wheelchairs close to the table. Carol noticed how kind everyone was being to them. And as she looked at the pain and fear in Gene's eyes, she knew why. Others saw it too. Carol could not keep from reassuring him that everything would be all right even though she wasn't sure herself.

"You're going to make it through this, Gene. You're going to be fine." Carol took the bloody towel from him and gave him a clean one in case it happened again. She gave him a few bites of her sandwich and held his glass while he took a few sips of water. "Do you still have a bad headache?"

Gene replied, "Yes. It's worse than a normal headache."

After they finished eating, they made their way slowly to the boarding area for gate 24. The handicapped area was completely packed. There was one empty seat on the end in the regular boarding area. They kept both wheelchairs close to them, Mike standing behind Gene. He wanted to protect Gene from anyone bumping his wheelchair.

A man next to where Carol was sitting immediately got up and said to Mike, "Please take my seat so you can be closer to your friends."

"Thank you, sir," said Mike graciously.

Gene tried to get the lid off his water bottle but dropped it, and it rolled a few feet away. A small blond-haired boy of about ten picked it up, smiled, and handed it to him. Gene thanked the boy. Carol helped him hold the bottle as he tried his best to take a drink. He spilled it on his shirt. Carol used the towel to wipe his shirt. A few minutes later, Gene's nose started bleeding again. Mike gently put a small pillow behind his neck. Carol used the white towel to wipe the blood. As she wiped his face, she couldn't help but notice the tears on his cheeks. There were some drops of blood on her blouse, but she didn't care; it was Gene's blood. Everyone around them in the small crowded area could sense the problems Gene was having.

John put a small piece of paper in Gene's pocket. "I love you, Gene. Please call me when you get home."

Gene's voice was very weak as he said, "I will."

Because it was so crowded, people were already lining up in the group A boarding area, which was close to where they were sitting.

A man in a pilot's uniform came up to their group. "Are you Gene and Carol?"

Carol replied, "Yes, and these are our friends Mike and John."

He shook hands with all of them and then put his hand on Gene's shoulder. "I'm Captain Tim Robinson, the pilot of the plane you'll be flying on. When they call for the first boarding group, which is the handicapped group, we want you to be the very first to board. The stewardess will come help you."

"That's very kind of you," said Mike. "If it is all right, I would like to take Gene onto the plane myself and help him get seated."

Captain Robinson, noticing the size of the two former football players, said, "That will be fine. He may need you to help him. I'll see you soon."

Suddenly, Carol could no longer hold back the tears. She walked away for a moment with her back to the guys and held her hands to her face to muffle her sobs. She was facing others waiting to board the plane, but she didn't care if they saw her crying. Many had looks of concern on their faces for what she and her small group of companions were going through.

She felt an arm around her. It was a young woman she had noticed standing in line near where they were sitting. "Is there anything at all that I can do for you?" asked the kind young woman.

Carol replied through her tears, "I just need to somehow stay strong for them. Gene is very sick, and we all love him so much."

"I can feel the love between all of you. I think you are probably the strongest woman I have ever seen. It seems like you are taking care of all three of them." She hugged Carol and went back to the line.

Carol had no sooner than sat down when they announced it was time to board the plane. A stewardess immediately appeared to board Gene and Carol first.

John took hold of Gene's hand. "Goodbye, Gene. Take care."

Gene nodded. He couldn't speak.

Carol stopped and kissed John. "I will miss you so much."

This time it was John who couldn't speak. Mike pushed Gene's wheelchair toward the door to the plane ramp as Carol followed. At the door, Gene turned and raised his hand in one last wave to John.

John had never felt so alone as he did at that moment. He put his face in his hands and cried silently. The nice young woman who had comforted Carol a few minutes earlier along with her husband came to John's side. They both embraced him.

"I'm Brian, and this is my wife, Holly. We are so close that we couldn't help but be involved in what is happening in your lives. We will give you and Mike our tickets so you can go with your friends."

Amazed at the generosity of the two complete strangers, John was overwhelmed with emotion. "We couldn't take your tickets."

At that moment, Captain Robinson appeared again. "John, you are coming with us. Mike is not leaving the plane."

"But we don't have tickets," said John.

"There were two TWA employees flying with us today. One of them saw Gene and remembered working with him at TWA years ago. They have given their tickets to you and Mike." Captain Robinson looked at Brian and Holly. "Would the two of you go ahead and help John board now."

There was not a minute of hesitation on their part as Brian pushed his wheelchair and Holly held his hand.

Then Captain Robinson made an announcement, "Is there a doctor who will be flying with us on Flight 721?"

A man sitting nearby waiting for a later boarding group raised his hand. "I'm Dr. Mark Landis. I am a surgeon. I do have a medical bag with me. This is my wife and son." His son was the ten-year-old boy who had picked up Gene's water bottle when he dropped it.

"Please, all three of you board now with John and his two friends and set as close to Gene as you can. And keep him safe, Doctor. Please, for the love of God, keep him safe."

They all moved rapidly.

A lady in line said angrily to Captain Robinson, "What is the holdup? This plane is going to be late."

Captain Robinson put his arm around her. "We will be on time. I promise you that. There is a young man on this plane who needs a little special love and care today, and I hope that all of you will help me give him and his friends that right now. We never know when any of us could be in his situation. Can I count on you, and actually can I count on all of you to love and help, especially Gene, but also his three good friends?"

To his surprise, all other passengers quietly cheered and clapped, and there was a unanimous yes.

When Captain Robinson boarded the plane, he walked back three rows to where his selected group had assembled. Carol was in the window seat, Gene in the middle, and Dr. Landis on the aisle. Across from them was John in the aisle seat, then Holly, and Brian. Behind Carol was Mike, Dr. Landis's son, Billy, and his wife, Judy. Captain Robinson noticed that Dr. Landis had reclined Gene's seat a little.

He asked Billy, who was directly behind Gene, "Do you have enough room?"

"Sure, he can lean back further if he needs to. I want to help too," said Billy.

They all couldn't help but thinking, *Out of the mouths of babes.*

Carol was impressed with how kind and attentive Dr. Landis was to Gene. He took his blood pressure and checked his heart at regular intervals. Gene had a slight fever, so Dr. Landis put a cool washcloth on his forehead. Dr. Landis spoke in a manner that seemed to calm Gene. He was worried about his trembling hands, his weakness, and his speech, but this was not the time to worry Gene more than he already was. Dr. Landis felt that Gene had another TIA possibly in the night or maybe after arriving at the airport. Although he didn't actually say this, Carol knew, and she was thinking the same thing, but neither one could be sure without more testing.

When Gene fell asleep, Dr. Landis talked to Carol, Mike, and John very quietly. "If you believe in prayer, pray for Gene now and that I can help him safely through this flight."

Judy and Billy were also very kind to all of them, and they seemed proud that Dr. Landis was taking such good care of Gene. Holly and Brian really seemed to connect with and genuinely care about John. But that wasn't unusual. John was very easy to love and make friends with.

Gene only slept for a short while. When he woke up, he put his hand on Carol's and said quietly, "I love you."

Mike heard and wondered what Carol's response would be.

"I love you too, Gene. I always have, and I always will," said Carol. She put his glasses on him and kissed him ever so gently on the cheek.

Mike was happy to hear them say that they loved one another, but then he also realized it was probably the saddest thing he had ever heard in his whole life.

As the plane landed safely and smoothly in Chicago, five minutes ahead of schedule, Captain Robinson came back to escort his special passengers off the plane. No one else attempted to leave before they did, and when Gene stood up to leave the plane escorted on one side by Mike and on the other side by Dr. Landis, everyone was completely silent.

There was a wheelchair waiting for Gene and one for John too. This time, Dr. Landis pushed Gene's wheelchair and Brian pushed John's. Brian went to get his van. Brian and Holly were going to take the four friends to Gene's apartment. Dr. Landis made an appointment to see Gene the next day in his office. He was a surgeon, but he had been a general practitioner. He really liked Gene, and he thought he could help him. Dr. Landis had originally wanted Gene to go directly to the hospital, but Gene assured him that he was feeling better and simply wanted to go home.

Carol and Mike went to pick up Gene's bag.

"I probably shouldn't have told Gene that I love him," said Carol sadly.

"It doesn't matter. He has known you love him for a long time," said Mike.

"What happened to us, Mike? We were good kids. We could have had it all. The world was ours," said Carol.

"It still could be. Maybe I'll get married, and Gene has a really good job," said Mike. "And John does well at the garage."

"What about me? Say something good about me." Carol suddenly felt really depressed. All she wanted to do was to go sit by Gene and love him.

"You have your daughter and the two boys. That's good," said Mike. "And you have a good job with the lobbyist."

"Yes, thanks, Mike. I guess I did do something right," said Carol.

Brian pulled up in a large blue van that resembled Mike's 1964 van that he had given to John when he went to Vietnam. At the same time, all four of them thought about the first California trip when they were all so young. That was a good trip, a really good trip.

CHAPTER

HEARTBREAK

When they arrived at Gene's apartment, he invited Brian and Holly to come in. It seemed as though they had known them forever. Since graduation rehearsal in 1964, no one had ever infiltrated their little group of four. Sam Hagan came close as did Janice and Roy, but they didn't make it.

Because of distance, their group didn't really exist anymore, but whatever was left of it had now been infiltrated by Brian and Holly. They were so kind, and all they wanted to do at the airport was to help John when he was alone and scared and crying.

As Carol sat on the sofa, Gene immediately sat beside her. Carol put a pillow on her lap. "Why don't you lay your head on my lap. It might make you feel better."

Gene did as Carol suggested. "Thank you. I like that."

Carol took his glasses off and very gently touched his temples. Carol asked Holly and Brian, "Do you have children?"

"No, but we hope to someday," said Holly.

Carol had made herself uncomfortable with her own question. She had tears in her eyes as Gene sat up and put his arms around her and held her close to him.

"Do any of you have children?" asked Brian.

"I have a son and daughter. I've been divorced for over two years," said Gene.

"I have a little girl and two boys," said Carol. "I'm married. Would someone call Greg and tell him I won't be home tonight. I'm worried about Gene, and I don't want to leave him."

For the first time they could ever recall, Gene, Mike, and John were without words. They always looked out for Carol and always had an answer, but not that night.

"If you want me to call him, I will," said Holly.

"No, I can't ask you to do that," said Carol quietly. "What about you, Mike. Would you call him for me."

Mike hesitated, "If you want me to and think he will talk to me, I will." And so Mike picked up the phone and did just that. "Hello, Greg. This is Mike McVary, Carol's friend."

"Hello, Mike," said Greg.

"Carol is going to stay in Chicago tonight. Her friend Holly will bring her home tomorrow," said Mike.

"What is the problem? I need her home, as do the children," said Greg.

"Her friend is ill. She doesn't want to leave tonight," said Mike.

"Why don't you bring her home tonight?" Greg sounded unfriendly and angry.

"Let me talk to him." Holly took the phone from Mike. "We can't bring Carol home tonight. We have all had an exhausting flight, and it wouldn't be safe to drive tonight."

"Where is Carol now?" asked Greg.

Holly hesitated, "She is trying to get a little rest."

"Who all is there?" asked Greg.

"My husband, Brian, Mike, John, Gene, and Carol," said Holly.

"Let me speak to John," said Greg.

"John, he wants to talk to you," said Holly.

"No, let me talk to him. He doesn't need to be mean to John too," said Brian.

"It's all right. I'll talk to him," said John.

Holly handed the phone to John.

"Greg, this is John." John's voice was quiet but strong.

"I need someone to tell me exactly what is going on there," said Greg.

"Gene has had a stroke. It happened the night of the reunion. The doctor in Kansas City thought it was a very mild stroke, but there was a doctor on the plane who was afraid it might be more serious, or he may have had a second stroke." John's voice broke slightly as he was fighting back tears.

"Thanks for explaining things to me, John. That's all I wanted to know. Tell Carol to stay through tomorrow or even the next day if she needs to," said Greg.

"I'll call tomorrow and let you know." With that settled, John hung up the phone.

Later that evening, as Carol and John were beginning to help Gene get ready for bed, he put his hand to his head and said the pain was much worse. He fell back on the bed, unable to move.

Mike was in the other room. He quickly came to Gene's room. He took one look at Gene and said, "I'm calling an ambulance."

A fire truck and ambulance arrived immediately. Mike and Carol answered all their questions as they stabilized and prepared Gene for transport to the hospital. They followed in Gene's car. John called Brian and Holly, who had only left Gene's apartment about twenty minutes earlier. They would meet them at the hospital.

As the long night turned into morning, Dr. Landis came to talk to them. He had been with Gene all night as had many other doctors.

"Gene has had a major stroke, which is the third. It is considerably worse than the other two put together. He is stable for the moment, but we must keep it from happening again. I'll come talk to you as soon as I know more." He took Carol's hand. "We are doing all we possibly can for him right now. Carol, will you come with me for a minute?" As Carol walked with him down the hall, he said to her, "He needs to hear your voice just for a minute or two."

As Carol entered the ICU room, there were several nurses and doctors there. She sat close to him. She spoke quietly and gently to her dear friend, "I'm with you. Gene. I'll always be with you. You are going to be well soon. Don't ever give up. I love you. I always have and always will. You are the best man I've ever known." For a second, he opened his eyes a little, and she could tell that he knew she was there. "I have your glasses. Whenever you are ready for them, just ask me." She knew that was the first thing he would ask for. She touched his hand and kissed him gently. Dr. Landis motioned that it was time to leave.

In the hall, Dr. Landis said to Carol, "That was beautiful, the way you talk to him. We are going to take good care of him. I promise you."

"Thank you," said Carol. "He is such a good man. He saved my life twice. I will do anything for him. I would give my life for him."

Carol went back to her friends in the waiting room. Holly had brought back some coffee and rolls from the cafeteria. Carol hated to think about Greg, let alone mention his name, but she did.

"Mike and Holly, I'm so sorry Greg was unkind to you on the phone."

"It's all right. At least he talked to John," said Holly.

Carol turned to John, "Thank you so much, John."

John took his hand and smoothed her hair back. "You know, if I could, I would change places with Gene. I can't stand seeing him like this. And you love him so much." John's voice trailed off. He put his arms around Carol, and she rested her head on his chest.

It was about noon when Dr. Landis returned. "Gene is stable. It appears the crisis is over at least for now." Dr. Landis sat down by Carol. "It's going to be a long hard road for Gene. He is young and basically strong, so the prognosis is relatively good. I want you to go in now. He has asked for you many times during the night."

Carol went to Gene's bedside with Dr. Landis. She had never before seen Gene like she did that day, so helpless and vulnerable. He couldn't speak, but she knew he could tell that she was there. Everyone else went in to see him one at a time that day, but Carol stayed through it all. She knew he wanted her there. He had many visitors that day. Some Carol knew or had heard Gene mention, whereas others were new to her. But they all had one thing in common, and that was their love for Gene. They all wanted the best for him.

Late that afternoon, John made another phone call to Greg. "I don't know how to say this, but Gene is in bad shape. He has had a third stroke, and it was a major stroke, much worse than the other two."

Greg could hear the heartbreak and despair in John's voice. "I know he needs Carol to be with him," said Greg. "Please tell her it is all right to stay. We'll be all right. I know it is hard for you too. You don't have to say anything else. Just keep me posted."

"Thank you, Greg. I'll talk to you later," said John.

With very little sleep, if any, or food, the vigil Carol kept by Gene's bedside the next four days was remarkable. She seemed to be the strongest one in the group. Gene slowly was coming back to them. He wasn't ready to leave just yet.

On the fifth day, Carol went home. Brian and Holly took her. Since they were coming back the same day, John went with them while Mike stayed with Gene.

THE HOMECOMING AND THE HEALING

They arrived in Springfield in the early afternoon. Greg had come home for lunch. The children were in school. Carol introduced Greg to Brian and Holly. As Greg briefly hugged Carol, John couldn't help but notice the sadness in her eyes.

"Thank you for bringing Carol home. I am sorry, Holly, if I was rude on the phone that first night. I just didn't know what was going on," said Greg.

"I understand. It was a hard time for everyone," said Holly.

"John, I want to thank you again for keeping me posted on Gene's condition," said Greg.

"That was the least I could do," said John.

"Brian and I just want to do anything we can for them," said Holly.

"Are the two of you staying at the hospital with Gene too?" asked Greg.

"As much as we can," said Brian. "We all just met at the airport in Kansas City, but it seems as though we have known them much longer. I wouldn't change that chance meeting for anything. John was alone while Mike was helping Gene board the plane. He needed someone with him, and we went to him. Just getting to know John and his wonderful friends has done more for us than we could ever do for them."

They didn't stay long that day because of the drive back to Chicago. Goodbyes were said. It was all that Carol and John could do to control their emotions, but somehow they managed to.

John had promised to call frequently with reports on Gene's condition. Carol knew what time he would be calling, and she was usually by the phone. If for some reason she was away, Greg would talk to John. The reports were not always good. They all knew that the quicker Gene could get into a regular therapy regiment and rehabilitation program, the better the outcome would be.

After several days, Carol needed to go back to Chicago. Greg and Carol had agreed that it would be good if Carol's mother, Stella, would come visit during Carol's absence to help with the children. Stella thought it was a great idea, and she would arrive in Springfield the same day Carol would leave for Chicago. Carol had taken her vacation time from work to be with Gene.

Even though John's reports were thorough, Carol was not prepared for what she found when she arrived at the hospital. Gene was unable to eat on his own. The tremors were gone probably because he was so weak. Gene was sitting up in a reclining wheelchair with a high back. There was a brace on his neck to keep his head stabilized. When she spoke to him, he knew she was there and he opened his eyes, but it took every ounce of strength he had to simply hold her hand.

John and Mike were with him. Brian and Holly were waiting outside the room. Everyone had a look of defeat on their faces. Carol really had no idea what to do, but she knew she had to do something. She started rubbing his hand and massaging his arm. She caressed his cheeks and kissed him gently, so very gently. She quietly talked to him in the same way that he had helped her talk to John so many years ago after John's accident. His eyes opened, and as the tears spilled out, she wiped them from his cheeks. She rubbed his shoulders and legs. She adjusted his pillow and combed his hair. Carol was not afraid to touch him.

Holly opened the door a crack and then closed it. As Dr. Landis started to enter the room, Holly said, "There is something remarkable happening in there. Carol has been there for about an hour.

There is a change in Gene. I can tell John and Mike see it too. They will follow her lead."

"I'll come back later. I'll give them a little more time together. There is so little we can do for him medically right now. We've tried everything. If anyone can help him, I think it could be Carol."

For the next three days, Carol stayed close to Gene constantly, leaving for a short while only when he seemed to be sleeping. On the third day, he whispered very quietly that he wanted his glasses so he could see her better. She put them on him. She knew this would be the first thing he would say. Carol was the only one who had understood what he said.

STELLA'S CAUSE

Things were going well with Greg and Carol's mother, Stella, and the children all loved Stella. Greg liked Stella and her honesty. Stella, on the other hand, had never been particularly fond of him. The children were in bed when John called to tell them about Carol's progress with Gene. They were glad to hear good news about Gene.

Stella said, "Carol has never had any medical training, but she knows how to help people. She always has. Sometimes that girl amazes me," Stella paused. "How much do you know about John?"

"Actually, very little," said Greg.

"He had a very hard childhood of poverty and abuse," said Stella. "He had polio when he was five, and he has had several eye operations. A few years ago, a roof overloaded with ice and snow fell on him. He was in a coma and in the hospital for almost six months. It was Carol and Gene who brought him back to life. Mike was away at college, but he also helped when he could," said Stella.

"Carol never told me that. I know very little about them. Mostly, just what Sam Hagen, our old boss, told me," said Greg. "He seemed to be very fond of all of them."

"I'm sure she hasn't told you much about them because it was before you were married, and she probably thought you weren't interested," Stella paused for a minute. "I met John for the first time right after they graduated from high school in 1964. It was obvious how infatuated he was with Carol. He was a young man who had been through so much. I told Carol once never to hurt John. She told me that she had no intention of hurting him, and she never did."

"I called John a cripple once. Sam really told me off for that. I actually like John," said Greg.

"I have never met anyone who doesn't love John, and he is so full of love for everyone. But you don't like Mike, do you?" asked Stella.

Greg just shrugged his shoulders.

"Mike had it all, handsome, rich, sophisticated, an infectious laugh, and a friendly personality. He was always smiling and nice to everyone, but he was somewhat rebellious, like Carol, and they paid for it. He was different when he came back from Vietnam, but I guess we all would be," said Stella.

"Sam told me that Gene was the one Carol loved, and he loved her," said Greg.

There were suddenly tears in Stella's eyes. "In some ways, Gene was a combination of both Mike and John, and yet he was completely different. He wasn't rich like Mike, but everyone loved him as they did John. He was class president for three years, and he won so many awards and scholarships. He was very popular. Gene and Carol were prom king and queen, and neither one wanted it. He was a great quarterback and like magic on the basketball court. But Gene never smiled or laughed, and I always thought he seemed so sad. The graduation speech he gave is something I'll never forget. He always went at everything fast and furious as though there was no tomorrow. He played hard, and he took risks. But Gene was genuinely good, and he followed the rules, which was the opposite of Carol and Mike. Gene didn't have a mark against him on his record, and Carol and Mike did. But Gene did love Carol so much, and she loved him. Do you love Carol, Greg? Do you love her as much as they did?"

"Sure, I love her. We have our differences, but I love her," said Greg.

"None of them ever had differences or ever argued. I think in the end, they all loved her enough to let her go. Gene would never stand in the way of the other two because they were his best friends. That's just the kind of person he was," said Stella. "It seems as though

I've said all this before, but I feel like tonight you have actually listened to me."

"Meeting John sort of got to me. I really liked the guy," said Greg. "And I feel really bad for what has happened to Gene. Now I want to talk to Mike, and I would really like to meet Gene. Maybe I also love Carol enough to let her go."

"It's too late for that, Greg. It was too late a long time ago," said Stella.

GENE'S FUTURE

Gene gradually improved over the next few days. As Carol prepared to enter Gene's hospital room one morning, a gray-haired man of about fifty-five spoke to her.

"You must be Carol. I'm Phillip York, Gene's boss at the advertising agency."

Carol shook his hand. "It is nice to meet you."

"Would you mind stepping into the conference room with me. I would like to talk to you for a moment," said Phillip.

Carol went with him to the conference room and sat across from him at a large table.

"Gene is one of my star executives. We talk a lot. We have quite a bit in common. He has told me all about you. I like what he has told me. I would like to offer you a job," said Phillip.

"But I don't live in Chicago. I live in Springfield," said Carol.

"We would pay for your move. It is a high-paying executive position. You would be able to climb the corporate ladder alongside Gene," said Phillip.

For a moment Carol was without words. "I'm married, and I have three children."

"Your salary would be so good that your husband could retire and become a house husband," said Phillip.

"But how do you know I would be qualified for such a position?" asked Carol.

"Because Gene told me that you were more than qualified," said Phillip.

"I do thank you, but I couldn't right now, but possibly in the future," said Carol.

"Don't wait too long. One never knows what the future holds," said Phillip. "Well, in any case, it was worth a try. Gene told me you were very smart and that you were the most beautiful, kindest girl he has ever known. From his description of you, I immediately recognized you."

"I've never been offered a really good job before. I'm a little overwhelmed," said Carol.

Phillip handed her his card. "Keep this in case you change your mind."

He put his arm around her as they walked to Gene's room. When they entered his room, Mike and John were already there. The first thing Carol noticed was that Gene's feeding tube had been removed.

Carol hugged Gene and kissed him on the cheek. "I just met Phillip. You have a very nice boss."

Phillip moved close to Gene and took hold of his hand. "You get well and back to work soon. I miss you, and I need you. We all do."

"These are Gene's friends, John and Mike," said Carol.

Phillip shook hands with both of them.

After Phillip left, it was very quiet in the room. They liked it best when it was just the four of them, for it was only then that Gene would try to speak. It was extremely difficult for him, and his voice was barely audible.

"Phillip is loud but nice," said Gene.

"It looks like you have a good boss," said Mike.

Gene tried to say something but couldn't get it out. He couldn't lift his hands to wipe his tears, and he became frustrated. Carol took his glasses off and cleaned them and dried is cheeks as John massaged one leg and Mike massaged the other.

They all knew how hard everything was for Gene, and they wanted to help him in any way they could, and the three of them would do just that. Never before had their dear friend asked for anything from them. He was their hero and the strongest of them all, and now he needed almost everything done for him

Gene Meets Greg;
Past Meets Present

During the next few weeks, Carol traveled back and forth several times between Springfield and Chicago. She enjoyed being alone with her thoughts on the four-hour drive. Stella had told Carol and Greg that if they ever needed her to care for the children, to just call and she would come.

There was talk of moving Gene to a rehabilitation facility in the near future, but since the third stroke had caused so much damage, Dr. Landis thought he needed a little more time in the hospital.

Carol told Gene that Greg wanted to meet him, and Gene had agreed to it, so on a warm summer day, Carol and Greg drove to Chicago. Mike and John would also be there. Carol was a little worried because Gene was only comfortable trying to speak in front of his three friends and Dr. Landis. He also felt somewhat comfortable with Brian and Holly. Carol was the only one who could really understand him completely.

When Carol and Greg entered Gene's hospital room, Mike and John were already there.

Carol said, "John, I know you and Greg have met."

John smiled and shook hands with Greg. "Greg, this is Mike."

They shook hands, but neither Greg nor Mike smiled. Then it was Gene's turn.

"Greg, this is Gene."

Gene lifted his left hand as much as he could, and Greg took hold of his hand and said, "I'm glad to meet you, Gene."

Gene simply nodded. Greg was just five feet eight inches and small framed. The size of the three guys was somewhat overpowering. He had met John before and knew he was quite tall, and although somewhat muscular, he was much slimmer than the other two. Gene and Mike were both taller than John and, by their builds, both obvious football and basketball players. Even though Gene was in a wheelchair, his broad shoulders and muscular arms and legs had not yet lost their tone.

It was somewhat intimidating to Greg, but then Gene spoke in a halting voice, very quiet and difficult to understand. "Thank you for coming, Greg. I'm sorry that I can't talk better. It's still a little hard for me."

"You're doing fine." Greg didn't normally feel compassion, but he did that day for the once strong athlete.

They were going to the cafeteria for lunch since it was the middle of the afternoon and it wouldn't be crowded. Gene still had the brace on his neck and a small pillow at the back of his head. There was a blanket over his legs and a brace on his right leg and his arms and hands rested on the padded arms of the wheelchair. Mike pushed Gene's wheelchair, followed by John, Carol, and Greg. Even though John used a cane, he still needed to hold on to Carol's arm occasionally, but he hesitated to do so in front of Greg.

In her gentle voice, Carol took John's arm and said to him, "It's all right, John. Greg doesn't mind."

John held on to Carol's arm as they walked to the cafeteria.

Mike arranged the seating in the cafeteria. Gene was between Carol and Mike on one side of the table with John and Greg on the other side. Greg was not prepared for what came next. Carol cut Gene's food into very small bites and mashed it, and she proceeded to feed him very slowly. When Carol stopped to take a bite of her own food, Mike would step right in to feed Gene. Greg had never been around anyone who had a stroke before, and he was surprised at how helpless Gene actually was.

In the cafeteria that day, Dr. Landis stopped by to talk to them and as always concentrated on how Gene was doing. Several nurses who had been with Gene at one time or another, other doctors, and hospital employees from the security and housekeeping departments also spoke and talked to Gene and his group of friends.

Greg was still somewhat intimidated especially by Gene, although he didn't really understand why. Gene was a sad, broken man who couldn't do anything for himself, and yet even in his present condition, people were drawn to him. Everyone seemed to love him and sincerely care about helping him, including Greg's own wife.

When they got back to the room, Gene tried so hard to talk to Greg, but the words wouldn't come. He was frustrated, but as usual Carol knew how to help him. She removed his glasses and took a cool washcloth and wiped his eyes as Mike uncovered his leg and gently massaged it. Carol adjusted the pillow behind his head and combed his hair.

John touched Greg's arm. "I talk to him a lot and help him with his speech. I'm not able to do some of the physical things that Carol or Mike can do for him."

"I'm sure you do all you can for him," replied Greg.

They would stay two more days before they returned to Springfield. Brian and Holly had dinner with them the next day. They helped with Gene also, especially stepping in when Carol or Mike and John were not there.

It was always extremely hard for Carol to say goodbye to Gene, and in turn, Gene hated to see her go.

As they pulled onto the interstate heading home, Carol asked Greg, "So now you have met Gene. What do you think of him?"

"He is a good man, probably even a great man. People love him, and they are drawn to him. He needs you so much, possibly more than he needs anyone else. The chemistry between the two of you is undeniable, but I'm sure you know that. Go to him whenever you want to. You are in all probability the only one who can make him well," said Greg.

"That is the most profound thing you have ever said to me," said Carol.

"Without taking away from what I just said, Gene loves you with every ounce of life that is left in him," said Greg. "But you already know that too, don't you?"

Carol paused before she replied. "I suppose. Gene is not like anyone else I have ever known. He has always been so strong and brave, and yet there is another side of him that is quiet and shy and frightened. It is like he is two different people. He is so sensitive and dependent now. It hurts my heart. I used to wonder why things are always so difficult for really good people like John and now Gene. I think I know the answer, but it is not really important. All I know is that he makes me a better person."

CHAPTER

THE ROAD BACK

One month later Gene was transferred to a rehabilitation facility. Carol was there to help with a smooth transition. John and Mike would arrive the next day.

His room was very pleasant and, of course, looked more like home than the hospital. Gene had showed great improvement. His speech, although somewhat slow and quiet, was very clear. Occasionally, he had difficulty with a specific word, but he never gave up. His hands seldom shook, and he had regained most of the strength in both arms and hands. The severe headaches had subsided to a degree, but his eyesight had not improved. He would still be using a wheelchair. His right leg seemed to have suffered most from the strokes. Dr. Landis felt that because he was young and strong, he would walk again.

Gene still tired easily and the move from the hospital to the rehabilitation facility had been overwhelming for him. He was resting in his new bed with a new view from his window and Carol sitting close to him. He took hold of her hand. "Do you have any idea how grateful I am to you for all you have done for me?"

"I know, Gene. There's nothing I wouldn't do for you. I would go to the ends of the earth to help you," said Carol quietly. "John, Mike, and I tried to do the same for you that you and I did for John so many years ago."

"The doctors tell me that it was all you, that you are the one who saved me and made me well, or at least almost well," said Gene.

Carol kissed his hand, and he continued, "You know, when I first moved to Chicago, I just thought it was important to make a lot of money and have a prestigious career, but I don't care about that now."

"What do you care about now, Gene?" asked Carol.

"I just want to see you happy. I'm glad I met Greg, but I felt he was just being nice to me because I was so helpless and ill, and he felt sorry for me. You just deserve so much more. You should be treated like a queen. Remember when we were king and queen. We didn't even want that honor, especially you," said Gene.

"That was your honor, not mine," said Carol.

"They voted for us because they liked us together," said Gene. "Why did you marry Greg?"

"We had fun at first, trips, parties. We had a few good years," said Carol.

"If we would have married, I would have treated you so good. I would have never hurt you or let anyone else hurt you," said Gene.

"Did we come close to getting married, Gene? Why didn't it ever happen?" asked Carol.

"We couldn't do it because of John and Mike. A part of me wanted you to be with John. I would never have stood in the way of the two of you. And Mike was my best friend," said Gene. "What I hate more than anything is the thought of Greg being unkind to you. In all the years we have known one another, do you realize we have never argued about anything and we have never said an unkind word to one another?"

"Yes, my dear sweet Gene, we have always treated one another with respect and the greatest kindness the world has ever known. That's what we were all about, and I will remember that forever. I have never known anyone else to equal you," said Carol.

"Nor I you," said Gene.

Gene's road back to good health was long and tedious. He had good days and bad days. Carol, Mike, and John were with him as much as they could be. No matter what they went through, so long as they stayed together, they would be all right. It was spring when Gene's strokes happened, and now it was summer. They were allowed to take Gene on short outings. These times provided some of the most significance togetherness they were ever to experience. They were older now, and their conversations were deeper and more stimulating. The one subject they did not touch on was that they knew, sooner than they really wanted, they would all have to go back to their lives. But the good side of that would be that Gene was well.

One afternoon they were sitting in Gene's living room at his apartment. Gene was still using the wheelchair. Carol was sitting between John and Mike on the sofa.

"You healed better and quicker than me, John," said Gene.

"Probably because I've had so much practice," answered John.

Carol moved to sit on the floor in front of Gene and began massaging his legs. Gene put his hands on her shoulders. "You're always working, doing something for me."

Carol rested her head on his lap. "I can't help myself. I just want you to be well and strong again."

"All three of you do so much for me without any pay. You are giving all your time to help me," said Gene.

"My dad has taken care of everything as far as travel is concerned for the three of us," said Mike. "If any of the four of us would ever have a money problem, my dad would take care of it. He wanted me to tell you guys that."

"But he has already done so much for me. I'm not sure I'm worth it," said John.

"I can assure you that he feels you are worth it and so much more. I think he loves the three of you more than he ever loved his own children. John, I think you are his reason for living. And, Gene, I have never seen him so deeply concerned about anyone as he has been about you these last few months. As for you, my sweet Carol, I think you know how he feels about you."

"You know, just yesterday, one of the nurses who works with Gene a lot told me she had never seen anyone like us, how close we are and how we treat one another," said John.

Carol buried her face in Gene's lap. She was crying. Gene kissed the top of her head.

"We've made her cry. I hate it when we or anybody else makes Carol cry," said Mike as he went to put his arms around her.

GENE GOES HOME AND BACK TO WORK

In early August, Gene went home. He had graduated to a walker and occasionally a cane, but this was at home. He didn't know yet how things would be at work. He would still use the wheelchair for long distances, but each day he seemed to be improving.

Carol, Mike, and John were all there for Gene the day he went home. His apartment was on the first floor, which was good, but there were a few changes that needed to be made so it would be more accessible for him, and his friends were going to take care of this for him. They helped Gene pack and stayed by his side as he said good-bye to all those who had helped him so much at the rehabilitation facility.

Gene had traded his small car for a van. Mike picked them up in Gene's new van.

"I like your van, Gene. It will make things easier for you."

"I wish I could drive it," said Gene.

"Patrick agreed to drive you to work in it until you are ready to drive," said Mike.

"Because of my eyesight, I may never be able to drive it," said Gene. "Thanks, Mike. I appreciate you talking to Patrick. You know something, John. I have always admired you so much. Now I feel like I'm walking in your shoes."

"Yes, but you're going to get well. I'll probably just get worse," said John.

"I don't know. I don't think my leg will ever be completely normal. They have already told me that my eyesight won't improve. Maybe stronger glasses, but I don't know how much stronger they can be. I just hope I can do my job," said Gene.

"Sometimes I just wish we could all be together again like we were in the house on Lansing Street," said John.

"Well, John, I guess we are on the same page, because I would like that too," said Gene.

"You guys do know that in all reality that is not going to happen, don't you?" asked Mike.

"We know. I just liked those years more than I ever expected to. We were never alone, and someone always had your back," said Gene.

"That was a good house, a really good house. I picked out a great house much better than I picked out a husband," said Carol.

"You don't usually make a joke, Carol. That was kind of funny," said John. "Why isn't anybody laughing?"

"It wasn't funny, John. She was just saying the truth," said Gene. Carol put her arms around Gene and buried her face in his hair.

"Is anyone really happy? I'm dating a nice girl, but I'm not happy. I don't know what's the matter with me," said Mike.

"I'm not particularly happy for obvious reasons. Just look at me. I have no strength at all. I hate this wheelchair. Everyone stares at me," said Gene.

"I love my daughter and the boys, and I'm married, but I have never felt so alone in my whole life. And I feel like I've lost all three of you," said Carol.

"Do you want to hear something really funny?" asked John.

"I think right now we would all welcome something funny," said Gene.

"I would like to go back to California and live with Jeremy. I always really liked him, but then I thought he is gay and I'm not, and I knew it wouldn't work. How come no one is laughing?" asked John.

"You know, Gene and I have always had a dark sense of humor. Right now, I feel more like crying than laughing," said Carol.

There was a long silence, and then Gene said, "I'm going to the office if someone will drive me. Would you drive me, Carol? I think Phillip would like to see you."

"It's strange you said that," said Carol. "I've been wanting to talk to him."

When Carol took Gene to his office the next morning. Mike and John stayed at the apartment to work on some projects to make things more accessible for Gene.

Carol parked in a lot in downtown Chicago as close to Gene's office as she could get. "I'm not going to be able to do this. There is no way I can walk that far," said Gene.

"You are going to have to use the wheelchair." Carol hugged and kissed Gene. "I'm so sorry. I know you don't want to, but there is no other way. They all love you there. It will be all right." Carol got the wheelchair out of the van and then helped Gene.

"I'm not so good, Carol. I can't walk, and I can't see. How am I ever going to be able to work?" Gene's hands were trembling again.

"This is just your first day, Gene. Let's at least go talk to Phillip. He is expecting us," said Carol.

Gene's office was on the thirty-seventh floor. As they entered the office, everyone warmly greeted Gene. His personal office was large and in the southwest corner of the building with a great view of the Chicago skyline. Phillip was glad to see them. They helped Gene get out of the wheelchair and sit at his desk. It was more difficult than he had ever imagined it being. The bright lights in the office were bothering his eyes, and he was unable to read the papers on his desk.

Phillip was reassuring. "It's just your first day, Gene. Things will get better."

"I know. I'll try to do my best," said Gene.

"Do you mind if I steal Carol from you for a few minutes?" asked Phillip.

"That's fine," said Gene.

"Why don't we just stay here and talk. I have no secrets from Gene," said Carol.

"I don't normally talk with a possible prospective employee in front of an actual employee, but in this case, I'll make an exception," Phillip smiled.

Carol shook hands with Phillip. "Thank you. There is nothing about Gene and I that has ever followed the norm."

"All right, Carol. The stage is yours," said Phillip.

"Let's pretend that I'm a prospective employee and this is the very first time I have met with you. I would like to take the tests and be interviewed as you would someone off the street," said Carol.

"Fair enough, but you come to me highly recommended by Gene," said Phillip.

"I know, and I thank you for that, Gene, but I'm not so sure of myself. I also don't believe this is something I can do right now but possibly in the future," said Carol. "I'll take the tests now if that is all right with you and also with you, Gene. Are you feeling all right?"

"I'm fine. The hardest part was getting here. Besides, I need to go through some of this correspondence," said Gene.

Phillip took Carol to a conference room and got her started on the test and the written interview. "I'll be back for the oral part in a while," said Phillip.

As Phillip went back to Gene's office, he realized how fond he was of Gene and this lovely young woman and, like Carol, he didn't want to leave Gene alone.

As Carol took the test as well as the essay part, which consisted of the actual preparing of an advertisement, Phillip slowly and methodically helped Gene in his office. He could tell how hard it was for Gene, but Phillip was a good man. He was not ruthless and cruel like some in his field, and he was determined that things were going to work out for Gene.

"Well, Gene, it's time for Carol's oral testing. I'll be back soon," said Phillip. "Do you remember Nick Jennison? He will assist me with her testing."

"Yes, I remember him. He helped test me," said Gene.

When Phillip entered the conference room, Nick was already there. He was telling Carol that they would give her the results tomorrow.

"Well, Carol, I see you have met Nick," said Phillip.

"Yes. He has been very kind," said Carol.

Nick smiled. "This part of the interview will only take about thirty minutes, but it is quite important. Actually, it is the determining factor."

Phillip and Nick took turns asking questions. Although the questions were brief, the answers needed to be considerably more involved and detailed. There was no hesitation on Carol's part. She was very vocal and knowledgeable. She answered everything quickly and she hoped to their satisfaction.

As the testing was completed, they both thanked her.

"I know you need to get back to Gene. We will see you tomorrow with the results," Phillip paused. "Do you think Gene will come back tomorrow?"

"Yes, he will be here," answered Carol.

As Carol walked back to Gene's office, she noticed that everyone seemed friendly to her. Gene was still at his desk looking somewhat overwhelmed. "I'm glad you are back. I missed you. How did it go?"

"I think it went pretty well. It was not easy but interesting," said Carol. "Are you all right? How are your eyes?"

Gene shook his head and turned to look out the window. Carol stood behind him and put her arms around him. "Some things I can read if the print is large enough, but so much I can't even see. It's not going to get better, is it?"

"I don't know. I really don't know," said Carol. Although she wanted to, she could not take the chance of giving him false hope.

The door was open a crack. Phillip came into the office. Gene hurriedly wiped his eyes. He didn't want Phillip to see him crying. He didn't turn around."

"You have both worked hard today. Why don't you go home and get some rest and come back tomorrow."

"We will. Thank you for everything, Phillip. You have been very kind to us today," said Carol. "Let's go home." Carol helped Gene to the wheelchair.

"Give me just a minute before we go by all the people," said Gene.

"Take as long as you want." Carol walked over and looked out the window. "Chicago is a big city, much bigger than Kansas City. So many buildings and so many people."

"I can't see them. Not just the people, but I can't even see the buildings," said Gene.

"I know, Gene. I know you can't," said Carol.

When they arrived at Gene's apartment, they could see that Mike and John had done a lot of work. There were grab bars in the bathroom and handrails on the stairs going in from the garage. There was also a ramp in the garage going up to the kitchen.

Mike and John didn't ask how the day went. They could tell by Gene's face.

Mike said, "Now before you say anything, we don't think you are going to need the ramp or anything else for very long, but my dad wanted you to have them while you need them. He's paying for everything."

"Thanks to all of you for everything you have done for me, and also thank your dad," said Gene.

"Dad wants to come visit you. Is that all right with you?" asked Mike.

"Sure. Your dad has always been so good to us," said Gene.

"You know, we are three guys and one girl like my family was. I think John replaced Danny. Dad has helped John a lot because he feels bad about his failures with Danny. Carol replaced Cathy. He has tried to help Carol when she would let him. He was always so impatient with Cathy. And you, Gene, have replaced my older brother, Ryan. He treated Ryan so badly at one time," said Mike.

"We are the same age, but you consider me an older brother?" Gene tried to smile a little, but he couldn't.

"Well, I'm just trying to say that we have sort of replaced the original family," said Mike.

"I know what you mean," said Gene.

There were a lot of things that John wanted to say to Gene that day. He hugged him and knew he didn't need to say anything because Gene knew that John more than anyone else could feel his pain and knew how discouraged he felt.

For that matter, they all felt his pain that day. Carol hoped that tomorrow things would be better at the office, but she didn't really feel that they would be. She knew it was going to take time, and although Gene had many good qualities, patience was not one of them.

Mike had tried to the best of his ability to help as did John, but they didn't feel that what they had done was enough.

"I'm really tired. I think I'll go to bed," said Gene quietly.

That night, they all went to the bedroom with him and helped him. He had been doing almost everything for himself but not that night. Mike and John said good night and went to their room.

Carol stayed with Gene and spoke to him in a soft quiet voice, "I love you, Gene, so very much. I appreciate everything you have done for me over the years. I'm going to make tomorrow better for you. Somehow I'm going to try to make it a really good day."

"I like for you to talk to me. It always makes me feel better. I love your voice. I can always feel the love and caring in it. No one except you has ever affected me that way." Gene closed his eyes, but he didn't let go of her hand.

She hadn't done it for a long time, but that night she nestled in the bend of his arm with her head resting ever so gently on his chest. She had to be careful not to hurt him. She would stay by him all night.

THE SECOND DAY

On the second day of Gene's return to work, everything seemed to go a little smoother, probably simply because they had been through it before. Gene's office was a little neater than the day before. The thought briefly went through Carol's mind that just maybe today would be better.

They had only been in the office for a few minutes when Phillip knocked on the door followed by Nick Jennison. "You look good today, Gene. You look well rested and a little happier," said Phillip.

"Thanks to Carol." Gene took hold of Carol's hand, and she put her arm around him.

"And this young lady standing by your side is who we want to talk about right now," said Phillip. "You said that you and Gene have no secrets, so I assume it is all right if we give you the results of your testing now."

"Please do. We are anxious to hear the results," said Gene.

"All of the tests we give are different. Yours was somewhat more difficult because of what we felt your abilities were, and you did not disappoint us. On all three sections of the testing and interviewing, your scores were the highest we have ever recorded. Whether you have a particular gift for the advertising industry, or you are just simply extremely smart, we can't be sure, but it doesn't really matter. You have surpassed everyone," said Phillip.

Nick added, "Your oral test was so impressive that I was in awe of you. I would not be able to do that well."

Gene rarely, if ever, smiled, but that day as he looked at Carol, there was a slight smile as he said, "Congratulations, Carol. I am so proud of you, but not at all surprised."

"Did you like the advertisement I wrote?" asked Carol.

"*Spectacular* is how I would describe it. We want to use it. It will represent big money," said Phillip.

"You have my permission to use it, but I am giving it and all the proceeds to Gene. I have already prepared a signed release form. I knew you would like it and want to use it." Carol reached into her purse and pulled out a signed release form showing her release entirely to Gene.

Phillip read it and handed it to Nick. Gene was without words, but nothing Carol did ever really surprised him.

Phillip said, "All I can say is, I don't know how you ever let this amazing woman standing beside you ever marry someone else. You told me once that you loved her since you were sixteen. You don't have to respond to that. I'm sure you both had your reasons. Do you accept her gift?"

"Yes, I accept it. Thank you, Carol. You never cease to surprise and amaze me," said Gene.

Phillip and Nick both shook hands with Gene and Carol and quietly left Gene's office.

Gene got up out of the wheelchair, and using his cane and holding on to Carol's arm, they walked close to the window.

Carol asked, "Are the buildings any clearer today?"

"No, I still can't focus clearly on them, but I can see you. You are always clear to me. Even when we are not together, I can see you and I always will. No matter where we go or how far apart we are, you will always be beside me," said Gene.

Nothing had changed and yet everything had changed. Gene was the kindest man Carol had ever known, and even though their destiny was to lead separate lives, he was the love of her life as she was his.

Later that day, when Carol approached Phillip about a more accessible parking place for Gene, he had already thought about it.

"Gene will have a parking place in the second-floor inside parking garage, the closest one to the door entering the building."

"Thank you so much, Phillip. That will help him a lot. Now I would like to pay for it," said Carol.

He took both of her hands in his. "There is no charge. It is my gift to Gene. He is a valuable employee, and I want him back with us. I don't want him to become discouraged and quit. I will do all I can to help him."

"Your generosity and kindness are appreciated by both of us," said Carol.

Carol also wanted to make sure Gene had a handicapped license plate. She knew that Gene didn't want this and also that he would need to accompany her to the office to obtain it. He did agree to go with her. They were very kind to Gene and without hesitation gave him a permanent handicapped license plate. They told him that when he recovered, he could turn it in for a regular license plate. His hand was trembling as he signed the documents in front of him. No one questioned him at all. The severity of his handicap was very evident, and Carol was grateful for the consideration they showed him.

There were two problems solved and one to go, the most difficult one. Carol had asked Dr. Landis to accompany her and Gene to the best optometrist in Chicago. His name was Dr. Charles Sanders, and Dr. Landis had known him for several years. When Carol and Gene met Dr. Sanders, it was reminiscent of the good doctor Alan had taken John to in Dallas, Dr. Wilson, so many years ago.

"It is good to see you, Dr. Sanders. This is my patient, Gene, and his good friend Carol. Gene had two TIAs, which were more serious than normal. They were followed by a major stroke, which took quite a toll on his eyesight. He also has severe headaches and has for a long time," said Dr. Landis.

As Dr. Sanders began examining Gene's eyes, he spoke directly to Gene, "Your eyes are very light. Have you ever been examined for retinitis pigmentosa?"

"I've had many eye exams. They just keep making my glasses stronger. I have a friend who has retinitis pigmentosa. He has had several operations," said Gene.

"It may not have presented before," Dr. Sanders paused. "You have probably always had poor eyesight and bad headaches. Is that correct?"

"Yes, I would get new glasses, and they wouldn't help much," said Gene.

"The good news is that I think we can help you, and I know you've heard this before, with stronger glasses, but we need to be sure we have the correct prescription. Possibly in the past it hasn't been correct. There is also a surgery that you may be a candidate for in the future, but I will not subject you to that right now. You have been through a lot," said Dr. Sanders.

"Thank you so much, Dr. Sanders," said Gene.

As Gene and Dr. Landis went to the front desk to make a future appointment, Carol stopped to thank Dr. Sanders. "Thank you for being so kind and helpful to Gene. He is very important to me, as is his eyesight," said Carol.

"I can tell that, and I am sure you are equally important to him," said Dr. Sanders.

Within a short while, Gene got his new glasses. They were much stronger and the lenses considerably thicker than ever before, but Gene didn't care because he could see somewhat better. The results of the test showed that he did not have retinitis pigmentosa.

Carol would be going home in two days, as would Mike and John. She wanted to talk to Patrick, Gene's friend, coworker, and neighbor before she left. She knocked on his office door.

"Come in," said Patrick.

"Hello, Patrick. I'm Gene's friend, Carol. I wanted to talk to you before I leave."

"I've been expecting you," said Patrick.

Carol was nervous although she didn't really know why. She was already crying, and she hadn't wanted to. "I'm sorry, Patrick. I'm leaving soon, and I hate to."

He sat by her and put his arm around her. "It's all right. I understand. You care so much about Gene, and you are afraid to leave him. I would be too." Patrick's voice showed deep concern.

"I haven't cried much during this whole ordeal, but all of a sudden it is as though I can't control it," said Carol.

"I'll tell you a little about me. Maybe that will help," Patrick's voice was very calm and reassuring. "I came to work here in Chicago from a small town in Iowa. I had heard how cutthroat and tough the advertising business was. But our boss, Phillip York, seemed to be a pretty nice man, and then he introduced me to Gene. We worked together on a few campaigns. Gene is probably the kindest man I have ever met, and he helped me so much in the beginning. I wouldn't have survived without him. He got things accomplished in a kind, gentle way while others had to be cruel and brutal to get things done. I don't know how he did it, but I admire him so very much, and he is truly an inspiration to me, even more so now after all he has been through."

"I'm so glad to hear you say that. I was so troubled at one time in my life many years ago, and Gene brought me back and made me feel my life was worth living. It was all him, no one else. He was so popular in school and always so strong. He was always a leader, class president, graduation speaker, and so smart, and he was a great quarterback and basketball player. He was never comfortable with all the attention and popularity, and he was somewhat shy. I met Gene when we were eight. I have always loved and worried about him," said Carol.

"So the two of you have always been together?" asked Patrick.

"Since we were eight, except for the last few years," said Carol.

"Are you engaged?" asked Patrick.

"No. I'm married and have three children. My husband allowed me to help Gene. It was something that I needed to do."

"I had no idea. I thought you two were in love," said Patrick.

"I love Gene more than life itself. I want only good things for him," said Carol. "He is so honest and good, and I just want so much for him to find lasting happiness."

"I know Gene was married and he has two children, but he doesn't talk much about himself," said Patrick.

"He loves his little children very much," Carol paused. "He is really very quiet, and he holds a lot inside. It is hard for him to open up and show his feelings. I don't want him to ever be hurt. Please, Patrick, don't let anyone ever hurt him."

"I'll try, Carol. I promise you, I will try," said Patrick.

"Gene is so important to me," said Carol.

"I know he is," said Patrick. "But please remember, this is a tough business, and people aren't always kind."

AN EVENING OUT

That evening they were all going out to dinner at one of Gene's favorite Chicago restaurants. It would be the four of them, plus Alan McVary, who had just arrived in Chicago. He would stay with Gene for a few weeks. He would help Gene at home while Patrick would take him to and from work as well as help him when he was at work. Patrick was also invited, as were Phillip York and Nick Jennison.

That particular day had been one of Gene's bad days. His leg had given out as he was going to a meeting earlier in the day. Patrick was walking beside him and was able to stop his fall. He was also having more weakness in his right arm than he had been experiencing.

Gene was using the wheelchair that night. In fact, he had been using it more than he thought he would. Carol had put a small pillow under his right arm as she had done in the past when it was bothering him.

But surprising as it may seem, there was someone else who seemed to be feeling worse than Gene that night, and that person was John. John was sitting directly across from Gene, and all of a sudden, out of nowhere, he just started crying. That evening they had their regular waitress. She was a pretty young woman and had always been especially attentive to John. Her name was Sandy.

"Are you all right? Is there anything I can do for you?" asked Sandy.

"I just can't stop crying. I feel so bad for what has happened to Gene. I know how he feels because I've felt it too. I hate so much seeing him going through it," said John through his tears.

Gene put his hand on John's hand. "Don't cry for me, John. I'll be all right. I've just had a hard day today," said Gene quietly.

Sandy brought back a cool cloth for John and a large glass of water. She wiped and dried his cheeks and put his glasses back on him. She noticed that he was trembling, so she held the glass as he took a drink of water. "It's not much, but I just wanted to help you a little."

Carol and Mike's eyes met. The both felt it was so reminiscent of the way Holly and Brian had treated John at the airport that fateful day. Everyone always loved John and simply wanted to help him.

Mike knew that Carol was on the verge of tears. More than anything, he hated to see Carol cry, but Patrick saved them.

Although Patrick was sitting at the other end of the table and hadn't heard all that was going on, he pulled up a chair at the end of the table between John and Gene and spoke to them reassuringly, "I know it has been a hard time for all of you, but it is going to get better. I'm going to take good care of Gene along with Alan. Not every day will be perfect, but we will make it. And we will be on his side all the way. We will protect him and never let anyone hurt him. I promise you that."

Patrick hugged both John and Gene that evening. When the food came, he stayed right between them. He knew that they might need some help. And as he saw Carol reach out to help Gene, he did the same for John.

There were eight really good people having dinner together that night. Their primary goal was to protect, especially Gene and John, from bad things and bad people that seem to always invade the lives of good people like themselves. But they knew this could not always be done.

As Mike studied his group of friends that night, he knew he wouldn't be able to be there for all of them. The one he wanted to protect the most was still Carol, and it always had been. But she would be the hardest for him to protect because she was married, and he didn't want to interfere. He just wished that things had turned out differently for all of them. He could still see them as they were sitting around the pool at his house and at Fairyland Park and in California. These were very brief moments in their lives, but they were the good times, the times he would always remember.

As they got up to leave, Patrick and Alan were assisting John when Sandy handed John a small bag and said, "It's just a piece of cheesecake. You always used to like it when you came here. I know you have had a hard time tonight, but maybe you can enjoy it later."

"Thank you, Sandy," said John quietly.

Mike pushed Gene's wheelchair as Carol walked beside them. She could tell how tired Gene was, and as he took off his glasses, she knew he had a headache. As soon as they got home, Carol knew what to do to relieve his headache.

That night, for very obvious reasons, Alan left Sandy a $500 tip. The $500 meant nothing to him. He knew it would mean a lot to her.

At Gene's apartment, Carol sat on the sofa in his room and put a small pillow on her lap. Gene sat by her and laid his head gently on the pillow as he had done many times before. She slowly and methodically massaged certain areas of his head. She knew where to touch to make him feel better.

"Do you want me to take your glasses off?" asked Carol.

"Not yet. I want to see you clearly." Gene looked at his trembling right hand. "I wish I could stop shaking."

As Carol put her hand on his, it immediately stopped shaking.

Gene said quietly, "I've always wondered how you make that happen. It's like magic."

"No, it's not magic. It is just love," said Carol.

"You know how I hate to see you, for that matter Mike and John too, leave tomorrow, don't you?" asked Gene.

"I know. I hate to leave," said Carol.

"What will you do?" asked Gene.

"I'll go back to work. I'll try to be a better mother to my children. And I'll try to salvage what is left of my poor, sad marriage," said Carol.

"I'm grateful to Greg that he let you spend time with me. I don't know what I would have done without you," said Gene.

"I often wonder why he did that. I think he actually liked you. But you know, everyone has always liked you and John. Do you remember how it was in high school?" asked Carol.

"All that attention. I was always so uncomfortable," said Gene.

"You know, while Greg talked to you and John, he hardly spoke to Mike," said Carol.

"You realize none of us could ever stand to see you hurt. But Mike was very vocal about it. If anyone ever made you cry, he simply couldn't stand it. He could see through Greg. He didn't trust him. I'm not sure I do either, but he is your husband," said Gene.

"What the four of us had was something very special. Not many people will ever have what we had," said Carol.

"Prom, graduation, California, and the house on Lansing Street were all very special to us. Even something as simple as Fairyland Park was special. A lady came up to me that day at Fairyland and asked me if we were all family. She said she had noticed us off and on all that day and was impressed by how kind and caring we were toward one another." A single tear ran down Gene's cheek.

"That's just the way we were. We never hurt or were mean to one another. We just loved one another so much. We sincerely wanted what was best for each of us," Carol paused. "That simple day at Fairyland showed how much we cared. We were so totally unselfish and uninhibited. Our only agenda was to take care of and help each other."

DEVASTATING SETBACK

Within a short while, Phillip York would take early retirement and resign his position at the advertising agency where Gene worked. Five other employees immediately quit, knowing they would not make the cut with the new head of the agency, George Meyer. George was fifty-six and well-known in the Chicago advertising world as ruthless and cutthroat. Although he didn't have a reputation for being nice, he did have several high-power, strong executives that he would be bringing with him. They had been working for him since the beginning of their careers, and he had trained them well and molded them into exactly the type men he wanted them to be.

Shortly before George's arrival, Nick Jennison went to Gene's office to talk with him.

"Come in and sit down," said Gene.

Nick spoke somewhat hesitantly, "Do you know much about our new boss?"

"Not really, but I hope you are going to tell me right now," said Gene.

"Of course, every man must make his own decision, but I haven't heard many, if any, good things about him," said Nick. "I don't think I'm the type he wants. Although not right away, I will probably be leaving soon."

"Nor am I the type he wants," said Gene. "But jobs are difficult for someone like me to get. I think I'll try to weather the storm. I believe Patrick is going to stay, or at least I hope so."

"Good luck to you, Gene, in the meeting this week. I hope we will continue to work together," said Nick.

"I need to ask you one thing before you leave, Nick. When Carol took the tests, you and Phillip said she had the highest score ever recorded. Were my scores even in the ballpark?' asked Gene.

"I assure you that your scores were excellent," said Nick.

"But they probably won't help much with George Meyer, right?" asked Gene.

"He's looking for the macho-man type, really tough, hard-core guys who will do anything to get ahead. I guess we will find out what happens in the meeting tomorrow morning." With this Nick left.

For the meeting the following morning, Gene's presentation was carefully and methodically prepared. His knowledge was extensive and thorough and without flaw if they chose to ask questions.

As Patrick drove Gene to work the following morning, Gene asked him, "Will you be in the meeting this morning, Patrick?"

"Not today. I'll be in the second meeting tomorrow. You're going to be in the meeting with the high-rollers today. You'll have all the fair-haired boys he brought with him from the other agency," said Patrick.

"I'm going to have to use the wheelchair to get there. Do you mind taking me?" asked Gene.

"Don't worry, Gene. I'll get you there," answered Patrick.

"It's probably a mistake. But because of the distance and the way I feel today, I know I can't make it on my own. My hand is shaking, and I know that will be very noticeable to them. I hope if I fail, it doesn't affect you," said Gene.

"Gene, you are my friend. I wouldn't be where I am today without you. You trained me in the very beginning. I don't like these new people. I am probably one who will be cut, but if I am, it's not your fault. I've enjoyed every minute that we have worked together." Patrick shook Gene's left hand. "Even if I do leave, I will always help you. That's a promise I made to Carol."

After a brief stop in Gene's office, Patrick pushed Gene's wheelchair to the conference room where George Meyer and his selected group of colleagues were already waiting. There would be about twenty-five employees in each group.

"Well, hello, Gene," said George. "You are early. That is a good quality. Since they have ranked you as one of their top employees, I think you should go first."

"I'll be happy to go first."

Gene knew it would be awhile before the meeting began so he sat alone and went over his notes. No one else spoke to him or was friendly toward him. Gene was sweating, his heart was beating fast, and his right hand was shaking almost out of control. He hadn't expected to be this nervous, but he was, and there was nothing he could do about it.

When the meeting finally started, after a few formalities, Gene was called upon for his presentation. As he carefully and slowly walked to the podium, John's speech that he had given twenty years ago at graduation came to mind, but it left as he turned to look at the faces before him. The faces had been friendly twenty years ago; today they were not. The first part of the presentation went well, but he noticed that each time he raised his hand to write on the board with the chalk, his hand was noticeably shaking. He couldn't stop it. And then he dropped the piece of chalk. On any other day with normal people who weren't out to destroy him as well as his career, someone would have simply handed him a piece of chalk but not today. He had to turn and move to his right to get a piece from the other board. Whether his leg gave out or he tripped on the edge of the board would never be known, but it didn't really matter.

Gene basically fell on his face, cutting his cheek on the board on the way down. His glasses fell off and landed just out of his reach. Several in the group started to help him but were stopped in their tracks by George Meyer.

"You can get up by yourself, Gene. Show us what you are made of. Get up. You can do it on your own."

Gene tried as hard as he could, but he could not get up. George was screaming his orders now.

"You don't need any help. You have to get up now. Prove to me that you are man enough to do it."

But he still couldn't. His leg and ankle were twisted and hurting terribly, but he didn't want them to know, not just yet anyway. He managed to get a handkerchief from his pocket to hold over his bleeding cheek.

George continued to be loud, heartless, and cruel in his encouragement—or to be more fair, in his abuse—to make Gene get up. He would later try to justify his actions by saying he didn't think Gene could be hurt by simply falling as he was standing giving a presentation, but the amount of blood pouring from his cheek should have been evidence in itself. Gene was on a blood thinner, and his leg was not strong enough for him to be standing for a long period of time.

George was now screaming, "You have to prove to me that you are not completely useless to this company. Get up now."

"I'm sorry, I can't do it. Would someone please hand me my glasses?" asked Gene.

Just as George's foot started to push Gene's glasses further away, a hand reached down to pick them up. It was Nick Jennison's hand.

Nick said, "I'm going to help Gene. I'm in a different category from the others here. Besides, my job doesn't really matter. You know that Gene just had a major stroke. He can't get up without help."

Nick put Gene's glasses on him and tried to help him up, but Gene was much bigger than Nick. Just then the door opened, and Patrick came in. Patrick and Nick had Gene in the wheelchair within a few seconds.

"Well, I see the housemaid has come to save the day," said George sarcastically.

"My friend needs help, and I'm here to see that he gets it," said Patrick.

As they started pushing Gene out of the room, he said quietly, "Stop for just a minute please. I'm sorry for ruining the meeting. It was no one's fault but mine. Please don't blame Patrick and Nick for my failure." Gene couldn't say anything else. Patrick and Nick took him back to his office.

"Will you be all right, Gene? I'm going back to see what happens in the meeting," said Nick.

"Thank you for helping me, Nick. I'll be fine. Let us know what happens," said Gene.

"I'm going to take you to the emergency room," said Patrick.

"All right. I'm afraid I have hurt my leg," said Gene.

They arrived at the emergency room in a short while. The first doctor to see Gene was Dr. Landis.

"How did you get here so quickly?" asked Gene.

"Patrick let us know you were on the way. Carol trained him well. I always want to be here for you. I know your history. What happened to you, Gene?" asked Dr. Landis.

"I basically fell on my face in front of a meeting," said Gene.

"Was it an important meeting?" asked Dr. Landis.

"It probably means my job. They are looking for a certain type of man. I don't believe I am what they want," said Gene.

At this point they took Gene for x-rays. Patrick went with him.

After examination of Gene's leg and ankle, Dr. Landis said, "We are going to put a brace on your leg, and we want you to try crutches instead of a cane for a while. They should give you a little more support. It is mainly a bad sprain, and your leg was twisted. Your leg is still weak. In addition to the fall, you also put a lot of strain on your leg trying to get up."

"They kept trying to make him get up on his own," said Patrick. "No one would help him. His boss wouldn't let them."

Dr. Landis had deep concern in his eyes as he looked at Gene. He put his hand on Gene's. "I'm sorry that happened to you. You deserved better treatment than that. Thank you, Patrick, for being there for him."

As they left the hospital, Gene asked Patrick to take him to his apartment so he could change clothes and go back to the office. He had blood on his shirt, tie, and suit. Gene had a bandage on his cheek. The cut was deeper than he had first thought and needed twelve stitches.

When they got back to the office, Gene stopped at Karen's desk. "Would you please ask George to come by my office this afternoon? I need to talk to him," said Gene.

Patrick helped Gene from his wheelchair to the desk chair. There was a knock on the door. It was George. Evidently, he was anxious to speak with Gene.

"Patrick, could we speak in private please?" asked George.

Patrick looked at Gene.

"It's all right. I'll be fine," said Gene.

Patrick didn't even look at George as he left the room.

"Let's sit on the sofa. It might be more comfortable."

Gene used the crutches as he slowly walked to the sofa. George followed close behind him. Gene pulled up his slacks a little and showed George the brace on his leg.

"My leg just isn't strong enough yet."

"I guess we had better talk about the elephant in the room," said George.

"I think I'm the elephant in the room. Maybe I should just leave now," said Gene.

"It's not you, Gene. It's your handicap. People in this industry have a difficult time dealing with someone who is handicapped. They don't know how to work with them and treat them. It is hard with coworkers but especially difficult with clients. If I keep you, we will lose clients because of you," said George.

"If that is the way you feel, then I suppose I should just leave now," said Gene. "I used to be able to get a job fairly easily. But since this has happened to me, the thought of job hunting scares me. I'm not sure I'm up to it."

Gene had on a light-brown suit, white shirt, and dark-brown tie. With his dark hair and pale-blue eyes, George thought how handsome he looked after what he had gone through that morning.

"All in all, you seemed to hold up pretty good through the ordeal this morning, but I honestly don't know if it's good enough to keep your job," said George.

"You know, I have a handicapped friend who, if he had been in my place this morning, would have gotten up. And he would have been smiling as he did it. He is an exceptional person, and he is very special to us. His name is John," said Gene.

"What is his handicap that would make him get up when you couldn't?" asked George.

"John had polio when he was five and wears a brace on his paralyzed leg. When he was twenty-three, a roof full of ice and snow fell on him. It injured his head and back and crushed his right arm and hand. He still has severe headaches from the accident. He also went through severe abuse when he was just a little boy. I told him once that he healed better than me. He said he had more practice than I did." There were tears in his eyes as he looked at George.

"I've never known anyone like that. I would like to meet him," said George.

"He will be here in two weeks unless you have fired me by then." Gene reached for a tissue. "As you can see, I'm crying now. I'm not that strong, tough man you are looking for."

"You know, Gene, I met with Phillip York a couple of times before he retired. I saw you at that time. He told me to give you a chance. He said I might be surprised. Phillip liked you very much. I asked him about the pretty girl who was with you. He told me that her name was Carol and that she was a remarkable woman," said George.

"We have been best friends, on and off, since we were eight years old. If it wasn't for her, I wouldn't be sitting here right now. I probably wouldn't even be alive. The doctors all told me that Carol was the one who saved me," said Gene as he took his glasses off and held his head in his hands. "I'm sorry, I have to stop talking for a while. I have no energy. I get so tired."

"Take your time, Gene. You have been through a lot. When you speak of Carol and John, you seem to get very emotional. Where is Carol now?" asked George.

"At home with her husband and children. She will be here in two weeks, the same time John is here," answered Gene.

"Can I meet her too?" asked George.

"I don't know why not," said Gene. "She applied for a job here once. Phillip had already offered her a job, but she wanted to do all the testing. She scored exceptionally high. Ask Nick Jennison. He has all that information."

"I may just do that," said George. "You know, I have no explanation for what I'm feeling, but I don't want to go out there and work in the rat race right now. I just feel like sitting here and talking to you. It seems strange. We don't even like one another."

"Just a minute, George. You don't like me. I have never said I don't like you. In fact, I haven't said a word against you," said Gene quietly.

"I have been very cruel to you, and you don't even fight back," said George.

"That's just what I'm worried about, George. I can't fight back. I'm not strong enough, and I may never be again," said Gene.

"But the thing is, you weren't always this way. You were a great athlete, president of the class for three years, and a graduation speaker. That last one alone would have made me go into a panic attack. I couldn't have given a graduation speech if I had wanted to," said George. "I've read your file, Gene. I know a lot about you."

"There is quite a story behind that graduation speech. You'll have to ask John about that. I would just cry again." Gene paused. "But I guess you are right. I was strong and outgoing at one time. I was never comfortable with all the attention and popularity. Sometimes I just wanted to disappear. Carol would help me do that by talking to me in her sweet, quiet, gentle way. It wasn't only what she would say to me but the way in which she said it and the love it always contained. She could always make my headaches go away and make me feel better. I miss her so much."

George noticed Gene's hand was trembling. He took hold of Gene's hand and said, "We'll have to go out for a drink or dinner some night."

"I take thirty-five pills a day, and most of them say no alcohol. If we went out to eat, I would just be a lot of work. You know Patrick has a pretty hard job," said Gene.

"I'm sorry I treated him badly," said George.

"He will be all right. I think he actually understands me and my friends," said Gene.

"I know I'll be meeting them in a couple of weeks. But would you tell me a little more about them if it is not too hard for you?" asked George.

"I think the four of us are closer than we've ever been to our own families. Carol and Mike met when they were twelve in junior high. Mike was a rich boy, and Carol was a poor girl from the wrong side of the tracks, and her mother never let her forget it. Mike said he fell in love with her the day he met her. I first met Carol when we were eight. Years later, I met both Carol and Mike in sophomore geometry. We were all just fifteen. I had never known anyone like her. The three of us met John the night of graduation rehearsal. I'll never forget that night. Carol was assigned to walk down the stairs and aisle in the practice processional that night with John, and he fell in love with her. He always says that was the best night of his life. She had to help him by holding his arm and by doing so, a school rule was broken. Mike and Carol didn't receive any awards that should have been theirs, not just because of that night. They tended to be somewhat rebellious, but they were just trying to help others. I ended up getting a lot of awards, and I felt as though I didn't deserve them. It has been twenty years ago, and I still haven't gotten over it." Gene rubbed his head. All the talking was exhausting him.

"What happened after graduation?" asked George.

"We went our separate ways. I went to a four-year college. Carol went to junior college. John went to work as an auto mechanic. Mike could have gone to the best university in the country, but instead he chose to go to Vietnam. I was afraid for him all the while he was over there. He was wounded in the head and received a Purple Heart. Even though he helps other veterans, he never talks about his time in Vietnam. Four years after graduation, we moved into the house on Lansing Street together. I feel those were some of the best years of our lives. I'll let them tell you the rest. They all speak better than I do." Although Gene spoke quietly and distinctly, there was something very sad in his voice.

"I would like to hear about the graduation speech and why no one ended up with the beautiful girl," said George.

"They will tell you all you want to know. Maybe they will even tell you something that might make you like me and want to keep me on," said Gene.

"Gene, I actually do like you. I made a bad mistake this morning that really hurt you. I'm sorry for that, and I hope in time you will forgive me," said George.

"It wasn't your fault. I'm just clumsy. I just tripped and fell," said Gene.

There was a knock on the door. Gene said, "Come in."

It was Patrick. "Could I get you something to drink?"

"Yes, I would like a cup of coffee, black," said George.

"I'll just have a glass of water," said Gene.

Patrick returned soon with the drinks. He was surprised that they were talking so long, but he thought that Gene was fighting for his job as well as his life, and in Gene's own quiet way, he was doing just that.

"Are you all right, Gene? You look a little tired," asked George.

"I stayed up too late last night trying to perfect my presentation only to fail so miserably," said Gene.

"You didn't fail, Gene. It was a very good presentation," said George.

"There is something else I would like to tell you about the four of us. I don't think John can ever talk about it again. Two days after graduation, we went to a beach just south of Kansas City. We just wanted a nice, quiet day swimming, having a picnic, and Carol wanted to build sandcastles, but it didn't turn out to be a sandcastle-type day. This is hard for me to talk about. There was a quote in the graduation speech. I said, 'There are thousands of stories in each of us, most of which would break your heart. This is one such story.'" Gene paused and took his glasses off and rubbed his eyes.

"I'd like to hear what you have to say, but if it's too hard for you, please don't continue," said George.

"You're going to meet John in two weeks. He has been handicapped all his life. I want you to like him." Gene was openly crying, but he didn't care, nor did George as he put his arms around him.

Gene continued very slowly, "John showed us his back, stomach, and groin area that day, all covered in the most brutal scars we had ever seen. He told us everything that day, how his father beat him and tried to starve him, and he also beat John's mother. His mother was pregnant, and the baby was born with brain damage. John will always take care of that little girl. If any of us had any innocence left, it was gone that day. We were only seventeen. I had a hard time handling it. I talked to my mom and dad, and they were very helpful and supportive. Mike couldn't even talk about it, but he finally did, and his parents have been very helpful to John throughout the years. But Carol never talked to anyone about that day. You see, she has her own story of abuse that we had been through with her two years before we ever met John." Gene paused. "I can't talk anymore, George. Would you tell Patrick that I need to go home?"

"I'll tell him. Thank you for letting me get to know you and your friends," said George. "I hope they don't judge me too harshly for what I did to you today." When he got up to leave, he hugged Gene, and then he was gone.

Within a few minutes, Patrick was sitting beside Gene. "He wasn't too hard on you, was he?"

"No, I'm just tired, and my leg hurts. I just need to go home," said Gene.

Patrick helped Gene to the wheelchair. "Are you ready? I know how you always hate this part, going by all the people."

GEORGE MEETS GENE'S FRIENDS

A week before George would meet Gene's three friends, Gene invited George, Alan McVary, and Patrick to go out to eat with him at their favorite Chicago restaurant, although not quite sure why he wanted George and Alan to meet. George left the office with Patrick and Gene that evening. As Patrick opened the van, the lift automatically came out and lowered to the ground for easy access. The passenger seat would transfer to the driver's seat when Gene was able to drive again. The seat was actually a wheelchair with a neck support and high back. As Gene got into the seat, George noticed there were many attachments that Patrick had to hook and lock before they were ready to drive.

Gene saw the look of concern on George's face. "See, I told you, George. I'm a lot of work. I can't do it alone."

"Is there something wrong with your neck?" asked George.

"I can only turn it so far, especially to the right," said Gene. "It's an old football injury."

"I saw you try to reach for the chalk without turning. I had no idea. Each day it becomes more my fault. I don't know what to say," said George.

"You had no way of knowing." Gene reached back with his left hand and took hold of George's hand.

Gene had every reason to be angry and upset with George, but he wasn't. George had never known anyone like Gene before. He was just incredibly kind, and George was completely overwhelmed.

They stopped by Gene's apartment to pick up Alan. "Alan, this is my boss, George Meyer. George, this is Alan McVary, my friend, and Mike's dad."

They shook hands and didn't seem to immediately hate one another. Gene and Patrick saw that as one step in the right direction.

Sandy was their waitress again. She immediately recognized Gene, Alan, and Patrick. She directed her question to Gene. "How is John? I've looked for him a lot since that night. I was so worried about him."

"We knew you were worried. We all were that night. He's better now. He will be here with us in about a week. We'll be back," said Gene.

"How about you, Gene, are you doing all right?" She gently touched the bandage on his cheek.

"It's just a small cut. I tend to be a little clumsy. This is my boss, George Meyer," said Gene.

Sandy greeted everyone warmly, and then she kissed Alan on the cheek and said, "I never got the chance to thank you personally. Did you get my note?"

"Yes, it was very kind of you," said Alan.

"I remember Carol saying you were all about kindness and caring for one another and returning one good deed with another. I never will forget what all of you have done for me." Sandy also hugged Gene and Patrick, and she was crying. "I'm sorry. I'm such a fool. Now I'm the one who can't stop crying. I wish there were more people in the world like you."

"Don't worry about crying, Sandy. I do it all the time. We are big believers in kindness, consideration, and helping others. It's Carol who has made us the people we are today. When John was injured in a terrible accident, I followed her lead, and together we healed him. She did the same with me. That's why we all love her so much." Gene wiped the tears from his cheeks as his eyes met George's.

The meal was delicious, and the service was above and beyond. George noticed how attentive and truly kind Patrick was to Gene. When Gene dropped his napkin, he had another one in a few seconds. Gene ordered steak, knowing it was always difficult to handle.

Patrick would help him when he had trouble cutting it. When Gene dropped something on his shirt and tie, Patrick wiped it off for him. Everything was done very discretely and quietly.

"So, George, Gene tells me you want to meet and talk with his small group of friends when they arrive next week," said Alan.

"I always like to get to know my employees' families, and Gene told me they are like family to him. I wish the circumstances were better," said George.

"They are four exceptional young people. I don't just say that because my son is one of them. I love them all very much, and I will always help them in any way I can." George sensed that Alan knew about the happenings of the past week and in all probability didn't approve.

"Your son, Mike, what is he like?" asked George.

"He's a lawyer now. He works a lot with homeless veterans trying to get housing for them as well as monetary and medical benefits. He is happiest when working with the veterans," said Alan. "He has always been the protector in the group of friends. You'll like him."

"But the question is, what will he think of me?" asked George.

"I don't know. What I do know is that he won't be happy about what happened to Gene last week," said Alan.

"Mike's a really good guy. The only person whom I have ever seen Mike dislike and who dislikes him is Greg, Carol's husband." This was an honest but yet uncharacteristic comment for Gene to make.

"Mike and Carol made a few enemies in high school, mostly teachers. Many thought they were rebellious, but as Gene mentioned, they were just trying to help people," said Alan. "Mike always wanted to take care of everyone, especially Carol. She is the healer in the group. When my daughter, Cathy, came home after two years strung out on drugs, I called Carol at work and asked her if she would help us, and help us she did. She stayed with Cathy until she was well. Mike was in Vietnam then, and Gene was away at college, but Gene came home on weekends and helped Carol with Cathy."

"Remember how she helped John after his accident and me? I wouldn't be sitting here right now without her help," said Gene.

"And John is the lover. He has enough love in him for everyone. And everyone always loves him," said Alan. "My beautiful wife, Colleen, loved John as her own son."

"So Mike is the protector, Carol is the healer, and John is the lover in the group. What does that make Gene?' asked George.

"That's easy, Gene is the hero. He always has been," said Alan.

"Were you in Vietnam, Gene?" asked George.

"No, because of my eyes I couldn't make it. I actually tried to enlist when Mike did," said Gene. "I'm legally blind in my right eye, and my eyesight isn't good in my left eye."

"Gene has been a hero to everyone. They didn't elect him president of the class for three years for no reason. I've always wished I could have been more like you, Gene," said Alan sincerely.

Patrick, who hadn't taken a big part in the conversation, suddenly had something to say. "I think the four of them are the kindest people I have ever met. It is as though they share a single thread that connects them for eternity."

"I like that, a single thread," said Gene.

"Will any of them accept me after what I did to their friend who is now, as strange as it may seem, my friend?" asked George.

"John will be fine," said Gene. "He loves everyone unconditionally."

"Mike will be all right. He has mellowed over the years," said Alan.

Everyone looked at Patrick. "Just a minute. My job is on the line here also. Please don't ask me to say what I think Carol's opinion will be. I think she will have questions for you. That is all I can say."

"Gene and Alan, what do you think Carol's opinion will be?" asked George.

Alan smiled. "Oh, she will definitely have an opinion, but she knows that the only opinion that really counts is Gene's."

"Carol will have a few questions. She doesn't like to see anyone hurt. She is very sensitive and yet strong. If she sees violence, she returns it with kindness. Of the three of them, I know what Carol thinks without even asking her. But as Alan said, the only opinion that counts, in the end, is mine," said Gene.

George knew he had his work cut out for him.

SEVEN QUESTIONS

When Carol, Mike, and John arrived at the office to meet George Meyer, Gene's boss, he hurried to meet with them when Karen announced their arrival. He greeted them warmly.

"It is a pleasure to meet you. I've heard a lot about you. I'm George Meyer."

"We have heard quite a bit about you too." Mike smiled slightly as they walked toward George's office. "I'm Mike, and this is John."

"I believe we are missing the young lady," said George.

"She stopped to talk to Patrick. She will be here in a minute," said Mike.

At that moment, Carol walked into George's office. She was even prettier than he remembered, but she didn't smile or speak as she shook hands with George. She sat on the sofa next to Mile as John sat in a chair close to George.

Mike was the first to speak, "I know Carol has several questions. I basically have some comments to make. We would like for John to start."

"Well, you definitely get right to the point. I really just wanted a friendly, informal meeting to get to know the three of you, but I can see it has escalated," George paused. "John, the floor is yours."

"I'm just a little nervous," said John slowly.

George took hold of John's left hand and noticed it was trembling, as Gene's often were. "Don't be nervous John. I'm a friend."

"I'm handicapped, as you can see, and I have been all my life. I think it is easier for me than it is for Gene. It's all still new to him. He is not always sure what to expect next. I had polio when I was five. I would fall a lot, but I would just get up and try again, and I always kept smiling. My mom liked it when I smiled, and it made her smile too. Carol and Mike, do you remember my mom?" asked John.

Mike pulled a chair close to John. "We remember her. She was a fine lady." John was teary-eyed, but he was still smiling.

"Your mother loved you so much, John." This was the first time Carol had spoken. Her voice was soft and kind and as beautiful as she was.

"She had cancer, and she died a few years ago," said John.

"I'm sorry you lost her, John," said George.

"I will always take care of my little sister, Meggie. She was born with brain damage because my mom was hurt badly when she was pregnant." John looked at Mike as his smile faded. "I can't talk about that right now."

"It's all right, John. You don't have to talk about anything you don't want to," said Mike.

"I have a degenerative eye disease. I've had three operations on my eyes. Sometimes they help me, other times not so much. I wanted to talk to you, so I sat close to you so I could see you. But I like to see Carol too, and she's far away," said John.

Carol pulled a chair up on the other side of John. "Is that better for you?"

"Oh yes. Thank you." John smiled at Carol. "I had a bad accident. A roof full of ice and snow fell on me. It hurt my head and back and crushed my arm and hand. Carol and Gene taught me how to write with my left hand so you could read it." John tried to lift his right hand to show to George, but he couldn't.

Carol lifted it up for him and pulled his shirt sleeve up a little. "He wants you to see his hand," said Carol quietly.

George took his scarred hand in his.

"I'm sorry that happened to you," said George.

John smiled at George and continued speaking, "When my dad used to beat me, he would call me bad names. He told me I would never graduate from high school or be able to hold a job. But I have done both. He said I would never have any friends, but I have the three best friends in the whole wide world. I was just a little boy. I didn't know why he hated me so much."

As Carol wiped tears from John's cheeks, Mike spoke to him quietly, "Come back from there, John. Don't go any further."

"I'll be all right. Mike always tries to protect me. They all do," said John. "You didn't mean to hurt Gene on purpose, did you, George?"

"No, I made a mistake, John, a bad mistake. I hope you can forgive me for it," said George.

John smiled and said, "I forgive you. I make mistakes too. When that roof fell on me, it cut my head very badly. I don't think as well as I used to. Carol, Gene, and Mike tell me I'm all right, but sometimes I can't remember things. I don't even remember the parts of a car like I used to. I think that is the worst part of being handicapped, when it affects your mind."

"I think you have a beautiful mind, and I like you very much, John," said George as he hugged John.

"Carol, my head hurts really bad. Would you rub it like you used to for me?" asked John very quietly.

"Of course I will," said Carol. "He started going someplace where he shouldn't. It always upsets him and makes his head hurt."

"I'll get you some water," said Mike.

As Mike stepped out to get the water, Carol and George helped John to the sofa. After he drank the water, Carol placed a small pillow on her lap, and John rested his head on it.

"Do you mind if he puts his shoes on your sofa?" asked Carol.

"No, I don't mind," said George.

"Carol knows just where to touch to make my head feel better," said John.

"How do you know that?" asked George.

"I remember where all the injuries were. You don't rub on the scar but around it in a certain kind of motion in the way it healed. His head is like a road map to me. I never forget it." Carol's voice was soothing, and the look on John's face was pain-free and content.

"Did anything I said help Gene?" asked John.

"My dear young man, I'm not so sure it is Gene who needs the help. I think it may be me." George noticed a scar going from the top of John's ear down his hairline and neck. "Is that from the accident too?"

"No, my dad did that. He threw me against the wall. I was a small boy. I don't hear well out of that ear. You see, George, I have a lot of handicaps," said John.

"I know, and I'm very sorry," said George.

"I don't mind. My friends have always taken good care of me," John paused. "Who has the floor now?"

"Carol has seven questions for you, George. They are my questions too," said Mike.

"Can you talk from there?" asked George.

"Yes. John's been through a lot today. I need to keep him close to me," said Carol.

"I believe we all do," said Mike as he pulled his chair closer so John could see him, and George did the same.

Carol began, "As Mike said, we have seven questions. Some are simple and can be answered with a yes or no while others are a little more involved. There is one question that the answer is very important to me personally. My decision will depend on your answer to that question alone, but the others are important to Mike, John, and me. Are you ready?"

"I think I'm as ready as I will ever be," said George.

"The first question is, have you ever known a handicapped person?" asked Carol.

"No. Not until meeting Gene and today meeting John" answered George.

"Do you stand by what you did to Gene as being the right thing to do, or do you regret your actions?" asked Carol.

"Even though similar situations have occurred in the company where I used to work, in this situation it was not the right thing to do, and I sincerely regret my actions. I have never done anything like this to a handicapped person, and I am not proud of it," said George.

"Do you hate Gene?" asked Carol.

"No. I really like him. He is a very kind man," said George.

"Did you know that without his glasses, Gene is legally blind in his right eye and even with them his eyesight is not good?" asked Carol.

"No. I noticed that he never took his glasses off, but I didn't know how bad his eyesight was," responded George.

Carol paused for a moment. "When Gene fell and you were trying to make him get up, were you screaming at him?" asked Carol.

"Yes. I'm afraid so," answered George.

"Were you trying to take away his dignity?" asked Carol.

"No. No one could do that. He left work and went to the emergency room. They took twelve stitches in his cheek and put a brace on his leg to relieve the pain. He went home and changed his suit, shirt, and tie because of the blood and returned to work that afternoon, dignity intact," answered George.

"Was anyone laughing?" This was Carol's final question.

"No. For the men who came with me from the other company, laughter would have been considered a sign of weakness. But no one in the room was laughing," answered George.

"I think you know the question I was particularly interested in the answer to, don't you?" asked Carol.

"Yes. I think it was number 5, was I screaming at him. I would have liked to say no, but I couldn't," said George.

"It was my own personal question. Gene could never stand for anyone to be loud and scream. But they were never screaming at him. Everyone always loved Gene." Carol was crying.

John said to Mike, "I'm sorry, Mike. George made Carol cry. Mike can't stand it when someone makes Carol cry." John put his arms around Carol as did Mike.

George turned his back to them and looked out the window. He had never in his whole life cried, and he wasn't going to start now. But he realized that he had probably just lost the best employee he had ever worked with and also the possibility of having an exceptional employee in the future.

But Mike wasn't finished just yet. "My two questions were, if you had ever known a handicapped person and the question about

Gene's eyesight. You answered them correctly." Mike hesitated. "I know there is a video tape of the first part of the meeting with Gene. We would like to see it," said Mike.

"Carol and John, do you want to see it also?" asked George.

"I very much want to see it," said John.

"And you, Carol? Please say no," said George.

"Since they want to, I will watch it with them. I won't leave them alone," said Carol.

George picked up the phone. "Nick, would you please bring us the tape of Gene's part of the meeting."

Within a few seconds, Nick entered the room with the tape and put it in the VCR. "If I were you, Carol, I wouldn't watch it."

"I'll be fine," said Carol.

Mike went to sit at the other end of the sofa. He put his arm around John as Carol did from the other side. They held hands in addition to comforting John. George thought how much he liked these three young people and how much he didn't want them to see the video. George didn't want to see it again. He was a little behind the three friends, and he could see them without them knowing he was watching.

As the video started, Mike almost immediately put his head in his hands and was crying. John put his arm around Mike and patted his back. Carol's eyes were glued to the screen. She did not take her eyes off the video until it ended, and then she turned and looked immediately at George. Carol walked over to George and stood directly in front of him as he stood up. Nick wasn't sure what was going to happen. For a brief moment, George thought Carol was going to slap him. He almost wished she would, but that was not Carol's character.

Then Carol spoke to George, "That was the saddest, most terrible thing I have ever seen. I feel so incredibly bad for you. You must be so humiliated." And then she hugged him.

For the first time in George's life, he felt a tear run down his cheek. George Meyer, who had never shed a tear in fifty-four years, was crying. But Carol didn't see it. She had already gone back to comfort John and Mike.

THE VIDEO

After the meeting ended at ten o'clock, Carol, John, and Mike stopped by Gene's office before they left. Gene was sitting at his desk trying his best to work. It was difficult knowing what his friends had been going through.

Carol hugged Gene and kissed him on the cheek as did John. Gene saw the tears in John's eyes and asked, "How did it go in there? He wasn't mean to you, was he?"

"No," said John. "I'm just sorry you had to go through that."

"Are you all right, Carol?" asked Gene.

"I'm fine. I'm just fine. But you're not fine, and John isn't either. And I love the two of you so much," said Carol.

"What about me?" said Mike.

Carol hugged Mike. "I love you too, you know that. But I don't worry about you like I do them. Just like me, Mike, you're fine. We will survive what went on in there, but will John? And Gene lived it."

"I'm all right, Carol. It was just the last part," said John.

"So you watched the video. Did you all want to?" asked Gene.

"I wanted to, and so did Mike. I didn't know anything could be so bad. I didn't know people could do that, especially to someone like you," said John.

"It was worse than I thought it would be," said Mike.

"And you, Carol, you didn't want to see it, did you?" asked Gene.

"No, I didn't want to see it," said Carol. "But I watched it with them. He didn't even answer my question right."

"Why don't you all go to my apartment and rest? I think I'll take off early. I need to be with you," said Gene.

When they got to the car, Carol immediately got into the back seat.

John asked, "Is it all right if I sit by you?"

"Sure. I'm just really tired," said Carol.

"At first I thought everything was going to be all right, but I can't get over the video," said Mike. "This is too dangerous a job for Gene. They are going to eat him alive."

"I talked too much. You should have told me to shut up," said John.

"No, John, you did fine. He said he wanted to get to know us. I just wish this hadn't happened to Gene, or to anyone for that matter," said Carol.

When they got to Gene's apartment, Carol said to Mike, "Tell your dad about it. See what he thinks. I need to go lie down."

John sat down by Mike and Alan at the kitchen table.

"Mike is it all right for Carol to be alone? We never used to leave her alone."

"It's all right now. We all have some thinking to do. Gene will be home soon. He is going to have some questions for all of us," said Mike.

"What shall I say, Mike? I don't want to make a mistake," said John.

"I want to see the video," said Alan.

"No, Alan. It is so terrible," said John.

"No matter how bad, I need to see it. I'm part of this decision whether I want to be or not." With this, Alan headed toward Gene's office.

A few minutes later, Patrick brought Gene home earlier than expected.

"Where's Alan and Carol?" asked Gene immediately.

"Dad went to your office. He wants George to show him the tape. Do you think he will?" asked Mike.

"I don't know why not," said Gene. "I'll be the only one who hasn't seen it. But I lived it. I don't need to see it."

"Carol's in your bedroom, Gene. She was so tired and sad. I'm worried about her," said John.

"Thanks, John. I'll go to her," said Gene.

Gene lay down on his bed beside Carol and pulled her close to him. She curled up against him and nestled in the bend of his arm with her head resting gently on his chest. They held one another tight, but neither one said a word. They didn't need to. Just as they both felt love for one another, they could both feel each other's pain.

At the office George showed Alan the video. Nick was also in the room.

When it was over, Alan asked, "May I have the video?"

George motioned for Nick to give it to him. Alan knew there were other copies, but that wasn't why he wanted it. Nick excused himself from the room without anyone asking him to leave.

The two men didn't speak for a few minutes. Alan did not like George. He simply didn't trust him. Gene had worked so hard after the strokes to get where he was before George stepped in and took it away from him. Alan felt so much love and respect and was so protective of Gene as well as Carol, Mike, and John.

Alan spoke hesitantly, "George, I feel as though I need to say something to you, but I don't exactly know what. I turned my life around. I wasn't always a good man. My youngest son committed suicide when he was sixteen, basically because of the way I treated him. My oldest son died when he was twenty-eight. He was gay, and at that time I didn't approve. My only daughter spent years on drugs and living with a guy who looked like Charlie Manson, and maybe was, for all I know. I had a beautiful, kind, caring wife, but I never told her I loved her. She died when she was forty-eight. As for Mike, I believe he went to Vietnam, against my wishes, hoping he would die there. Thank God he came back. But those four young people, Gene, Carol, John, and also Mike have made me a better person. But the thing is, no matter how many good deeds I do or how much I try to help John and improve his life, I can never change the past. I'm the one who knows that probably better than anyone."

"So you think that what I did was bad and there is no recovery from it?" asked George.

"Gene is such a good man. He has never hurt anyone in his whole life. He has a lot of extra work to do now. I wish I was the man that Gene is. He is the one I wanted my sweet Carol to marry, even over my own son.," said Alan.

Alan picked up the video and left. Neither man had anything else to say. Alan was anxious to get back to the apartment and the four people he loved. When he opened the door, he saw Carol and Gene first sitting on the sofa. Gene had his arm around Carol. He hurried to them and sat on the floor in front of them. He put his head in their laps and cried.

"I'm so sorry that happened to you," said Alan.

Carol put her hand on Alan's head and kissed him gently. Gene put his hand on his back and said, "I'll be all right, Alan. Don't worry about me."

When Mike and John came into the living room from the kitchen, what they saw needed no words. Mike sat on the floor with his arm around his dad, and John sat on the sofa by Carol. They stayed that way for a while. It was as though they were afraid to let go.

Later that evening, the phone rang. Gene answered it.

"Hello, Gene. This is George."

"Hello, George. Is everything all right?" asked Gene.

"Not really, but I am trying to make it right if I can. I was wondering if you would bring John to see me tomorrow. I forgot to ask him something, and there are a couple of things I need to say to him," said George.

"I don't know why not. But he is a little fragile after this morning. It was kind of hard on him. He will probably want someone to be with him," said Gene.

"He can bring anyone with him. I know I need to be gentle with John. I promise I won't hurt him," said George.

"We will be there," said Gene.

Gene and Carol went to the room Mike and John were sharing.

"Where's John?" asked Gene.

"He went to dad's room. He's scared, and he wanted to talk to him," said Mike.

"You had better come with us, Mike," said Gene.

Gene knocked on the door.

"Come in," said Alan.

Alan and John were sitting on the sofa. Alan was holding John tightly, and John's head was on his shoulder. Carol immediately sat down by John.

"What's wrong?" asked Carol in a comforting voice.

"I'm afraid," said John.

"What are you afraid of?" asked Gene.

"Go ahead. It's all right to tell him," said Alan.

"I'm afraid something is going to happen to you in the night, Gene. The thought won't leave my head," said John.

"He needs you to sit here by him, Gene," said Carol as she moved over to a chair.

Gene took hold of John's hand. "Do you remember, on our second trip to California, when Mike was in Vietnam, how you, Carol, and I slept in the big king-size bed, and Carol was feeling bad, but she was better in the morning?"

"Yes, I remember. I liked that," said John.

"What if we do that tonight in my big bed?" said Gene.

"Great, then I can watch you all night," said John.

"Yes, you and Carol can both watch me all night." Gene smiled slightly, but Carol saw sadness and worry in his eyes.

"Mike and Alan, you guys can come too," said John.

"No, we'll be fine," said Alan.

John started to get up, but Gene stopped him. "Just a minute. There is something I need to ask you first about you being scared. Did it have anything to do with the meeting with George this morning?"

"No, he was nice to me," said John. "I'm just afraid you're going to have another stroke and die in your sleep."

"Don't worry about me, John. I'm going to be all right. At least I think I am," Gene paused. "Did you hear the phone ring just before we came in here?"

"Yes, who was it?" asked John.

"It was George. He said he forgot to ask you something, and there is something he wants to say to you. He wants you to come talk to him tomorrow," said Gene.

"Just me all by myself?" asked John.

"No, someone can be with you," said Gene.

"Can all of you come?" asked John.

"It would be best if it is just one," said Gene. "Tomorrow night we will all go to that restaurant you like so well. We will all be together then."

"Would you go with me, Carol?" asked John.

"Sure, John. I'll go with you," said Carol.

"I'm so tired," said John. "Gene and Mike, do you remember how you guys used to almost carry me when I could hardly walk?"

"We remember, John," said Gene. "You know I can't do that now, John. But I think there are two people here who can help you."

As Alan and Mike helped John to Gene's room, Carol and Gene followed. Alan gently removed John's leg brace and helped him get ready for bed. Carol changed the bandage on Gene's cheek and helped him to bed. His brace had to stay on all night. John watched Carol take a pink nightgown from her small blue carryon.

"You've had that bag for a long time, Carol. Maybe you need a new one," said John.

"I'm kind of attached to this old bag like I'm attached to you, Gene, Mike, and Alan. I am very fond of it. It is like an old friend to me because it has been with me through everything, sort of like you guys," said Carol.

On this Mike and Alan said good night and left the room.

When Carol came back into the bedroom, she had on the pretty pink gown. She had brushed her hair. It was almost to her waist and hung over her shoulders in waves and curls.

John started to move over so Carol could be in the middle as he said, "You look so pretty."

"Thank you. I think you should stay in the middle tonight, John," said Carol.

"You need to be in the middle tonight, John," said Gene.

They talked for a long time that night. "Remember in California, how young we were?" asked John.

"I sure do. I wish I was that same guy," said Gene.

"You are, Gene, just twenty years older like all of us," said John. "Carol, you look the same but maybe even prettier."

"You guys have always told me I'm pretty, but I've never really thought so," said Carol.

"I've always thought you were the prettiest girl in the world, but it is so much more. It's also the way you talk and treat everyone and the way you touch me. Your touch can make my hand stop shaking or my head stop hurting. I think John will agree with that," said Gene.

"I agree with everything," said John.

"I'll tell you guys a secret, but maybe it's not. When I went to prom with the three of you, I felt like the luckiest girl in the world because I was with the three nicest, most handsome guys," said Carol.

"John and Mike were handsome. I never thought I was," said Gene. "I have always had too many things wrong with me."

"Oh, Gene, I have always thought you were handsome beyond words. My friend, Linda, always compared you to President Kennedy. She thought you had every bit as much charisma as he did," said Carol. "I loved you all so much."

"And we loved you," said Gene.

"I loved you, Carol, but it is strange, I always felt younger than Gene and Mike, and I'm actually the oldest," said John.

"I think you are forever young, John. You never age," said Gene.

"Mike and Alan have aged, and you have too, Gene, but like George said, you have dignity. I like that word. Do I have dignity?" asked John.

"Very much so," said Carol.

"What about charisma, do I have that? I like that word also," said John.

"You have that too, John," said Carol.

"I would like to talk all night, but I am really sleepy," said John.

Carol kissed John on the cheek. "Go to sleep, my sweet John. I'll see you in the morning."

"Good night, Gene and Carol. I love you both," said John.

"And we love you, John," said Gene.

Carol got up and went to the other side of the bed and kissed Gene. "Good night, Gene. Sleep peacefully. I love you."

"And good night, Carol. I love you too," said Gene as Carol wiped a tear from his cheek.

As Carol went back to her side of the bed, they both reached out to touch and hold John's hand. Carol picked up his scarred hand and kissed it. He always liked it when she did that. And Gene took hold of his other hand and of Carol's hand.

That night, Carol was awake long after Gene and John had fallen asleep. Carol thought it had been a strange and yet amazingly wonderful day and evening, but she wondered as she had many times before if this was the last, or next to last night, they would all be together. She would have liked to know just how much time they had left together.

ALWAYS GO WITH YOUR HEART

When they woke up the following morning, the first thing John did was look at Gene and ask, "Are you all right, Gene?"

"Yes, John, I'm fine," said Gene as he smiled slightly at his friend.

"I woke up three times in the night and checked you. I'm not afraid anymore. You're going to be all right," said John.

"I love you so much, John. You're a really good guy," said Gene.

"I love you too, John," said Carol.

John got up quickly. "I have to get ready. I need to look really good today."

Carol smiled at Gene. "Well, John's up, so everyone else will be soon."

"Did you notice he just gets up, snaps the leg brace on, puts his glasses on, and is on his way? I can't even put my brace on by myself. I ask you to put my glasses on me, and I can hardly get up," said Gene.

"Well, like John said, it is easier for him. He has had more practice," said Carol.

"Will you please help me get up," asked Gene.

Carol helped Gene get up. She sat beside him and put her arms around him. She knew how frustrated he was because there were so many things that he couldn't do.

Mike walked by the open door and came into Gene's room. "Can I help you get ready this morning, Gene?" asked Mike.

"Yes. I would welcome it," said Gene.

Carol went to get the wheelchair and brought it to Gene's room.

"I'll take you and John this morning and wait in Gene's office until you are finished. It will be easier for John that way," said Mike.

"Thanks, Mike," said Carol. "I'll get ready."

Mike helped Gene to the wheelchair and took him to the shower. He gently removed his leg brace. Mike had helped Gene with a shower many times since his strokes, but today it was different. Mike helped him shave, brush his teeth, and comb his hair, and then he took him back to the bedroom to help him dress.

"Thank you, Mike. I can't seem to be able to do anything this morning. I need to get back to where I was. I never thought you would have to do so much for me," said Gene.

"You've been doing lots of things for yourself. You've just had a little setback," said Mike.

"You will never know how grateful I am to you, Mike. Thank you for everything," said Gene.

"I only wish I could do more for you," said Mike.

Patrick came to pick Gene up before the others left. Carol thought Gene looked very nice. He had on a gray suit, light-green shirt, and gray and green striped tie. "John and I will be in to see you after the meeting," said Carol.

"Bye, Gene. We'll see you later," said John.

John had on a navy-blue suit and light-blue shirt and tie.

"You look good, John," said Carol. "In fact, you all look good except me. I'll go see what magic I can work."

When Carol came back, she had on a white blouse, a light-gray A-line skirt, and a red belt. Her hair was loose and full and beautiful.

"Wow. You did that quick," said Mike.

"Remember, I'm low maintenance, and I travel light," said Carol.

As they got in the car that day, John sat in the front seat with Mike.

"Well, John, you usually sit with Carol," said Mike.

"Since you didn't get to sleep with us last night, I wanted to sit by you now so you don't feel left out." John reached over and patted Mike's hand on the steering wheel.

"John, I think you are probably the nicest guy in the world," said Mike.

"Thanks, Mike. I hope I do all right today," said John.

"You will. Always go with your heart," said Mike.

"That's so strange," said Carol.

"What's strange?" asked John.

"What Mike just said to you. 'Always go with your heart.' Ryan said that to me many times. In fact, it is the last thing he ever said to me," said Carol.

"I remember," said Mike.

"Did you do what Ryan said, Carol? Did you always go with your heart?" asked John.

"No. I never did. I guess I wasn't smart enough to," said Carol. Carol could see Mike looking at her in the rearview mirror, but he didn't say anything. He didn't have to.

When they arrived at the office, Mike let Carol and John out so John wouldn't have to walk so far. John was using his cane, but Carol was holding on to his bad arm.

Karen called George and announced their arrival. He met them at the door to his office.

"Come in. I'm glad you could make it, and I am glad you are with him, Carol."

"I thought Mike would have been the better choice, but John asked me," said Carol.

"He made a good choice," said George. "You both look extremely nice today."

"Thanks, George. You look nice too," said John.

"The first order of business is something I forgot to ask you in our last meeting. Gene told me to be sure to ask you about his graduation speech," said George.

"I like that question. That's a good question," said John. "I was talking to Gene after graduation rehearsal, and he said he had a graduation speech written, but he didn't like it. He was going to rewrite it. That was the first time I ever really talked to Gene, Mike, and Carol. I told him that I had a speech written and he could have it if he liked it. He read it, and the next day he told me he would use it. I was so happy because I was really proud of that speech. Nobody knew who I was before he gave the speech, but afterward everybody knew me."

"And rightly so, John. Gene had a hard time with the emotional parts, but he made it. There wasn't a dry eye in the auditorium. It was very sad as well as inspirational," said Carol.

"And I bet you could give it to me word for word right now, couldn't you, John?" asked George.

"Yes, I could," said John.

"Gene tells me you are an auto mechanic and a very good one," said George.

"I'm not so good anymore. It's harder for me now," said John.

"I have a proposition for you," said George. "I think you are a very inspirational speaker especially talking about your handicaps. I think you would be a very good motivational speaker, speaking before groups like my employees so they would have a better understanding of handicapped people. And maybe even speaking at schools and universities. I think you would appeal to young and old alike. You are very genuine and extremely likeable."

Without saying a word, Carol pulled a chair up close to John and took hold of his hand. He was shaking and without words. Carol took her hand and smoothed his hair back across his forehead.

"John, did you understand all George just said to you? You like to speak and tell your story, don't you?" Carol spoke in a very clear, calm voice to John, and George immediately knew he had talked too fast for him.

"There would be a lot of people who would be strangers. I don't know. I would have to think about it," said John hesitantly.

"It wouldn't necessarily be a lot of people in the beginning. Let's say maybe just a small group in this office. People who want to be there, people you know, like Gene, Patrick, Nick, and me and a few others. I would choose wisely," said George.

"I was scared last night, George. I thought Gene was going to have another stroke. I watched him in the night, and he was fine this morning," said John.

"You take very good care of Gene. You are a good man," said George.

"Do you want to think about George's offer? Do you need a little more time?" asked Carol.

"Time, I need more time. But thank you, George, for thinking I could be a motivational speaker," said John.

"You can get back to me. Here's my card," said George.

"That's a nice card. I always wanted a card with my name on it," said John.

"Now, John, tell me why you, Gene, and Mike ever let this remarkable woman sitting by you get away from you," asked George.

"That's an easy question. She married Greg and had a little baby girl. She wanted a baby," said John.

"But one of you could have given her a baby," said George.

"I will never be able to father a child because of my problems. Mike was all confused and really messed up after Vietnam. And Gene, he loved Carol so much, but there is something inside him that keeps him from being entirely happy and making long-term commitments. He told me that once. We have to be really careful with Gene, Carol knows. That's why I watched him last night. I was afraid he would die in his sleep. Of us three guys, Gene would have made the best husband for Carol. I hope someday he will be happy because he is a really good man," said John.

"I know, John. I know he is." George hugged John and reached out and took Carol's hand. He could tell by her face that what John had just said had torn her heart out, but he had no idea what to say to her.

In Gene's office, Mike was sitting in the window looking at the traffic below. "You know, Dad and I have noticed some changes in John lately. I didn't say anything because it is mostly Dad who notices the changes."

"I've noticed, and so has Carol, but I don't think she wants to admit it yet," said Gene. "What do you and Alan notice?"

"He's more dependent and childlike. He doesn't make decisions on his own, and sometimes he doesn't remember how to do something or simply can't do something he has done hundreds of times. We have been worried about him," said Mike.

"What do you think about me? All those things could apply to me too except the childlike part," said Gene. "But I know what you mean. Sometimes I think John seems like he is about eleven or twelve. But John is smart. He is really smart. You know John is a very special person. I doubt that there is anyone else like him in the world. We just need to hold him and love him and keep him safe and close to us for as long as we can."

Just then there was a knock on the door. It was Carol and John.

"You guys won't believe what just happened." John was so excited he could hardly speak. "I can't talk. Carol, you tell them."

"George thinks John would be a good motivational speaker, speaking about his handicaps and handicapped people in general, starting with small, well-chosen groups at first and then maybe talking at schools and universities if he enjoys it," said Carol.

Mike was first to speak. "Well, it sounds like George may have hit on something this time."

"It would be something for us all to look into for you," said Gene.

"So you guys don't think it is a completely crazy idea?" asked John. John was so excited his glasses were crooked, and his hair was messed up again. Gene straightened his glasses and smoothed his hair down. "Will you all help me? I can't do anything without you."

"We will always help you, John," said Gene as John hugged him. Carol saw the tears in Gene's eyes, and she quickly looked out the window as Mike was doing. She didn't want John to see her tears. Mike reached over and put his arm around Carol and pulled her close to him and kissed the side of her forehead.

That evening as they had promised John, the five of them went back to their favorite Chicago restaurant. They were seated at their usual table, and once again Sandy was their waitress. She greeted them all warmly, especially John.

"It's been a while since I've seen you, John. Are you feeling better?" asked Sandy.

"I'm much better than last time," said John.

"You all look exceptionally good tonight," said Sandy.

"John had a job interview today. He may be a motivational speaker and speak about his handicaps" said Mike.

"I would love to hear you speak. Let me know when I can come to one of your meetings," said Sandy.

"I will," said John.

Sandy took their orders and left their table.

"You embarrass me, Mike. I have not decided yet," said John.

Mike put his arm around John. "I'm sorry. She just seems to really like you."

"But I have a girlfriend. You're getting married, Mike, so Carol is my and Gene's girlfriend," said John sincerely.

There was silence for a moment. No one knew what to say.

"I shouldn't have said anything to Sandy. Do you forgive me?" asked Mike.

John smiled and hugged Mike. "Of course I forgive you. I love you, Mike."

"And I love you too," said Mike.

It was very quiet at Gene's apartment that night. This was their last night together. Carol would fly back to Springfield the next day. Mike and John would fly back to Kansas City. Alan had chosen to stay with Gene. He had no immediate commitments, and he knew Gene needed him.

Carol helped Gene that night, as she always did. She removed and changed the bandage on his cheek. She kissed the scar.

"Does it hurt?" asked Carol.

"Not when you touch it," said Gene.

Carol nestled in the bend of his arm with her head resting gently on his chest. "I love you, Gene. Please never forget that."

"I won't. It's what keeps me alive," said Gene.

There was a quiet knock on the door.

Gene said, "Come in."

It was John, and he had been crying. "I can't sleep."

"That's because we need you here with us," said Gene in the kindest, gentlest voice Carol had ever heard. "If you can help me move over a little, you can sleep on the other side of me like Carol."

John very gently helped Gene move a little, and he lay down beside him and hugged him. Carol got up quietly and went to John's side of the bed. She took his leg brace off and his glasses, and then she got a cloth and dried his cheeks and eyes.

"You've been crying for a long time, haven't you?" asked Carol.

"Yes, but I won't cry now," said John. "I'm with you and Gene now."

Carol kissed him on the cheek and went back to her side of the bed and once again found her favorite spot next to Gene. Gene kissed both Carol and John on the forehead.

Just in the Nick of Time

After saying a difficult goodbye to her Chicago and Kansas City friends, Carol returned home to her family in Springfield. Carol's mother had stayed with the children. Carol had flown to Chicago, so Greg was there to meet her when the plane landed in Springfield.

"How do you get everything in that little blue bag?" said Greg as he briefly kissed Carol on the cheek.

"I travel light. I always have," said Carol. "How are the children and Mom?"

"They're fine. They miss you, but they love your mom. It's good to have you back home," said Greg.

"It's good to be back. It was really hard this time, harder than ever before," said Carol.

"How is Gene?" asked Greg.

"Do you really want to know, or are you just being polite?" asked Carol.

"I really want to know. You don't believe me, but I like Gene. I'm sorry for what happened. I assume you met the man who treated him so disgracefully," said Greg.

"Yes, we met him. He tried to get on our good side. He wants Gene to stay now, or so he wants us to believe," said Carol.

"So who did he win over, or maybe let me guess, probably John, Mike, and Alan," said Greg. "But not you, right?"

"You're right. He hurt Gene so badly. Not just physically, but there is something that just isn't quite right with him. He is in a lot of pain, and he can't seem to do many of the things he had mastered. He uses the wheelchair and crutches now. He can't seem to get by with a cane anymore," said Carol. "Gene has never hurt anyone, and for someone to be so cruel to him, it hurts my heart. I just keep asking myself why he treated him that way, and there is no answer. It didn't have to happen. It could have all been avoided. There is a video of the first part of the meeting when Gene fell. I didn't want to see it, but Mike and John did, so I watched it with them. It upset John very much, and Mike couldn't even watch it."

"But you were more or less forced to watch it, and you didn't even want to," said Greg.

"I couldn't stop watching. I tried to make some sense out of why it happened, but I couldn't," said Carol. "He had been doing so well and, in just a few minutes that horrible George Meyer took it all away from him. Without even blinking an eye, he destroyed all the work Gene had done to recover and probably even his career."

"Are Mike and John all right?" asked Greg.

"Mike's fine. We're not so sure about John. The bond of love between John and Gene is extremely strong," said Carol. "George wants John to be a motivational speaker and talk about his handicaps. I actually think he would like to do it if Gene would be able to go with him."

"I can see that. He is likeable and friendly," said Greg.

"John has become very forgetful. Mike told me he forgets how to do things he has done a hundred times. He's very dependent and childlike. Those are Mike and Alan's opinions, not mine or Gene's. They see him so much more than we do," said Carol.

"What do you think?" asked Greg.

"He's very sensitive. One night he kept checking on Gene all night. He was so frightened. He thought Gene was going to have another stroke in the night and die," said Carol.

"John made many calls to me when Gene was very sick. He was always nice to me and gave me good and correct information," said Greg.

"And thank you for being kind to him. I really appreciated it," said Carol. "I just don't want people to take advantage of him or hurt him. He seems so young and innocent at times. If he decides to do the motivational speaker job, someone would have to be with him all the time."

"There are a lot of people who could take turns helping him, Mike, Alan, you, me, and Gene when he is better," said Greg.

"You? Do you mean that you would be willing to do that?" asked Carol.

"Yes. I find it interesting," said Greg.

"John has had so many bad things happen to him. It would be wonderful if just once something good could happen. He always tries so hard," said Carol.

Several weeks later, there was a phone call from John one afternoon at Carol's house. Carol was at work that afternoon. Greg answered the phone.

"May I speak to Carol?" asked John quietly.

"Hello, John. This is Greg. Do you remember me?"

"Yes, I talked to you many times when Gene was sick," said John.

"Carol is at work right now. She told me you might be a motivational speaker. You would be very good at that John," said Greg.

"That's why I called. George sent me a box of business cards with my name on them and a title of motivational speaker. I really want to try it, but I don't know if I can. I don't know what to do," said John. John sounded nervous and scared and as though he had been crying.

"I'll tell you what, John, I'll have Carol call you as soon as she gets home, or better yet, let's stay on the phone for a while. You sound a little upset. We'll talk for a while. Carol will be home soon. Are you alone?" asked Greg.

"Yes, I'm alone," said John. "I fell and hurt my leg. It's hard to walk. My mouth and teeth are bleeding," said John. He was crying.

"Did this just happen? Are you all right?" asked Greg.

"It happened a little while ago. I'm just confused. Carol knows how to help me when I get like this," said John. "I'm hungry and I'm so cold and I'm shaking."

"I want you to stay on the phone with me. Whatever you do, don't hang up," said Greg. "Tell me about this speaking job."

"I want to do it, but I've never traveled alone, and I would probably have to," said John.

"We could all take turns traveling with you, Carol, Mike, Alan, Gene if he can, and me. I'd like to go with you too," said Greg.

"That's nice of you, Greg," said John. "You're a nice man. Remember that time you came to visit Gene when he was really sick?" asked John.

"Yes, I do," said Greg.

"I was having a hard time walking that day. I had my cane, but it was a long way to the cafeteria. I needed to take hold of Carol's arm, but I thought you might not want me to. Carol told me that it was all right and that you didn't mind. When I took her arm, I could walk better. I never thanked you for that, but I want to thank you now," said John. "Tell Carol I appreciate all she has ever done for me and Gene too. Whenever Carol has been there to help me, Gene has been there too."

"John, I'm glad I was able to do something to help you. I really like you, John. You are a really good person," said Greg. "I think Carol has just turned in the driveway. Hold on, John. Whatever you do, don't hang up."

"I'll hold on," said John.

Greg met Carol on the porch. She had picked Julie up at school.

"John is on the phone. He is scared and crying and alone. He needs to talk to you. I've been talking to him for quite a while. He seems so sad, and he can barely speak, and he fell and hurt his leg and mouth."

Carol hurried to the phone and started talking to John immediately. She didn't stop to think what she was going to say, but she could sense the seriousness in Greg's voice.

"Hi, John. It's Carol. Are you all right?"

"I just needed to talk to someone. Greg talked to me. He was nice to me. I'm scared. I just want my friends," said John.

"Have you called Mike?" asked Carol.

"He's not home. I left a message," said John.

"Try relaxing and take some deep breaths like I showed you. Think some of your favorite thoughts, like California and the house on Lansing Street. Don't let any bad thoughts in," said Carol.

"I'll try. I'm breathing like you showed me right now," said John.

"I can tell by your voice," said Carol.

"George sent me some business cards with my name and motivational speaker below it," said John.

"That's very nice, John, but if it's speaking in front of people that is bothering you, maybe you shouldn't do it," said Carol.

"I don't want to disappoint you," said John.

"John, you could never disappoint any of us. We just want you to be happy and safe and well," said Carol. "We are very proud of you, and we all love you so much."

"I worry about Gene. I want us all to be together," said John.

"Gene is going to be fine. He has just had a setback, so it will take him a little longer to get well. He loves and cares about you very much, John," said Carol.

"Somebody is at the door," said John.

"See who it is, but don't hang up the phone yet," said Carol.

"It's Mike and Alan," said John.

"Let me talk to Mike for a minute," said Carol.

John handed the phone to Mike.

"I've never heard him talk like this before. Please don't leave him alone," said Carol.

"We are going to take him to the emergency room," said Mike. "We got his message. It was frantic. I was afraid we might be too late."

"Thank you, Mike. Keep him safe. For the love of God, please keep him safe," said Carol.

"I'll call as soon as we know what's wrong," said Mike. As Carol hung up the phone, she put her head down on the desk. Greg put his arms around her. There was nothing he could say.

Late that evening, Carol and Greg's phone rang again.

"Hello, Greg. This is Alan McVary, Mike's dad."

"Hello. Just a minute and I'll get Carol," said Greg.

"I would like to thank you for keeping John on the line today until Carol got home and could talk to him," said Alan.

"I was glad I could help," said Greg. He handed the phone to Carol.

"Hello, Alan. It's Carol. Is John going to be all right?

"Yes, he's here with us now," Alan hesitated. "He wasn't in such good shape when we found him. He was so thin. I don't know how long it's been that he hasn't eaten. No matter how bad things were, John was always hungry. I guess it's because his dad tried to starve him when he was a little boy." Alan's voice trailed off, and Carol knew he was crying.

Mike picked up the phone. "I'm sorry. Dad can't talk anymore. He just wanted to thank you and Greg. Thanks to the two of you, we got to him in time. I'm so sorry, Carol. Dad feels so bad. We failed our friend."

"You had no way of knowing," said Carol. "Don't cry, Mike. You and Alan are our rocks. You two aren't supposed to cry."

"We took him to the emergency room. They checked him out. He has some cuts from falling. And he hurt his good leg and his hip. He hurt his mouth. That's why he wasn't talking well. Dad's going to stay with him all night. He won't leave his side. He keeps asking for you and Gene. I'm going to let you talk to John for a few minutes, and then I'll call Gene," said Mike. There was a short pause.

Carol looked at Greg and shook her head. "How am I supposed to compose myself in a minute?"

"If anybody can do it, you can," said Greg.

"Hi, John. It's Carol."

"I'm sorry, Carol. I should have eaten," said John.

"You'll be all right now, my sweet John. Mike and Alan aren't going to leave you," said Carol.

"The girls were visiting Charlene. I was all alone," said John.

"I'm so sorry. Were you afraid?" asked Carol.

"Yes. I couldn't find you and Gene," said John. "I looked for you and Gene in the night. I even went outside, but I couldn't find you."

"You were just having a bad dream. I'm sorry we weren't there for you. Never forget how much Gene and I love you," said Carol. "Mike will call Gene for you tonight. Will you be able to talk to him?"

"Yes, I will talk to him," said John.

"If you ever need to talk to me, just call me. If I'm not here, talk to Greg. He loves you too," said Carol.

Carol hung up the phone. "You didn't mind my telling him that, did you?" said Carol.

"I didn't mind at all. I do love him. He is your friend, and I'll do whatever I can for him," said Greg.

A little later, when Mike called Gene, John was so emotional that he couldn't even speak. Gene was devastated about what had happened to his friend and that he couldn't be with him.

CHAPTER

STRANGE TRAVELING COMPANIONS

When Greg came home from work the next day, Carol was sitting outside with Julie. Greg hugged Julie and sat down by Carol.

"Do you know anything else about John?" asked Greg.

"Not really. Alan is taking him to another doctor tomorrow. Poor Alan is so distraught. He loves John so much. Gene would very much like to go visit John, but I can't go with him right now because of work," said Carol.

"Is Gene unable to travel alone?" asked Greg.

"It's too difficult for him to travel alone right now. He has had too many setbacks," said Carol.

"I'll go with him," said Greg.

"You would really do that for Gene," said Carol.

"Yes, I would be doing it for you, John, and Gene," said Greg.

"You would both be staying with Mike and Alan," said Carol.

"That's all right," said Greg.

"Greg, you need to know that in Gene's own words, he is a lot of work," said Carol.

"You tell me what to do, and I'll do it," said Greg.

"Do you want me to tell you right now?" asked Carol.

"You might as well." Greg pulled a notebook out of his pocket.

"Gene, of course, can't drive now. He needs help with his leg brace. He wears it all night. Without it he is in severe pain. And sometimes he needs help getting up in the morning. He needs help with a shower and shaving. His right hand is still weak, and his left hand trembles. Sometimes he needs help with cutting his food. He needs help dressing and putting on his shoes and socks. He uses crutches now, but only for short distances. He can't walk very far. He takes thirty-five pills a day, and he needs help with that. He is very sensitive and embarrassed about all the help he needs. At night be sure he knows where his glasses are. He can't see without them," Carol paused.

Greg shook his head. "It just makes it more unbelievable what they did to him at work. That should have been a friendly, safe place for him."

"You're right. It should have been, but it wasn't. I think I'm the only one who would like to see him quit. He can't face looking for another job right now. Even though I understand that, I can't accept him staying there. I am afraid he is going to be hurt again," said Carol.

"Are you sure he won't mind me accompanying him?" asked Greg.

"He won't mind. He wants to see his friend. There is a very special bond between Gene and John. There always has been," Carol paused. "Gene has always been such a proud, brave man. He is still that same man, but this has taken a lot out of him. But even though he has suffered and been through so much, he still has his dignity, and he is still incredibly kind and caring. That's why it is so sad what they did to him at work. Gene has never hurt anyone. He was even kind when he was a little boy. Please take good care of him, and don't let anyone say or do anything to hurt him."

"I promise you. I'll take good care of him," said Greg.

Greg would drive to Chicago to Gene's apartment. They would take Gene's van to the airport. They would leave Thursday afternoon and return the following Tuesday.

Gene greeted Greg warmly. "Greg, I can't tell you how grateful I am to you for doing this for me." Gene reached out with his left hand to shake hands with Greg.

"I'm glad to be able to do something for you and for John," said Greg.

"John is pretty special to all of us," said Gene as he took off his glasses and wiped his eyes. "Did Carol tell you that I cry a lot?"

"No, she didn't. Gene, I know how hard this is for you. I would cry too. I know you don't know me very well, but I do care about you and John. I'm here to do anything I can for you," Greg hugged Gene.

"Thanks, Greg. I'm glad you'll be traveling with me. My suitcase is already in the van," said Gene.

They made it to the airport and through the terminal in good time. When it was time for the handicapped boarding, Gene and Greg were asked to board first. At the door to the plane, Greg helped Gene with his crutches and to a seat close to the front of the plane. It was a connecting flight, and there were already about twenty-five passengers on the plane.

The stewardess started to take his crutches and put them with his wheelchair, but a voice behind her said, "There won't be anyone in the window seat so he can keep them in case he needs to use them." Then the pilot stepped up to shake hands with Gene. "Hi, Gene. Remember me? Captain Robinson."

"Of course I do. It's good to see you," said Gene.

"I hope this will be a better flight than the last one," said Captain Robinson.

"Captain Robinson, this is my friend Greg. He is Carol's husband. Do you remember Carol?" asked Gene.

"Yes, I remember her well. It is a pleasure to meet you, Greg. If you need anything at all, please let us know," said Captain Robinson.

"Thank you. Also, I want to thank you for visiting me in the hospital," said Gene. "I've never forgotten it."

"Everyone was rooting for you, and they were all praying for you," said Captain Robinson.

"I needed all the help I could get that day. I've never forgotten the kindness everyone showed to me," said Gene.

As Captain Robinson went back to the cockpit, other passengers started to board the plane.

"Did Carol tell you much about that flight?" asked Gene.

"Not much. That was before I ever met you," said Greg.

"They said I shouldn't fly alone, so Mike got our reservations changed so Carol and I would be on the same flight. We had to wait a while and everyone in the boarding area could tell something bad was happening to me. My nose was bleeding, I was shaking, and I could barely walk. Mike boarded the plane with Carol and me to help me to the seat. John was alone, and he was frightened. Brian and Holly went to help him." Gene paused to wipe his tears.

"I remember Brian and Holly. They brought Carol home. John was with them," said Greg.

"They became our good friends," said Gene. "They offered John and Mike their tickets so they could be with us, but two TWA employees were on the plane, and they gave their tickets to Mike and John. They remembered me. I worked at TWA right after college with them. I guess they could tell I was in bad shape. There was a doctor on that plane. His name was Dr. Landis. He is still my doctor today,"

"Was John all right when he got on the plane with you?" asked Greg.

"Yes. He can't be alone. We shouldn't have let this happen to him. We didn't know his sisters weren't at home. I just hope he will come back to us. John couldn't even talk to me when Mike called. Sometimes John goes to bad places in his mind where he shouldn't go, and I'm afraid that someday he may not come back to us. That's why I'm so thankful to you for going with me to see him. Since he had that dream about me having another stroke and dying in my sleep, he hasn't been quite the same," said Gene.

"I'm glad to be of some help. I've never done anything for you guys," said Greg.

"Oh, but you have, Greg. You take good care of Carol, and you gave her a beautiful daughter and the two boys. She loves all of you very much," said Gene.

Now it was Greg's turn to have tears in his eyes. "I'm not such a good husband or father. I've never cried before. I don't know what's the matter with me."

"You made it a lot longer than I did. The first time I ever cried, I was eighteen years old and in California. I was so glad my dad couldn't see me cry. He was against men showing their emotions at that time anyway. He changed later. You would never guess who made me cry that first time," said Gene.

"It was probably either John or Carol," said Greg.

"You're right. It was Carol," said Gene.

"Should I ask what happened, or would we both start crying again?" asked Greg.

"Oh, I'll probably cry, but I think it was something that was just sad to me." Gene paused for a moment. "We were talking about getting married and having children the previous night. We were staying with Ryan and Jeremy. Ryan was Mike's older brother, and he was gay. The next morning Ryan and Carol were walking on the beach, and we were all watching them. Mike was upset because he could tell Carol was crying, and he could never stand it when someone made Carol cry. We knew they were probably talking about us. Ryan thought Carol loved Mike, and Jeremy thought she loved John. When they came back inside, Carol made an announcement. She said she was going to stay with Ryan and Jeremy and be their surrogate and have as many babies for them as they wanted. Everyone was silent for a while, and then they all laughed, except me. I remember I just looked out at the ocean, and I felt tears running down my cheeks. Carol came up behind me and put her arms around me. She said she was just kidding, and she had just tried to make a joke but didn't do it well. But I knew how much she loved it there, and she wanted to stay." Gene took off his glasses and looked out the window and wiped his eyes.

"I knew she went to California with you guys, but she never said much about it. Of course, I hadn't met her yet," said Greg. "Do you remember Sam, her boss at the insurance company?"

"Carol liked working for him. He took us out to eat a couple of times, and he used to visit when we lived in the house on Lansing Street," said Gene.

"He told me I wasn't the right man for Carol and that we shouldn't get married," Greg hesitated. "He told me that you were the one who loved her, and she loved you. Look, I didn't say that to make you feel bad. Everyone loved Carol then."

"It's all right. I know you didn't mean to hurt me," said Gene. "This isn't the first time this has come up. You see, I always felt that she loved John. I always thought that if there was any chance, they would end up together that I would never stand in the way, but that never happened."

Gene sounded very sad, and Greg was sorry that he had taken him to that place in his past.

"Oh god, I told Carol I wouldn't hurt you, and I think I have done just that. Forgive me, Gene. I didn't mean to go there," said Greg.

"Nothing you said has hurt me, Greg. You just told me Carol loved me. That doesn't hurt me," said Gene. "She thinks I'm more sensitive and fragile than I really am. It's just that I've been through a lot in the last few months, and I'm not doing so good."

"I'm not a very good man. I don't deserve Carol," said Greg.

Gene took off his glasses and wiped his eyes again. "You may regret getting involved with us. We are not just your everyday run-of-the-mill people, especially me. Like I told you, I'm a lot of work," said Gene.

"I've never stepped away because something or someone was a lot of work, so I don't intend to do it now," said Greg.

"You know something. I think John would really like to try that motivational speaker job. Mike told me he is really proud of the business cards George sent him," said Gene.

"Let's try to make it happen for him," said Greg.

"It's a good idea. Just so at least one of us can travel with him and be with him at the meetings," said Gene. "Well, it looks like we are almost there. I can see the Kansas City lights. It is still like home to me. Is it your home too, Greg?" asked Gene.

"No, I'm actually from Peoria, Illinois," said Greg.

They both smiled a little, and then the plane landed. They were first to leave the plane as they had been first to board. They both said goodbye to Captain Robinson and thanked him.

As they entered the terminal, the first people they saw were Mike and John. John was in the wheelchair Jeremy had given him years ago, and he was holding a small box. Mike wheeled Gene as close as he could to John. Gene hugged and kissed John with as genuine a greeting as Mike and Greg had ever witnessed.

"What do you have in the box, John?" asked Gene.

"My business cards with my name on them. I wanted you to see them," said John quietly, and he appeared to be on the verge of tears.

"Those are really nice cards, John. Can I have one, and I bet Greg would like one too. Do you remember Greg?" asked Gene.

"Greg needs two, one for Carol. Hi, Greg. Where's Carol? Is she coming?" asked John.

Greg knelt down by John. "She couldn't come today. She will come to see you soon. She will like your business cards," said Greg. Tears were running down John's cheeks.

"Well, let's get you up to the baggage claim area, and I'll go get the van. Greg and Gene, do you each have a checked in bag?" asked Mike.

"Yes, we each have one bag," said Greg.

John would not let go of Gene's hand as they made their way to the baggage claim area.

Greg had the bags when Mike pulled up in the van. "I tried to fix my van so it would be more like yours for safety reasons. Mine has some of the same equipment your van has."

"You did a really good job," said Gene.

"Let me get John in first. Then I will come back and show Greg how everything works," said Mike.

Mike took John to the other side of the van and picked him up out of the wheelchair and gently set him in the seat and put the seat belt around him. Mike had picked John up as though he had lost a lot of weight. Greg and Gene both noticed, but neither one said anything.

"Greg, I'll show you how this works," said Mike.

"You do good work, Mike. It's pretty close to Gene's van," said Greg.

"I'm glad you are here, Greg. We all need you. John needs you."

For a moment Greg saw tears in Mike's eyes.

John was curled up in the corner of his wheelchair with his head against the window. John was having a hard time talking.

"Did you hurt your mouth and teeth when you fell?" asked Gene.

"Yes. When I fell, I hit my mouth and teeth on the cement. Alan's going to take me to the dentist," said John.

"Who's that you've got there, John?" asked Gene.

"It's Cathy's teddy bear. Mike got it from her room. He said she doesn't need it anymore. Gene, do you remember the little white kitten you won for Carol at Fairyland Park?" asked John.

"Yes, John, I remember it," said Gene.

"When we went on the Ferris wheel, she held it against her heart for a long time. I wonder if she still has it." asked John.

"Did it have a little pink collar with diamonds?" asked Greg.

"Yes, it did," said John.

"She still has it," said Greg.

"I'm glad because she liked it so much," said John.

"I know she did, John. She named it Snowball," said Gene.

"I like that name. That's a really good name for that little kitten," said John.

"Give me your hand, John. I would like to hold it for a while," said Gene.

"It's my bad hand. Do you mind? That's the one Carol always wants to hold." John was crying more now. He missed Carol so much.

"I know. It's the one I want to hold too, John." As Gene took hold of John's hand, it felt like a child's hand, and as he moved his hand up John's arm, he realized how thin John was. He knew by the way Mike had picked him up and put him in the van that John had lost a lot of weight. John was tall, and although he was rather thin, he had been fairly muscular in his arms but not anymore.

When they arrived at Mike's house, Greg was able to get Gene out of the van while Mike took care of John. Alan met them at the door.

"Gene, it is so good to see you. And, Greg, thank you for bringing Gene here. We need you both so much right now." He hugged and kissed them.

In the living room, Gene used his crutches to get to the sofa. Mike picked John up and set him by Gene. He was still holding the box of cards and the teddy bear.

"Alan, shall I show them my leg?" asked John.

"Yes, John, it's all right," said Alan.

"Gene, will you help me pull my pants leg up?" asked John.

Mike went over to John. "Is it all right if I help you, John? Gene can't bend over that far."

"It's all right, Mike." John patted Mike on the back.

Mike gently pulled up his pants leg to show them his good leg. It appeared to have many cuts and bandages on it as well as a brace.

"Gene, when I fell, I hurt myself really bad. I hurt my hip too."

"Where did you fall, John?" sked Gene.

"I went to the garage. I wanted to work, but I couldn't do anything. Then I fell," said John as he buried his face in Gene's chest. "That's when I hurt my teeth and mouth too. I can't walk good now." John was still crying. He couldn't seem to stop.

"John, remember how I told you that you healed better than me?" asked Gene.

"But not this time. I really messed up bad this time," said John as he rubbed his head and eyes.

"Do you have a headache?" asked Gene.

"Yes," said John.

Gene got a small pillow from the back of the sofa and put it on his lap. "I know I'm not as good as Carol, but I'm going to rub your head like she does. I've seen her do it many times." Gene rubbed very gently. He knew his hands were so much bigger than Carol's. He knew she rubbed around the edge of the scars outward in the direction the wounds healed.

John looked up at Gene with tears in his eyes and said, "You're pretty, Gene, but not quite as pretty as Carol."

Gene bent over and kissed John gently on the forehead.

Mike said, "I'm going to pick up a couple pizzas. Any special requests?"

"I like pepperoni," said John.

Alan went to the kitchen to get drinks, and Greg went to help him. "We didn't say everything on the phone. It is just that we thought he would snap out of it. He has had problems before, but he has always been all right. I'm so sorry." Alan sat down at the table and put his head down and cried.

"He will be all right. You have all taken good care of him over the years. John's got a job to do, and he wants to use his business cards," said Greg.

Alan stood up and hugged Greg. "Thank you again for bringing Gene."

"I hope we can all help John. Carol thinks so much of him," said Greg.

"I know. We are all going to help him. I'm not sure how just yet, but we are going to help him," said Alan.

Mike returned with the pizzas, putting one piece on a plate for John.

"You used to eat a lot more than that, John. Aren't you hungry?" asked Gene.

"I just can't eat much anymore. I'm too nervous," said John.

Gene put his arm around John. "Why are you nervous, John?"

"I'm just worried about you, Gene. I can't get over it. I'm worried something is going to happen to you," said John.

"John, you have to stop worrying about me. You will get sick if you don't eat. Where do you want me to sleep tonight?" asked Gene.

"With me, please," said John.

"I will. Now let's have another piece of pizza," said Gene.

"John, do you remember the nice doctor in Dallas, my friend, Dr. Brett Wilson? He helped you many years ago," said Alan.

"I remember him. He was really nice to me," said John.

"I'm going to call him tonight. He's at KU Medical Center here in Kansas City now. Maybe he can work us in tomorrow. Would you go see him, John?" asked Alan.

"Yes, I'll go. Maybe he can help me," said John.

"Well, that's settled. I'll call him now. You guys had better get some rest. You look really tired, Gene." Alan hugged Gene as well as Greg and John. "I love all of you, and I'm glad we are all here."

"I feel honored that Gene let me come with him," said Greg.

"If you two are ready, Greg and I will help you to bed," said Mike. Mike helped John to his wheelchair.

Gene stood up and tried to use his crutches, but he felt too weak.

Greg noticed immediately. "I'll get your wheelchair, Gene."

When they got to the bedroom, Mike had already put John to bed. "I'll give you a shower and wash your hair in the morning. Now I'm going to take your braces off." When Mike took the brace off John's good leg, John cringed in pain. "I'm sorry, John, I didn't mean to hurt you." Mike handed John his teddy bear. "Hold on to it tightly. I'm going to help Gene now."

"Would you like for me to help Gene or stay by John?" asked Greg.

"It hurt John when I took the brace off. Please make sure he is all right," said Mike.

Greg sat on the bed beside John. "I'm sorry it hurt so much, John."

John reached out as much as he could with his bad hand and touched Greg. "Carol always holds my bad hand. Would you do that for me?"

Greg took hold of John's bad hand and kissed it and gently rubbed it.

As Mike was helping Gene get ready for bed, Gene was having a hard time brushing his teeth. "I can't do anything tonight. I'll wait until morning." Gene held on to Mike's arm to keep his balance. "Mike, you are doing so much for everyone. You never signed up to be a caregiver. You are not even getting paid."

"But I am getting paid, a hundred times over. You, John, and Carol are my best friends. You're the only real friends I've ever had. I would do anything for the three of you. It kills me to know all you have gone through just to have a setback. And to see John like he is right now, I know it hurts you as much as it does me. I think it would destroy Carol to see him like this. You know, before my mom died, she told me to always take care of the three of you. She was so worried about you when you had the concussion and hurt your neck and leg playing football. We were all concerned, but she seemed to be worried the most. She said you might need me more than anyone," said Mike.

"I was only sixteen, my parents were away, and I was in so much pain. She held me in her arms, like I was a little boy, she fed me, took my temperature, gave me medicine, and washed my face. She was so kind to me, as though she really cared about me and loved me," said Gene.

Two good friends cried that night together. When they composed themselves, they went back to the bedroom where Greg and John were waiting. Mike very gently helped Gene from the wheelchair to the bed and then helped him to lie down on his back.

Then Mike went to John's side of the bed. "Do you have anything you want to talk about tonight, John?"

"If I go to the doctor tomorrow, can somebody stay with me?" asked John.

"Somebody will always be with you, John. I promise, we will never leave you alone," said Mike.

"Will the doctor hurt me?" asked John.

"No, we won't let anyone hurt you. If they want to do something to you that you don't want them to, please tell us," said Mike.

"I will," John hugged Mike.

Mike took John's glasses off and put them on the nightstand.

"Mike, would you please get me a pill from my jacket pocket?" asked Gene.

Mike got a Nitroglycerin tablet for Gene. "Are you all right? Is it a bad pain?" asked Mike.

"I'll be all right. It's just a slight pain. I need to stay as strong as I can for you, guys." Gene took hold of Mike's hand.

"I'm going to stay here with them for a while. Would you like to stay with me?" asked Mike.

"I'll stay," said Greg.

"Greg, would you please put my business cards with my glasses. I forgot I had them with me."

John handed Greg his box of cards.

"They are right by your glasses," said Greg as he took the cards from John.

"Thanks, Greg." John turned to Gene. He reached over and kissed Gene on the cheek. He knew Gene wasn't feeling good.

Mike and Greg sat with their friends for a long time that night. John fell asleep soon. Gene's breathing seemed regular a little later, and he eventually fell asleep. Mike motioned for Greg to go with him as they quietly left the room.

Down the hallway, Mike stopped and put his head on the banister. Greg put his arm around Mike as Mike said, "How much more can they take? They have both had so many bad things happen to them. I feel so helpless."

"You're doing everything for them, Mike. You are very kind to them," said Greg. "I wish Carol was here with you to help you. I know everyone would feel more secure with her here. She always seems to know what to do."

"Carol is the kind and gentle one. It's out of character for me, but I'm doing the best I can. I just hope I can do enough," said Mike.

"You are doing a good job, Mike. They love you very much," said Greg.

"We'll see what happens tomorrow at the doctor's office. Good night, Greg. I'll stay with them tonight," said Mike.

As he had done many times before, Mike would stay in the room with Gene and John all night. It was Mike, not John, who felt he needed to watch Gene that night. Whenever Gene asked for a Nitroglycerin, it worried Mike, as it did Carol. He decided not to mention it to Alan.

Toward morning, Mike noticed that Gene was sleeping peacefully and his breathing was still regular. He went to John's side of the bed. John was awake.

"Be very quiet. I'm going to let Gene sleep while I help you get ready. He didn't go to sleep right away last night."

Mike already had John's clothes, braces, and glasses in the small room outside the bathroom. Mike took John directly to the shower and set him on the chair in the shower and washed his body, hair, and teeth. He was very careful with his injured leg. As Mike had asked him to be, John was very quiet. Mike dressed John in a light-blue, long-sleeve shirt and navy slacks. John always wore long sleeves because of his arm. He very gently put the braces on John's legs. He shaved him, combed his hair, and put his glasses on.

"Dad's already up. I'll take you to him. Be sure not to eat because of the tests you'll take today." On the way out of the room,

Mike handed John's box of business cards and teddy bear to him. He knew John would want them.

Alan and Greg were both at the kitchen table. "I'm sorry, you can't have breakfast today," said Alan.

John smiled, "It's all right, I don't mind."

Gene was awake when Mike went back to the bedroom. "It would be easier, Mike, if I just stayed here. I'm just too much work," said Gene.

"Not today, my friend, and you are not too much work. You're my work, and I love you, and John loves you. This is a big day for him," said Mike.

"Thanks, Mike. I just hope you know how much I appreciate all you have done for me," said Gene.

"I know, Gene, I've always known," said Mike. "Do you have any pain this morning?"

"Not that kind," said Gene.

After breakfast, they left for the doctor's office. John was cold and shivering so Mike got a blanket out of the back of the van and put it around him. Because there were five of them, they were taken to a conference room and told Dr. Wilson would be there soon.

When Dr. Wilson arrived, he went around the table and warmly greeted everyone. It's good to see you, Alan."

"Dr. Wilson, this is Greg, Carol's husband," said Alan.

"I remember Carol very well," said Dr. Wilson. "Hello, Gene. Alan told me what happened. I am so sorry."

"Thank you. We appreciate you seeing John," said Gene.

"Hello, Mike," said Dr. Wilson. "And here's my old friend, John."

John moved his chair over a little, and Dr. Wilson pulled up a chair by John. John seemed very shy. He was curled up in the corner of his wheelchair as close as he could get to Gene, and he was trying to hold Gene's hand with his bad hand. John still had the blanket around him.

Dr. Wilson spoke to John very softly. He knew from what Alan had told him that this would not be easy.

"What do you have with you, John?"

"This is Cathy's teddy bear, but Mike said I could use it. Carol has a kitten named Snowball. Gene won it for her a long time ago," said John.

"And what is in your box?" asked Dr. Wilson.

"These are my business cards," said John. "Gene's boss, George, gave them to me. He wanted me to be a motivational speaker, but I'm not doing so well now."

John struggled to open the box but couldn't, so Dr. Wilson helped him. John took a card out of the box.

"I want to give you one of my cards."

"Thank you, John. I want to hear you speak," said Dr. Wilson.

"It might be in Chicago," said John.

"That would be fine. I like Chicago." Dr. Wilson smiled at John, and even though John smiled a little, Gene saw how afraid John looked.

"John, you don't have to answer any questions because Alan has told me everything. But what I need to do is examine you. Will you let me do that?" asked Dr. Wilson.

"Can Gene stay with me?" asked John.

"John, I won't be able to help you," said Gene.

"Can two people come with me?" asked John.

"For special people like you, sure," said Dr. Wilson.

"Mike needs to be with me too, in case he needs to lift me." John put his hand out to touch Mike's hand. "Gene is hurt, and he can't help lift me."

John would have many tests that day. Gene, Mike, and Dr. Wilson stayed with him through everything. They did not leave his side. Eight hours later, the tests were finished. Alan tried to get John to eat a little since he hadn't eaten all day. Then they took him home and put him to bed.

THE PHONE CALL AND THE ROAD MAP

Dr. Wilson would work long into the night along with many others so they could have the results for John and his friends the following day.

That evening at about eight thirty, Dr. Wilson went to his office and made a phone call. Dr. Wilson had talked to Gene while John was having the tests that day. Gene had told Dr. Wilson how close Carol and John had always been, and after the accident that had damaged John's head so badly, she had always been able to help him with the pain. Gene told him that Carol had said John's head was like a road map to her. Dr. Wilson pulled a crumpled piece of paper from his pocket with Carol's phone number on it. He dialed her number. She answered the phone on the first ring.

"Hello, Carol. This is Dr. Brett Wilson, John's doctor. Do you remember me?"

"Of course. You were so kind to John. I never forget kind people," said Carol.

"How much do you know about John's present condition?" asked Dr. Wilson.

"As you probably know, my husband Greg is there with them. He called me yesterday and just a few hours ago. He has told me everything. He knows I should be there in his place, but I can't be there right now. If John has surgery and before, I will be there," said Carol. "I love him so much."

"We know you do. He speaks your name often. If he has any memory problems, where you are concerned there is definitely no memory loss," said Dr. Wilson. "There is one thing in particular that Gene told me that I would like for you to tell me about. You told Gene that John's head is like a road map to you."

"After the accident, he would get terrible headaches. No medication would help him. He would get them when he was nervous or afraid. I would sit on the sofa with a pillow on my lap and gently lay his head on the pillow. As Gene told you, his head is like a road map to me. I knew where every scar was, and I remembered how they healed. I would massage very gently just outside the scar in the direction I remembered the scar healing. Soon his body would relax, and his headache would go away. This happened on a regular basis," said Carol.

"Thank you, Carol. You have been very helpful," said Dr. Wilson.

"May I ask specifically how I have helped you?" asked Carol.

"You said he would get the headaches when he was nervous or afraid. He was definitely nervous and afraid when he was alone, and he fell at the garage. He couldn't work, and he wasn't eating. I'm sure you can imagine how scared he was. He is also very worried about Gene and has been for some time now. I was afraid he might have a brain tumor, and I don't believe he could handle that type of surgery. I think it is more of a nervous disorder that can be treated without surgery. I know that Greg told you that we will do surgery on his hip to stabilize it. We will help his eyesight and hearing. It will be the first time he has ever had hearing aids. There is a 90 percent hearing loss in his injured ear and a less severe loss in the other ear. I think we can help him, and at least get him back to where he was and hopefully better," said Dr. Wilson.

"You know, Dr. Wilson, John has always been a very special person. Recently, those close to him have mentioned that he is childlike, but you see I noticed that the very first time I ever met him. They feel he is forgetful and gets confused, but he has been through so much. He has always been so smart, gentle, kind, and loving. He is also so honest and genuine. John is not a king or a prince, but right now he is the most important person in the world to us. His life and happiness are very important," said Carol. Dr. Wilson could tell she was fighting back tears. He wished he was near so he could comfort her.

"He is important to me also, and I know how much you and the four guys with him today love and care about him. I will help him with all that you have told me tonight. I look forward to seeing you. Goodbye for now," said Dr. Wilson.

"Thank you, Dr. Wilson. I'll see you soon," said Carol. As Carol hung up the phone, she wiped her tears away.

In Kansas City, Dr. Wilson sat at his desk for a while, and he could feel an occasional tear run down his cheek. He was a doctor, and doctors don't cry. But he remembered years ago when he first treated John. He had brought Dr. Wilson to tears then too. Then it had been because of the terrible scars he had seen on his body. And now it was because he just wanted so much to help John. He loved and was impressed with John's wonderful group of friends.

He remembered what Carol had said about John not being a king or prince, but to her and their friends, he was the most important person in the world. He only hoped that it was within his power to help John.

John's Happiness and Gene's Heartache

John and Greg were eating breakfast the following day as Alan was preparing breakfast for Mike and Gene. John was having a hard time eating his cereal and eggs.

"Can I help you, John?" asked Greg as he put his arm around John.

"Yes, I can't do it this morning," said John.

"What's the matter, John?" asked Greg.

"I'm just too nervous and really scared," said John.

"We will all be there with you today. He is a very nice doctor and really smart. He's going to help you," said Greg.

John smiled a little and took a bite of the cereal Greg offered him. Then Greg offered him a bite of egg and a drink of milk. John put his head on Greg's shoulder, but he kept eating the small bites of food that Greg continued to feed him.

Gene and Mike came to eat their breakfast.

"John, did you eat a good breakfast?" asked Gene.

"Yes, Greg helped me," said John. John still had his head resting on Greg shoulder.

Gene tried to eat a few bites of his egg, but he dropped the eggs and fork on the floor. Gene tried to pick it up, but he couldn't. Mike came to help him.

"I'm sorry, Mike," said Gene.

"Don't worry, Gene. It's all right. Can I get you something else?" asked Mike.

"No, I've had enough," Gene paused and took hold of Mike's arm. "I'm going to need the wheelchair today."

"I'll get it," said Mike. Mike slowly helped Gene to the wheelchair. "Is it your leg?" asked Mike.

"Yes. It's really bothering me today," said Gene.

Mike helped John to the van, and Greg helped Gene, and they headed toward the doctor's office. In the van, Gene reached out and held John's hand. John immediately noticed that Gene's hand was trembling, and he patted it gently as Carol had done to him many times.

Dr. Wilson was waiting for them in the conference room. He had many reports and x-rays in front of him. After initial greetings, Dr. Wilson said, "And how's my favorite patient today?"

"I'm all right," said John.

"You're not afraid of me today, are you, John?" asked Dr. Wilson.

"No, I just worry about all the test results," said John as he continued to hold tightly to Gene's hand.

"I think I know where we will start. Can you come a little closer to my desk?" asked Dr. Wilson.

"Gene too?" asked John.

"Gene too," said Dr. Wilson.

Mike immediately moved them both closer to the doctor's desk with John a little to the side.

"John, these are your new hearing aids, one for the left ear and one for the right. Let me show you how to put them in your ears." Then Dr. Wilson took his own hearing aids out of his ears and showed John how to put them in.

"Gene, Dr. Wilson has hearing aids too, just like you, and now I also have them," said John.

"I first got mine when I was much younger than you. I was just a little boy. How old were you, Gene?" asked Dr. Wilson.

"I was sixteen. I had a concussion playing football that affected by hearing," said Gene.

"Now let's put them in together." John watched closely what Dr. Wilson did, and he did the same.

John's eyes became very big, and he smiled. "I can hear so much better. Thank you, Dr. Wilson."

"We will have your new glasses in a few days. They will be stronger, and you will be able to see so much better," said Dr. Wilson. "John, have you ever seen an x-ray?"

"Yes, after my accident," said John.

"This is your hip. We are going to make a small incision and insert a pin in your hip. It will keep your hip from hurting and keep you from falling. All the cuts on your leg will be healed before we put the pin in your hip. You will be able to walk, but you will probably still have to use the cane," said Dr. Wilson.

"That's all right, because I'll be able to walk," said John.

"I'm going to give you some pills to take every morning for your headaches and your eyes, and one pill will help you with anxiety. Will you be all right with taking them?" asked Dr. Wilson.

"Yes, I will," said John.

"Does everything sound agreeable to you?" asked Dr. Wilson.

"Fine. I am anxious to get my hip fixed so I can walk and get my new glasses. I promise to take my pills," said John. "Thank you for everything."

John put his arms out, and Dr. Wilson knew he wanted to hug him, so he moved closer so he could.

As everyone got up to leave the room, Dr. Wilson said, "Gene, could I talk to you for a few minutes?"

"Sure," said Gene.

John touched Gene's arm. "Do you want me to stay with you?"

"Not this time. I'll be all right," said Gene.

Mike pushed John's wheelchair out the door and closed it behind him.

Gene took his glasses off and took a tissue from Dr. Wilson's desk and wiped his eyes.

"Gene, are you going to be all right?" asked Dr. Wilson with compassion. "I could see the pain in your eyes when I was talking to

John, not just physical but emotional. I was afraid you were going to break."

"You were right. I was pretty close to losing it. John is tearing me apart. I need Carol with me. She always takes the brunt of it. She knows how everybody feels, and she always knows what to do and say. I just feel completely helpless," said Gene.

"I would like to try to help you, if you will let me," said Dr. Wilson.

"I don't want to die. I want to live to see John get better. I just feel completely defeated, like there is no hope for me," said Gene.

"There is always hope. What happened to your cheek?" asked Dr. Wilson.

"I fell on my face giving a presentation at work. I was trying to reach for a piece of chalk. I cut my face and twisted my leg. My boss screamed at me to get up, and I couldn't. He wouldn't let anyone help me. He wouldn't even give me my glasses. He just kept screaming at me in front of everyone. He doesn't like handicapped people," said Gene through tears.

"I can't stand to know you were abused like that," said Dr. Wilson.

"He met Carol, John, Mike, and Alan when they visited me a few weeks ago. Carol had several questions for him. She thinks I should quit. Mike and John wanted to see the video of the meeting. Carol didn't want to see it, but she watched it with them. Alan has the video," said Gene.

"Could I see it?" asked Dr. Wilson.

"Yes. I haven't seen it. I lived it," said Gene. "My boss has been described as cutthroat and ruthless. He wants the macho man type who will do anything to get ahead. I'm not that man. Even if I wanted to be, I couldn't. I'm not strong enough anymore."

"Do they know what caused your strokes?" asked Dr. Wilson.

"High blood pressure, heart disease, football injuries to my neck and a really bad concussion. I have it all. I have always had severe headaches and poor eyesight. Mike always wanted me to play baseball, but the ball was too small. I couldn't see it. So I played football and basketball," said Gene. "I can't go out there now, but they need to go home."

"I'll see if Alan will bring me the tape," said Dr. Wilson as he went to where Gene's friends were waiting.

"Is everything all right?" asked Alan.

"Not really, but I'm trying to help. Gene needs some understanding and encouragement right now. He's not feeling so good," said Dr. Wilson.

"Can I go see him?" said John.

Dr. Wilson put his arm around John. "Not right now, John. Gene told me about something very bad that happened to him. You know about it. It's how he got the scar on his face and his painful leg and the setbacks. I'm going to try to help him if I can. He loves you very much, John. He loves all of you. Alan, would you bring me the video of the meeting?"

"Yes, right away," said Alan.

John seemed to understand, and he waved to Dr. Wilson as they went out the door. Dr. Wilson went back to his office.

"Gene, would you like to talk to Carol? I know that Greg is her husband and that he traveled here with you. I also know that you love Carol more than life itself and she loves you."

Without a word, Gene dialed Carol's number. She answered immediately.

"Hello, Carol. It's Gene."

"It's good to hear your voice. Is everyone all right?" asked Carol.

"John's doing well. Everyone else is fine, except me. I'm not fine, Carol. I'm with Dr. Wilson. He wants to try to help me," said Gene.

"Gene, if anyone can help you, it could be Dr. Wilson. Let him try. He is a good doctor," said Carol. "Gene, we all love you so much. There is no one else in the world as good as you. There never has been before, and there never will be again. John needs you so much, and so do I. I always have. Please stay with us, Gene. I need to see you and touch you and be with you."

Gene was on the verge of tears. He couldn't speak.

Dr. Wilson took the phone. "Carol, this is Dr. Wilson. I'll keep him safe. I'm going to try to help him."

"Thank you. I love him so much," said Carol.

"I know, and so does he," said Dr. Wilson.

"Please tell her not to worry about me," said Gene.

"He doesn't want you to worry about him," said Dr. Wilson.

"You don't need to tell him what I'm saying to you, but it's too late. It was too late a long time ago because I'll always worry about him," said Carol.

At that moment, Alan returned with the video. "You wanted to see it, Dr. Wilson, so here it is." As Alan looked at Gene's face, he put his arms around him and said, "May I stay here with Gene? He is like a son to me."

"It's all right, you can stay. You don't mind, do you, Gene?" asked Dr. Wilson.

"I don't mind. I need him," said Gene.

"Unless you want to watch it with me, I'll go to the room next door to watch it," said Dr. Wilson.

"I don't want to see it again, and I know Gene doesn't want to see it," said Alan.

As Dr. Wilson left the room, Gene spoke quietly to Alan, "Thanks for staying with me, Alan. Dr. Wilson asked me to call Carol. Just in a few minutes, she calmed me and made me feel better with her voice and her words. She has always been able to do that for me."

"I'm not sure what it is, but she has always affected me that way too," said Alan. "Gene, know that if it was feasible, I would take your pain away. I'm old, my life is almost over, but you are young with your whole life in front of you. I just wish I could trade places with you." Alan had his arms around Gene until Dr. Wilson returned.

"That definitely was not pleasant to watch," said Dr. Wilson. "As a doctor, to me what he did was a criminal act, and he should be punished. He shouldn't be allowed to get away with those despicable actions. I am so sorry that it happened to you."

"In his defense, he didn't know that I couldn't turn far enough to the right to reach the chalk, and he didn't know my eyesight was so bad," said Gene.

"Gene, you don't need to defend him. He is a cruel man and quite probably will continue to be. He is a bully. He may have been nice to your friends, but he will go back to his old ways. That is a work environment that I hate to see you subjected to," said Dr. Wilson.

"I just don't think I can get another job right now. I don't think I am physically capable of it," said Gene. "Carol definitely wants me to get another job. I usually agree with her, but I just don't think I can now."

"What do you think, Alan?" Asked Dr. Wilson.

"As I mentioned earlier, Gene is like a son to me. I fully understand how difficult it would be for him to find another job today. But I also know that he would be an asset to any company lucky enough to hire him. I know how difficult it was for you to return to work, Gene, even before the terrible treatment you received. I hope to see you get back to where you were before the setback," said Alan. "I wish so much that I could protect you, Gene, because you need it now, but I can't. I can help you, but I can't really protect you like I can John."

"You have done so much for me, Alan, and for all of us. I thank you for that," said Gene.

Dr. Wilson handed the video to Alan. "Thank you for letting me see it. It gave me a better understanding of what Gene is dealing with. People who are handicapped need to have more protection than they do today. Maybe someday they will."

"I agree with you, but when that happens, it may be too late for me and for John," said Gene. "Speaking of John, I need to go to him now. I just want to be with him."

"Call me before you leave for Chicago," said Dr. Wilson. "I want to help you, Gene."

As Gene looked at Dr. Wilson, there were tears in his eyes. "You have helped me, more than you realize. Just the fact that you understand and care and are showing concern about what happened is very special to me, and I thank you for that," said Gene.

Three fine men left the conference room together. After Alan secured Gene's wheelchair in the van, he took a handkerchief from his pocket. He took Gene's glasses off and wiped his eyes and cheeks.

"I think I'll leave my glasses off for a while. My eyes are very tired," said Gene.

Alan handed Gene his glasses, and they headed home.

MIKE, TEACHER AND SWIMMER

When they arrived home, everyone was glad to see them, especially John. He met them at the door.

"Are you all right, Gene?" asked John.

"I'm not sure, John," said Gene. "I don't feel so good right now."

"I was worried, but I knew you were with Alan and Dr. Wilson, and I know they wouldn't let anything happen to you because they love you like I do," said John. "Greg called Carol a while ago, and after he talked to her and his children, he let me talk to her. She was happy for me, and she said she will be here when I have my surgery."

"I'm glad you got to talk to Carol, and I'm happy for you too, John," said Gene. "John, would you ask Mike if he will come help me?"

Mike came to Gene quickly. "What's wrong, Gene?" asked Mike.

Gene spoke quietly, "I want to sit on the sofa, and I can't do it on my own, and I need a Nitro."

Mike got the Nitroglycerin tablet from Gene's pocket and gave it to him and helped him to the sofa. Mike gently lifted Gene's feet up and put a cover over him.

"John, I'm going to help you sit by Gene. Don't lean against him, just hold his hand." Mike could tell this pain was worse than usual.

"What's the matter with Gene?" asked John.

"He's having a pain in his heart. He needs to stay quiet and still after he takes the pill," said Mike. Mike sat down by John. Mike did not take his eyes off Gene, nor did John. After a while Mike said, "He seems to be breathing a little better now."

Two hours later, Gene woke up. "I knew you were both with me, and I could feel John holding my hand."

"John, I was taking care of Gene, but I was also doing something else. Do you know what I mean?" asked Mike.

"I know what you mean," said John. "You were teaching me how to take care of Gene too."

"You're right, John. You are very smart," said Mike.

"Thank you guys for taking care of me," said Gene.

"We love you, Gene," said John.

Mike helped Gene to the wheelchair to take him to the bedroom. "I'll be back for you in a few minutes, John," said Mike.

"Don't forget me," said John.

"I assure you, John, I will never forget you." Mike smiled at John.

A few minutes later Mike came back. "I'll be here with you all night, but right now I'm going to ask Greg to come in for a while."

When Greg came into the room, Gene and John were both asleep.

Mike went out to the pool. No one swam much anymore, but Alan kept the pool cleaned. Alan himself would swim laps occasionally. But that night Mike swam lap after lap. He swam fast and every different stroke he could remember as he used to do with Carol, Ryan, and Richard so many years ago. He swam until he felt as though his arms and legs would fall off. But it felt good to push himself to the limit and beyond.

When Mike went back into John and Gene's bedroom, Greg said on his way out, "That was some good swimming you did out there."

"Thanks," Mike smiled.

Two days later Gene and Greg went home. This goodbye was especially hard for Greg. He had grown very fond of all four men, especially John, but he truly loved all of them. John had completely stolen his heart. Gene called Dr. Wilson before they left Kansas City. He told him that he was actually feeling better and that John was doing great. Dr. Wilson seemed pleased and told Gene that he would see him in two weeks.

After Gene's phone call, Dr. Wilson sat in his office alone for a while thinking about this wonderful group of friends he had become involved with. Dr. Wilson was fifty. He had never been married or had a family. His father had been Alan McVary's friend. When his father died, Alan had helped him through medical school. He remembered the first time Alan had brought John to him. John was only eighteen, as were Carol, Gene, and Mike, and Dr. Wilson had been able to help him then and many times through the years. And now he so much wanted to help Gene.

He was anxious to do John's surgery in two weeks. He was also anxious to see Carol in two weeks. Carol was so kind, smart, and easy to talk to. Dr. Wilson was in love with her and had been since she was eighteen. But no one knew. Others loved her too, Greg, John, Mike, Alan, and especially Gene. They all loved her. He wished he could see and talk to her more often. She intrigued him. He liked to watch her and study her. No one had ever affected him that way before. He was thinking of Carol as his wife and the mother of his children. He thought at that time that these thoughts would stay in his heart, but that was not to be. He couldn't help but love her, but then he realized that he didn't just love Carol, but he loved her friends as well and the kind, tender way they all treated and took care of one another.

John's Surprise

Gene returned to Kansas City two weeks later for John's surgery. This time Carol was with him. John and Mike were there to meet them when they got off the plane. Carol embraced John.

"You look good, John. I'm so glad to see you. I love your new glasses and your hearing aids. Can you hear me better now?"

"Yes, much better. I've missed you so much, Carol," said John. "And I've missed you too, Gene."

Gene took hold of John's hand. "And I've missed you, John."

"Well, I'll tell you what. I've missed you guys too," said Mike.

"Is Alan with you?" asked Gene.

"No, he stayed home tonight," said Mike.

As they walked to the baggage claim area, Mike asked, "How many bags?"

"Just one for me," said Gene.

"I just have my blue bag. Can you hold it for me, John, while I push your wheelchair?" asked Carol.

"Sure," said John.

Carol opened the blue bag and pulled out a little white stuffed kitten with a pink collar with diamonds. "Do you remember Snowball? Greg told me you asked about her."

"She came to visit," said John.

"Oh gosh, you two are making me cry already," said Mike. "I'll go get your suitcase."

When they arrived at the house, Alan was waiting for them in the living room. Mike helped both Gene and John to the sofa. "Thank you, Mike. That feels good after the plane ride," said Gene.

John was sitting between Carol and Gene on the sofa. John had been hiding his mouth with his teddy bear. Carol noticed he had a hard time talking and pronouncing some words.

All of a sudden Carol said, "John, look at me and smile."

John did as she said.

"No, smile bigger like when I tickle you," said Carol.

John smiled bigger.

"John, you have braces on your teeth. How cool is that. You look so good," said Carol.

"We wondered how long it would take you to notice," said Alan. "He hurt his mouth and teeth really bad when he fell."

John turned to Gene and smiled. "That's great, John. Alan is taking very good care of you."

Carol said, "I'll tell you a secret, John. I always wanted braces, but my mom said we couldn't afford them. I never wanted to smile in pictures because my teeth were so crooked. My mom told me I wasn't pretty enough to be a movie star, so I didn't need braces. Even now I never like to smile big."

"This is strange," said Gene. "I always wanted and needed braces too, but my parents couldn't afford them either. I never smiled so no one saw my teeth, but they go every which way, and I've always had the big space between my front teeth."

"I always loved your teeth," said Carol. "But then I love every-thing about you."

"Well, guess what. I wanted braces too," said Mike. "My teeth were small but crooked. I never liked the way they looked. Ryan and Cathy had braces, so I wanted them too."

"I always thought your teeth were fine, Mike," said Alan.

"And I always liked your smile, Carol. It was gentle and sweet, just like you," said Gene.

"You forgot kind and sensual," said Mike. "Carol had the most inviting, kindest smile I had ever seen, and it held a little mystery. I could never stand bigmouthed girls with a smile that went all across their face."

"You guys are funny. I never knew you all wanted braces," said John.

"Well, John, you now have something that the three of us have always wanted," said Carol. "You have always had a wonderful smile. Now it will be even better."

"You know that I would pay for braces for all of you if you still want them," said Alan.

"No, not now, thanks. I have one child with braces and two more who will need them soon," said Carol.

"Thank you, but even though I know I really need them, I've got too many other things going on now," said Gene.

"I guess not. We'll let John have this one. You'll be the only one of us who has straight teeth," said Mike.

"And, Mike, you always smiled from the very first day I met you. You have always had a beautiful smile," said Carol. "Do you remember my friend, Janice? She loved your smile. She loved you."

"I never knew that," said Mike. "I'll tell you who loved you, Carol. Nathan, Jessie, and David all liked you."

"I knew about Nathan because he told me, and David loved me since the third grade, but I never knew about Jessie," said Carol.

"I remember Nathan. He was in my gym class, and he was really tall," said John. "Nobody even knew me."

"We got to know you. You are all ours. You were the sweetest, best-looking guy in the whole class, and I got to walk with you in the graduation processional. I was the luckiest girl in the class," said Carol. "You three guys were not only cute, but you were the nicest guys I had ever met."

"Girls always scared me. I thought they were to forward and loud, but not you. You were perfect," said Gene.

"I agree with Gene," said Mike. "You were always so good to everyone. I had never known anyone like you before or since. There was one guy who was really shy, but he was a nice guy, Terry Sheley. I guess he saw us together, and he wanted to know if you were my girlfriend. I think he wanted to ask you out."

"He should have asked me out. I liked him too," said Carol. "After prom, my good friend Linda Conley asked me all about you, John. She said she wished she had met you sooner. Do you remember her?"

"Yes, she was pretty," said John. "Do you remember Lanna Talbot?"

"Yes, she was beautiful," said Carol.

"She was the only girl I ever asked out," said John. "She said no, and it really hurt my feelings."

Carol hugged John. "I'm sorry, John. No one should have ever hurt you."

"You've never hurt me, Carol. You're always nice to me," said John.

"I never trusted girls," said Mike. "Most of them weren't very nice to me."

"Girls acted like they wanted to go out with me, but then they didn't like me. I hardly ever could get a second date," said Gene. "You were the only one who was ever nice to me, Carol, but because of Richard, we never went out. None of the girls ever talked to me like you do. I think they just wanted to go out with me because I was an athlete."

"It was so hard then. I liked you three guys so much, and I tried so hard to stay loyal to Richard," said Carol.

"You did a good job. You discouraged many prospective suitors," said Mike.

"You know I loved my mother, but she never let me forget that I was a poor girl from the wrong side of the tracks. She made me feel like I wasn't worthy of you guys," said Carol.

John hugged Carol. "My mother loved you. She thought you were pretty and nice. I was poor too, probably poorer than you."

"My mother loved you, John. She thought you were too nice for me. She was always afraid I was going to hurt you. I told her I would never hurt you, but she didn't believe me. Did I ever hurt you, John?" asked Carol.

"No, you never hurt me," said John as he wiped the tears from Carol's cheeks and kissed her.

"Well, I started this, so I might as well finish. Are you ready, Mike?" asked Carol.

"Sure, I can take anything," Mike smiled.

"My mom thought you were too sophisticated and too rich for me," said Carol. 'She thought I had no sophistication whatsoever."

Mike walked over to Carol and kissed her. "Your mother was wrong. I always loved you. What did you think of Carol, Dad?"

"I think you know the answer to that," said Alan. "Colleen and I loved you like a daughter, and it would have been the most joyous moment of our lives if you and Mike had married."

"And, Gene, I always leave you for last because you are the most difficult," said Carol.

"Difficult, I've been called that before," said Gene.

"I just mean it is hard for me to say what someone thought of you because I know you won't agree," said Carol. "My mom thought you were too handsome, too popular, and definitely too good for me. She didn't think I was popular, or at all pretty, and she didn't even think I was good. My mother loved you, Gene. You were the only guy I ever dated that she loved."

"She was a nice lady, but totally wrong about everything," said Gene. "My parents loved you. I think you know that."

John moved over a little on the sofa. "Carol, you need to sit between me and Gene."

Carol put her arms around Gene, and they kissed gently and sweetly. "It's been so long ago, but it still hurts, doesn't it? I've always wondered why people say such cruel, hurtful things. It is almost as though they try to say something that will hurt you forever, something you will never be able to forget. I've never said anything like that to anyone."

"Don't you realize that is why we all love you so much? You never hurt, you only heal and help and love us," said Gene.

"I think we should go to our favorite pizza place," said Mike. "Would you go with us, Dad?"

"No, you can bring me something back," said Alan.

"Mike, is it handicapped-accessible?" asked Gene.

"No, but I know a way in," said Mike.

When they arrived at the Pizza Inn, they went in through a side door directly to a table.

Upon entering a restaurant, especially in Kanas City, Carol always looked around to see if there were any people she knew there, and tonight there was. Roy, one of Gene's best friends and football and basketball teammates, was there with two young boys, probably his sons. He saw her the same time she saw him. He immediately came to their table.

"Hello, long time no see," said Roy.

Gene held out his trembling left hand to shake hands with Roy. "Hello, Roy," said Gene.

Roy pulled up a chair between Carol and Gene.

"Hi, Carol, Mike, and John. It great to see you guys," said Roy.

"Are those your sons?" asked Carol.

"Yes, they are ten and eleven now," said Roy.

"Gene and I are here for John's surgery," said Carol.

"Something serious?" asked Roy.

"It's my hip," said John. "I fell."

"Good luck to you, John," said Roy. Roy hesitated and seemed to be having trouble making eye contact with Gene. "How are you, Gene?"

"I'm not so good right now," said Gene.

There was another uncomfortable silence. "We were best friends. I'm sorry I haven't been to see you," said Roy.

"It's all right," said Gene quietly.

"How's beautiful Janice?" asked Mike.

"She left me and the boys and went to New York," said Roy. "Well, I better get back to the boys."

After Roy left, Mike said, "That was awkward. Maybe someone should have told him you are not contagious, Gene."

"Don't be too hard on him, Mike. Like everyone else, he just didn't know what to say," said Gene.

John put his hand on Gene's arm. "If I get to be a motivational speaker, maybe I can help people like Roy to understand and know how to talk to people like us."

"That would be good, John. It is long overdue," said Carol.

"John speaks much kinder than I do," said Mike. "I think Carol has rubbed off on you, John, and that's a good thing."

As Roy got up to leave, he brought his boys to their table. "I would like for you to meet my sons, Rodney and Blake. Boys, these are my friends from high school, Gene, Mike, John, and Carol. Gene was my best friend. Carol was your mom's best friend." They all noticed the tears in Roy's eyes. "How long will you be here, Gene? I would like to get together with you."

"We just got in today. We'll be here a week. I'm staying with Mike. Give me a call," said Gene.

"I will," said Roy.

Gene knew at that moment that he would be hearing from Roy.

On the way home, John was exceptionally quiet.

Gene asked, "Do you feel all right, John. You're so quiet tonight. Is there anything you want to talk about?"

"I'll be fine, Gene. You know how I am. I'm just a little nervous about tomorrow," said John.

"We'll all be there with you tomorrow. Even if you don't see us for a little while, we will be there," said Gene.

Carol was in the front seat with Mike. She looked out the window. She didn't want them to see her tears. Mike reached over and took hold of her hand.

That night after Mike and Carol helped John and Gene get ready for bed, Mike said, "We have an early morning. I'm going to stay here with you two tonight. Is that all right with you?"

"Sure, I like it when we are all together," said John.

That night John would sleep in the middle. That was his favorite place. Gene was very tired and went to sleep right away. John fell asleep shortly thereafter. Carol couldn't sleep. She got up and went to sit by Mike on the sofa.

"Do you mind if I sit by you?" said Carol.

Mike pulled Carol as close to him as he could, and she put her head on his shoulder as she always did Gene. Mike kissed Carol, and she returned the kiss. "I love you, Carol, and I will forever."

"I love you too Mike," Carol paused. "I'm so afraid for John right now and Gene too."

"I know. So am I. That's why I wanted to stay here tonight," said Mike.

They held one another tight most of the night, dozing off occasionally. As long as they had one another, they could help their friends through anything.

SURGERY DAY

Only one person could go to the surgery prep room with John. Mike went with him so he could help him change into a hospital gown. In a few minutes, a nurse came to the waiting room and asked Carol to come to the prep room.

"Is everything all right?" asked Carol.

The kind nurse replied, "He's getting a little teary-eyed. He is so sweet, but I think he is a little scared. He has mentioned your name several times."

"May I take his teddy bear to him?" asked Carol.

"Sure, that will be fine," said the nurse.

When Carol saw John, he seemed to look so young. She bent over and kissed him. "I brought your teddy bear to you."

"Thanks, Carol. This is my nurse, Becky. She gave me something to make me drowsy," said John. "I'm just a little scared."

"Don't be afraid, John. You are going to be fine," reassured Carol.

At that moment, Dr. Wilson came into the room. "Hello, Carol and Mike, and here's my favorite patient, John. It will be all over before you know it. You will do fine."

John smiled at Dr. Wilson. They could tell he was getting sleepy and relaxing.

"Mike, do you have my glasses and hearings aids?" asked John.

"Yes, I'll keep them safe for you," said Mike.

Carol held John's hand as they wheeled him down the long hallway. Gene and Alan were waiting at the point where Carol would have to let go of John's hand.

"I'll see you later," said John as he disappeared through the operating room doors.

As they went to the waiting room, they all felt concern for their friend, but both Carol and Gene seemed to be on the verge of tears. Mike helped Gene to a sofa in the waiting room.

"It might be a little more comfortable, and I need to sit by Carol," said Gene.

Mike sat on the other side of Carol, and Alan sat across from them. Gene put his arm around Carol, and she put her head on his shoulder.

"My tears got his teddy bear wet," said Carol.

Mike took a handkerchief from his pocket and dried the teddy bear. "Is that better?" asked Mike as he kissed Carol on the cheek.

"Thanks, Mike. I love all of you so much," said Carol.

"We love you too, Carol," said Gene.

The waiting room was full that morning. Everyone seemed to be looking at them, but they always did attract attention—the pretty girl with the long red hair holding the teddy bear; the handsome young man in the wheelchair; the nice-looking, red-haired man who could be the girl's brother; and the distinguished older man who seemed to be protecting them all.

"He's going to be all right. Don't worry, Carol," said Gene.

"John's been through so much. He looked like a little boy when they took him away," said Carol.

Mike reached over and smoothed Carol's hair back. "Just think how happy he is going to be. He will be able to walk."

"You know something, the only thing I want to do is take care of John forever. I'll never leave him," said Alan.

Two hours after they had taken John to surgery, Dr. Wilson came into the waiting room and directly to the group of four. Mike and Carol stood up. Mike had his arm around Carol's waist.

Dr. Wilson put his hand on Carol's arm. "The surgery went well. John is in recovery. There is a slight problem with his blood pressure, and he is having a hard time waking up. We will watch him closely for a while, but he will be fine."

"Thank you so much, Dr. Wilson," said Carol.

Dr. Wilson touched the side of Carol's face and smoothed her hair back just as Gene and Mike often did. Alan and Gene's eyes met, and for a moment they thought it looked as though Dr. Wilson was going to hug or even possibly kiss Carol, but Mike beat him to it.

Mike held Carol tightly and said, "I'm so relieved and happy."

"I'm going to go back to recovery and stay by John. I don't want him to wake up and see strangers," said Dr. Wilson.

Gene reached his left hand out to Dr. Wilson. "Thank you for coming to talk to us."

Carol sat down by Gene and hugged him. She gently kissed the scar on his cheek, and as she rubbed his hand, she noticed that it stopped trembling. A short while later, Mike helped Gene to the wheelchair. Gene didn't want to hold them up when it was time for them to go to John. Although Carol couldn't help Gene by lifting him and helping him to the wheelchair, she always checked the locks and adjusted the seat pad and pillow for his arm.

Their timing was perfect because soon Dr. Wilson returned to the waiting room.

"John is in his room. I will take you to him. Carol and Alan took hold of hands and walked with Dr. Wilson as Mike and Gene followed. When they got to the room, John's eyes were shut, and he looked very peaceful. Carol sat as close as she could to John and took hold of his bad hand. She knew he could feel her touch and would know it was her.

"Hi, Carol. Where's Gene and Mike and Alan?" asked John.

"They are all right here with me," said Carol. "How do you feel, John?"

"My leg hurts a little, and I have a headache, but it's not bad," said John quietly.

"It will be better soon," said Carol.

"Please don't leave me alone, Carol," said John.

"I won't leave you. I'll stay with you tonight," said Carol.

Just then a tray of food was brought to John.

"I bet you are hungry. Do you think you can eat a little?" asked Mike.

"I'll try," said John. "Gene and Alan, I can't see you very well."

"Is that better?" asked Alan as they moved closer.

"Yes. That's much better," said John. "Do you feel all right, Gene? Do you have any heart pain?"

"I'm fine, John," said Gene.

John had a very nice nurse named Selina. "John, you are so considerate. You've just had surgery, and you are concerned about your friend," said Selina.

"John is very sweet and loving. That's the way he always is," said Carol. "Is it all right if he sits up a little more?"

"I'll move him up a little. He can't sit completely up just yet, but he will be able to soon," said Selina. "Who do you have here?"

"Cathy's teddy bear and Carol's little kitten. They let me use them," said John.

"That's very nice of them. They must love you very much," said Selina.

"This is Carol. Cathy's far away," said John.

"Do you think you can eat a few bites of food?" asked Selina.

"Can Carol help me? I can't use my right hand," said John.

Selina looked at John's hand and touched it gently and said, "Sure she can."

"Can he have his glasses and hearing aids?" asked Mike.

"That's fine," said Selina.

Mike opened the bag and took John's glasses out first. "I took good care of everything for you." Mike put his glasses on him. Then he opened his hearing aid box. John was able to put them in his ears himself.

"That's very good, John. I'm so proud of you," said Gene. "In fact, we are all proud of you. You're the bravest person I know."

"Me? I'm not brave, you're the brave one. I'm actually kind of scared," said John.

"You seem pretty brave to me too," said Selina. "What are you afraid of, John?"

"I just don't want to ever be alone," said John.

"I think someone is going to stay with you all night. Do you know who that is?" asked Selina.

"That would be Carol." John reached his bad hand out to Carol, and she gently took hold of it.

"And you would be right. I'm going to be right here in this room with you all night," said Carol. "Now can you eat a few more bites for me?"

"I'm going to leave you for a while now," said Selina. "I'll be back later to take your vitals and give you some medicine. Will that be all right with you?"

"Yes, that will be fine," said John.

There was a sofa that made into a bed in John's room, but Carol sat in the recliner near his bed. She wanted to be sure that if he woke up in the night, he would be able to see her.

John ate breakfast the next morning with Carol's help. Then he began his first physical therapy session. It was hard for him, but he did the best he could. Gene, Mike, and Alan arrived a little later to see John. He was so glad to see them, but he couldn't stay awake. He fell asleep holding his teddy bear and Carol's little white kitten.

They were trying to be quiet because they knew John needed his rest. Mike was looking at John sleeping.

"What's wrong, Mike?" asked Carol.

"It seems like John gets younger. Just look at him. He looks like he is eighteen," said Mike.

"It's just the teddy bear and the kitten," said Carol.

Mike shrugged his shoulders. "I guess you're right."

They didn't know Gene was listening, but he had heard everything they said.

"I think John is forever young. I don't believe he will ever age."

Discharge Planning

On John's third hospital day, a woman from discharge planning came to John's room. She asked to speak to the person responsible for John's care. Alan said he would be in the absence of John's sisters, but he wanted Carol and Gene to be part of the discussion. John was sleeping. Mike would stay with him. Alan, Carol, and Gene followed the lady, Ruth Morris, to a conference room.

"We need to discuss John's discharge. Will he be going to an assisted living facility?" asked Ruth.

"No. He will be coming home with me," said Alan.

"Where was he living when he fell?" asked Ruth.

"At his home. His sisters were away, and he was alone," said Alan.

"I have talked with John. He should never be left alone. What is his degree of retardation?" asked Ruth. "Who was caring for him?"

"John is not retarded. He is very smart." Carol couldn't hold back any longer. "He has been taking care of himself forever."

"I was under the impression that he hadn't eaten for a long time and that he fell and was unable to walk. From my meeting with him, I felt he had mental disabilities," said Ruth.

Gene spoke very calmly to Ruth, "John will never be left alone. Someone will always be with him. We will take him to outpatient physical therapy. If he needs a nurse or a companion, we will hire them. We will take care of him."

"Carol, I see you have an address in Springfield, Illinois. Gene, I see your address is in Chicago. Are these addresses correct? How can you help care for John from that distance?" asked Ruth.

"Yes, those addresses are correct. We travel to Kansas City frequently." Carol tried to speak in a calm voice as Gene had done. "John has no mental disabilities. He had polio and was severely abused as a child. When he was twenty-three, a roof covered in ice and snow fell on him. He had severe head and back injuries, and his right arm and hand were crushed. Gene and I worked countless hours with him to teach him to write with his left hand." Carol stopped to wipe her eyes. "I'm sorry, but I love John so much. We all do. We need to protect him and keep him close to us. John is thirty-eight. Some think he is childlike. But I thought that the first time I ever met him. I loved that about him. He is holding the little kitten and teddy bear because they make him feel better."

"Very well said. That is all I needed to know. We will release John today to you, Alan. I'm sorry I asked if he was retarded. He is a beautiful man, and I really like him. Now you may all go to him," said Ruth.

"Thank you," said Alan.

When they went back to the room, John was still asleep. Carol gently kissed his cheek and sat close to him. Gene did the same.

Mike asked Alan, "Did everything go all right in there?"

"We can take him home today," said Alan.

"I'm glad. I was afraid they might make him go to an aftercare place. I don't think that would work for John," said Mike.

"He will be with us. That is where he needs to be," said Alan.

John opened his eyes. "I felt somebody kiss me, and then somebody else kissed me," John smiled. His nurse Selina was also by his bed.

"So who do you think it was who kissed you?" asked Selina.

"Oh, I can always tell. It was Carol and Gene," said John still smiling.

"You're right, John. We are taking you home today," said Gene.

"I'll be glad to go home," said John.

Mike combed John's hair and put his glasses on him just as his lunch came. John's lunch consisted of a pork chop, green beans, and mashed potatoes and milk. John tried so hard, as he always did, to eat his green beans and cut his meat, but he kept dropping his food; and even though the meat was tender, he couldn't cut it.

"Carol, will you please help me. I'm embarrassed."

"John, you know I'll always help you. You never need to be embarrassed about anything," said Carol. She knew he was embarrassed because Selina was in the room.

"Dad, would you like to go to the cafeteria with me? These two can go all day without eating but not me," said Mike as he bent over and kissed Carol on the forehead. "Can we bring you two something?"

"I could eat a tuna salad sandwich," said Gene.

"That sounds good to me too," said Carol.

"We will be back in a few minutes. How about a piece of cheese-cake, John?" asked Mike.

"That would be good," said John.

"You have cleaned your plate, John. You are doing so much better. I'm so proud of you," said Carol as she wiped a small piece of food from his cheek.

"Thank you, Carol. Would you check my braces?" said John as he smiled big.

"They are perfect. I'm going to get something for us to drink. Do you want anything?" asked Carol.

"No, I still have my milk," said John.

Carol went down the hall to the breakroom to get the tea. Carol sat down at a table and put her head in her hands and cried. She felt an arm around her. It was Selina.

"I just wanted to tell you how much I admire you. You are just so incredibly good to that wonderful guy in there. He is the sweetest patient I have ever had. The other guys love him too, don't they?"

"We all love him. He is very special to all of us. That lady from discharge planning thought John was retarded and would be going to an assisted-living facility. It hurt me so much that she thought that.

John worries so much about Gene. He is afraid something is going to happen to him," said Carol.

"That woman was stupid to say that," Selina paused. "What's wrong with Gene?"

"He had three consecutive strokes within a two-day period. The first two were mild, but the third was a massive stroke, and now he has had some setbacks. It's not just John that worries about Gene. We all do." Carol's eyes were filling with tears, and she was overwhelmed by the concern of the kind nurse.

Selina sat down by Carol. "You know a lot of patients come and go here. Most I don't remember, but John is a patient I will never forget. I just love John. He is so sweet and innocent. I like the way you feed him and check his braces. I like the way Mike shaves him and washes his face, and the way Gene combs his hair and makes sure he has his glasses and hearing aids. Alan watches him so closely and makes sure he has his kitten and teddy bear. But what touches me most is the way he always wants you to hold his poor scarred hand. He says it makes his hand feel better. I like the way you talk to him and the way Gene pushes his hair back. Whenever I go into that room, it is like it is erupting with love and kindness." Selina was also crying.

"I had better get back to them," said Carol.

"I'll carry the tea for you," said Selina.

As they left the breakroom, Alan and Mike were just heading back to John's room. Mike immediately looked at Carol. "What's the matter, you've been crying?"

"I'm all right. I just get emotional once in a while," said Carol.

Mike put his arm around Carol, and they went back to John's room.

Alan handed John his cheesecake. "That looks good," said John.

Gene took hold of Mike's arm. "Mike, would you help me sit on the sofa? It might help my back a little"

"Sure." Mike wheeled Gene to the sofa and slowly helped him move from the wheelchair to the sofa.

"Could I get you a pillow, Gene?" asked Selina.

"That would be nice," said Gene quietly.

When she handed him the pillow, she noticed how cold his hands were. "You're cold. I'll get you a warm blanket. Is anyone else cold?" asked Selina.

"I'm a little cold," said John.

"We can't have that. I'll bring you one too," said Selina.

When Selina returned with the blankets, she put one on John and the other one on Gene's lap and covered his legs. She noticed the scar on his face.

"What happened to your cheek, Gene. That looks recent, and it must have been very deep."

"I fell. I'm a little clumsy," said Gene.

"Nobody would help him get up," said John. There was an uncomfortable silence.

"Well, I'm going to leave for a while. I'll get the discharge papers ready. I'll be back in about two hours," said Selina. As Selina left the room, she wondered what had happened to Gene, but it didn't seem right to ask.

Carol opened Gene's sandwich for him and sat by him. Mike sat at the other end of the sofa.

Mike asked, "Is the tuna salad good?"

"Yes," said Carol. "It is delicious. Would you like a bite?"

"No, that's all you have eaten all day," said Mike.

"You two are funny," said John.

"Really. You think we are funny," said Mike. "How about your cheesecake. Can I have a bite of that?"

"Yes, you all can. Carol, Gene, and Alan can have a bite too," said John.

"John, you are just too good. We are not going to take your cheesecake," said Alan.

After they all finished eating, Carol talked to John very quietly, "John, Alan and Mike are here by you. I'm going to sit by Gene for a while. He's very cold and can't seem to get warm. I'm going to see if I can help him."

"He can have one of my blankets," said John.

"No. You need your blankets. If he doesn't get warm, I'll get one from Selina," said Carol.

"Is Gene asleep?" asked John.

"No, I'm just resting my eyes, John," said Gene.

Carol kissed John's bad hand and then went to sit by Gene. She held him as close to her as she could. "Do you want me to take your glasses off?" asked Carol.

"Yes, thank you," said Gene.

About one hour later, Dr. Wilson came into the room. Selina was with him.

"Hello, John. How's my favorite patient today?"

"I'm fine," said John.

"John, would you be mad at me if I ask you to stay another night?" asked Dr. Wilson.

John held out his left hand to Dr. Wilson. "I would never be mad at you. You helped me to walk again."

"John's blood pressure has been up a little. We don't want to take any chances. We will give him some different medicine and see what happens tonight. He can probably go home tomorrow," said Dr. Wilson. "What's the matter, John? Your eyes are filling with tears."

"I don't think Gene feels so good. I worry a lot about him," said John.

Dr. Wilson pulled a chair up by Gene. "What's the matter, Gene?"

"My back was hurting sitting in the wheelchair, and I just got really cold. Other than that, I'm probably as good as can be expected," said Gene.

"Let me listen to your heart and check your blood pressure," Dr. Wilson hesitated. "Your heart is a little fast. Have you been getting enough rest?"

"I think so, but sometimes I have a hard time relaxing," said Gene.

"I know it is easier said than done, but just try to stay as calm as you can," said Dr. Wilson.

"I'll try. Thank you, Dr. Wilson," said Gene.

"John, I have an idea," said Alan. "Why don't I stay with you tonight, and Carol can go home with Gene and Mike."

"That would be fine. Then Carol can watch Gene," said John.

"Carol, would you please hand me my crutches?" asked Gene.

403

Carol got his crutches and helped him up. Mike came to help too. Gene slowly and carefully walked to John's bedside. Alan got up out of the recliner so Gene could sit by John.

Gene took hold of John's bad hand and spoke quietly to him, "John, have I told you today what a nice guy you are?"

John thought for a minute. "Maybe not today, but I think you did yesterday."

"If Carol, Mike, and I leave, will you make a promise to me? Will you eat a good dinner tonight with Alan?" asked Gene.

"Sure, Gene. I can do that," said John.

"And you won't be afraid tonight without Carol, will you?" asked Gene.

"I won't be afraid. Alan will be here." John smiled, but Carol could see the tears welling up in his eyes.

They were silent as they left John's room and rode the elevator down to the lobby.

"Well, I guess I'll go get the van," said Mike. Mike put his arms around Carol. "You won't be here when I get back, will you?"

"I can't leave him. I've been with him every night since he has been in the hospital. I have to stay," said Carol.

Mike kissed Carol and went to get the van.

Carol sat down by Gene and held his hand. "You knew I was going to stay too, didn't you?"

"I had a feeling. That's part of why I love you," said Gene.

Carol kissed Gene through her tears.

When Mike brought the van to the lobby door, Carol said to both of them, "I love you two. I'll see you tomorrow."

They waved as they drove away.

As Carol went back to John's room, she knew she was doing the right thing. "I changed my mind. I want to be here with you guys tonight."

Alan hugged Carol, as did John.

"I'm glad you're staying with me. You've been with me every night," said John.

Carol was glad she stayed because some of the new medicine didn't agree with John and he couldn't eat much of his dinner. They had stopped John's pain medication because of his blood pressure, and his hip and leg were hurting. Alan napped but didn't sleep much. Carol pulled the recliner as close as she could to John's bed and held his bad hand into the wee hours of the morning when Selina was finally able to give him something for his pain.

"I'm putting something for pain in your IV. You should be pain-free soon, and you'll be sleepy," said Selina.

"Thank you, Selina. You've been so good to John," said Carol.

John just smiled and felt very sleepy as he waved to Selina as she left the room.

When John was sleeping soundly, Alan stepped out of the room for a while. Dr. Wilson was in the hall.

"Hello, Alan. Is everything all right?"

"John's sleeping soundly now. I can tell Carol's worried about John and Gene. She didn't like it today when that woman from discharge planning thought John was retarded," said Alan.

"That should never have happened. I'm so sorry," said Dr. Wilson. "I thought she was going to leave with Mike and Gene."

"She couldn't leave him," said Alan.

"I'll check on her," said Dr. Wilson.

"Thank you," said Alan.

Carol was sitting on the sofa looking out the window. Dr. Wilson took her in his arms and held her close to him. He wiped her tears and pulled her hair back. Carol didn't pull away. She let him comfort her and hold her in his arms.

"I'm so sorry John was in pain," said Dr. Wilson. "And I wish I could help Gene."

"You've helped us all so much." Carol touched her finger to his lips. "You have been kind to all of us and loved us since we were eighteen."

"I'll tell you a secret, or maybe it's not. I love you the most. I fell in love with you the first time I met you," said Dr. Wilson. "I've never done anything like this before."

"It seems so natural," said Carol.

"I wish I could help Gene for you," said Dr. Wilson.

"It would be wonderful to have Gene well. I live for that day," said Carol.

"Do you mind if I call you sometime? I love to talk to you and hear the sound of your voice," asked Dr. Wilson.

"I don't mind," said Carol.

"You are so caring and smart. You should have been a doctor. I love the way you treat all the guys, but I especially love the way you treat Gene. You give him hope and make him feel good about himself. It would be so easy for him to give up, but you never stop helping and encouraging him."

"I'll do anything I can for him," said Carol. "People have always told me that I'm smart, but I've never felt smart. In important things like life choices, I'm not smart at all. Thank you for comforting and caring about me. I needed that."

THE BASKETBALL

Early that evening, as Mike and Gene arrived home without Carol, Alan, and John, the phone rang as they entered the front hallway.

"Hello, this is Mike. Gene's here. Just a minute," said Mike. "It's for you, Gene. It's Roy."

"Hello, Roy," said Gene.

"Can you and Mike go to the Riverside Inn with us tonight? We will meet in the bar and have dinner there later," said Roy.

"Roy, you guys would all have more fun without me. As I always say, I'm a lot of work," said Gene.

"You're the one everyone wants to see, Gene. We are doing this for you," said Roy.

"Since you put it that way, I would love to see you guys. Would you mind driving over here, and we will take Mike's van? It's handicapped-accessible," said Gene.

"We will be there in thirty minutes," said Roy.

"We'll be looking for you," said Gene.

"You know, Gene, they just want to see you. I wasn't really close to that group," said Mike.

"You were part of both the basketball and football teams, and you're invited," Gene hesitated. "I need you, Mike. I can't do it without you."

"I'll go with you. I'll let Carol and Dad know in case they try to call us," said Mike.

"Thanks, Mike. I owe you more each day," said Gene.

Mike just smiled and hugged Gene. "You don't owe me a thing, Gene. Never forget how much I care about you. I would do more for you if I could."

When Roy arrived at Mike's house, Jessie was with him. Jessie had been the smallest guy on the basketball team, but along with Gene and Leon, he was one of the best.

"Hello, Jessie. It's good to see you," said Gene.

Jessie hugged Gene and greeted Mike. "It's good to see you, guys. I didn't make it back for the reunion."

"Well, I'll tell you, Jessie. You didn't miss much, just me having the first of three strokes," said Gene. "I'm sorry. That wasn't funny. It wasn't even meant to be."

"You guys probably remember, Gene always had a dark sense of humor," said Mike.

"That's what everyone has always told me," said Gene.

"I'm not laughing, Gene. We all just wanted to see you, not for any particular reason," said Jessie sincerely. Next to Gene, Jessie was always one of the kindest and most well-liked in the group. "Remember, you, me, Roy, and Nathan were all best friends, I guess because of basketball, long before you were friends with Carol, Mike, and John. The four of us were on the football team together too. You were the best quarterback ever. I've missed you, Gene."

"I've missed you guys too. I love you all. Let's go party. I'll try not to ruin it," said Gene.

"We'll take my van. It makes things a little easier," said Mike.

As they were driving, Gene asked, "So who all will be there?"

In 1984, only one of their teammates was deceased, and that was Jeff Moore, who had been killed in Vietnam in 1966.

Roy answered, "Nathan, Dennis, Rodger, Fred, Terry, and Leon. Leon is coming all the way from Quebec to see you, Gene." After playing in college, Leon went on to play professional basketball.

"I sure wish John could be here. Leon was always his favorite. John always knew when he was going to be on TV, and we would watch him play. Remember, Mike?" asked Gene.

"I remember," said Mike.

When they arrived at the Riverside Inn, Roy helped Mike get Gene out of the van.

"Jessie, you know what the worst thing was about going back to work?" asked Gene.

"What was it, Gene?" Jessie put his hand on Gene's shoulder.

"Going by all the people with someone pushing me in a wheelchair. Everybody stared. They don't mean anything by it. They just don't understand or know what to say to handicapped people," said Gene.

As they went into the bar, the other six guys were already there. Mike pushed Gene's wheelchair next to Nathan. They had always been best friends. Mike sat on the other side of Gene.

Gene held out his left hand to Nathan. "It's good to see you, Nathan."

Nathan's voice was quiet. "I've missed you, Gene. I'm sorry I haven't called."

"It's all right, Nathan. Don't worry about it," said Gene.

A pretty young woman came to take their drink orders. "Hi, Gene, do you remember me?"

Everyone looked at her, but no one, not even Mike, recognized her.

"Of course. I remember you, Linda Conley, one of Carol's best friends," said Gene. "I don't see very well, but I do remember you. It's good to see you."

"How's Carol? We haven't talked for a while," asked Linda.

"She's fine. She is with John right now. He just had surgery," said Gene.

"Will he be all right?" asked Linda.

"He's having a hard time, but he will be all right," said Gene sadly as a single tear ran down his cheek. "I'm sorry. I just get emotional when I think about John. He's been through so much."

Linda hugged Gene and wiped the tear from his cheek. "What can I get everyone to drink?"

"For me, just water. I take too much medicine that alcohol doesn't mix with," said Gene.

Linda took the other drink orders.

Leon was sitting across the table from Gene. "Gene, I heard you say John is in the hospital. Can he have visitors?"

"Sure, he would love visitors," said Gene.

"Tomorrow morning we will all go see him," said Leon.

"It would really surprise him, and he would be so happy," said Gene.

Mike could tell Gene was on the verge of tears, and he wasn't sure how Gene would feel about crying in front of his old friends. But Gene decided to speak through his tears.

"I'm not the same guy you all remember from high school. I cry a lot, but don't think anything of it. I imagine you all know, but in case you don't, I'll tell you what happened to me. At the reunion last spring, I had a minor stroke, and on the plane going home, I had another stroke. When I got home, I had a massive stroke, which basically left me a prisoner in my own body. It affected my right arm and leg, my neck, and my eyes. Unfortunately, it also affected my heart. My speech is still a little slow, but it has improved. I was doing better, but a few weeks ago, I had a setback." Gene paused and touched his cheek. "I cut my cheek and hurt my leg. I can't talk anymore." Gene looked at Mike.

"It's all right, Gene. You did fine." Mike put his arm around Gene.

They could all tell how sensitive and fragile Gene was. Terry, who was sitting by Leon, got up with Leon's help. Gene noticed immediately that Terry's right hand was paralyzed and he was walking with a cane. They came to Gene's side of the table. He spoke in a halting voice and was difficult to understand.

"I cry a lot too, Gene. I had a stroke six years ago."

"I'm sorry, Terry. I didn't know," said Gene.

Mike moved over so Terry could sit by Gene. Terry had been the tallest one on the team, and he was always very quiet and shy.

"As you can tell, I don't talk very well and probably never will. Since I always stuttered anyway, it just makes it worse," said Terry.

"We'll have to talk more, Terry. We have something in common," said Gene.

There was silence for a moment, and then Rodger broke it, "I was in Vietnam, like Mike. I got wounded in the head."

"So did I," said Mike.

"Did you hate it there as much as I did? I haven't been the same since. I can't stop taking the pain pills," said Rodger.

"I hated it too. I thought I would die there, but I came home. I called Carol and Gene from the airport and asked them to come pick me up and to bring me a T-shirt and jeans. I had to get the uniform off because people were throwing rocks and rotten food at all the veterans and screaming at us, even wounded ones like me. I felt like I was back in Vietnam. When I went home, I couldn't leave the house for several days."

This time it was Gene's turn to comfort Mike, as did Terry.

"Well, I'm no war hero or any kind of hero," said Fred. "I've been married three times and have two kids by each wife. I can't seem to get it right. I'm an insurance agent."

"I have seven kids by the same wife," said Dennis. "I live in a small town in Western Kansas and don't have a very good job, but we get by. I work in construction when the weather is decent."

"I have a pretty wife and a son and two daughters, and I still play basketball. I guess I have a lot to be thankful for," said Leon.

"I'm engaged to a pretty girl with long red hair named Carol, but it's not the Carol you remember. I met her in law school. I finally became a lawyer. She is a little younger than me," said Mike.

"I'm married to Vicky and have two beautiful little girls. My wife is pregnant with a little boy," said Jessie. "I'm a high school government teacher, and I coach football."

"I have two sons. They are ten and eleven. I married Janice, my high school sweetheart, but we are divorced now," said Roy. "I'm an orthopedic surgeon."

"I'm divorced, and my son is eight, and my daughter is four. They are great kids. I'm very proud of them," said Gene. "I work at an advertising agency in Chicago."

"I'm not married. I've never even had a girlfriend. I worked at the post office, but I lost my job when I had the stroke. I haven't been able to get another one," said Terry.

"Nathan, you're awfully quiet," said Gene. "I remember in senior year, you were voted most likely to succeed."

"That didn't happen. Maybe the vote put a curse on me," said Nathan quietly. "I don't have a wife or children. I haven't been to war, and I don't play basketball anymore. I don't even have a job. I don't have much of a life. I tried to kill myself two years ago, but I couldn't even do that right."

Gene put his arm around Nathan. "I'm sorry, Nathan. I didn't know. You don't have to say anything else. I need to keep in touch with you. I want to help you."

Their table was ready in the dining room. Nathan pushed Gene's wheelchair. Mike stepped back and let him do so. Leon walked with Terry.

Mike knew he needed to sit by Gene so he could help him, but he wasn't quite sure who needed to sit by Gene the most, Nathan or Terry, but Terry saved him.

"I think Gene and Nathan need to talk. Mike, sit here between me and Gene. Leon will help me, won't you?" said Terry.

"You know I would do anything for you, Terry," said Leon.

Linda was their waitress in the dining room too. The food was very good, and the service was excellent. Gene and Terry both ordered a steak. Neither one seemed embarrassed when their friends had to help them with it.

"Gene, I think you are the only one in this group who remembers me," said Linda.

"John Kelley isn't here, but he remembers you. He thought you were pretty," said Gene.

"He was so sweet and innocent, and he seemed so young. He was really tall and so kind but just so very young," said Linda.

"I remember you, Linda. I wanted to ask you out, but I didn't know if you would go out with a black guy," said Leon.

"You should have asked me. I definitely would have gone out with you," said Linda. Leon just smiled. "How about you, Terry. Do you remember me?"

"Yes, I remember you now. I never dated. I was too shy," said Terry.

"Gene, do you remember that time Sarah asked Carol to fix her up with you for a date to that dance right after you had a football injury?" asked Linda.

"I'll never forget that night," said Gene. "She didn't like me. She was really mean to both me and Carol."

"Carol was so loyal to Richard, but she really wanted to be with you. Did you know that?" asked Linda.

"I had a pretty good idea," said Gene.

"I suppose I should shut up while I'm ahead, but you and Carol always seemed so right together. I could always tell by the way she looked at you and the way you looked at her. There was so much chemistry between you and Carol. What happened, Gene?" asked Linda.

"Life happened, Linda. We went separate ways," said Gene.

Everyone was looking at Gene, and he suddenly felt very uncomfortable.

Linda hugged Gene and kissed him on the cheek. "I've always thought you were the nicest man I've ever met. I didn't mean to say anything to hurt you, and I am sorry if I did. But you have to know how much Carol loved you and how perfect the two of you were together."

"But we're not so perfect now, are we, Linda? I would never expect a woman to take care of me in this condition because I am about as far from perfect as anyone can be and still be alive." Gene took his glasses off and put his hand over his eyes.

Mike put his arm around Gene. "It's all right, Gene. We all understand. Since they're all going to see John tomorrow, I know you wanted to tell them a little bit about him. I'm going to do that for you. Is that all right with you?"

"Yes, Mike. Thank you," said Gene.

"Gene, Carol, my dad, and I have always tried to take care of John and keep him safe. He can't be alone, but he was alone for a while, and he didn't eat, he was cold, and he fell and hurt his hip, his good leg, and his mouth. Years ago, he was in a bad accident, and his right arm and hand were crushed and his head was injured as was his back. In many ways he is like a little boy, and that is why Carol has stayed with him every night. We love him very much. We just want him to be well," said Mike.

"We'll come by your house in the morning. We have a present for John," said Leon.

When Linda brought the bill, Mike immediately took it. It was a large bill, but Linda had given them good service, and Mike felt she had been especially attentive and kind to Gene, which pleased him greatly. Mike left her a large tip reminiscent of the tip left by his dad to Sandy at their favorite Chicago restaurant a short while ago. Also, Linda had always been a good friend to Carol.

They met at the McVary house the next morning and took two vans to the hospital to visit John. As they walked into the hospital, everyone looked at the ten extremely tall, handsome men. Even though Gene was in a wheelchair, his height of six feet five inches and his muscular build were still evident, and he was undoubtedly the most handsome man in the group. When they got to John's floor, Gene saw Selina at the nurses' station.

"I know this is too many visitors, but we have a gift for John. This is my basketball team from high school."

"There is no way I would turn a group of such good-looking men away. If you don't mind, I'll go with you in case anyone says anything to you. I also want to see John's face," said Selina.

Mike and Gene went in first followed by Leon and then everyone else. Carol was sitting in the recliner holding John's bad hand. Alan was sitting on the sofa. John was lying on his back holding his teddy bear and kitten.

Carol said to him quietly, "John, you have company. Let me put your glasses on you."

John smiled, but his eyes and cheeks were still wet from crying. He had a bad night.

"Hi, Gene and Mike," said John quietly.

"You have some visitors this morning," said Gene.

Then Leon stepped up.

"It's Leon," said John excited.

"We brought you a basketball, John. We all signed our names on it," said Leon.

"Thank you. I love it." John tried to sit up but fell to the side.

Carol and Leon could tell it had hurt him. They helped him sit up and put a pillow by his side.

"Do you remember any of these guys?" asked Leon.

"Come closer, guys. John can't see too well," said Carol quietly.

"I know all of you. It's Roy and Jessie. Behind them, it's Nathan, Rodger, and Terry. Terry was always the tallest. And behind Leon is Dennis and Fred. I can't believe you guys came to see me," said John.

Terry moved closer to John. Carol got up and let him sit in the recliner.

"We had English together. Do you remember?" asked Terry.

"Yes, you were always nice to me," said John. "Your hand is like mine."

"I had a stroke like Gene," said Terry.

John reached out to hug Terry. "I'm sorry, Terry. It hurt Gene really bad."

Nathan said, "I was next to the tallest and then Gene and Rodger."

"I remember. I was in your history class, and you liked Carol," said John.

"Yes, I certainly did," said Nathan.

Carol had gone to look out the window so John wouldn't see her tears.

Roy, Jessie, Dennis, and Fred all hugged John. Leon was still holding John's bad hand.

"Thank you for holding my bad hand. Carol always does that for me," said John.

Nathan walked over to the window where Carol was. He put his arm around her.

"It's nice of you guys to come to see John. He will never forget it. Are you all right, Nathan? Has life been good to you?" asked Carol.

"We all told our stories last night. I'm not sick like Gene and Terry, but my story was the worst. I didn't even want to talk about myself, but I had to say something. I always loved you, Carol. You were the most beautiful girl I had ever seen," said Nathan.

"I loved you, Nathan. You were always so nice to me. Thank you for being good to Gene," said Carol.

"Gene loves you so much. He always has," said Nathan. "He was my best friend when we were in school. I've lost all my friends."

"You haven't lost Gene. He will always be there for you, and so will I," said Carol.

Mike brought Gene to where Carol and Nathan were.

"Are you all right, Nathan?" asked Gene. "Sit down, and let's talk for a while."

"I'm just disappointed in myself," said Nathan.

"It's over, Nathan. Whatever you did, it's too late to change it, but you must go on. You are one of the best guys I have ever known," said Gene. "We've all made mistakes, Nathan. I've definitely made my share of mistakes." Nathan was still looking out the window, and there were tears in his eyes.

"I'll talk to you guys later. I need to check on John." Carol went to John and sat on the end of his bed.

Terry and Leon were still sitting on each side of John. He was still holding his basketball and admiring the signatures. But he still hadn't let go of his teddy bear and kitten.

"You know something, Carol, In English whenever we had to do something in a group, I never had a group, but Terry would always ask me to be in his group," said John.

"Thank you for that, Terry. John has always spoken fondly of you," said Carol.

"He has always been my friend, like you, Leon, Gene, and Mike. I'm just sorry I haven't kept in touch with everyone," said Terry.

Carol hugged Terry and kissed him on the cheek. Then she walked over to Leon and kissed him and took his hand. "You came such a long distance, and we all appreciate that so much. You know, you were always John's favorite," said Carol.

"Gene told me. I just wish I was closer so I could help you all more," said Leon with tears in his eyes. Carol didn't expect to see Leon of all of them cry.

The guys all said goodbye to John as well as Gene, Carol, and Alan, one by one. Mike would take them back to his house to get the other van.

Carol had forgotten how kind and wonderful they had always been and still were, and she hoped her three guys could keep in contact with all of them. The leaders had always been Gene, Leon, and Jessie; kind, gentle, shy Terry, always Leon's best friend; sad, tragic Nathan, who had loved Carol so much; sweet Dennis, who she could tell was now a good husband and father; Roy, who had loved her friend Janice—she wondered what had happened; successful, happy Jessie, always so agreeable and just a really good guy; Leon, John's favorite, always taking care of Terry and doing good things for so many; Rodger, who admitted he needed help and Mike the "protector," who would help him; Fred, who had led the senior class as vice president, under Gene as president, now unable to find love even though Carol had always seen him as loving and caring; Mike, always so pleasant and friendly; dear John, the "lover" who loved everyone and was loved by all; and her wonderful Gene, the "hero" to so many and the best man she had ever known.

Alan had left with Mike to take Jessie to get his van. After they were all gone, it was just Carol, Gene, and John.

Carol sat by John and held his hand. "You enjoyed that, didn't you, John?"

"Yes, they are really good guys. I didn't think they would care about me," said John.

"They all care very much. They hated to leave you," said Carol.

"But you, Gene, Mike, and Alan always stay with me," said John.

"We will be with you as much as we can, John. We promise you will never be alone," said Gene.

"Gene, will you help Terry. He was always good to me when others weren't. He seems so sad and alone," said John.

"I'll help Terry all I can," said Gene.

Just then Selina came in with John's lunch. "John, as soon as you eat, we are going to discharge you. Are those tears I see?"

"I'm just crying for my friend Terry. He is very sad and alone, and Gene is going to help him," said John.

"And which one is Terry?" asked Selina.

"He's the tallest one. He had a stroke like Gene," said John.

"I know who he is now, and I am sure Gene will help him," said Selina.

Mike came back just in time to take them home. John had his basketball, his teddy bear, and his kitten, and Carol, Gene, Mike, and Alan, and those were all he needed at the moment.

HELP FOR THREE FRIENDS IN NEED

After dinner that evening, Gene sat on the sofa, and Carol helped him lift his legs up, and then she sat by him. Mike helped John sit by Carol.

"Carol, would you please rub my head. I have a bad headache," said John.

"Of course I will," Carol said as she reached for a pillow.

Mike helped John get settled, and Carol gently touched his head.

Gene asked John, "Did I do all right rubbing your head the other night?"

"You did fine, Gene, but your hands are bigger than Carol's. I love you, Gene," said John.

"And I love you too, John, very much," said Gene.

Mike was in the hallway when the doorbell rang.

"Hi, Leon, come in," said Mike.

"I know you haven't been home long, but I need to talk to all of you," said Leon.

As they went into the living room, Leon saw the threesome on the sofa.

"Hi, Leon," said John. "I got to come home."

"That's great, John. I'm glad you're home," said Leon as he pulled a chair up close to the sofa where Gene, Carol, and John were sitting.

"We should move. This doesn't look too good the way we are sitting here," said Gene.

"You guys are fine. Mike and Alan, come over here by us."

Mike pulled up a chair, as did Alan.

"You are five of my favorite people. I know two of you are going home tomorrow. I hate to see that happen," said Leon.

John reached out for Gene's hand and looked up at Carol. "I'm going to miss you so much."

"I know, John. We will miss you too, but we'll come back soon," said Carol.

"I would like to stay a little longer if it can be arranged," said Gene.

"I'm not ready to go home tomorrow either," said Leon. "There is something I need to do while I'm here. That's why I came to talk to you this evening. I couldn't sleep last night. I'm glad we all got together, but there are some of our friends who I am really worried about, and I don't know what to do."

"I know, Leon. I'm worried too," said Gene.

"Rodger was living in a shelter for homeless veterans, but he had to leave, and, Mike, I know how close you and Rodger always were," said Leon.

Mike put his arm around Leon. "Don't worry, I'm not going to let him live like that. I'm going to help him. He will never be home-less again. The only problem is that I have to find him first."

"Thanks, Mike. And then there is Nathan. He was always one of your best friends, Gene. I had no idea what his life was like," said Leon.

"Carol and I had an idea this morning," said Gene. "I have a friend who helps me to and from work as well as when I am at work. He lives in the same apartment complex where I live. So far, either Carol, Mike, John, or Alan have been there to help me at home, but I don't know what the future holds."

"When I get well, I'll be able to help you again," said John.

"I know you will, John, but right now, I thought maybe Nathan could help me," said Gene.

"That would be great," said John. "But what about Terry? I'm worried about him too."

"I know, John. Of all of them, I'm worried about Terry the most," said Leon. I've asked him to come home with me, but he said no. I wanted to have him closer to me."

"Terry was my good friend too. I'll help him, Leon," said Gene.

"I've tried to give him money, but he won't take it. I don't know what to do for him," said Leon.

"Maybe he would come here. Would that be all right, Mike?" asked John.

"It would be fine with me. Terry is one of the nicest guys I have ever known. We were senior instructors together in physical education class," said Mike.

"I've known Terry forever. He is like a brother to me," said Leon. "I went to an elementary school that was all black except for Terry. He lived with his grandma in a tiny house next door to me. Kids were mean to him at school and in the neighborhood. He was treated like an outcast even by the teachers. One morning Terry came to our door. He was only ten, and he was carrying a small suitcase. He told us his grandma was dead, and he had to go away, or they would put him in an orphanage. He thought they would be mean to him there. My mom told him she would never let that happen, so he came to live with us. He always said he wouldn't take up much room. I shared my room with him. He kept his few things in one little corner. He had a blanket and a pillow, and he slept on the floor, but I finally convinced him to share my bed. He always slept on the edge, so he didn't take up too much room. We became really good friends. Terry was probably the best and most loyal friend I have ever had. He was so painfully shy, and he stuttered, but he was my friend, and I never noticed that he was different from me. We started playing basketball together and then football. We both kept getting taller and better at the games. When we were sophomores, I had a hard time talking him into trying out for the teams, but he did, and he made it on both basketball and football teams. As I said we were like brothers, and as brothers do, we grew apart. I went to college, and Terry got a job and an apartment. He never dated or had a girlfriend. I guess he was too shy. I didn't even know he had a stroke six years ago. I had no idea." Leon was crying, and he had to stop talking.

Carol put her arms around him. Alan was also becoming emotional after listening to Leon's story. Everyone was quiet for a few minutes, and then the person least likely to speak in the room that day did so.

"Mike, would you help me move closer to Gene, and please put that red pillow by my side. I can't sit up very good yet, and I have something to say."

Mike did as John asked. John reached out and took hold of Gene's hand.

John began speaking, "I know I'm not very strong, and I know I can't stay alone. Mike has a job and needs to get back to work. Carol and Gene will be going home soon. Although I know Alan will stay with me, there are things he needs to do. He is retired, but there is still a lot of business he needs to take care of. And there may be other reasons that he may have to leave. If it would be all right with everyone, I would like for Terry to live here with us and be my companion. I know what a good person he is. He has always been nice to me and cared about me. I would like to return the kindness he has showed me by doing something for him. I have been able to save a little money, and I can pay him. What do you think?"

"That is probably the best idea I have ever heard," said Gene. "But it is entirely up to Mike and Alan."

"It is really a good idea, John. As I told you, I have always loved Terry," said Mike.

"I'm all for it. It would solve future problems," said Alan. "But you keep your money, John. I will pay him."

Carol hugged John. "I think you are the smartest person I know."

Leon was excited and could hardly speak. "Is it all right if I go get Terry and bring him over here to talk to you now?"

"It's fine with us," said Mike.

"Shall I tell him on the way here?" asked Leon.

"That might be good since Terry is so shy," said Carol.

"Thank you, John." Leon hugged and kissed John. "Thank you for giving my friend his life back." Leon left to go pick up Terry.

"John, you never cease to amaze me," said Gene. "No one knew what to do except you."

"I have another idea too. Are you guys ready for it?" said John.

"The floor is yours, John," said Carol.

"When I get well or at least better and become a motivational speaker, I could have guest speakers on the stage with me to speak on subjects close to their heart: Rodger could speak on war and being wounded and being homeless, Nathan could speak on suicide and unemployment, Gene and Terry, if he can, could speak on strokes and the resulting handicaps," said John.

"John, that is a great idea. I have always known how smart you are, and you are an excellent speaker," said Carol.

Carol moved back to the sofa between John and Gene. They were all anxious to see what Terry's reaction would be.

"We had a couple cookouts for the basketball team here," said Alan. "I remember Terry. He was so polite and quiet. One conversation I had with him was about college. He said he wouldn't be going to college. He was going to work at the post office. I didn't know that he lived with Leon's family and had no family of his own. I would have paid for his college if I had known he had no family. He was a good student, and he was good at multiple sports, football, basketball, track and field, tumbling and gymnastics, and swimming."

A few minutes later, Leon returned, and to everyone's relief, Terry was with him. Terry immediately walked over and sat by John. He was crying, and he couldn't speak.

John patted him on the back and said, "Don't worry, Terry, Gene and I cry a lot too, and so does Carol. I need someone with me because sometimes I forget things and I get scared."

"Thank you, John, and thank you, everyone," said Terry very quietly.

"Mike managed to get our plane reservations changed. We will be staying three more days, and he made reservations for three. I hope Nathan will go home with me," said Gene.

"That makes me very happy, Gene," said John.

"I had a feeling it would," said Gene.

"I'm staying three more days too," said Leon.

Without a word, Terry went to Leon and hugged him. "You've saved me so many times," said Terry. "Do you remember that time when I was nine and all those boys beat me up at school and you stopped them? You have always been there for me."

After Leon and Terry left, John seemed very tired.

"Why don't you let Mike and Carol help you to bed, and I'll be in soon. I have to make a phone call," said Gene.

"We'll see you in a while, Gene. Don't forget us," said John.

"I assure you, John. I won't forget you," said Gene.

Gene went to the phone in the back hall and dialed a number scribbled on a napkin he took from his pocket. "Hello, Nathan. It's Gene."

"Hi, Gene," said Nathan.

"Nathan, would you have lunch with Carol, Leon, and me tomorrow?" asked Gene.

"Sure. May I ask what's going on?" asked Nathan.

"I have a job offer for you. I want to help you. We all do," said Gene.

"Thanks, Gene," said Nathan as he choked back tears.

"We'll pick you up at noon," said Gene.

"I'll be ready," said Nathan.

With that settled, Gene went to the bedroom where John and Carol were waiting for him.

Physical Therapy

John's first outpatient physical therapy appointment was at eight thirty the next morning. Carol, Gene, and Mike went with him. The first appointment would be an evaluation with John's physical therapist, Rachel. John wasn't quite sure what to expect.

As Rachel greeted them, she looked at both Gene and John and asked, "Do I have two patients today or just one?"

"John's your patient. I'm beyond all help," said Gene.

"No one is ever beyond help," said Rachel in a friendly voice as she shook Gene's left hand and greeted Carol and Mike.

"I'm Gene, and these are our friends, Carol and Mike."

"John, can you climb up on the examining table for me?" asked Rachel.

"I'll need to help him," said Mike. "Is it all right if he keeps the pillow? He can't sit up too well yet."

"Whatever will help him. I have another pillow if he needs it," said Rachel. "I like your teddy bear, John. You don't need to be afraid of me."

"I'm just afraid I can't do what you want me to do," said John.

"I'm actually just going to talk to you today and a brief exam. If you don't want to talk, one of your friends can talk for you," said Rachel.

"Carol can answer for me," said John.

Gene smoothed John's hair back and straightened his glasses. Gene knew that John always felt loved when he did this for him.

"So what happened to John?" asked Rachel.

Carol spoke quietly yet distinctly in the reassuring way that always made the three guys feel good. As she spoke, she held John's bad hand.

"John had a bad fall. He hurt his good leg, his hip, and his mouth. He just had an operation on his hip. His other leg was paralyzed by polio when he was five. In an accident years ago, his right arm and hand were crushed, and he had severe head and back injuries. Before this last fall, he was walking with a cane."

"And Carol lets me hold on to her arm. That always helps me walk," said John. "When we graduated from high school, Carol walked with me, and I held her arm. I couldn't have done it without her."

"John has been through a lot more, but we don't always talk about it," said Carol.

"May I see your hand, John?" asked Rachel.

Carol ever so gently picked up John's hand and helped him reach toward Rachel.

"I'm sorry so much has happened to you, John. Can you lift your arm?"

"No," said John as he tried but it didn't move.

"Did you all go to school together?" asked Rachel.

"Yes. I'm thirty-seven, like they all are," said John.

"I would have guessed you much younger," said Rachel.

"I don't talk so good, and my head hurts, and sometimes I forget things," said John.

"John, you are the smartest, nicest guy I know, and don't you ever forget that," said Gene.

"If you will all come back this time tomorrow, I will have a plan all worked out for John. I'm going to consult with my manager because we must be sure we don't do anything to hurt you. You have my promise that we won't hurt you, John," said Rachel.

"We will see you tomorrow," said Carol. "Do you have any questions, John?"

"No, I don't have any questions. Thank you, Rachel," said John as he smiled at Rachel.

As Mike helped John to the wheelchair, Rachel asked Gene, "Do you mind if I ask you what your condition is?"

"I don't mind. I had three consecutive strokes and recently a fall that set me back quite a bit," said Gene.

"What did the strokes affect?" asked Rachel.

"My right leg and arm, my eyes, my neck, and my voice, but it has come back, not quite normal but close. My neck is actually an old football injury, but the last stroke seems to have made it worse," said Gene.

"May I examine you tomorrow?" asked Rachel.

Gene looked at Carol.

"Thank you for caring. What time do you want him?" asked Carol.

"I'll examine him right after John. I'll have a nurse with me," said Rachel.

As they walked to the car, John asked, "Is Rachel going to help you too, Gene?"

"I'm not sure, John. It would be nice, but I'm not sure it's possible," said Gene.

There Is Hope for the World

When they arrived home, Mike and John got out of the van. Leon was there waiting for them.

"We will see you later," said Gene to Mike and John. "We are going to have lunch with Nathan."

As they started to back out of the driveway, Mike came out to the van.

"I hate to ask, but John would really like to go with you."

"Sure, I just didn't think he would be up to it," said Gene.

When Mike came back with John, Leon helped him into the front seat. "You don't mind sitting up front with me, do you, John?"

"Not at all," said John as he smiled at Leon.

As they drove to pick up Nathan, John asked Gene, "It won't make Nathan nervous having me with you, will it, Gene?"

"No, not at all. Nathan is not shy. Last night there were a lot of us in the room when Terry came back with Leon, and that went all right, and Terry is very shy," said Gene.

When they arrived at Nathan's apartment, Leon went in to get him.

As they were walking to the van, Leon said, "We have one more person with us. John wanted to come."

"That's great, I love John," said Nathan.

Carol moved to the third seat so Gene and Nathan could talk.

Nathan looked back at Carol. "I didn't mean to take your seat."

"It's all right, Nathan. Don't worry," said Carol as she smiled quietly at Nathan.

"You know, I remember a lot about you, Carol, but what I remember most is your sweet, quiet smile and the comforting way you always talked to me. I always felt like you cared," said Nathan.

"I did care, Nathan. I always cared about you, and I still do," said Carol.

When they got to the restaurant, Nathan pushed Gene's wheelchair while Leon took care of John. Carol sat between Nathan and Gene, and John sat by Leon. Leon wanted to help John. He knew John would like that.

"Nathan, we were very upset with what you told us the other night. It broke our hearts. We care so much about you. We want to help you," said Leon. "Carol, why don't you ask him?"

Carol took Nathan's hand and spoke to him in the kindest voice he had ever heard, "Gene wants to offer you a job helping him. He has a friend who lives in the same apartment complex where he lives. His name is Patrick. He takes Gene to work and brings him home and helps him during the day at work. Until now someone has always been with Gene at night and during the time he is home. It has been me, Mike, Alan, or John until John got hurt, but we might not always be able to be there for him. And speaking for myself, I worry about him when he is alone. He needs someone to stay with him, help him, travel with him, and be kind to him. The last one, be kind to him, is why I would like for it to be you because I know you love him as I do."

As Gene took his glasses off and wiped his eyes, Carol put her arm around him and kissed him gently on the cheek.

"Gene wanted me to ask you for him. It is very emotional for him because he cares so much about you as we all do."

"I would be honored to do it. Even the fact that you want me to is overwhelming to me after I have messed my life up so much. But I'll do a good job. I promise you that with every ounce of life I have left in me. I love you, Gene. You were always my best friend." Nathan was also crying.

Carol put her arms around Nathan. "Everything is going to be all right now."

"Nathan, we'll talk later. I can't seem to speak right now," said Gene.

"That's fine, Gene, I understand," said Nathan as he reached over and touched Gene's hand.

John was having a hard time eating his sandwich. Leon cut it up in smaller pieces so John could handle it better. "Thank you, Leon." When the waitress asked about dessert, John said, "Could I have a piece of cheesecake, please?"

"Of course," said the waitress.

Leon and Nathan both decided to have a piece also.

"Do you guys know, the reason I like cheesecake, besides the fact that it is delicious, is that it sticks to the fork so it's easy for me to eat and I don't drop it," said John.

"John, I love you so much. Only you would think of that." Carol reached across the table and touched his bad hand.

Leon hugged John. "I love you too, John. You make me think there is hope for the world."

"You make me smile, John. I haven't smiled for a long time," said Nathan.

"Good. You are all so nice. I'm glad I made you smile because I love all of you so much," said John. "Are you all right, Gene? You are really quiet today."

"I was just thinking about the big job we have ahead of us this afternoon," said Gene.

"We had better go. Mike and Terry will be waiting for us," said Leon.

CHARITY FOR THE HOMELESS CAMP

They were all going to the homeless camp to search for Rodger as well as help the other homeless people they would encounter there. At Mike's house, they loaded several boxes into the van.

Mike said to Leon, "I'll drive. This is a strange place to find."

Carol made sure that Terry sat in the middle seat by Gene. Nathan, Leon, and Carol sat in the back seat, and John sat in the front seat with Mike. John looked back at Terry and reached his hand back.

"Terry, I had physical therapy this morning," said John.

Terry took hold of John's hand. "Did it go all right for you?"

"I think so. They are going to try to help Gene too," said John.

Gene looked at Terry. "It's a long shot, but I'll try anything. I don't have much to lose."

"I've tried a lot of things. They told me they couldn't help me. They say it's been too long. It was my fault. I waited too long. No one told me differently." Terry turned and looked out the window.

Then he felt John squeeze his hand. "I'm glad you are going to stay with me, Terry."

"Thank you, John, and all of you for caring about me," said Terry.

As the group drove toward the Seventh Street traffic way, they all knew the challenge ahead of them would be the most difficult yet. They were going to look for Rodger, Mike's friend, the homeless Vietnam veteran.

"Don't forget to tell me where to turn, Carol. Does the street have a name?" asked Mike.

"No, the streets down there don't have names," said Carol.

"Well, Carol, I thought I knew everything about you. How do you know about this area and that homeless veterans will be there?" asked Gene.

"They will be there. I have no doubt about that. Many years ago, in 1955, I was nine and Ethan was eleven, our grandmother used to take us there to feed the hobos, as she called them. She would cook for days before we would go there. She would prepare a feast for them. My dad would take us there. He would help us carry the food, but then he would go back and sit in the car while we served them. That is the only thing I ever remember doing with my dad." Carol paused and wiped her eyes. "There were veterans then there too from World War II. My grandmother was so kind to them, and they all thanked her and us. They have always stayed there, under the bridges and in the old deserted buildings."

"I never knew that, and I grew up fairly close to here," said Gene.

"My grandmother fed them in her backyard too. Shortly after she died, a homeless man came to her back door and asked for food. I was there, and I heard my aunt tell him that the lady who used to feed them was dead and there would be no more food. She told him to tell the others. He said he would tell them. They had a strong line of communication between them because no one ever came to her door again. When that man left that day, he stood in the alley and waved to me, and I waved back. I recognized him as one who my grandmother had fed and been kind to."

Carol had been leaning forward, responding to Gene's question, but everyone else had heard. Her hair was covering her face. Gene pushed it back and kissed her gently on tear-stained cheeks.

"This is where you turn right, Mike. We are almost there," said Carol. "Now turn left and at the end turn right."

And then they saw them, like a carpet that seemed to cover miles. There were hundreds of men as well as many women and children, living in tents and cardboard houses and taking cover under blankets hanging over ropes stretched between trees.

"We will take the food out first. There probably won't be enough, but many won't eat, and others have their own food. We will split up in three groups—Leon and John, Mike and Gene, and Nathan and Terry will go with me. We need to find those who have influence or seem to be in charge and ask about Rodger. We won't be able to cover the whole area today. We will come back tomorrow and bring more food and some blankets. It will be winter soon," said Carol. "There aren't many children. Maybe we could bring some of the stuffed toys from Cathy's room."

As they got out of the van, some of the people walked toward them, but they didn't come too close. Most stayed back in their shelters. One little girl of about ten or eleven came running up to Carol and put her arms around her. She had long red hair like Carol. She was barefoot and dirty, but Carol immediately bent down and hugged her.

Within a short while, the sandwiches, drinks, fruit, and cookies were gone. Then they separated and started walking among the people. They each had a bag of candy, chips, and crackers to distribute. They started talking to those who seemed to have some authority and asked them if they had seen Rodger. They each had a picture of him. It was an old picture, but he hadn't changed much. They told the people that he was six feet five inches tall, very thin, and had shoulder-length blond hair.

In the area where Carol, Terry, and Nathan were, several remembered Rodger. One older lady said she thought he would be back tomorrow. And then Carol heard a voice from the back of the camp say, "Carol, Carol Sullivan, is that you?"

A man came running toward her but stopped a few feet away. They never came too close to those trying to help them for fear of scaring them. But Carol wasn't afraid. She went toward the man.

"Ricky Salerno, is it really you?" said Carol.

"Do you remember me?" asked Ricky.

"Yes, you were in Vietnam. I worked with your wife, Donna, at the insurance company a long time ago," said Carol. "We rented a house on Lansing Street with two other girls until you and Donna married."

"When I was in Vietnam, Donna had my baby. She died in childbirth, and so did my baby," said Ricky. "I couldn't imagine that happening in this day and age."

"I'm so sorry, Ricky. I loved Donna," said Carol. "I didn't know."

"I've never been able to go on," said Ricky.

"We will help you, Ricky. Do you want help?" asked Carol.

"Yes, I want and need help," said Ricky.

"We'll be back tomorrow. Do you see that tall, red-haired man over there? That's my friend Mike. He is a Vietnam veteran too. He is going to help you," said Carol. "Stay in this area. I'll bring him to you tomorrow."

"Thank you. God bless you all for helping us," said Ricky as he went back to his shelter.

The little girl was still holding Carol's hand. Her name was Melanie, and she wanted an address so she could go to school. She didn't want food, toys, or clothes. All she wanted was an address.

"How long have you been here, Melanie?" asked Carol.

"A few days. We will probably move soon. My mother doesn't want to stay in the same place too long," said Melanie.

Gene frequently looked at Carol to make sure she was safe. He noticed that the little girl was still with her. "Carol is not going to be able to leave that child," said Gene.

"She'll be all right. She knows why we are here," said Mike.

As Carol was talking to a young woman, Nathan said to Terry, "I'm in awe of her. She doesn't know a stranger. She can talk to anyone. She always could."

When Carol saw the other groups were going back to the van, their group did the same. They were soon all in the van except Carol.

"Goodbye, Melanie. We will be back tomorrow. Will I see you then?" Carol took her sweater off and put it around Melanie.

"We might be gone. I never know. But if I'm not here, don't worry about me. I'll be fine," said Melanie.

They waved as Mike slowly drove away. Carol was sitting by Gene, and he put his arms around her. Carol said through her tears, "You know all that little girl wants is an address so she can go to school. She doesn't even have an address."

John looked back at Carol. "Are you all right, Carol?"

"Yes, John, I'm fine," said Carol.

"Did you see the little boys that were talking to me? They seemed to like me," said John. "I wonder why."

"You had five little friends. You look a lot younger than the rest of us, except Leon, he looks pretty young," said Carol.

"How did you know there were five boys? I didn't know you could see me," said John.

"John, every few seconds I looked at you and Leon, and the next few seconds I looked at Mike and Gene, and I always knew Terry and Nathan were close to me," said Carol.

"Wow, you are amazing, Carol," said John.

"No, not amazing, just observant and careful. They all seemed like good people there today, but they aren't always all good," said Carol. "You know, people have lived here in this exact place long before we were born, probably when my mother was a little girl, and they will be here long after we are gone. When I came here with my grandmother it was mostly older men. Today they are younger, and there are many women and children. It's strange," said Carol.

"What's strange?" asked Leon.

"But for the grace of God, those people out there could be any one of us. And actually one of us is still out there. Rodger is out there," said Carol.

"We'll find him tomorrow. We have to find him before it's too late," said Mike.

Carol put her hand on Mike's shoulder. "We'll find him, Mike. Somehow, someway we will find him."

A Baby Bird with a Broken Wing and Leg

On John's second day of outpatient physical therapy, he was a little more relaxed. He was still very weak, and they knew they couldn't work him too hard or for too long. Sometimes he reminded Carol of a baby bird with a broken wing and a broken leg.

When John was finished, he sat quietly by Mike as Rachel and Brad, a nurse, examined Gene. Carol stayed close to Gene. In his own way he was as fragile as John, possibly more so.

"Do you live here in Kansas City, Gene?" asked Brad.

"No, I was born in Kansas City, but I live in Chicago now," said Gene.

"Where is your most severe pain right now?" asked Brad.

"My leg and back," said Gene without hesitation.

"How about your neck and right arm?" asked Brad.

"With my arm, I'm never sure if it is going to work or not. My neck hurts when I turn it too far to the right. It has been that way for a long time from an old football injury, but it seemed to get worse after the stroke," said Gene.

Brad took Gene's vitals. Rachel evaluated his range of movement of his leg, arm, and neck.

"Am I beyond all help? I'm beginning to feel that way," said Gene.

"I will meet you in the conference room in fifteen minutes. I need to check on something," said Brad. "And, Gene, there is hope. You have heart disease, high blood pressure, football injuries, and a serious neck injury, but physically you are a very strong man. But I do have one question. When you played football, how many concussions did you have?"

"Five," said Gene. "One was exceptionally bad. I could barely hear or see or walk for a while."

"Did they send you back out to play that night?" asked Brad.

"Yes, about thirty minutes later," said Gene.

Rachel and Carol helped Gene sit up, and Mike helped him to the wheelchair. As they waited in the conference room for Brad, Rachel could not help but notice the deep, genuine concern Carol and Mike showed for their two friends.

When Brad returned, he spoke to John first, "John, you are going to make a fine recovery. As Dr. Wilson told you, it will be necessary for you to use a cane, but you will be able to walk. We will go easy with you and not push you too hard mainly because of your arm and hand." Brad reached over and took John's bad hand in his hand. "My only regret is that I can't do anything for your hand and arm."

John patted Brad on the back with his good hand. "That's all right."

"You are a fine man, John," said Brad. "And now for this other fine man sitting by you, I'm giving you the name of a friend of mine in Chicago who I know will be able to help you. He is the head of a physical therapy group that works primarily with stroke patients. He will try everything. He will not give up on you. I promise you that."

"Do you think there is the remote chance that I could be normal again?" asked Gene.

"Yes, and I think it is a strong possibility. It has only been six months. You have some more recovery coming your way. I just wish you hadn't hurt your leg and had a setback," said Brad.

"Thank you. I will call when I get back to Chicago," said Gene.

As they walked out of the conference room, Carol bent over and hugged first John and then Gene.

"Even the thought of you both being well makes me the happiest I've been in a long time," said Carol. "Never, ever forget how much I love the two of you."

THE CHILDREN OF THE HOMELESS CAMP

Leon, Nathan, and Terry were waiting for Mike, Gene, Carol, and John to pick them up after physical therapy to help in the search for Rodger. They once again had food for the homeless people as well as stuffed toys for John to distribute to the children and also some blankets.

They were all quiet in the van going to the homeless camp. Mike was very worried that they wouldn't be able to find Rodger and if and when they did that it would be too late.

When they arrived, the people walked toward their van, but as the day before, they kept a comfortable distance. When Mike helped John out of the van and handed him the bag of stuffed toys, the five little boys who John had befriended the previous day started passing the toys out to the smaller children. They took nothing for themselves.

Nathan and Leon passed the blankets out especially to those who didn't seem to have a blanket. And as the day before, the food and drinks went fast. Carol took Terry's arm and motioned for Mike to come with them. They were headed toward the section where they had found those who knew Rodger.

Terry talked very little. It was so hard for him. But he seemed more comfortable talking to Carol than to anyone else.

As they walked, Carol asked, "Didn't you used to wear glasses, Terry?"

"Yes, but I fell and broke them. Since the stroke, I fall a lot," answered Terry quietly.

"Can you see all right?" asked Carol.

"No, my eyesight is bad. I've worn glasses since I was five," said Terry.

"We'll get you some new glasses," said Carol.

"Thank you, Carol," said Terry.

Ricky Salerno approached Mike. Mike gave him an address and told him that he would meet him there tomorrow.

Mike had a bag of food for the people in the area where they were. Carol had a blanket to give to someone. The elderly lady approached them who had told Carol she thought Rodger would be there today.

"Hello, I have a blanket for you, and Mike has some food," said Carol.

"Thank you so much," said the lady. "Rodger is here. He is in the green tent right over there. He went to VA yesterday. He wasn't feeling well. He talks about Mike a lot. Please see if you can help him."

"I will. Wait here for me," said Mike.

As Carol and Terry waited for Mike, Melanie, Carol's friend from the day before, came up to them.

"Hello, Melanie, would you like a sandwich?" asked Carol.

Melanie still had Carol's sweater on that she had given her. Melanie ate the sandwich in a few bites. Carol handed Melanie a small white stuffed dog. She hugged the little dog close to her heart.

"I'm sorry. I told you a lie yesterday. I thought you might be my mother because I look like you. The lady with me yesterday is not my mother. I don't have a mother. I was born in a place like this, and my birth mother left me. I thought the nice, handsome man in the wheelchair was my father because I can tell he loves you," said Melanie.

"That's my friend Gene. He's not married. He is the father of two children, and I have three children. I'll be going home to them soon," said Carol.

"What about him?" Melanie nodded toward Terry. Carol realized she was still holding his arm, but she didn't let go.

"Terry is my friend just as Gene is. I love both of them very much. They are wonderful men," said Carol.

"Some people think I am strange and weird. Do you think that, Carol?" asked Melanie.

"No, I think you are beautiful," said Carol.

"I say strange things. I don't want an address anymore. It doesn't matter. Thank you. Goodbye," said Melanie.

"Goodbye, Melanie," said Carol as she bent over and kissed her.

Melanie left then and soon disappeared in a large group of people. Carol wiped the tears from her cheeks. Terry put his arm around her.

"I'm sorry. That was hard for you. You were so kind to her."

"But I can't help her. There is nothing I can do," said Carol.

Just then Mike and Rodger came out of the tent. Mike was very solemn.

Rodger said, "Hello, Carol and Terry. Mike is going to help me."

"We are glad he found you," said Carol.

"So am I," said Rodger.

It was a long walk back to the van. Carol and Terry were far behind Mike and Rodger.

"Are you all right, Terry?" asked Carol.

"I'll be fine, but please don't let go of my arm," said Terry.

"I won't. Let's just take our time. If you ever need anything or just want to talk, please call me. If you ever need to ask me anything about John, don't ever hesitate to call. I love you, Terry, and I love John and Gene and all the guys. I want you to all be fine and happy. I will do anything for you guys," said Carol.

"I know. You're the only person I can talk to," said Terry.

When they got to the van, everyone else was already there. John was in the back seat between Leon and Nathan, and he was very happy. Carol and Terry would sit in the middle seat by Gene.

"Carol, since you are the smallest, you get the smallest seat," said Gene.

"I hope I don't crowd you too much, Terry," said Carol.

"I don't mind," said Terry.

When they got home, Mike and Rodger got out first.

"Leon will help John," said Mike.

"All right. Do you and Rodger need any help?" asked Carol.

"Not right now," said Mike.

Nathan helped Gene, and Carol and Terry followed them into the house. Carol suddenly realized that she hadn't let go of Terry's arm during the entire ride home.

"I'm sorry, Terry. I didn't let go of your arm," said Carol.

"I like for you to hold on to my arm. It helps me walk and makes me feel secure," said Terry.

In the living room, Gene was already on the sofa with his legs up. John was sitting close to him. Carol sat by John. Terry started to get a chair from the dining room.

"Sit here by us, Terry. It's more comfortable," said Carol.

Terry sat by Carol. She reached out and touched his hand. Like Gene, Terry never smiled, but Carol knew that he was happy in his heart and secure knowing he would be John's companion.

After Mike got Rodger settled in Danny's old room on the third floor, he returned to the living room. Alan was also there.

Mike began speaking very hesitantly, "I need to tell you all about Rodger. He has more problems than I ever realized. He is addicted to prescription drugs as well as other drugs and alcohol. The pain in his head from the wounds he received in Vietnam is almost constant and unbearable for him. They want to admit him to the VA hospital. He doesn't want to go there, but he needs professional help. I don't know what to do."

Carol got up and went to Mike. She sat on the footstool by his chair and took hold of his hand. "Mike, we have done a lot in our time for many people, and you and Gene have done so much for me. When we were only sixteen, you two saved me. You saved my life twice. But this might be too big for us, Mike. I want to talk to Rodger in the morning. Is that all right with you?"

"Yes. I need you to help me to help him," said Mike.

They were all amazed by Carol, even Leon who always seemed to have an answer for everything. Of course, nothing Carol ever said or did surprised Gene, and that was one of the reasons he loved her.

It seemed as though there should have been so much for them to talk about that night, but for whatever reason, there wasn't. It was John once again who broke the awkward silence.

"You guys know something, those five little boys whom I made friends with yesterday, all they wanted to do today was pass out the stuffed toys to the smaller kids. They didn't even take food for themselves. They gave that to the little kids too."

Carol went back to the sofa and sat between John and Terry. "You know what I think, John. I think that because you are such a great guy and so kind that you rubbed off on those boys. They saw how good you treated people, and they wanted to do the same."

"Well, Terry and Nathan, I'm going to take you home. I think everyone is tired tonight," said Leon.

As Terry got up to leave, Carol said, "I'll pick you up at nine o'clock tomorrow, Terry."

"Thank you. I'll be ready," said Terry.

As they walked to the car, Nathan said, "Terry, why don't you sit up front with Leon."

Terry got in the front with Leon. "You probably wonder why Carol is picking me up at nine o'clock," said Terry.

"I don't know that it's any of my business," said Leon.

"Carol noticed that I wasn't seeing well. She asked me about my glasses. I fell and broke them. She is going to help me get some glasses tomorrow," said Terry.

"I should have done that for you," said Leon.

"Don't worry, Leon. Carol wants to do it for me. No girl has ever talked to me or been nice to me like she is," said Terry.

Mike helped John to bed that night as Alan helped Gene. Carol followed them into their room. Alan and Mike said good night and left.

Carol sat on the sofa. "Why are you over there all by yourself, Carol?" asked Gene.

"I'm just thinking," said Carol.

"We miss you, Carol. We need you to be here with us," said John.

"So my question is, who should be in the middle tonight?" asked Gene.

"I think John should be," said Carol.

"No. Not tonight," said John. "Carol should be. You need to be close to Gene tonight."

Carol went to the bathroom and put on her gown and brushed her hair and teeth. Then she got between them in the big bed.

"Just like California, but then again not really," said Carol.

"It's as close as we can get," said Gene.

"Don't worry if I get up early in the morning, John. I have to talk to Rodger first and then meet Terry at nine o'clock," said Carol.

"I know about Rodger, but why are you meeting Terry?" asked John.

"Terry broke his glasses, and he is having trouble seeing. I'm going to take him to get some new glasses," said Carol.

"Thank you for being nice to Terry," said John.

"I hope you have pleasant dreams, John," said Carol.

"I heard you today when you asked Terry about his glasses. One of us should have noticed and helped him. But it is always you. You help everyone," said Gene.

"Right now, I think Terry needs us to help him more than Rodger and Nathan and everyone else put together. I have never seen anyone so sad and lonely in my whole life. We need to be very kind and gentle with him. He is so sensitive about talking and about everything for that matter," said Carol.

"I'll be good to Terry," said John.

"I know you will, John. You are good to everyone. That's why I'm glad Terry is going to be here with you," said Carol.

Gene kissed Carol on the cheek. "Thank you for helping my friends, all of them. And thank you for helping me."

THE HEALER

Carol fixed a breakfast for Rodger of scrambled eggs, bacon, toast, and orange juice and took it to the third floor. She knocked very quietly on the door.

Rodger said, "Come in."

Rodger was sitting in a chair looking out the window. Carol could tell the bed hadn't been slept in.

"Would you eat a little breakfast for me this morning?" asked Carol.

"I'll try. It looks good," said Rodger.

"Rodger, do you know how much we all love and care about you?" said Carol.

"I know. Mike was always my best friend. He has to be so disappointed in me," said Rodger.

"He just wants you to be well and happy," said Carol. "It wasn't your fault that you were wounded so severely. He is devastated about what happened to you."

"It would be so much easier for me and everyone else if I just died," said Rodger.

"Not for Mike or me or Gene or any of your friends," said Carol. "We all love you so much. Gene and I have to go home tomorrow. It is very hard on us, especially Gene, to leave. Leon will be leaving tomorrow too. John has not yet recovered completely from his surgery. Mike is overwhelmed and just not in a good place. Poor Alan is trying so hard to help everyone. And Terry is so sad and alone. In many ways I worry about him more than anyone. He has always been so painfully shy, and now he has so much trouble speaking that he is embarrassed. I've tried so hard to help him, and I actually think that he says more to me than to anyone. You finished your breakfast. Did you have enough?" Carol reached over and smoothed his hair down.

"I've had plenty. It was a good breakfast. Thank you. It has been many years since anyone has fixed me breakfast," said Rodger. "I feel bad for Terry too. I always liked him. Do you think Mike would let me stay here and help all of them? I'm bigger than Mike. I could help him lift John. I could help Alan with driving and taking John to appointments. I could be useful to them."

"But could you get by without the pills and alcohol?" asked Carol.

"Yes, if I had a purpose in life," said Rodger.

"But what about your pain. Can you live with it?" asked Carol.

"I can try," said Rodger.

"I have seen both Gene and John in some of the most excruciating pain imaginable. I know what it is to live with pain. I could always see it in Gene's eyes. I could never understand how people could be so cruel to him." Carol was crying, and Rodger comforted her.

"Would you do something for me, Carol? Would you lie by me on the bed for a few minutes?" asked Rodger.

"Yes, I will," said Carol.

Carol and Rodger lay on the bed together. She rested her head on his shoulder.

"Do you have any idea how many guys in the class of 1964 were in love with you? Mike, Jessie, Nathan, John, Terry, and me and probably others. But the one who loved you the most was always Gene. I always thought you two would get married, but I guess that wasn't meant to be." Rodger had his arm around Carol, and she was holding his hand. "It is strange, but right now I have no pain, I have no pain pills and no alcohol.

Carol kissed Rodger. It was a gentle, heartfelt kiss, and he returned the kiss. "I need to go now. Do you want to go downstairs with me and talk to Alan and Mike?" asked Carol.

"All right. I'll go," said Rodger.

Carol took hold of Rodger's hand, and they went downstairs. Mike, Alan, John, and Gene were all at the table eating breakfast.

"Have you eaten, Rodger?" asked Alan.

"Yes, Carol brought breakfast to me," said Rodger.

"I'm going to be gone for a while. I think you have a lot to talk about," said Carol. "Alan, may I use your car? I need to take Terry someplace this morning."

Alan handed Carol his car keys. "Bring Terry home to us, Carol. Bring him home to stay."

When Carol arrived at Terry's apartment, he was waiting for her with a small, tattered suitcase, probably the same one he had with him when he went to live with Leon. Carol helped Terry to the car.

"Let me move the seat back a little. Are you comfortable?" asked Carol.

"I'm fine," said Terry. "You always make me feel comfortable."

Carol talked to Terry quietly and reassuringly as they drove to the optometry office. Terry wasn't afraid to talk to Carol as he seemed to be to others. When they arrived at the office, Carol took hold of his arm and walked with him.

"Terry needs to have his eyes checked. He broke his glasses some time ago. He has worn glasses since he was a small child," said Carol.

"If you will come with me back to the doctor's office, we will check your eyes," said the clerk.

"Is it all right if I accompany him?" asked Carol.

"Yes, that will be fine," said the clerk.

They dilated Terry's eyes and examined them extensively. He was basically unable to read the eye chart. His new glasses would be ready in about two weeks and they would call him. He was told they would be exceptionally strong. Terry and Carol went to pick out some frames.

"They will probably be really thick," said Terry.

"That's the same news Gene usually gets. Gene doesn't think his glasses can get much thicker. But don't worry, Terry, you'll get used to them quickly and be able to see so much better," said Carol as she put her arm around him.

"You are always so kind and make me feel better," said Terry as they began looking at frames.

Carol smiled slightly at Terry and asked, "Do you have any preference?"

"I can't see well at all now, but I like Gene's frames and John's frames too," said Terry.

Carol knew right where to look. "I think these are identical to Gene's frames." She put them on Terry. "They look very nice on you."

"They feel good. I'll take your word as to how they look," said Terry.

When they went to pay, Terry reached for his billfold.

Carol put her hand on his. "No, I'm paying. It's my gift to you."

"I've never had anyone do something like this for me before," said Terry.

"Well, now you have," said Carol kindly. "Let's get something to eat. What would you like?"

"Anything is fine with me," said Terry.

"I would like for it to be your choice today, Terry," said Carol.

"I like Mexican food," said Terry shyly.

"I do too, Terry. We have something in common," said Carol.

They were seated in a round booth. Carol liked that because it would make it easier to help Terry if he needed it, but he seemed to do quite well on his own.

"I like sitting by you," said Terry as he took hold of Carol's hand. He seemed embarrassed and started to pull his hand back.

"It's all right, Terry," said Carol as she held on to his hand. "Terry, do you understand about John and his problems and why he is so special to us?" asked Carol.

"Yes, Gene told me a lot about John," said Terry.

"If Gene told you, then I know it is right. Gene loves John as much as I do. They have always been very close," said Carol.

"I love him too," said Terry as he reached out and touched Carol's hair. "I just like to touch you. Do you mind?"

"I don't mind at all, Terry," said Carol.

"I felt bad for John in school. He didn't have any friends, but we became friends," said Terry. "When John walked with you in the graduation processional, all the guys were jealous. Every guy in that class would have changed places with John."

"That was only the second time I had ever met John, and I couldn't help but love him. He was just so sweet and innocent. Some worry about John because they say he is childlike, but you see, that was one of the first things I noticed about him and one of things I loved the most. But John will be fine, and I am so glad that you are going to be with him. You are much stronger than John and much more logical. John lets something get hold of him, and he can't seem to let it go. He becomes a little obsessed. He had a dream that Gene was going to have another stroke and die in his sleep, so he wanted to watch him all night. One night he even went outside in the dark hunting for Gene and me."

At this point they finished eating, and they left the restaurant.

"I'll take good care of him and protect him," said Terry. "I love to talk with you. I don't feel shy and scared. I'm not afraid to talk to you because I know you will never make fun of me or laugh at me."

"Not in a million years, my sweet Terry. I would never make fun of you," said Carol as she kissed Terry on the cheek and then on the lips.

He returned the kiss. It was sincere, sweet, and from their hearts. He ran his fingers through her hair, and she wiped the tears from his cheeks.

"Terry, this doesn't have anything to do with John, Mike, Nathan, Gene or anyone else. It is just between you and me. I just wanted to kiss you because I love you. Please forgive me if it is wrong," said Carol.

"It's not wrong. I just wish..." Terry paused.

"What do you wish, Terry?" asked Carol.

He couldn't finish, but it didn't matter. Carol knew what he was trying to say.

A DIFFICULT FAREWELL

When Gene, Carol, and Nathan left Kansas City to fly back to Chicago, there were many tears. Since emotions were running so high, Mike would have preferred to just take the three of them to the airport, but John, Terry, and Rodger wanted to go. Mike knew how hard it was going to be.

As they entered the terminal, Carol asked Terry, "Will you be all right walking to the gate with us, or would you like a wheelchair?"

"I want to walk if I can hold on to your arm," said Terry.

"That would be fine, Terry," said Carol.

Alan also had gone with them. He knew when Carol left, Terry would be very sad and lonely, and he wanted to be there for him.

At the gate, Carol and Terry sat down. Gene and John were close. Everyone was looking at them. But today, for whatever reason, it was bothering Gene. He was holding his head, and Carol knew he had a bad headache. Alan, Mike, Nathan, and Rodger left them alone to say their goodbyes.

"John, it is very important to Gene and me to know that you and Terry are going to be all right without us," said Carol.

John's eyes were flooded with tears. "I wish you and Gene could stay."

"I know you do, but it won't be long before you will all come to Chicago," said Carol.

"We can't wait to see your program. Terry will come with you. Everyone will be with you," said Gene.

John reached in his jacket and pulled out Carol's little white kitten that Gene had won for her so long ago. "You need to have Snowball with you. It will help you to remember me and Gene."

"Thank you, but I could never forget you or Gene or Terry or any of the guys," said Carol.

It was time for handicapped boarding. Gene and Carol kissed and hugged John one last time, and Gene shook hands with Terry. The other four guys said their goodbyes, and Nathan said goodbye to Terry. Then Nathan pushed Gene's wheelchair to the plane entrance. All that was left was for Terry to let go of Carol's arm.

"I will miss you," said Terry. "I can't talk to anyone like I can talk to you."

"No more than I will miss you," said Carol. She kissed him very gently, and he returned the kiss.

And then Carol hurried to catch up with Gene and Nathan. At the entrance to the plane ramp, Carol turned and waved to everyone one last time with the little white kitten in her hand.

Nathan sat in the window seat and Gene in the aisle seat. "Carol is going to be very sad. We will keep her between us," said Gene.

When Carol got on the plane, she quickly took her seat. She took hold of Nathan's hand and rested her head on Gene's shoulder. "I held my tears back until I got on the plane, but I can't anymore. John really got to me when he handed me the kitten, and it hurts me so much to leave Terry," said Carol. "Nathan, I am so glad you are going to be with Gene."

As Carol settled back and wiped her tears, Gene took his glasses off and handed them to her. "Would you put my glasses in your bag? I'm suddenly very tired and cold."

"I'll ask the stewardess for a blanket," said Carol.

The plane was ready for takeoff. When the stewardess brought the blanket, Gene was shivering. Carol felt his hands. "Your hands are like ice." She covered him with the blanket and put her hands under the cover to warm his hands. "Do you have a chest pain?" asked Carol.

"No, I'm just so tired," said Gene.

"Just close your eyes and rest," said Carol quietly.

The pilot came back to talk to Gene. It was Captain Robinson. "Hi, Gene. You're not looking so good today."

"I'm not feeling so good right now," said Gene.

There was an empty seat across the aisle from Gene. Captain Robinson asked the man in the center seat to save it for a doctor whom he wanted to be close to Gene. He walked several rows back and talked to a young man.

"The stewardess told me you are a doctor."

"Yes, I'm Dr. Jason Allen." He shook hands with Captain Robinson.

"I have a passenger on this flight who is not feeling well. He is a fine young man and a good friend of mine. He had a massive stroke about six months ago. There is a vacant seat across the aisle from him. Would you mind helping him for me and taking care of him. He is a very special man."

Dr. Allen immediately got up and picked up his bag. "I'll do anything I can for him. Please take me to him."

Dr. Allen followed Captain Robinson to Gene. He sat in the seat across from him. "Gene, this is Dr. Allen. He is going to be here with you on this trip. Please let me know if you need anything."

Gene shook his head yes. Carol handed Gene his glasses. "Would you please put them on for me?" asked Gene.

Carol did so very gently. "Dr. Allen, I'm Carol, and this is Nathan. We're Gene's friends."

"I'm pleased to meet you," said Dr. Allen. "How are you feeling right now, Gene?"

"Cold, weak, and shaky. My leg hurts really bad. I could hardly make it to the seat," said Gene. "We have been here for a week for our friend's surgery. I couldn't sleep last night knowing we would be leaving today."

"Is your friend all right?" asked Dr. Allen.

Gene took his glasses off and put his hands over his eyes, and he was crying.

Carol put her arms around Gene. "Our friend is getting better each day. It has been a long week. We had some difficult goodbyes at the airport."

Dr. Allen very gently took Gene's vitals and pulled the blanket up a little higher on his chest. "Do you have a Nitro with you, Gene?"

"Yes, in my pocket," said Gene.

Carol reached in his pocket and got one out of the small bottle.

"I think you should take it and rest. Your heart is a little fast and irregular. Hopefully, when the plane lands, you will feel a little better. I'm going to stay right here by you all the way to Chicago," said Dr. Allen in a very kind voice.

"Thank you, Dr. Allen," said Gene. He seemed to be a little more relaxed and soon fell asleep.

Nathan put his arm around Carol.

"Sometimes I'm so afraid for him," said Carol as she rested against Nathan's shoulder.

"It's all right, Carol. I'm afraid too. I just hope I can do a good job," said Nathan.

"You will because you love him just as I do," said Carol. "Do you think John and Terry will be all right?"

"Not really. John loves you and Gene so much. He will miss you guys terribly, but I think you both know that. As far as Terry is concerned, you are the only person he can really talk to. Mike will try to help Terry all he can. But Terry is in love with you. You know that too, don't you?" asked Nathan.

"I know he is. I've always tried to be kind to him and help him. I love him as I do all of you guys," said Carol.

Carol reached over and took Gene's glasses and put them in her bag. Then she very gently wiped the tears from his cheeks. Dr. Allen was watching Gene closely.

"Gene is a very quiet sleeper," said Carol.

"That's good," said Dr. Allen. "Right now he is resting well, and he has a regular heartbeat."

"He was doing so much better, but he has had some setbacks since his stroke. He was abused at his job because he is handicapped. He fell and twisted his leg badly and cut his face." Carol gently touched the deep scar on Gene's cheek. "Gene is the kindest man I have ever known. It hurts my heart that he was mistreated. I love him very much."

"Gene is very tall and muscular. Was he a football player?" asked Dr. Allen.

"Yes, he was a football quarterback and on a championship basketball team along with Nathan," said Carol.

"I was his teammate in both sports, and he was the best on the teams. Just knowing Gene and being on teams with him made some of the best years of my life. And now he is helping me by giving me a job. I owe my life to him," said Nathan.

"Gene saved my life when I was just sixteen. I was abused and wanted to die, and Gene and Mike made me want to live, and they kept my horrible secret. I also owe my life to him," said Carol.

"Those are very powerful testaments from both of you. I could tell from my brief conversation with him that he was a very special, good man. That quality is something one cannot hide. I am so sorry that people were not kind to him at work," said Dr. Allen.

"I have often wondered why really good people are often mistreated. I will never understand why it happens that way," said Carol.

"There are too many bad people in the world, but I am one of the good ones. I am going to take care of your friend for you. I feel honored to be allowed to do so," said Dr. Allen. "I don't really know you three, but I can tell you are good people, and I like you all very much."

Carol reached out and shook Dr. Allen's hand as did Nathan.

Gene slept peacefully through the entire trip. When he woke up, the plane was ready to land.

"Carol, do you remember our flight to Kansas City last spring when I was still well? We were so glad to see one another, and we talked so much."

"I remember it well," said Carol.

"On this flight all I did was sleep," said Gene.

"This was a very different trip. Things will get better," said Carol. Carol got Gene's glasses out of her bag and put them on him.

"Thank you. I wondered why I couldn't see." Gene reached over and took Nathan's hand. "I'm glad you are going to be staying with me. I really need you," said Gene.

"I just hope I'm good enough," said Nathan.

"You'll do fine, Nathan. We have no doubt about your ability or your dedication," said Carol.

"How are you feeling now, Gene?" asked Dr. Allen.

"I feel extremely weak. I don't know if I'll be able to walk," said Gene.

Just then two young men who had been sitting behind Dr. Allen stood in the aisle between Gene and Dr. Allen.

"Excuse us, but we were so close we couldn't help but overhear. When it's time, we would be honored to help you to the wheelchair. We are both on the football team at Kansas State University. I'm Cory Johnson, and this is my teammate Jordan Harmes. Jordan is a fullback. I'm a quarterback. What were you?" asked Cory.

"I was also a quarterback. It seems like a lifetime ago," said Gene as he looked at Carol.

"You were a very good quarterback too, wasn't he, Nathan?" asked Carol.

"He was the very best," said Nathan.

"Thank you, Cory and Jordan, for offering to help him," said Dr. Allen.

When the plane landed, Gene's two new friends helped him stand. Gene was taller than both of them. Nathan went to get the wheelchair as close to the door as possible. Dr. Allen took Carol's hand, and they followed. Captain Robinson hugged both Gene and Carol as he said goodbye. They all thanked Dr. Allen, Cory, and Jordan.

Immediately Carol saw Patrick in the terminal. She introduced Patrick to Nathan. Patrick hugged both Carol and Gene and went to get Gene's suitcase. Carol was glad to have Gene and Nathan home.

A New Vocation

As John healed from his surgery, he thought more about the motivational-speaker job. One day as John, Terry, Rodger, and Alan were having lunch, the phone rang. It was George Meyer. Alan handed the phone to John

"Hello, George," said John.

"Hello, John. Gene told me your surgery went well. How is your recovery coming along?" asked George.

"I'm getting stronger each day. I'm anxious about becoming a motivational speaker. Terry is anxious too. He is my companion. He is with me all the time," said John.

"Is he with you now? Can I talk to him?" asked George.

"He's here with me, but Terry has a hard time talking. He had a stroke like Gene six years ago, and it affected his voice. But he will be with me, and you will meet him when I have my first speaking engagement," said John.

"You tell Terry for me that I can't wait to meet him," said George. "Do you have your speech ready yet?"

"Oh, I've had it ready for a long time. I'm more than ready," said John.

"For some reason, I knew that is exactly what you would say. I'm very proud of you, John," said George. "I look forward to seeing you real soon. Goodbye for now."

"Goodbye, George. Thank you for calling," said John.

"Should I start working on a speech too?" asked Rodger.

"Yes, I think you should," said John.

Alan noticed the frightened look in Terry's eyes. He took hold of his hand. "Don't worry, Terry. You won't have to speak," said Alan.

"But what if Gene talks about strokes?" asked Terry.

"Gene would be the speaker. If you didn't have to talk, would you be on the stage with him?" asked Alan.

"Maybe, if I didn't have to speak," said Terry.

As Alan looked at the three guys sitting at the table that morning, he thought how much he liked them and how uniquely handsome they all were: John—so youthful-looking and kind and sweet; Rodger—a little rough around the edges but somewhat like a gentle giant; and Terry—so handsome and distinguished as long as no one asked him to speak.

"I'll tell you what I would like to do for you three. I would like to take you shopping and get each of you at least two new suits, shirts, ties, shoes, socks, and anything else you need. Then we will get your hair cut and styled. We will do all this before John's first speaking engagement," said Alan.

"Sounds fine to me. I really need a haircut." Rodger pushed his shoulder-length blond hair back.

"I'm not so thin anymore. I'm filling out a little, so I could use a new suit," said John.

Alan was still holding Terry's hand. He felt so protective of him. When they went out, Rodger or Mike usually pushed John's wheelchair. Alan always walked with Terry as Carol would do if she was there.

"And how about you, Terry?" asked Alan.

"That would be fine," said Terry.

Within a short time, plans were underway for John's first motivational-speaking engagement. It would be in Chicago in a conference room in the same building and on the same floor as Gene's office. George had talked to Mike and Alan as well as Gene and Carol to settle on a date when they could all be there.

With the details all worked out, George prepared the invitations. Almost everyone who received an invitation said they would be there. There would be all familiar faces in the audience: Leon and Olivia (his wife); Roy and Janice (they were back together); Jessie, Dennis, and Fred (all from the basketball team); Mike, Alan, and Cathy McVary; Sandy (the Chicago waitress who was always so kind to John); Dr. and Mrs. Mark Landis and Billy; Dr. Brett Wilson; Phillip York, Patrick Monohan, Nick Jennison, and George Meyer (all from Gene's office); Captain Tim Robinson; Brian and Holly; Linda Conley (Carol's friend from Kansas City); Sam Hagan (Carol's Kansas City boss and their fifth friend); Jeremy (from California); Karen (George's secretary); Charlene (her husband Victor), Darla, and Meggie (John's sisters from Dallas and Kansas City); twenty people from Gene's office handpicked by Gene; fifteen others from the office building who had requested to attend. Gene, Terry, Rodger, Nathan, and Carol would be on the stage or in front with John.

Greg could not attend because of work responsibilities, but Greg and Carol's mother, Stella, both called John several days before and wished him well.

Carol would arrive in Chicago two days before the conference. John, Mike, Alan, Terry, and Rodger would arrive one day before.

John had made a special request that Carol talk to George Meyer about two potential points of concern he had. Carol, for the first time, wasn't certain how to mention this to Gene. As Carol, Gene, and Nathan were sitting in the living room shortly after Carol's arrival, Carol mentioned that John wanted her to tell George two things.

"If he doesn't want me to talk to George, I assume it must be about me," said Gene.

"One is. I would actually be more comfortable if I tell you or you go with me to talk to George," said Carol.

"It's all right, Carol. It's John's program. Do as he asked," said Gene. "Please come sit by me."

Carol sat by Gene. "John wants George to know, he will be using the wheelchair to get to the venue, but when he talks, he will be standing. He also wants him to know that there is one part of his speech that he can't say without crying, but he knows if I am there that I can calm him and stop his crying."

"Can't he leave that part out?" asked Gene.

"No, that's not an option," said Carol.

Nathan was sitting across from them. "That's probably the part about you, Gene. That can't be left out."

"Is that right, Carol?" asked Gene.

"Yes, it's the part about you," said Carol.

"Do you want me to go with you to talk to George?" asked Gene.

"No, I'll be all right," said Carol.

When Karen told George that Carol was there to see him, he seemed to be almost expecting her visit.

"Hello, Carol. Please come in and sit down," said George graciously. "How's John, our featured speaker?"

"He's a little nervous but also excited," said Carol. "He has two concerns that he wanted me to discuss with you."

"And what might those be?" asked George.

"John will need to use the wheelchair to get to the venue. Once he starts speaking, he will stand. He was worried you might not approve," said Carol.

"That will be fine. Please tell him that I understand he has just had surgery," said George.

"There is a part of his speech that he cannot give without crying. It is not an option to leave it out. It's the part about Gene. He wants me to help him. If he turns to me, I will go to him and calm him in a few seconds. It usually works. Hopefully it will then," said Carol.

"Tell John not to worry. If he cries, it will probably just make him appear more vulnerable and likeable," said George. "You seem very worried and a little sad."

"I just want it to work out for John and Terry too and all of them for that matter. It would be good for them to have something go right just once," said Carol.

"I want to meet Terry. Will he speak?" asked George.

"No, he will be by Gene. He will push Gene's wheelchair to the front, but he will not speak," said Carol.

"I see more tears in your eyes as you mention Terry," said George.

"I'm just really worried about him as well as Nathan, Rodger, and Gene. I think John will do fine," said Carol.

"I don't know the others, but I am sure Gene will do a good job," said George. "Why are you worried about Gene?"

"I always worry about Gene, ever since he was a little boy," said Carol.

"You love him so much. I've known that since the very first time I met you," said George as he hugged Carol. "I respect all you do for your friends."

As Carol returned George's hug, she seemed to relax a little. "George, I feel you are just pretending to like me and that you actually wish I wasn't here."

"That is definitely not correct. I know you are very smart. I saw your test and interview scores. Gene told me once that I should ask Nick about those scores, and I did just that. You scored higher than anyone we have ever interviewed," said George. "John is a fine young man, and I want this to be a positive experience for him. If you weren't here with him, I don't think he would be able to do this, so don't think for a minute that I don't want you here."

Carol had no explanation for what she was feeling, but she suddenly had a sense of security with George. "Please be kind to Terry and help me with him. I'm not sure what to do for him."

"You know, I have never had a daughter or a son. I feel protective of you and Gene and John. I feel protective of Terry too, and I've never even met him," said George. "Will you ever forgive me for what I did to Gene?"

"I just don't want something like that to ever happen again, and I'm afraid it will. I'm so afraid it will," said Carol. "I don't know if he could survive something like that again. He's just not strong enough. Protect him for me, George. Please protect him."

John Kelley, Motivational Speaker

On the day of John's first motivational speech, John was in a very good place in his life. He was happy and speaking well that day. He was excited and well prepared. No one could have been better prepared than John was on that fateful day.

"Hello, everyone. My name is John Kelley, and I am from Kansas City, Kansas. I have multiple handicaps, and that is what I am going to speak to you about today. There are many people who have never known anyone who is handicapped.

"When I was five, in 1951, I had polio. It left my left leg paralyzed. I wear a brace on my left leg, and today it is two inches shorter than my right leg. Sometimes symptoms and pain of polio return in later life. My good leg hurts and is weak at times. This caused me to fall recently, and I injured my good leg and my hip. I now wear a brace on that leg also.

"I have had a degenerative eye disease since I was very young, but it was not diagnosed as retinitis pigmentosa until I was thirteen. I had an operation at that time and the correctional glasses. My grades improved in school, but I was far behind my classmates. I have had two more eye operations. Without glasses, I am legally blind. I did drive a car, but I haven't been able to drive for several years now. I am thirty-eight now. I haven't been able to drive since I was twenty-seven.

"My father abused me all through my childhood. He threw me against a wall when I was twelve, and it cut my ear and head open.

I have a severe hearing loss because of that injury. He also beat me repeatedly, but those scars have healed.

"In my opinion, my most severe handicap occurred when I was twenty-three. I was working at a garage as a mechanic. The roof covered with ice and snow fell on me. I had many severe head injuries, and my back was hurt. But the worst injury from that accident was that my right hand and arm were crushed. I have not regained the use of my right hand and arm and never will. This was very hard for me because I was an auto mechanic and I was right-handed. The head injuries from that accident have given me terrible headaches, and as I get older, I sometimes forget things. I don't think or speak as well as I did before the accident.

"Many handicapped people are the subjects of severe bullying in school and in the workplace. The bullying I received happened to me at my home, and the bully was my father. He told me I would never graduate from high school or be able to hold a job. I have done both of those. He also told me I would never have any friends. But I have the three best friends in the whole world, Carol, Gene, and Mike, and they are here today. They have helped me a lot as has Mike's dad, Alan, who is also here today. Carol, Gene, Mike and I graduated together and went to senior prom together.

"Last spring, my friend Gene had three consecutive strokes. The first two were mild, but the final stroke was a major stroke. He was only thirty-seven years old."

This was where John was crying, and he stopped and turned to Carol who was behind him. Carol comforted him for a moment and then he began speaking again.

"He is handicapped now with some of the same problems that I have, but his prognosis is actually better than mine. He can possibly make a complete recovery, and I hope I can help him as he has always helped me. He also has very poor eyesight, which became worse after the strokes. He is almost blind in one eye. If anyone chooses to not get to know him because of his handicaps, they will be missing out on knowing a truly wonderful man and a real hero to me as well as many others.

"If you meet someone who is handicapped, just start a conversation with them. Most like to be friendly and talk. If they drop something, pick it up for them. If they fall, help them up. These are small things, but they could be the beginning of a wonderful relationship or friendship.

"My friend, Gene, is using a wheelchair right now. He always tells anyone who wants to do something with him that he is a lot of work. That may be true, but it is good work, and just because someone is handicapped doesn't mean that they can't go out and do things with their friends. We may not be able to do everything that you can do, but we can do a lot of things. We may be a little slower. We may need a little help. We may do things in a little different way from others. But we try hard to do all we can and be accepted.

"For my entire life, I have been handicapped. It has been hard never knowing what it would be like to be normal. But in some ways, I may be the lucky one. You see, my friend Gene was normal all his life until he was thirty-seven years old and had his stroke. He was a football quarterback and a basketball forward. He was a graduation speaker and president of our class for three years.

"It is important for us to have interaction with all kinds of people. I like to talk to people and learn about them as I want them to be interested in me and learn about me. Accept us, help us, and be kind to us. We are really not that much different from anyone else. I know most of the people in this audience today, and I love all of you, and in turn, I hope you love me."

As John finished his speech, it was obvious that it was well received. There were many tears shed in the audience that day. And then John was ready to introduce Rodger.

"I would like to introduce our next speaker, my friend Rodger," said John.

Rodger showed no signs of nervousness as he walked to the podium.

"My name is Rodger Hartman. I am a Vietnam veteran. I was homeless and addicted to prescription drugs as well as other drugs and alcohol. I had a head injury in Vietnam, which caused me a lot of pain. My friends Mike, Carol, Gene, John, and Alan have all helped me. I thank them for giving me a chance because I was at a very low point, and without them, I wouldn't have made it. Those five people are very special to me, one in particular I credit with giving me the incentive to try and be successful. I'm not going to single that person out now because that person knows who they are, and they are all wonderful, caring people."

"Thank you, Rodger. The next speaker is my friend Nathan," said John.

Nathan reluctantly walked to the podium.

"My name is Nathan Ellis. A little over two years ago, I tried to commit suicide, but I failed. I had no home, no family, and no job. I felt hopeless, and I had no purpose in life. And then my best friend from high school, Gene, convinced me to work for him because he needed me. I thank him for that. Everyone has to feel needed."

"Thank you, Nathan," said John. "The next speaker is one of the best friends I have ever had, Gene."

Terry slowly pushed Gene in front of the podium, and John handed him the microphone.

"I'm Gene Sandusky. John spoke about me in his speech. As he said, I had three consecutive strokes, two minor TIAs followed by a massive stroke. It is a long, hard road back, and I have had setbacks, but I hope to work hard and make a full recovery. I also have heart problems and a history of football injuries, including five concussions and a severe neck injury, but I will never give up, not only for myself but for all those who have worked so hard to help me. This is one of my best friends from high school, Terry Sheley. Terry had a stroke six years ago, which affected his leg and arm but mostly it affected his voice. I hope he will make a full recovery also, and I want him to know that I will be by his side all the way. My stroke has made me a prisoner in my own body. I need help with everything. So what John said is very true. If I should drop something, please pick it up for me because I can't. It's a long road back. Thank you."

Before Terry moved Gene's wheelchair, he hugged him.

The first meeting was over. It had gone well and on schedule, and almost everyone seemed to be talking and happy. Gene seemed quiet and a little emotional, and then Carol noticed Terry. There seemed to be panic in his eyes. She knew he didn't want to be in front with those who spoke because he was afraid someone would ask him a question. Carol immediately took his hand. "Let's go sit and rest in one of the seats at the back."

They walked together to the back of the room and sat down. Terry seemed very relieved.

"You are so nice to me. All these people here that you know, and you stay with me," said Terry.

"I can't explain it, Terry, but I just want to sit by you and hold your hand. We don't have to talk or do anything," said Carol.

"I like it that everyone seems to love John, Gene, Nathan, and Rodger. They did a really good job," said Terry.

"They like you too, Terry, and just between the two of us, I think everyone liked Gene's speech the best, but that doesn't surprise us, does it? Everyone always loves Gene," said Carol.

Carol smoothed Terry's hair and straightened his tie just as Dr. Wilson and George Meyer approached them.

"It went well. John and everyone else did a great job," said George.

"John did fine," said Carol.

"And this nice young man sitting by you must be Terry," said George.

"He has been working as John's companion. Terry, this is George Meyer, Gene's boss and the sponsor of this event, and this is Dr. Brett Wilson, the doctor who operated on John and also Gene's doctor," said Carol.

Terry held out his left hand to George and then to Dr. Wilson, but Carol continued to hold his right arm, which was his paralyzed arm and hand.

"Thank you, Terry, for being John's companion. He loves you very much," said George.

Terry simply nodded.

"Terry, would you come to see me? I may be able to help you. I'm sure this wonderful woman sitting by you would bring you to my office," said Dr. Wilson.

"If he wants to come, I will bring him," said Carol.

"I will," said Terry. "Thank you."

Dr. Wilson moved to the seat on the other side of Terry and took hold of his hand. The short sentence that Terry had just said was the first Dr. Wilson had heard him speak. Suddenly, he felt very protective of Terry. He was a very handsome young man, and he could tell his sweet Carol loved him. He knew at that moment that he would do everything in his power to help him. George liked Terry too.

"Terry, will you be at John's next program with him?"

"Yes," said Terry.

"Will you speak alongside Gene?" asked George.

Terry immediately looked at Carol.

"George, do you mind if I answer for him?" asked Carol.

Dr. Wilson was still holding Terry's hand, and when speaking was mentioned, he held tightly to Dr. Wilson's hand. Dr. Wilson felt as though he needed to protect Terry from George. Terry, of course, knew what George did to Gene, and he was frightened of him.

"No, I don't mind," said George.

Carol put her arm around Terry. "Terry has a difficult time speaking, especially in front of an audience. Terry is very shy, and he has a hard time getting the words out because of the stroke. Sometimes people have made fun of him and hurt his feelings. It hurts my heart that people have treated him badly because he is one of the kindest people I have ever known, and he always has been ever since we were in school together."

"I'm sorry, Terry, I understand," said George.

Terry looked at Carol with tears in his eyes and quietly said, "Thank you."

Gene and Leon were watching and weren't quite sure what George might have said to Terry to upset him.

"I think we had better go talk to them," said Gene.

As they went back to where Carol and Terry were, Leon asked, "Why are you all the way back here?"

"We just wanted to get away from the crowd," said Carol.

"Are you all right, Terry?" asked Leon as he hugged Terry.

Leon noticed the tears in Terry's eyes. Carol got up and moved over to sit by Gene so Leon could sit by Terry.

"Dr. Wilson and George, Terry is my brother. He lived in a little house next-door to me with his grandmother. She died when he was just a little boy. He came to our front door with his little suitcase. He was going to run away because he was afraid they would put him in an orphanage and be mean to him. My mother promised she wouldn't let that happen to him, and she took him into our home and raised him. We lived in an all-black neighborhood, and Terry was the only white boy in our elementary school. I tried to protect him, but he stuttered, and the kids beat him up a lot. We went all through high school together, and we played football and basketball with Gene, Mike, Nathan, and Rodger. I love Terry very much."

Carol hugged Leon and said, "Gene and I will always take care of Terry when you can't be with us. We love him very much too."

CHAPTER

THE WOMEN

John was thriving as a motivational speaker. He was very good, and each time he spoke, he made his speech a little better. George was a good promoter for John. His office prepared the programs and sent out invitations to specially selected groups and individuals. George also acquired some engagements at universities, high schools, and elementary schools. Everyone thought John would particularly like speaking before the young people, but he loved them all, the children and adults.

In a very short time, John completed twenty-eight seminars in the Chicago area arranged by George and another twenty-two seminars in the Kansas City area arranged by Alan. Sometimes he would do as many as four seminars in one day. Carol, Gene, Terry, Nathan, and Rodger made it to all the Kansas City events as well as the Chicago events. Greg was able to attend five seminars in Chicago.

Nathan and Rodger both expanded their speeches as John did his. Gene and Terry were not as comfortable in front of the groups as the other three, but they did their jobs. Gene was looking very tired, and Carol as well as Alan and Dr. Wilson were worried about him, but he wanted to continue.

At the end of the seminar, John always asked for questions. There were never any reporters or media in the audience. The seminars were never publicly advertised. George did a good job of protecting John as well as Gene. Usually the questions were polite and stayed within the subject matter of the seminars, handicaps and disabilities primarily within the workplace.

At one of the final seminars scheduled in Chicago, Carol noticed two nicely dressed women entering the conference room. They appeared to be in their late thirties. They took a front row seat directly in front of the podium where Gene and Terry would be during Gene's presentation.

Dr. Wilson and Mike were on the sidelines with Carol. They noticed the two women also.

"Do you think those two are reporters?" asked Mike.

"I don't think so," said Carol. "Their clothes are too fancy."

"They seem to have some type of agenda," said Dr. Wilson. "Look at their notebooks and briefcases."

As Carol took her place on the stage behind John, she made sure she could see the two women. She noticed they took a lot of notes.

John was exceptionally good that day as was everyone else. When he opened the floor to questions, many hands went up, including the two women in the front row. He answered several questions from the back of the room, and then he called on one of the women in the front row.

Her voice was very powerful and determined to get an answer to what Carol, Mike, and Dr. Wilson all felt were extremely rude, inappropriate questions.

"You are five exceptionally nice-looking young men. I would like to know if any of you are married, and if not, why, and what are your occupations other than motivational speakers?

John didn't hesitate. "I'll answer first. I have been an auto mechanic since I was sixteen. When the owner retired, I bought the shop from him. I expanded the shop, and I now have twelve people working for me. I still work there and do detailing on cars and many other things, but because of some injuries I have had, I can't do as much as I used to do. I am single. I had a beautiful, wonderful girlfriend. She was kind and gentle, and I would have loved for her to be my wife, but she wanted to have a baby. Because of some of the injuries I suffered, I was told I would never be able to father a child. She married someone else and had a baby, so I am very happy for her."

"Did you ever consider adopting?" asked the woman.

"We did talk about it, but because of my disabilities, I would not have been able to adopt," replied John.

"I loved a girl when I was in school, but she was in love with someone else," said Rodger. "When I graduated, I went right to Vietnam. I was there for a long time and then in the hospital. I am clean from the drugs and alcohol that once ruled my life, but I still think it would be difficult to have a wife and family. Right now, I am working as a caregiver."

"You are all so tall. Were you all basketball players?" asked the woman.

"Yes, we were all on the same basketball and football teams except John, but he has always been our friend," said Rodger.

"I've been out with several girls in my life, but the girl I really liked was dating someone else," said Nathan. "I am a caregiver, and I like that kind of work. I like being needed. I'm in a better place in my life now than I was a few years ago. I think now I could be a husband and father, but I don't know if I will ever find anyone to love me. I have a lot of baggage sort of like Rodger and all of us for that matter."

Carol wanted so badly to save Gene and Terry. She just wanted to rescue them take them away, and as her eyes met Mike's and Dr. Wilson's, she knew they felt the same way. But it was too late.

"And what about you, Gene?" asked the woman.

It was so obvious to Carol, Mike, and Dr. Wilson that the woman had been waiting for this moment with Gene in mind as her primary target.

Gene began slowly. He basically had no other choice except to speak, but he did not want to. He was a very private person and somewhat shy, and he did not like to talk about his personal life. They could tell this was bothering him.

"I am a senior vice president at an advertising agency here in Chicago. I worked there before I had my stroke, and I have continued to work there. I am divorced, and I have two young children. I always tell people, even those who just want to go out and eat, that I am a lot of work. It is difficult even for me to realize and accept all the things I cannot do. If I don't improve, I would hate to make someone take care of me for the rest of my life. I cannot take care of myself or my two children without an excessive amount of help. I had a very sweet, kind girlfriend a long, long time ago who would probably accept me as I am today, but I would not wish myself on her or anyone else." Gene took his glasses off and wiped his eyes. "I also cry a lot, and that is not very masculine or appealing to most women."

"And how about you, Terry?" asked the woman.

"I think we are going to stop here," said Gene as he turned to John. "John, help us out here please."

John immediately walked down to Terry and put his arm around him. "Terry is my companion. I need a lot of help doing things that he can do, and I can't. I help him with one thing that I can do and he can't, and that is speaking. As Gene said, it is not easy being handicapped. Terry is very shy. He has never had a girlfriend, but there is someone he loves very much. Have we answered all your questions?"

"Yes. Thank you," said the woman.

The seminar ended, much to the relief of Gene and Terry. The women went to talk more to John, Rodger, and Nathan.

Carol immediately went to Gene. Mike pushed his wheelchair to the back of the room. Dr. Wilson walked with Terry. Carol gave Gene a drink of water. He choked on it, so she held the glass for him. He was sweating, so she wiped his forehead and cheeks with a cool cloth. This was unusual because Gene was usually cold, and as she touched his hand, it was like ice. He was very pale, and she could see his heart beating through his shirt.

"If we stay here with Gene and Terry, maybe they will leave them alone," said Carol. But this was not to be. As the two women left, they started walking toward Gene and Terry.

Carol immediately stepped forward. "Did you ladies enjoy the seminar?" Carol asked in a very sincere voice.

"Yes, it was very good. We would like to book John's seminar for our sorority. My name is Sharon Beliot, and this is Cassandra Turner," said Sharon.

Carol quickly handed her one of George Meyer's cards. "George is in charge of booking engagements for John. Please feel free to call him."

Sharon diverted her attention and question directly to Gene. "They are very protective of you, Gene, but I need to ask you a question. You don't remember me, do you? University of Kansas, class of 1968. We had several classes together," said Sharon.

"I'm sorry, I don't remember very well anymore. I have a lot of health issues," said Gene.

"You were always studying and very smart. You were very quiet, and you never smiled. I thought you were the most handsome man I had ever seen," said Sharon.

"I wish I was that man today. I'm surprised you even recognize me," said Gene quietly.

"You're still the same man. I recognized you immediately," said Sharon. Terry was still holding on to Carol's arm although he was standing a little behind her, but there was no escaping Sharon. "I'm sorry, Terry, if I made you uncomfortable. I didn't mean to."

"Thank you." Terry's voice was barely audible as he reached out his left hand to Sharon.

"You seem like such a sweet, gentle man," said Sharon. "I hope you do well, Terry, and you also, Gene. Gene, you are very genuine in your presentation, and I understand the problems you have."

"Thank you. I'm glad you came to talk to us," said Gene.

Sharon and Cassandra left.

"Well, at least we know they are not reporters," said Carol. "Let's get our group together and go home." Carol bent down and hugged Gene and kissed him on the cheek. "I know you are not feeling well, Gene. Would you like for Dr. Wilson to check you here or shall we wait until we get home?"

"I can make it home. I just want to get out of here," said Gene quietly. "I'm just tired and weak. It's like every ounce of strength has been drained out of me."

"Mike, please see if John, Nathan, and Rodger are ready," said Carol.

Dr. Wilson got his bag and checked Gene's vitals. "I know you don't want me to do this now, but you are not looking good." Dr. Wilson attended most of the seminars for that particular reason. Gene had basically hired him as his personal physician. "I don't like seeing you have the stress that those women caused. It is not good for you."

"Thanks for taking care of me, Dr. Wilson. I can't seem to take care of myself anymore," said Gene.

Mike came back and went to get the van. They all just wanted and needed to go home.

CAROL AND GENE WERE INSEPARABLE

At Gene's apartment that night, there were nine friends sitting in the living room talking and enjoying good food together. It had been a long day; in fact, the whole month had been busy. John had made many speeches that month, and they had all helped him.

"This was a strange seminar today. Those two women threw me off a little," said Nathan.

"It was different, but I didn't mind it so much," said John.

"John, your response was handled very well," said Alan.

"John didn't miss a beat. It was as though you were ready for them. I'm very proud of you, all of you for that matter," said Carol.

"Thanks, Carol." John hugged Carol.

"You know, as we were all talking about our past loves, I realized we were all talking about the same person," said Nathan.

"And I wonder who that could have been," said Mike.

"How does it feel, Carol, knowing that all eight guys in this room love you?" said Nathan.

Carol was sitting by Gene. He put his arm around her, and she rested her head on his shoulder. "You are going to make Carol uncomfortable," said Gene.

"I'm not saying it for that reason. I love you, Carol. I would never hurt you," said Nathan.

"I have an idea. Why don't we vote as to who loves Carol the most. Of course, if everyone votes for themselves, then it would be a tie. But Carol has a vote too, so she would break the tie," said Mike. Mike always liked to vote.

"You guys are silly. I'm nothing special and never have been," said Carol.

"You are special. You are the only person I can talk to," said Terry.

Carol got up and went to Terry and hugged and kissed him, but she returned to her seat by Gene. Rodger was making nine slips of paper and passed them out to everyone.

"I can't decide, so we need to vote for two," said Alan.

"That will work," said Rodger. Everyone put their choices down quickly. Rodger picked up the slips of paper. "Alan, would you help me tally the votes?" Rodger and Alan tallied the votes together. "Go ahead and read them, Alan."

"Are you ready?" asked Alan. "Mike and John both received three votes each. Terry received four votes. The winner had a vote from everyone but himself, of course. With a total of eight votes, the winner is Gene."

"Well, the guy in the worst shape of anyone in the room and with the shortest life expectancy just won. I'm sorry, Carol." Gene hugged Carol, and everyone could see the deep sadness and tears in his eyes. "But I would not classify myself as a winner, especially the way I feel right now."

"Sorry, everyone, I guess this wasn't so much fun," said Mike.

"It's all right, Mike. You know Gene has always had a rather dark sense of humor," said Carol.

Gene took his glasses off and rubbed his eyes. "I don't think I have a sense of humor at all. Have you guys noticed that none of us laugh anymore. Mike and John smile a little, but why doesn't anyone laugh? When did we stop laughing?"

"I haven't laughed since Vietnam. It hurts my head to laugh," said Rodger.

"I used to laugh a lot. I guess if there is ever something really funny, I'll laugh," said Nathan.

"I'm too tired to laugh. I'm going to bed," said Alan. As he walked by Carol and Gene, he hugged them both. "I wish things could be easier for you two. Always know that if there was anything I could do to help you, I would do it in a minute."

"We know, Alan. You have helped us a lot, and we thank you for that, and we love you very much," said Carol.

As John and Terry got up, Rodger and Nathan came to assist them.

"Are you two coming to bed tonight?" asked John.

"I'm going to stay right here tonight. As long as I don't move, there is no pain," said Gene.

"I'm going to stay here with Gene," said Carol.

John hugged and kissed them both, and Terry gently touched Carol's hand.

Dr. Wilson said, "Gene, I'm going to check your vitals before I go to bed. Is that all right with you?"

"Yes," said Gene.

"I'll move," said Carol.

"No, stay right where you are," said Dr. Wilson. "His heart beats better when you are close to him."

Gene reached out and touched Dr. Wilson's arm. He had no strength. "Thank you for keeping me alive. I'm not so sure I'm worth it."

"Gene, you have to know how important you are to me," said Carol. "Please never forget that. We may not always be together, but I will love you forever."

Mike hugged them both. "I can't speak right now, but I love you, guys. I'll see you in the morning.

"Good night, Mike," said Carol.

Dr. Wilson spoke to Gene quietly, "Gene, I'm not going to give up on you. You are very important to a lot of people, including this wonderful girl sitting by you. Your life matters, Gene, and I'm going to do everything in my power to help you."

As Dr. Wilson looked at Carol and Gene, he realized how much he loved them both. He wanted to comfort and hold Carol, but Gene and Carol were inseparable that night. Nothing could come between them. The kind, pretty girl with the long, red hair and the gentle, handsome young man in the wheelchair, who could barely move without assistance, were both very important to Dr. Wilson, and he wanted so much to help them.

"Gene's losing weight. He can't eat much." Carol gently touched the scar on his cheek. It was three inches long and ran from the outside corner of his eye toward the corner of his mouth.

"It won't hurt him to lose a little weight. He is a big guy, but he does need to eat. I thought you were asleep, Carol," said Dr. Wilson.

"No, I shut my eyes once in a while, but ever since John's dream, I stay awake and watch Gene as John would do," said Carol.

"You really need your sleep. You have to stay strong for him," said Dr. Wilson.

"I'm fine. I'm just fine, but Gene isn't. He's not fine at all, but I love him. What am I going to do, Brett? Whatever in the world am I going to do?" asked Carol.

CHAPTER

GENE'S HEART

Gene was not feeling any better than he had the previous night when he went to work the next day, but he had a scheduled appointment with three prospective clients. When Patrick picked Gene up, he noticed that he didn't look well.

"Are you all right, Gene?" asked Patrick.

"It's been a long week. I'm just tired, and I don't have much strength," said Gene.

"Are you sure you are up to going to work?" asked Patrick.

"No, but I have to. I have three prospective clients coming in to meet with me," said Gene.

As Patrick was helping Gene out of the van, he said, "If you need to go home, please call me."

"I will. Thank you, Patrick," said Gene.

As Gene waited for his clients to arrive, he noticed that his left hand was trembling uncontrollably, and he couldn't seem to move his right hand.

Then there was a knock at the door. It was Karen and the three clients. Gene greeted them and began explaining the advertising program that he had prepared for them. They had a lot of questions, and after about an hour, Gene couldn't continue.

The lady in the group seemed to be concerned about him. "Are you all right? Do you need some help?"

"I'm so sorry. I'm going to call George to help," said Gene. He couldn't even remember George's number, so he called Karen. "Karen, would you ask George to come to my office? I need his help."

When George arrived, he immediately saw the pain in Gene's face and the absolute terror in his eyes. "Relax, Gene. I'll take over."

George finished the presentation Gene had prepared. After a few more questions, the clients were ready to sign the contract. Gene was unable to witness the signatures. George called Karen to be a witness.

As the clients left, the lady in the group said, "I hope you feel better soon, Gene."

"Thank you," said Gene quietly.

When they were alone, George sat down across from Gene. "I'm not sure what to say, Gene."

"I'm a failure. I can't do it. I felt this way at John's seminar yesterday. I could hardly speak or move. Would you call Carol for me? I need her," said Gene.

George did as he asked. Carol said she would be there soon. George went to get Gene a glass of water. When he returned, he asked Gene, "Do you want me to call your doctor?"

"Not right now," said Gene.

"Would you like to lie down?" asked George.

Gene shook his head no and started crying. "Where's Carol?"

"She's on her way. She will be here soon," said George. "I'm so sorry, Gene. You were doing so well."

When Carol arrived, Nathan was with her. She went to Gene and put her arms around him. He was still crying, and he couldn't seem to speak. Carol looked at George. "What happened to him?"

"He had been meeting with his clients for about an hour. He called and said he needed help. He was unable to continue," said George.

"I'm sorry, Gene. You've been working so hard," said Carol.

Gene tried to take his glasses off, but he couldn't. Nathan helped him. "How many Nitros have you taken, Gene?" asked Carol.

"I've taken three. They haven't helped yet," said Gene. "I have to quit, George. I can't do my job."

"Why don't you take a leave and think more about what you want to do. Don't make a hasty decision," said George.

"All right," said Gene.

"We will take the van and leave the car for Patrick. Will you please tell Patrick for us?" asked Nathan.

"I'll tell him," said George. "Gene, I have grown very fond of you. I want you to succeed. I'm so sorry this happened. I want you to stay with us. No matter what, I don't want you to quit. Somehow we will work things out. You two take good care of him."

"We will," said Carol. Carol dried Gene's cheeks and eyes and put his glasses back on him. "We have to go by all the people to get out of here. I'm so sorry. I know how much you hate that."

They left quietly. No one said anything to them. It was as though everyone knew.

"Gene, we are going to stop at the emergency room if it is all right with you," said Carol.

"It's all right. I'm scared. I'm really scared," said Gene.

"Nathan, will you ask Karen to call Dr. Wilson and ask him to meet us at the emergency room. He will contact Dr. Landis," said Carol.

When they arrived at the ER, both Dr. Wilson and Dr. Landis were waiting for them. Gene was immediately taken to an ER room. They worked with him quickly taking his vitals and blood work and other tests. They were not wasting any time. There were so many people in the room with Gene that Carol and Nathan waited in the hall. Carol was crying. Nathan put his arms around her and held her tight. "Don't cry. He is going to be all right."

Carol held tightly to Nathan. At this point she was as scared as Gene was. "I love Gene so much. What are we going to do, Nathan?" asked Carol.

"He loves you so much, Carol. I don't know if he will ever be able to love anyone else the way he loves you. I have never seen any two people who love one another as much as the two of you. It's beautiful but also sad because I know the two of you will never be together," said Nathan.

Dr. Wilson motioned for them to come into the room. It was just Dr. Wilson, Dr. Landis, Carol, and Nathan. Dr. Landis moved a chair close to Gene. "Sit close to him, Carol, so he can see you as he wakes up. Hold his hand. He will know you are with him."

Carol did so. As she held his hand, she could feel him very weakly move his fingers to hold her hand, but he didn't open his eyes. "I'm here, Gene. Nathan and I are both here with you," said Carol quietly. "Is he all right?"

"They've given him something to help him relax and hopefully sleep a little. He just can't take too much stress," said Dr. Wilson. "They will have a room for him soon."

"Nathan, sit by me please," said Carol. "I don't know what I would do if you weren't here with us. Please don't leave. Gene needs you so much."

Nathan pulled a chair up by Carol and put his arm around her. "I'm not going anywhere. I'll be here for both of you," said Nathan as he kissed her on the cheek.

Dr. Wilson and Dr. Landis looked at one another. Dr. Landis knew of Dr. Wilson's love for Carol, but she did not seek comfort from him. Instead, she turned to Nathan, although he knew she did care for him.

A while later, Dr. Landis said, "They have a room for Gene. They are taking him to the ICU."

"The ICU? What's wrong?" asked Carol.

Dr. Wilson put his hands on her shoulders. "They want to watch him closely tonight. All the tests are back. It's his heart. The Nitros aren't going to help this time."

Carol buried her face in Nathan's chest. "Should I call Alan and Mike?"

"Yes, you probably should. The tests don't look good. We will stay with him until they come for him. There is a private room at the end of the hall if you want to call from there," said Dr. Wilson.

Carol gently kissed Gene on the cheek and touched his hand.

"Nathan, please stay with her. That is going to be a difficult call to make," said Dr. Wilson.

"I will," said Nathan.

The two doctors watched as Nathan put his arm around Carol, and they walked down the hall.

"What are his chances?" asked Dr. Wilson.

"Without surgery, fifty-fifty. With surgery, a little better, but he is not a good candidate for surgery," said Dr. Landis.

"Shall we tell Carol that?" asked Dr. Wilson.

"Not right now, but she probably knows anyway. She always seems to know everything where Gene is concerned," said Dr. Landis.

Carol hesitantly dialed the phone. "Stay by me, Nathan."

"I'm not going anywhere," said Nathan.

Carol prayed silently that Mike or Alan would answer the phone, but it didn't happen. "Hi, John. It's Carol."

"Hello, Carol. Is something wrong? You sound like you've been crying," said John.

Carol paused and tried to compose herself. "Who is there with you, John?"

"Just me and Terry. Mike is at work. Alan and Rodger went grocery-shopping," said John.

"Please have Terry get on the other phone," said Carol.

"All right," said John.

"Are you there, Terry?" asked Carol.

"I'm here. What's wrong, Carol?" asked Terry.

"Gene is very sick. He is in the ICU. It's his heart," said Carol.

"We will tell Alan as soon as he gets home. We will come there. I'm sure Alan will call you," said Terry.

Carol could hear John on the other line crying. "Don't cry, John. Please don't cry."

John could hardly talk. "Tell Gene I love him."

"I'll tell him, John," said Carol. "Please tell Alan I will call back when I have more information."

"We'll tell him," said Terry.

Carol hung up the phone. "Of all five of them, I didn't want John to answer that phone call. If something happens to Gene, I don't know what it will do to him."

Nathan took hold of Carol's hand, and they walked together to the ICU.

In another part of the hospital, Dr. Wilson called Greg. Carol had asked him to.

"Hello, Greg. It's Dr. Brett Wilson."

"Hello, Dr. Wilson," said Greg. "Is something wrong?"

"Yes. Gene is in the ICU. He has a serious heart problem. He was on the verge of having a heart attack."

"I'm sorry. The poor guy can't get a break, can he? I grew very fond of him when I flew to Kansas City with him awhile back. How bad is it? What are his chances?" asked Greg.

"He has about a fifty-fifty chance. With surgery, the odds are a little better, but he isn't a real good candidate for surgery," said Dr. Wilson.

"Carol's mother is here. Tell her to stay as long as she needs to," said Greg.

"Thanks, Greg," said Dr. Wilson. "I'm glad I met you when you were in Kansas City."

"Same here. You took such good care of John. Now please take care of Gene. I'm not sure how it would affect John if something happened to Gene. He loves him very much, as does Carol. But the strange thing is, I love him too," said Greg.

"I'll do the best I can. I love Gene too. In fact, I love all of them," said Dr. Wilson.

"Please keep me posted," said Greg.

"I will," said Dr. Wilson.

When Alan and Rodger returned to the house in Avalon Manor, the first thing they noticed was John sitting in Gene's usual seat on the sofa. He had his head on Terry's shoulder; he was crying, and Terry had his arm around him. They hurried to them.

"What's the matter, John?" asked Alan.

John could barely speak, so Terry spoke for him, "Carol called. Gene is in the ICU. It's his heart. They want us to come there. Carol will call back soon."

Alan sat by John and held him close. "Don't worry, John. Gene will be all right. He's a survivor. The four of us will go to him as soon as we can. Mike will probably have to come later. He has a trial this week." Alan reached out and hugged Terry and Rodger also. "You are all like my sons, just as Gene is. I love you all so much. We will stay together."

A few minutes later, Mike walked in the front door. As he looked at the group in front of him, no explanation was needed as he said, "Oh my god. It's Gene, isn't it? I knew something was going on with him. I just didn't know what it was."

"It's his heart. He is in the ICU. They want us to come," said Alan.

Mike threw his briefcase to the floor. It came open, and papers fell out. He beat his fist on the desk. He immediately picked up the phone.

"Hello, Elizabeth, this is Mike. I know you have been following the trial closely. Can you finish the trial for me? My friend in Chicago is in the ICU. I need to go to him. Thank you. I'll call you soon." Mike hung up the phone, and he was crying.

Rodger went to him and hugged him. He picked up Mike's papers and put them back in his briefcase. Mike was sitting at the desk when the phone rang. It was Carol.

"Hello," said Mike.

"Thank God, you answered, Mike. I was so afraid John would. The doctors say Gene has a fifty-fifty chance. With surgery, the chances are better, but they don't feel he is a good candidate for surgery. The problem is that they may not have a choice," said Carol through her tears.

"I think we can get a red-eye flight tonight. That way we will be there in the morning if they do surgery," said Mike.

"Thank you, Mike. We need you. We all need you, but Gene needs you the most," said Carol.

Nathan took the phone. "She's crying too hard. She can't talk. I have the van here at the hospital. Let me know flight number and arrival time, and I'll pick you up."

"I'll let you know. Take care of them both until we get there," said Mike.

"I won't leave them," said Nathan. "Dr. Wilson will stay with Carol when I come to pick you up."

"Thanks, Nathan." Mike hung up the phone. As he did so, he put his hands to his head and cried. Gene had always been his best friend, and he had felt for some time now that Gene would be leaving this world long before him. Not necessarily today or tomorrow, but he just didn't think Gene would be with them much longer, and even though she had never said so, he knew that Carol had these same feelings.

John was still sitting by Alan on the sofa. John was very upset. Terry went to Mike and comforted him.

"Terry, I'm glad you, Rodger, and Nathan are with us. We need you guys especially now," said Mike. "I'll make reservations for us on a red-eye flight tonight. Can you all be ready soon?"

"We'll be ready, Mike. Whenever you tell us, we will be ready," said Alan.

A short while later, Mike told everyone they had reservations at eleven thirty at night. He had already talked to Nathan, and he would be picking them up. Terry and Rodger went to get ready and pack. Mike walked over to his dad and John still on the sofa.

Alan looked down at John. "He cried himself to sleep. What shall I do?"

"Dad, why don't you go pack, and pack for John too. I'll sit with him," said Mike as he put his arms around John and took him from his dad.

John reached up and touched Mike's cheek. "I'm sorry, but I cried so much I went to sleep. You're crying too, Mike. You don't usually cry."

"I'm worried about Gene too, just like you are, John. I love him and respect him very much. He has been my best friend long before I knew you. We need to try and be brave for both Gene and Carol. She is very sad right now too, John," said Mike.

"I'll try, Mike, but I just love Gene so much," said John.

"I know you do. I know. Dad is packing for you," said Mike. "I don't have to pack. Do you know why?"

"Why, Mike?" asked John.

"Well, I didn't unpack when we got home last night," said Mike.

They were at the airport and through security in good time. Mike and Rodger took care of John and checking the bags. Alan stayed close to Terry. During John's motivational speeches, Gene and Terry had become very close. Terry could talk to Gene as well as he could talk to Carol, but he liked being close to Alan too.

"Terry, I'm going to get you a wheelchair. It will be faster and will make it easier for you," said Alan.

"Thank you, Alan," said Terry.

As they waited at the gate for the plane, John held tight to Mike's hand. When they boarded the plane, John sat between Mike and Rodger. Mike put his strong arm around John and held him close to him. Alan and Terry sat behind them. Terry had not let go of Alan's hand. Alan hugged Terry to protect him, just as Mike was protecting John.

For whatever reason, the flight seemed shorter and faster than usual. Nathan was there with Gene's van to pick them up. Alan sat in the front with Nathan.

Alan asked Nathan quietly, "Is there any change?"

"Carol touches his hand. He moves his fingers slightly, but he can't grasp her hand. He knows she is with him." Although Nathan spoke softly, they all heard him.

When they arrived at the hospital because it was the middle of the night, they had to stop at the security desk for entrance to the ICU. Before they were asked any questions, Dr. Landis appeared.

"Dr. Wilson and Carol are in the waiting room. I will take you there," said Dr. Landis.

No one said anything on the way up in the elevator. They could tell something had happened. Although no one knew what, they had a feeling it probably wasn't good.

As they arrived at the ICU waiting room, Dr. Landis said, "Carol and Dr. Wilson are in there. I'll be back soon."

Carol was sitting close to Dr. Wilson on a sofa. He had his arm around her. Mike sat by Carol, and she immediately put her arms around him.

"Oh, Mike, he coded. They had to take him to surgery." Even though her voice was quiet, everyone heard what she said.

"They are doing his surgery sooner than they had planned. They had no choice," said Dr. Wilson.

"I didn't get to see Gene, Carol. I didn't get to tell him how much I love him," said John.

"I told him, John. He knows you love him," said Carol. "Oh, sweetie, you are shivering. Here, please take my blanket. I don't need it," said Carol as she put the blanket around John.

"Dr. Landis and I are both keeping a close watch over Gene. Dr. Landis is in surgery with him right now. He doesn't do heart surgery, but he wants to be there for Gene. I'll be back soon to let you know how it's going," said Dr. Wilson as he left them.

"He must have coded right after I left," said Nathan.

"You had been gone for about fifteen minutes when it happened. I was so scared. It was terrible. I thought he was going to die," said Carol in a very quiet voice. "But he didn't die. He opened his eyes, and I told him that I loved him, and I told him you loved him too, John. He heard me, and then they took him to surgery. And I suddenly had this overpowering feeling that everything was going to be all right."

Four hours after they took Gene to surgery, Dr. Wilson told them Gene was in recovery and that the surgery went well.

A little later, Dr. Landis came to talk to them. "Gene is awake. Dr. Wilson will not be leaving his side for a while. Right now, I will take Carol and one other person to see him. He needs to be very calm and quiet for a while."

Without hesitation, Mike made the decision as to who should go with Carol. "Terry, would you go with Carol please."

"Yes, thank you, Mike," said Terry. No one questioned Mike's decision as Terry took Carol's arm and they followed Dr. Landis.

Gene was connected to many monitors, tubes, and wires. They both sat close on his left side. They knew he wouldn't be able to see them well. Carol gently touched his hand, and he responded. His fingers grasped her hand a little stronger than yesterday. He opened his eyes slightly.

"It's Carol and Terry, Gene. We love you. We love you so much," said Carol.

"I love you both," said Gene. His voice was weak, and he couldn't really turn his head.

"You're going to be all right, Gene, probably better than before," said Carol very softly. Carol bent close and kissed him on the cheek.

"I want you to be well soon, Gene. I can talk to you like I can to Carol. I love you." Terry's voice was as quiet and calm as Carol's.

Gene's voice was barely audible. "Stay by me for a while please. Dr. Wilson is going to stay with me too."

Carol and Terry sat by Gene talking to him quietly. Carol always amazed Dr. Wilson. She had told Gene that he would probably be better than before. That was true, but no one had told her that. She just knew.

They went in to see Gene in groups of two throughout the day. The last one to go in was John. Carol went with him. He was trying hard to hold it together. He wasn't sure that he could, but he did. He was as calm and quiet as everyone else had been. It was as though he had cried all his tears and there were none left.

Later that afternoon, Alan called George Meyer. "Hello, Alan. I've been anxious to hear from you. How's Gene?"

"He's out of recovery. He's speaking. It will be a difficult and long road back, but Gene will make it." Alan's voice broke. He was crying, and George could tell.

"Alan, if you want to talk later, we can," said George.

"No, I want to talk now. I'm sorry, but as I told you before, Gene is like a son to me. We need to cancel John's future speaking engagements," said Alan.

"I'll take care of that. I'll also cancel the Kansas City engagements," said George.

"You know, George, John is a great speaker, and he has done a very good job. But the fact is, the people were coming to see Gene. Everyone wanted to hear him speak and ask him questions. He was the star, and between you, me, and Carol, we know it put too much stress on him. Carol worried about him from the very beginning. But he wanted to do it for John, and he did," said Alan.

"I know, and I take part of the responsibility for that," said George.

"You don't need to do that, George. This was for John. He made a lot of money, and he did a great job. It was his idea to include Gene and the other guys," said Alan.

"I guess I will always feel guilty about Gene and what happened to him at my hand," said George, somewhat melancholy. "The clients who were meeting with Gene the day he got sick have called several times asking how he is doing. They care about him, and they do want to work with Gene and only Gene. Please tell him that for me, of course, at the right time. Let him know that I've asked about him and that I also care. I'll come to visit him, but I'll wait a little while. Take care of him, Alan."

"I will as best I can. Goodbye, George," said Alan.

Gene's recovery was slow, but over the next few days, some progress was made. Late one night, as Dr. Wilson was leaving Gene's room, Gene had a question to ask him. "Brett, I have something I need to ask you. Do you have time?"

"I always have time for you, Gene. I thought you were sleeping," said Dr. Wilson.

"Is my mind and head all right?" asked Gene. "Have they been affected by everything that has happened to me?"

"As far as I know, they are perfect. What would make you ask that question?" asked Dr. Wilson.

"I just wondered. So much has been affected," said Gene. "You know I don't see well without my glasses, and I have always had such bad headaches. My eyes and headaches have been worse since the strokes. Everything is a blur. I can't even see the clock. But what is strange is that whenever Carol comes in the room, her face and everything about her is basically clear. Terry is usually with her, and he is also clear. I don't understand. I have always had poor eyesight. When I was three, I wore thick glasses and had a patch over my right eye for a long time, even after I started school. It didn't help, nothing did. I couldn't see the board at school. My grades were bad. Kids made fun of me. One day I got lost walking home from school. I was scared. It was dark when I got home, but I saw my house clearly, like I see Carol."

"I have no explanation but…" Dr. Wilson paused. "Carol loves you so much, and she always has. I think she would give her life for you. As far as Terry is concerned, I think he loves Carol as much as she loves you."

"Do you think she loves him?" asked Gene.

"She loves him, but I don't know if she is actually in love with him," said Dr. Wilson.

"You love her too, don't you, Brett?" asked Gene.

"Yes, ever since I first met her when she was eighteen. She was so pretty, smart, sweet, and mature for her age," said Dr. Wilson.

"Does she know?" asked Gene.

"She knows, but she is not in love with me," said Dr. Wilson.

"You do know that her marriage has ended, don't you?" asked Gene.

"I know," said Dr. Wilson. "As Nathan said in your living room a few nights ago, there were eight men who loved Carol there that night, but you, Gene, are the one who loved her the most."

"Do you realize I haven't talked this much for a long time?" said Gene.

"I know. You probably should rest," said Dr. Wilson.

"Did you know that for many years, Carol and I didn't see or talk to one another?" asked Gene.

"Whose choice was that?" asked Dr. Wilson.

"It was mutual. It was right after she got married," said Gene.

"Don't worry too much about seeing Carol and Terry so clearly. It probably has something to do with love and just simply being glad to see them as you were glad to see your house when you were lost," said Dr. Wilson. "But there is something about Carol that is spellbinding, and she knows what I am going to say before I say it. That's part of the reason that she has always fascinated me. She is complicated and interesting, but she is also incredibly gentle and kind, especially in the love she shows for you."

"You would like to be her husband, wouldn't you?" said Gene.

"Maybe at another time and in another place and if she would have me. But I'm a lot older than Carol. If she can't be with you, I would choose Terry over me any day," said Dr. Wilson.

"Thanks for talking to me, Brett. Everybody seems afraid to talk to me except Carol, she's not afraid of me," said Gene.

"You're right, Gene, she is definitely not afraid of you, but she is afraid for you. I think that everyone should just once in their life have a love like you and Carol have. I have never seen anything so beautiful," said Dr. Wilson.

"Even with me in a wheelchair?" asked Gene.

"That's not even a factor as far as she's concerned," said Dr. Wilson.

"Speaking of a wheelchair, the nurses want me to walk tomorrow. Do they know I can't?" asked Gene.

"Probably not. We will surprise them tomorrow," said Dr. Wilson.

JOHN'S GOOD HEART

Initially after surgery, Gene had seemed to be doing fine, but on the tenth postsurgery day, he had a slight setback. It seemed as though setbacks had become a part of his life and ultimate survival. Gene had a brace on his neck to stabilize and strengthen it reminiscent of shortly after his stroke when he had the same problem. His neck had been problematic since the football injury in 1964, but it was worse now. He was in bed just slightly elevated.

"Carol, would you please ask John to come in. I need to talk to him," said Gene quietly.

"I'll go get him. Do you want us to stay?" asked Carol.

"Yes, you, Terry, and Dr. Wilson need to be here," said Gene.

Carol went to the waiting room where John was sitting between Alan and Rodger. Alan had his arm around John. Mike and Nathan were sitting nearby.

"John, would you come with me. Gene wants to talk to you." Carol's voice was quiet.

"Alan, Mike, Rodger, and Nathan too?" asked John.

"No, John. Gene just wants to talk to you," said Carol.

"Where's Terry? Who else is with Gene?" asked John.

"Terry and Dr. Wilson are in the room with him. I'll be with you too, John," said Carol.

John got up. He hugged Alan and then took Carol's arm, and they slowly walked toward Gene's room. "What does Gene want to talk to me about?" asked John shyly.

"I'm not sure. Gene loves you so much, John," said Carol.

"What shall I say to him?" asked John.

"Just love him. Don't be afraid of him. He is still the same Gene who has been with us through so much. When the roof fell on you, Gene and I arrived at the hospital at the same time, and we walked through the emergency room doors together to be with you. You were in bad shape, but we never left your side," said Carol. "The lights in his room are very dim. The bright lights hurt his eyes."

John held tight to Carol's arm as they walked close to Gene's bed. "He's asleep," said John.

"He's just resting his eyes, John," said Carol.

"Carol, would you please put my glasses on me," said Gene.

Carol picked up Gene's glasses from the nightstand and put them on him, and then she pulled up a chair close to the bed for John. "Sit close to him so he can see you, John. He can't turn his head. I'm going to sit by Terry."

"Hi, Gene," said John quietly.

"Hi, John," said Gene. "I'm sorry about your seminars. But you, Rodger, and Nathan can still do them."

"No. We all need a break," said John. "I'm sorry. It was hard on you and Terry."

"We wanted to do it. We did it for you, John. Remember how I always used to smooth your hair down and straighten your glasses?" asked Gene.

"I remember," said John. "It always made me feel like you loved me."

"I would do it now, but I can't seem to raise my arms. I love you, John. Always know that," said Gene.

John sat by Gene for a long time that evening. He touched Gene's hand gently. Gene tried to take hold of John's hand, but he didn't have the strength.

Carol and Terry sat close that evening. He had his arm around her, and she rested her head on his shoulder.

Dr. Wilson could feel the love in the room that night. Dr. Wilson felt that he treated everyone kindly, especially Carol, but she was to seek comfort and love from Terry and Nathan, not from him, although he loved her so much. And as several nights ago, when no one could come between Carol and Gene, now no one could become between John and Gene. He envied their love, and he wished he could share it.

None of them were sleeping, but they were all very quiet late into the night. And then John said quietly, "Gene, could I give you my heart? I think it's good."

"No, John. You might need it," said Gene.

"But you are a better man than me, Gene. You are my hero," said John.

"I'm no hero, John. Mike is a hero, and so is Rodger. They both went to Vietnam, and they were wounded," said Gene.

"But you are so good, Gene. You are a really good person. Just ask Carol," said John.

"Gene is the best man I have ever known," said Carol as she put her arms around John. "John, I'm sure your heart is good. I wish everyone had as good a heart as you do."

"I want to stay here by Gene. I don't want to ever leave him," said John.

"John, you need your rest," said Gene.

"John and Terry, you both need to go home with the other guys. Gene's had a rough day. I'll be staying with him all night," said Dr. Wilson.

As John and Terry left Gene's room, Carol sat in the chair close to Gene. "Are you coming with us, Carol?" asked John.

"I can't leave Gene tonight," said Carol. "I'll see you guys in the morning."

When John and Terry walked into the waiting room, Alan put his arms around both of them. "Gene had a bad day, and his neck really hurts," said John. "Carol and Dr. Wilson are going to stay with him tonight. They said we should all go home."

"But you don't want to leave, do you, John?" asked Alan.

"I just love Gene so much, and I'm worried about him. I didn't cry in front of Gene, but I can't help it now," said John.

Alan held John in his arms. "I'll stay with you. You can sleep right here. Mike, Rodger, and Nathan, you better all get some rest at home. Would you stay here with us, Terry?"

"Thank you for asking me to stay with you and John," said Terry. "I'm really worried about Gene too."

"I know, Terry. I know you are worried. I'm worried about this guy too." Alan looked down at John who had fallen asleep on his lap. "If something happens to Gene, I don't know what it will do to John. He loves Gene so much."

Terry smoothed John's hair back as Gene used to do. "Thank you, Alan, and I thank John too for giving me a job and letting me live in your home. I tried to get a job, but no one would hire me. I felt so alone until you helped me. And I can talk to you, John, and Gene like I can to Carol. Do you think Gene is going to be all right?"

"I hope so, Terry. But I just don't know for sure," said Alan. "He has so many problems, and they are not small problems."

"Gene has always been so kind to me even when we were in school," said Terry.

"That's the way he has always been. He is an exceptionally good person. I don't think he has ever hurt anyone in his entire life," said Alan.

Back in Gene's room, Carol did not leave his side all night. She would gently hold his hand, kiss his cheek, or smooth his hair. She talked to him quietly and lovingly. He always knew she was there.

Once when Carol stepped out of the room for a short while, Gene became slightly restless, and Dr. Wilson knew he was looking for her. He moved close to Gene and sat in the chair where Carol had been sitting. "Carol will be right back, Gene."

When Carol returned, Dr. Wilson got up and motioned for her to sit by Gene. He briefly opened his eyes and then relaxed as she touched his hand. "He seems to know the moment you leave," said Dr. Wilson quietly.

"He always has. He feels secure when I'm by him. He knows I won't let anyone or anything hurt him." Carol's voice was so soft and kind and caring.

Dr. Wilson put his hand on her shoulder. "How long can you go without sleep?"

"It's all right. I dozed off a little. He just needs to know that I'm here with him," said Carol.

"Is there anyone else he responds to as he does to you?" asked Dr. Wilson.

"Terry and Mike. And Alan and Gene have also become very close. Everyone else seems to be afraid to be alone with him. Terry is so quiet and gentle, and Terry and Gene have known one another for a long time, and they are very close. Since Terry has also had a stroke, he feels some of the same pain that Gene does. They have that in common. And as for Mike, he is able to do so much for Gene. Mike and I know some things about Gene that no one else knows. The three of us have shared so much for such a long time. Mike loves Gene as much as Terry and I do, but he stands back because he knows Gene wants me by him, and he knows how much Terry needs Gene." Carol's voice was so gentle and tender, but it was laced with a tinge of sadness.

Dr. Wilson put his arms around Carol and kissed the top of her head. "I only wish I could help you and Gene more."

Carol put her hand on his. "You are his doctor. You have saved him."

"My dear, sweet girl, it is your love that has saved him." Dr. Wilson pulled up a chair close to Carol and Gene. "I want and need to be close to Gene also just as you do. I'll help you protect him. But I also want to protect you. Do you mind?"

"I don't mind. We both need you, Brett. You treat him so good. Do you notice how peaceful he looks? He can feel our love for him." One single tear ran down Carol's cheek. Dr. Wilson gently wiped it away with his finger.

"Gene is so vulnerable right now. He can't walk or move his neck without excruciating pain. He can't move his right arm and hand, and his left hand is so weak that he can barely use it. His back hurts, and I think his terrible headaches have increased," said Dr. Wilson.

"Do you know that Gene is almost blind in his right eye and has been ever since he was a little boy?" asked Carol.

"No, I didn't know that. I knew his eyesight was very poor, but I thought it was mostly caused by the stroke," said Dr. Wilson. "But he did tell me that he wore a patch on his eye when he was a little boy and he couldn't see well."

"It got worse after the stroke. He would look out the window in his office, and he not only couldn't see the people below, he couldn't even see the other buildings," said Carol.

"Have you and Gene been friends for a long time?" asked Dr. Wilson.

"We met when we were eight. He was so small and not very strong, and he fell down a lot. I was about a head taller than him. He had a very serious heart surgery when he was eight. He went to Chicago for the surgery, and we didn't see him for a very long time. He never talks about it," said Carol. "So many bad things happened to Gene when he was very young. I wish he had a better life now, and I would like to see him have some happiness."

"I noticed the scar, but I could tell it was from a very long time ago. I've also noticed the scar on his neck. How did that happen?" asked Dr. Wilson.

"That was a football injury. I was in the front row, cheering for him, the night it happened. He landed on his head, and I saw his neck turn to the right. He was out of the game for a while, and then they made him go out and play again. He also had a bad concussion and hurt his leg that night. They did surgery on his neck," said Carol. "He never wanted anybody to know about the heart surgery when he was a little boy or the neck surgery. I think Mike and I are the only ones who knew, except his family, but now you know."

"Thanks for telling me. He was probably afraid he wouldn't be allowed to play sports if they knew about it," said Dr. Wilson.

"I'm sure you are right. He was a great quarterback. He also played basketball." Carol's voice was full of love and admiration for her good friend. Gene opened his eyes a little. "Look who's waking up. Good morning, Gene." Carol kissed him on the cheek.

"Have you two been here all night?" asked Gene quietly.

"We most certainly have. We don't want to leave you," said Carol.

"You never get sleepy, do you? But what about you, Brett. Don't you get tired?" asked Gene.

"No. I don't want to leave you either," said Dr. Wilson.

At that moment, they brought Gene his breakfast. "It looks good. Can we help you with it?" asked Carol. "I'll raise your head a little."

Carol and Dr. Wilson cut Gene's food in small pieces and fed him carefully and with the greatest love imaginable. They moved slowly because they didn't want him to feel hurried. "I'm sorry, Gene. I forgot to put your glasses on you." Carol cleaned his glasses for him as she always did. "Is that better?"

"Yes, thank you. I can see you better now. You look pretty. I wish I could put my arms around you, but I can't. Do you remember how you used to lie in the bend of my arm and rest your head on my chest?" asked Gene quietly.

"I remember, Gene. That's always been my favorite place to be. I remember everything we have ever done together as well as every minute we have spent together." Carol gently hugged Gene and held him close being careful not to hurt him.

Terry knocked quietly on the slightly open door to Gene's room. "I don't want to interrupt, but may I come in?" asked Terry.

"Of course, Terry. Come sit by us," said Carol as she pulled up a chair close to Gene's bed.

"John's hip was hurting, so Alan took him home," said Terry.

"Have you been in there all alone?" asked Carol.

"Yes, but I didn't want to bother you," said Terry.

"Terry, you never have to be alone. You should have come to us." Carol hugged Terry. "We all love you very much."

"You stay right here with me. I need you," said Gene as he reached out as much as he could to Terry. Terry put his hand on Gene's.

"You ate a good breakfast, Gene. I'm going to take your tray and see what the physical therapy plan is for you today. I'll be back soon," said Dr. Wilson.

When Dr. Wilson left the room, Carol and Terry noticed Gene's eyes filling with tears. "I want to get well, but I'm not sure I will be able to do what they expect from me."

"I know you can't do it right now, Gene. We will stay with you," said Carol.

"Please don't let them hurt my neck. That is the one thing I can't stand," said Gene.

"I promise I won't let them hurt you," said Carol. "My dear, sweet Gene, I'll never let anyone hurt you. Do you remember when we took John for physical therapy in Kansas City, they gave us the name of the clinic here in Chicago where all the therapists specialize working with stroke victims? They are the therapists you will see today."

"Thank you. That's why I love you. You always take care of everything," said Gene.

"I only wish I could take care of everything for you. I'll do my best," said Carol.

Dr. Wilson returned to Gene's room with two therapists. "Gene, these are your therapists for today, Drew and Nicole. They work with stroke patients. These are Gene's good friends, Carol and Terry."

Before they started, everyone could see the fear in Gene's eyes, and his hands were trembling. Carol immediately went to Gene and put her hands on his hands. "I'll be right here by you, Gene. It's going to be all right."

Drew spoke kindly to Gene. "Today I am just going to evaluate you to determine how we can work with you and not hurt you. We will never hurt you, Gene. Is it all right if we examine you?"

As Gene looked at Carol, there were tears running down his cheeks. Carol spoke to Drew. "Gene's been through a lot. He has had several setbacks and a great amount of pain."

Drew and Nicole examined Gene very gently as Carol sat close to him. When they were finished, Nicole said, "Now that wasn't so bad, was it?"

"No, it wasn't bad," said Gene.

"We will be back tomorrow. We will have a plan set up for you and your friends to approve," said Drew.

"That will be fine," said Gene.

As Drew and Nicole left, they stopped and talked to Terry. "May I see your hand, Terry?" Terry slowly lifted his right hand. Drew gently took his hand and turned it over and examined it. "How long ago was your stroke, Terry?"

"Six years ago. I was thirty-one when it happened. I had a bad head injury playing football, like Gene did. They think that's what caused it." Terry's voice was very soft and difficult to understand.

"May we try to help you?" asked Drew.

"Yes," said Terry.

Drew smiled and said he would see them tomorrow.

Carol was sitting by Gene holding his hand. Terry sat by them and put his hand on top of Carol's hand.

"We will do it together, Gene. I'll protect you too, like Carol does. I won't let anyone hurt you."

The three close friends sat together in silence. They needed no words. Their tears and the love in their eyes for each other said it all.

THE SEMINAR

As Gene's condition stabilized and he went home and back to work, Carol continued working for the lobbyist in Springfield. His name was Curt Woodson. Carol liked the job. She attended many Senate and House meetings where there were discussions of bills up for passage. She also frequently traveled to meetings and hearings in Chicago with Curt and sometimes alone.

One day Curt told Carol that he would be having a seminar in Springfield with many speakers coming from Chicago to speak on various bills that were coming up for votes in the legislature. One bill was for the passage of laws to make things more accessible for handicapped people especially in large cities like Chicago and also laws to prohibit discrimination or unfair and bad treatment of handicapped people in the workplace.

Carol immediately thought of Gene and discussed it with Curt. "I have a friend who lives and works in Chicago and is handicapped. He would be excellent speaking on that subject at the seminar."

"Really. You know, there is not a lot of money involved, in fact, very little," said Curt.

"Money is not important to him. He would like to help. It is a serious problem that he is faced with daily," said Carol.

"How would he travel here?" asked Curt.

"He has a specially equipped van and a caregiver who would travel with him," said Carol.

"What's his name?" asked Curt.

"His name is Gene Sandusky. His caregiver who would also speak is Nathan Ellis, and there is another friend who might attend, but he will not speak. His name is Terry Sheley," said Carol.

"Go ahead and set it up," said Curt.

"I'll call Gene. Do you want to talk to him?" asked Carol.

"I trust your judgment," said Curt.

That evening Carol called Gene and extended the invitation to him. Although Carol knew Gene did not like to speak publicly, because he was being asked to speak in favor of the passage of a bill to help handicapped people, he agreed to speak. John was visiting his sister in Dallas so he would not be attending. Terry was staying with Gene, so both Terry and Nathan would accompany Gene to Springfield. They would arrive the day before the seminar. Carol gave them the address of the office and asked them to stop by when they arrived in Springfield to meet Curt and the others who would be involved in the seminar.

They arrived at about two in the afternoon. the day before the seminar. As they entered the office, everyone was eager to meet them.

Carol made introductions. "These are my good friends from Chicago, originally from Kansas City, who will be speaking at the seminar, Nathan Ellis, Terry Sheley, and Gene Sandusky. These ladies will all be at the seminar working in different capacities. They are my coworkers, Cecelia, Michelle, Ellen, Nadine, and my supervisor, Anna. This is Henry Jacobs, and this is my boss, Curt Woodson."

Curt immediately shook hands with Nathan and Terry. As Curt reached out to shake hands with Gene, he noticed how Gene struggled to lift his left hand as much as he could. Curt moved closer to Gene so it would be easier.

"It's good to meet all of you. I've heard a lot about you, Gene."

"That could be good or bad," said Gene. "I'm honored you want me to speak at your seminar."

"It came from Carol, so I assure you it was all extremely good," said Curt. "The honor is ours."

Carol hugged Gene. "We have known one another for a long time, since we were eight. Gene is a really good man, the best man I have ever known." Curt noticed the tears in both Carol and Gene's eyes as did everyone else. "Gene has helped me many times. I've learned so much from him."

"We have been through a lot together," said Gene quietly. "Carol has been with me through some of the worst times of my life, and she has saved me. She is very important to me."

Everyone in the room seemed to be a little emotional.

"Why don't we go to the conference room and talk a little about tomorrow," said Curt. Curt led the way followed by Nathan and Gene, Terry and Carol, and Anna.

After they went into the conference room and shut the door, Cecelia said to Ellen, "Gene is so handsome, and he loves Carol very much as she does him. I've never seen caring and consideration so strong between two people that is immediately obvious."

"He seems incredibly nice, and I feel bad for him because he is severely handicapped," said Ellen. "I wonder what his prognosis is."

"I want to attend Gene's part of the seminar. I'm looking forward to hearing him speak," said Nadine.

"I think we will all be attending his group session," said Michelle. "In the face of tremendous odds against him, he seems so dignified and kind."

In the conference room, Curt explained the activities of the following day to them, and then he asked, "Terry, will you also be speaking?"

"I had a stroke six years ago. My voice was severely affected," said Terry.

Gene answered further for Terry. "Terry will not be speaking, but he will be up front with me, Nathan, and Carol, if that is all right with you. Sometimes I need help, and I need them close to me."

"That will be fine, Gene. Let me know if I can be of any help to you," said Curt.

That evening they went to Romanesque, Carol and Curt's favorite Italian restaurant in Springfield. Anna went with them. Curt would have liked to sit by Carol, but as Carol sat by Gene, he could sense that was where she wanted and needed to be.

Gene ordered lasagna, which was one thing that he could manage to eat, but Carol and Nathan were very attentive and helpful to him as they always were. Anna was sitting by Terry, and she was actually encouraging him to talk. Carol liked to see this because Terry seldom talked to anyone. Anna and Curt were seeing a different woman from the Carol they were accustomed to seeing. She definitely had the qualities of a caregiver as well as a woman who was deeply in love with a very kind, gentle man.

After dinner, they took Curt, Anna, and Carol back to their office to their cars. Carol would go home for a short while to care for her daughter and talk with her mother, but later that evening she would go to the hotel where Gene, Terry, and Nathan were staying. She would stay with them for several hours to help Gene get ready for the next day, but then she would return home to make her preparations for the seminar.

When Carol arrived at the hotel that evening, Nathan opened the door for her. Terry was sitting at a table. There were two double beds in the room. Gene was propped up with pillows in bed. He had on a T-shirt and warm-up pants. Carol went to him and sat on the bed beside him.

"Would you two be more comfortable if Terry and I would leave for a while?" asked Nathan.

"No, we want you to stay with us," said Carol.

"Are you sure?" asked Terry.

"We are sure," said Gene. "We just need to be close for a little while."

Carol slowly lay down beside him. She nestled in the bend of his arm with her head resting gently on the right side of his chest. She kissed him, taking special care to not hurt his neck. Carol and Gene were probably closer that night than they had been in some time. Nathan and Terry both noticed the undeniable love, tenderness, and need they had for one another. There was little conversation. Carol was like a feather on his chest. It made Gene feel that he was still alive to know how much she cared for him.

"I need to leave and let you get some sleep so you will be ready for the seminar tomorrow," said Carol.

"You have no idea what it means for me to have you close to me if only for a short while," said Gene.

"I know, because I feel the same way," said Carol.

"I'm going to follow you home so you'll be safe," said Nathan.

"I'll be all right. This isn't Kansas City or Chicago. It's just Springfield," said Carol.

"It is just very important to the three of us to know you are safe," said Nathan.

"All right, since you put it that way. I'll see you guys in the morning," said Carol as she kissed Gene one more time and hugged Terry and then left with Nathan.

When they got to Carol's house, Nathan got out of the van. Carol walked to him, and he hugged her tightly. "Thank you, Nathan, for taking such good care of Gene."

"I always will. I love him as you do," said Nathan as he smoothed her hair back.

"Keep him safe tonight," said Carol.

"I will my dear, sweet girl. I will do anything and everything I can for Gene," said Nathan.

Carol kissed Nathan so gently and kindly. He had never been kissed like that before. He had never felt loved before as he did at that very moment. Carol was the only woman he had ever loved, or for that matter, ever would love.

"I'll see you in the morning, Nathan," said Carol.

When Nathan got back to the hotel, Gene and Terry were both still awake.

"Is she all right?" asked Gene.

"She's fine or as fine as she can be without you next to her," said Nathan. "You know, Gene, sometimes I wonder if you realize how much she loves you. Her every thought is of you."

"I know, Nathan. Thank you for being with me and taking care of me and Carol. We are both so grateful to you and Terry," said Gene.

Nathan hugged Gene and then helped him lie down.

At the seminar the next day, Gene's session was packed. Terry, Nathan, and Carol looked very nice, as did Curt and Henry and all the girls from the office. But Gene looked exceptional, and the attention was directed toward him. He had on a light-gray suit with a light-blue shirt and matching light-blue tie. His hair was dark and full at a length where it seemed to curl a little and lie in natural waves. His pale-blue eyes matched his shirt and tie.

Nathan spoke first, explaining the bills coming up before the legislature as Terry and Carol passed out handouts. When Nathan finished speaking, he pushed Gene's wheelchair in front of the podium and adjusted the microphone to compensate for the fact that Gene could not turn his neck. Gene was a very big man, and even in the wheelchair, his six-foot-five height was evident. His broad shoulders seemed to hide some of the weight he had gained. He looked incredibly handsome.

Carol, and probably everyone else for that matter, couldn't help but notice how everything Nathan did for Gene was done with a high degree of gentleness and kindness. He was very careful never to hurt Gene, and he protected him from being hurt by anyone else or any outside forces. As Carol had often said, she would give her life for Gene, so would Nathan. Gene began speaking in a soft, gentle, yet extremely strong voice. He was charismatic and dignified, and all eyes were on him.

"Good morning. My name is Gene Sandusky. I know personally what many of you and other handicapped people experience in their everyday existence, especially in a large city like Chicago which is where I live. I am lucky to have a kind caregiver like Nathan and good friends like Carol and Terry as well as many others who help me on a daily basis. Without them, I would not be able to be here today. I need their help to survive."

Carol noticed the tears on Gene's cheeks. She gently wiped them with a tissue.

Gene continued, "I'm sorry. I get very emotional when I talk about those who help me. Their kindness and their ability to help me is overwhelming. Within a two-day period, I had two minor strokes followed by a massive stroke. I have a heart condition for which I have had two surgeries. I have also had head injuries, including five concussions and a neck injury requiring surgery from playing football in high school. I am legally blind in my right eye and have poor vision in my left eye. I take extensive physical therapy daily in the hope of possibly improving my quality of life. In the meantime, my caregivers and I fight obstacles every day. I'm not sure what the outcome will be. This is my good friend, Terry Sheley (Terry walked up to where Gene was sitting and put his hand on Gene's shoulder). Terry had a stroke six years ago. He has been told that no more can be done for him. He is thirty-eight, the same age that I am. Terry's stroke primarily affected his voice and also his leg and arm. My friend John, who could not be here today, had polio when he was five. Someday there may not be people like John who are handicapped because of polio. But being handicapped will never be eradicated. The illnesses and injuries that have made me a prisoner in my own body will always occur, so there will always be people like me. But there is another bill that I am also very concerned about as I am sure many of you are. That is the bill involving the abuse of handicapped people in the workplace. When I returned to work after my strokes, I was treated very badly. At that time, I was improving to the point where I could use crutches. For a normal person, what happened to me would not have been serious, but at that stage I was still far from normal, and it was a devastating setback for me. I was giving a presentation, and I fell on my face, which for some could have been a laughing matter, but for me it definitely was not. I was attempting to turn to the right to get a piece of chalk, but I cannot turn my neck to the right. I lost my balance and fell, cutting my cheek and twisting my leg and ankle badly. My glasses fell off just out of my reach. I was screamed at and ordered to get up. No one was allowed to help me. I took a blood thinner, and my cheek was bleeding profusely. There was blood on my suit and shirt as well as on the floor. I was finally able to get some tissues from my pocket to hold over my cheek, and someone handed me my glasses. But until a kind friend came into the room, no one would help me up. This was a very bad setback for me, not only physically, but emotionally and mentally also. Handicapped people need to be understood better and extended a little more consideration because it's very difficult or impossible to do many things others take for granted. It was so hurtful and cruel, but I did return to the same job. I have tried to help those same people who were in that fateful meeting to understand handicapped people and maybe to try to show just a little kindness. For many of us, probably myself included, these bills will not pass soon enough to help us, but for those who come after us with the same problems and for small children who are handicapped it is not too late and they can be helped. Thank you for letting me speak to you today. Now, I will turn the podium over to Curt Woodson."

Gene received a standing ovation, and many were emotional. As Curt approached the podium and took the microphone, he said, "Thank you, Gene. That is a hard act to follow. I have never heard someone speak so directly from their heart before, and I thank you for that. I am so sorry that happened to you, and I wish you the very best. I hope you realize how much we appreciate you being here and speaking to us. I know it wasn't easy for you. Gene, you have my sincerest respect and admiration."

Curt spoke for a few more minutes as Carol went to help Gene. She took his glasses off and wiped his cheeks and eyes and gave him a drink of water.

All eyes were on the gentle, soft-spoken, handsome young man in the wheelchair and the dedicated, kind young woman who seemed to care for him and about him so much.

At the luncheon, Gene, Carol, Nathan, Terry, Anna, and Curt sat together. The lunch consisted of a pork chop, vegetables, and a salad which were all difficult for Gene to handle, but Carol and Nathan helped him very discretely and with the love they always showed when caring for Gene.

Carol also helped Terry. Anna was very kind to Terry as she was the previous night, and he was able to talk to her.

Many session participants as well as Carol's fellow employees complimented Gene on his presentation. Everyone wanted to talk to him, and he met with them each individually and with genuine concern and care. Many of the participants in Gene's session had some form of disability, and Gene, with Carol's assistance, made certain that no one was left out and any questions they had for him were answered. Carol was so proud of Nathan and Terry, and especially Gene. As Curt had indicated in his thank-you speech to Gene, although his condition was so devastating, he still cared for others and sincerely wanted to help those he came in contact with that day. Of course, that didn't surprise Carol because that was one of the many reasons she loved him. In fact, everyone loved Gene that day, but they always had ever since high school or even when he was eight sitting on her Grandma's lap.

"Thank you so much, Gene," said Curt. "Your session was one of the best we have ever had. And thank you, Carol, Nathan, and Terry. You all made it possible. We will have a couple of hours before the banquet. I look forward to seeing you there."

"Curt, I was wondering if you would mind if I rest on the sofa in the conference room at the office. I have very little energy, and my back and neck are bothering me," said Gene quietly.

"That's fine. I will meet you there," said Curt.

When they arrived at the office, Carol took a pillow and blanket from the van to make Gene more comfortable and Nathan and Terry both stayed with him.

As Carol passed Anna's office, Anna said, "Carol, come in and sit down a minute." Michelle was also there. "Is Gene all right?"

"He just needs to rest for a while. Everything is so hard for him," said Carol. They noticed her eyes were flooded with tears.

"Carol, can I give you a hug?" asked Michelle as she put her arms around Carol. "Gene is a beautiful, strong man, but I know how fragile he is, and I can tell how much you love him."

"Thank you. Everyone has been so kind to him, and I appreciate that so much. I just want to help him any way I can. I don't think there is anyone else in the world as truly good as Gene. I feel so fortunate to be his friend," said Carol.

Later, after Gene had rested, Nathan and Terry took him to the men's room and helped him wash his face and comb his hair and get ready for the evening. As Gene was waiting at the front of the office for the others, Anna took him a bottle of water with a straw.

"Thank you, Anna. Do you mind holding it for me?" asked Gene.

"Not at all," said Anna. "Do you need anything else?"

"No, thank you. Anna, you have all been so kind to us. We really appreciate all you have done for us," said Gene.

Anna was sitting by Gene when Carol came out of her office. Terry and Nathan were with her. "Thank you, Anna. You have been very kind to my friends," said Carol.

"They are all so nice. They are easy to be kind to," said Anna. "You are three of the most polite, kind, and attractive men I have met in a long time. And you are all so tall."

"Nathan and Terry are attractive, definitely not me," said Gene. "We all played basketball together in high school a lifetime ago."

"Gene is very modest. He was the best-looking guy in the class. He was prom king and leap year prince," said Nathan. "Not to mention, he was the best basketball player ever, and he was a big part of taking our team to a state championship."

"How the times have changed," Gene spoke with sadness in his voice. "There's nothing left of that man now."

"I'll tell you something else, Anna. Carol was prom queen, and she gave her crown away to little Bonnie. Carol fixed her hair and brought her a dress for the prom. Bonnie didn't have a date, but she got to dance with Gene that night. That was such an unselfish act on your part, and you made her so happy," said Nathan.

"It wasn't the real prom. It was an alternative prom," said Carol.

"It was better and more fun than the other prom, and more people went to it," said Nathan.

"You always treated everyone so good," said Terry as he wiped a tear from his cheek. "Remember when those girls laughed at me and bullied me in English? You took up for me. You were my friend when no one else would be."

"As you can see, Anna, I managed to get really good friends in these three wonderful people. I don't know how I got so lucky," said Gene.

"I think you are pretty wonderful too," said Anna as she hugged Gene very gently. "And I also think you are the most handsome man I have ever seen."

"Anna, if I could move, I would give you a hug, but unfortunately I can't," said Gene.

At that moment, Curt came out of his office. "I guess it is time to leave. Is something wrong? Everyone looks so sad. What's wrong Terry?"

"Nothing, I'll be fine," said Terry.

As they got in the van, it was just the four of them. "It's been a busy two days," said Carol. "Are you all right, Gene? I know this has been hard on you."

"I'll be fine. It's just my neck and back," said Gene.

They were all quiet in the van on the way to the venue. Carol held Gene's hand and spoke quietly to him. When they arrived at their destination, Nathan was exceptionally gentle helping Gene out of the van and pushing his wheelchair. He could feel Gene's pain as they all could.

Terry asked Carol quietly, "Does it show that I've been crying?"

"No, Terry, not at all," said Carol.

The meal that night was steak and all the trimmings. They, of course, helped Gene, but he wasn't particularly hungry. At one time, he asked Carol to take his glasses off and dry his eyes.

"I can hardly see tonight. I guess it's the lights," said Gene. "I sometimes wonder who will die first, me or my eyes. I hope I do. I can't imagine not being able to see you."

Carol gently put his glasses back on him. "Is that any better?"

"Yes, it is. Thank you. In case you don't know, I love you." Gene's voice was very soft and weak.

"I know you do. And I love you. I always have and always will," said Carol.

They were the first ones to leave the dinner that night, but they really didn't care. The guys were heading back to Chicago early the next morning.

After they left, Michelle was crying. Anna comforted her and asked what was wrong. "I just feel so bad for Carol and Gene. She loves him so much as he does her, and he is so sick. He seems like such a good man."

"He works so hard to get better. Let's just hope that he can recover," said Anna.

When they got to the hotel, they quickly and gently helped Gene get ready for bed. Carol stayed by him as she had the night before, but he went to sleep soon. He didn't even wake up when she kissed him goodbye, but she could tell he knew she was leaving. Gene always became a little restless when she left him.

Nathan held Carol close to him as they walked to the van. "Did you notice that Gene refused the stipend that Curt offered him?" asked Carol.

"I noticed, but Gene still insisted on paying me and Terry," said Nathan.

"Gene has always been so good to everyone, but people haven't always been so good to him, people like George Meyer. I will always wish that had not happened, and I'm so afraid something like that is going to happen again," said Carol.

"I've never trusted George since the first time I met him," said Nathan.

"Nor have I. I just wish Gene didn't still work for him, but I know he still can't face looking for another job," said Carol. "Oh, Nathan, he seemed so fragile tonight. I worry so much about him."

"Always know, Carol, that I love Gene like a brother, and I will protect him," said Nathan. "I'll take good care of him, and I'll watch him closely. I will make a promise to you. Nothing will ever happen to Gene on my watch. I won't let it. That's my goal."

And Nathan stood by his words. Nothing would ever happen to Gene on Nathan's watch.

DOWNWARD SPIRAL

When Gene became physically well enough, he spent countless hours in physical therapy at the clinic specializing in stroke and cardiac rehabilitation. Nathan would take him there every day after work and on weekends, either waiting for him or working with him. Gene was doing well. He was walking unassisted. His arm, back, and neck were considerably better. He could even drive short distances alone just so he didn't attempt to drive at night.

But suddenly, without warning or for any particular reason, there was a change for the worse in Gene's condition. One Saturday when Nathan returned home from grocery-shopping, he found Gene sitting on the sofa with his head in his hands staring at the floor. It was noon, and he still had his robe on. Nathan sat by Gene and put his arm around him.

"Are you all right, Gene? Shall we get ready to go to physical therapy?"

"I'll be fine. I can't go today," said Gene. "I can't do it anymore."

"You've worked really hard, Gene. You are almost well. We should go out tonight and celebrate," said Nathan.

"You go, Nathan. I'll just stay here," said Gene.

"I'm not going without you, Gene. I'll stay with you," said Nathan.

"I feel like I'm going backward. I could walk better a couple weeks ago," said Gene.

Gene sat in the same position all day. Nathan sat by him and held him in his arms. He knew what Gene had just said was true, but he didn't want to say anything. There were tears in Gene's eyes as he said, "I wish Carol was here, but she might not like me. I've gained so much weight."

"You've gained weight before. Besides, it's not that much. You look fine. It seems more to you than it actually is. You'll be able to take it off now that you are well," said Nathan. "Carol loves you unconditionally."

"I don't think I can do it again. I'm just tired," said Gene.

"You just need to rest, Gene," said Nathan. Gene was much bigger than Nathan, but he felt as though he was holding a small child in his arms.

Late that night, Nathan received a phone call. His dad in Kansas City was quite ill, and they wanted him to come. He told Gene the following morning.

"Take my car, it's yours. I'm giving it to you," said Gene.

"That car is almost brand-new. I can't take your car, Gene," said Nathan.

"The van is all I need. I owe you, Nathan, so much more than I have ever paid you," said Gene. "I'm scared driving. I don't think I can see well enough."

"Your eyesight is improving, Gene," said Nathan. "You need someone to stay with you."

"I'll be fine. If I need to go somewhere at night, Patrick will take me. But I don't want to drive in the daytime either. I won't go anyplace. Please don't worry," said Gene. "I just get confused."

"I'll be leaving first thing Monday morning, said Nathan. "You know I have to tell Carol. I promised her."

"I know. It's all right. She won't hate me," said Gene.

"No, I assure you, Carol won't hate you," said Nathan. "I told you once not too long ago how much she loves you. Do you remember?"

"I remember. I was really sick then," said Gene. "But my head and mind were in a better place then, and I wasn't so depressed."

"I'll let you know about my dad," said Nathan.

"Have a safe trip, Nathan," said Gene.

Nathan left for Kansas City early Monday morning. He wanted to stop in Springfield and talk to Carol. He would stop at her office and take her to lunch. He called her so she would be expecting him. When he walked into the office, Anna was the first person he saw.

"Hello, Nathan. It's good to see you," said Anna.

"Hello, Anna," said Nathan. "I didn't think you would remember me."

"I remember all of you. How's Gene, and how's Terry doing?" asked Anna.

"Terry's fine," Nathan paused. "Gene has good days and bad days. His physical condition has improved. I hope he will be well soon. He just needs a little more time."

Carol came out of her office and greeted Nathan with a hug. "We will go to Romanesque. It's quiet," said Carol.

As they got in the car, Nathan said, "Gene gave me his car and too much money. I wasn't comfortable taking it."

"He owes you a lot, Nathan. He wants you to have it," said Carol.

As they sat in a secluded booth in the quiet restaurant, Nathan couldn't help but think how kind and gentle Carol had always been to him and how much he hated to tell her what he needed to.

"I told you about my dad and why I have to leave, but that's not why I wanted to see you," said Nathan.

"I know," said Carol. "Mike used to say that I knew everything where Gene was concerned. This time I hope I'm wrong."

"You probably know," said Nathan. "I told you once that nothing would ever happen to Gene on my watch, and I kept my word. But now I notice many of the same traits in Gene that I had before I tried to kill myself."

"I so hoped that I was wrong, but I knew what you were going to say. I'm planning to leave in the morning. Will that be soon enough?" asked Carol.

"That will be fine. He's not quite there yet, but he has changed so much," said Nathan.

"My poor, sweet Gene. I never thought he would go there. He's the one who saves others, now we need to save him," said Carol. "Tell me what you notice. Tell me what to look for."

"I know you two have talked on the phone, but I'm not sure how much he has told you. He won't go to physical therapy anymore, and he doesn't take his medicine. He has a hard time doing his job, and he calls in sick a lot. He's very quiet, almost shy, and he is incapable of making decisions. He is extremely depressed, and sometimes he simply can't get out of bed. He won't even go out to eat. He has gained a lot of weight. He has a hard time carrying on a conversation even with me. The only reminder left of the Gene I used to know is his kindness. He is still incredibly kind, almost too kind," said Nathan.

"I have to save him, Nathan. I have to find a way to save him," said Carol.

"Gene has always been one of my favorite people," said Nathan. "I always remember him in high school and how popular he was, yet, he was always humble and kind. Everyone loved him."

"It always made him sad that everyone loved him. He never understood why he was so well-liked. He never felt he deserved it, but he did, more than anyone," said Carol. "I think Mike should know and be there too. I need him. Do you think the others should be there? Rodger won't be able to make it. He is in the hospital and will be there for quite a while."

"John should come. He loves Gene so much. Alan loves him like a son, and there has always been a special bond between Gene and Terry," said Nathan.

"They will all be able to help me with him. Thank you, Nathan, for taking care of Gene," said Carol.

Carol left early the next morning for Chicago. She couldn't get there soon enough. She arrived late morning and went directly to Gene's office. George Meyer was standing by Karen's desk. Carol spoke to them and noticed how solemn George looked.

George took Carol's hand and said, "I'm glad you're here. Gene needs you with him. He's a good man, but he is in a bad place right now. Save him, Carol. You are probably the only one who can do it. Are the guys coming?"

"They will be here in the morning," said Carol.

"Tell Gene to take some sick leave. He won't want to because he has used so much already, but he is definitely sick. Good luck," said George.

Carol took a deep breath. She wasn't exactly sure what to expect, but she told herself that she could handle it and help him. He was still the same Gene she knew and loved. She knocked on the door.

"Come in," said Gene.

Carol immediately noticed the quietness of his voice. She went to him and kissed and hugged him. "I'm here now, Gene. Everything will be all right."

"Will you sit by me on the sofa," said Gene. He seemed glad and relieved to see her, but his voice was also weak and incredibly sad.

Carol reached for his crutches. "You've got some new crutches. You have Canadian crutches. They should be easier for you to use."

"I just got them a few days ago. I couldn't walk very well, and I kept falling, so they put some new braces on my legs," said Gene. "I thought I was well, but I guess not. I'm scared, Carol. I'm really scared. I don't understand what's happening to me."

Carol helped him with his crutches, and they walked the few feet to the sofa and sat down. She put her arms around him and held him as close to her as she could.

"I need a haircut. Do you think my hair is getting too long?" asked Gene.

"I love your hair. I think it looks nice," said Carol.

"With you by me, I think I might just make it," said Gene.

"You better make it. You are in my heart, Gene. If anything ever happens to you, it will tear my heart apart. There is nothing to be afraid of because I'm going to be by you," Carol paused. "Could I get us some lunch?"

"I have no appetite. I don't eat much, but I still can't seem to lose weight," said Gene.

"Gene, you are six feet five inches tall. You have to eat to stay strong," said Carol.

"Maybe some soup. Is that all right?" asked Gene. He seemed to seek approval on everything, and just as Nathan had told Carol, he was unable to make decisions.

"That will be fine. I'll be back soon," said Carol.

"Please hurry. I miss you when you leave me," said Gene. He spoke very slowly.

As Carol walked to the cafeteria, she could understand the solemn look on George's face as well as the concern in Nathan's eyes. When Carol returned with the soup, she noticed Gene hadn't moved. She took a bite of her soup to check the heat. And then without even asking, she fed Gene half spoons of his soup. He ate every bite she fed him.

"Is there anything I can help you with here in the office?" asked Carol.

"No, I'm all caught up. I just haven't brought in any new clients lately," said Gene.

"What's wrong, my sweet Gene? You seem so tired and sad," asked Carol.

"I don't know what's wrong. I can't talk right. I keep forgetting my words. Will you please help me, Carol?" asked Gene.

Carol hugged and kissed him ever so gently. "I'll do whatever I can for you. We'll figure out what's wrong. I love you, Gene. That never changes."

They stayed close together for a long time that afternoon. Carol talked quietly and kindly to Gene, the way that he used to like so much and always made him feel better. She held him in her arms and smoothed his hair and caressed his cheeks. When they left the office that day, everyone was gone. She knew he would like that.

When they got to the lobby, Carol said, "I'm parked about a block away. Wait here for me, and I'll pick you up."

"I think I can make it," said Gene. "I need to stay with you. Don't leave me."

When they got outside, Gene had to sit down on a bench. A young taxi driver got out of the first cab and came to them and asked, "Can I take you somewhere?"

"I'm parked a block away. Would you mind taking us there?" asked Carol.

The driver spoke kindly to Gene and helped him into the cab. When Carol tried to pay the driver, he said there was no charge.

"Gene has been in my cab many times. He is always very kind and a generous tipper. I've noticed a change in him lately. I feel honored to be able to help him."

Carol hugged the taxicab driver. She couldn't speak.

When they got to Gene's apartment, Carol fixed them a sandwich, and they tried to watch TV for a while, but Gene couldn't seem to concentrate. Then she helped Gene get ready for bed. She made sure he took his medicine. There was something special about that night. He rested peacefully because he knew she was beside him and she would protect him as she had when he was a little boy. She was sure to keep her hand on his all night so he would know she was there.

Gene hugged his friends when they arrived the next day. Carol had told Mike what to expect, and she knew he would tell the others. They were all so gentle and kind with Gene, especially Alan.

Carol was sitting by Gene on the sofa. Alan sat on the other side of him and put his arms around him. "You know, Gene, I often think of that time you stayed at our house when you had that bad concussion playing football. You were only sixteen. Colleen was so kind to you and comforting you, and I was not. Did you ever forgive me for that?"

"I forgave you, Alan, a long time ago. I was a big baby that night," said Gene.

"No, you weren't. You were just a boy and all alone. If you will allow me to, I'll make it up to you now. I'll love you and take care of you like I should have done then," said Alan.

That night, John was tired and went to bed early. Mike and Alan went to help Gene with a shower. Terry was sitting alone in the living room. As Carol walked toward him, she could feel tears burning her eyes. Without a word, he put his arms around her and held her tight as she cried, and he comforted her.

A short while later, Terry went to the room he shared with John, and Carol went to her place beside Gene. She took hold of his hand, and even though he was asleep, she could feel him squeeze her hand. He knew that she was by him.

Early the next morning there was a quiet knock on Gene's bedroom door. "Come in," said Gene. It was John.

"Is it all right if I lie by you two for a while?" asked John.

"Of course, John," said Gene kindly. "I wondered where you were."

"I stayed with Terry. He needs me sometimes, just like I need him," said John.

"Terry is a good man, John. He loves you very much," said Carol.

John snuggled close to Gene and took hold of his hand. "Terry also loves you, Gene, and he loves Carol. He talks about you two a lot."

"John, I met Terry the same time I met you, in sophomore physical education class. Remember our teacher, Mr. Dalton, and our senior instructor, Richard, Carol's boyfriend?" said Gene.

"They all treated me good, but you were the very best, Gene. You helped me make a basket in an actual basketball game. I'll never forget that," said John. "I'm sorry, Gene. I didn't mean to make you cry."

Gene couldn't speak, so Carol spoke for him as she hugged him. "It's fine, John. Gene is just very emotional right now. It's nothing you said. He was just reminded of better times."

Without a word, Carol and John helped Gene get ready for the day then they joined the others. Mike and Alan had prepared a good breakfast. As Gene tried to eat, he dropped his toast on the floor. A few minutes later, Mike offered Gene a donut, and he also dropped it.

He cried and said, "I'm sorry. I can't seem to do anything."

"It's all right, Gene. Don't cry." Carol put her arms around him and held him close to her. Her eyes met with Alan and Mike. Alan sat close to Gene. "We want to help you, Gene. We'll do whatever you want today." Alan took hold of Gene's hand. "We are here for you, Gene. Is there anything you would like to do, go to the lake or to a movie?"

"I'm afraid of falling, Alan. I'm just really afraid," said Gene.

"We'll take good care of you, Gene. I promise we won't let you fall. We could even take the wheelchair if it would make you more comfortable," said Alan.

"I don't know, Alan. I can't make decisions anymore," said Gene.

"I can," said John. "I'll help you, Gene. Remember when we went to the zoo and you really liked it? Let's go there."

"That's all right with me, just so you all stay by me," said Gene.

"Then it's settled. We will go to the zoo," said Alan. "We will all be with you. There won't be a thing for you to worry about."

"Gene, do you remember how it used to always make me feel loved when you smoothed my hair down? Now I want to fix your hair." John took a comb from his pocket and combed Gene's hair. "You sure have a lot of hair, Gene."

"Thanks for combing it for me, John," said Gene.

That day turned out to be a very memorable day for all of them. Mike drove, and John sat with him. Carol and Terry sat in the back. And Alan and Gene sat in the middle. Even though Mike stayed close to John that day, and Carol never let go of Terry's arm, the emphasis and attention of all of them was centered on Gene. They talked quietly to him, touched him, and gently loved him without reservations. Gene was their primary concern, and they focused on him in an attempt to transfer their energy and strength to him.

Gene knew that the five people with him that day loved him and cared deeply for his recovery. Gene was aware that he was on a downward spiral, and he also knew that his friends only had one agenda and that was to make him well, but he had to let them in and allow them to help him.

When they stopped at a small café, Alan stayed by Gene while the others went to get the food and drinks. Alan would not leave Gene's side. He talked quietly and kindly to him. He held his hand. He took Gene's glasses off and cleaned them, and he wiped the tears from his eyes and cheeks. When the others brought the food back, Alan helped Gene with his drink and cut his sandwich in small pieces, as he knew Carol would do. Over the years, Alan had watched Carol closely and learned from her how she cared for her friends and made them feel special and loved. They walked slowly through the park so they could hold on to each beautiful moment as long as possible.

During that whole week, they never left Gene's side. They nurtured and encouraged him. If Gene wanted to stay home, they all stayed with him. If he agreed to go out, they made suggestions, but the final decision was always up to Gene. They prepared food for him that was nourishing and healthy.

Gene had an unnatural fear of falling, so Mike stayed close to him, especially when they were outside, so he could help him if he should start to fall. Mike was his protector, and he would not let Gene be hurt.

John kissed Gene and combed his hair and loved him more than he ever had before. Although John had always loved Gene, it was more powerful now than it had ever been because John knew how much Gene needed him and his love.

Carol orchestrated the outings, the food, made sure he took his medication, massaged his back and legs, and tried to put his mind at ease. She concentrated on all she could do to heal him.

Terry and Alan both loved Gene so much, and he could feel their love. The strong bond that existed between Terry and Gene was undeniable. Alan worked hard encouraging Gene and staying by his side constantly.

And Gene was trying so hard to get well. He was their hero. He always had been and always would be. Gene knew he couldn't do it alone. He was willing, agreeable, and determined.

The next day they went to an afternoon movie and out to eat at their favorite Chicago restaurant. The movie wasn't crowded, so Alan helped Gene from the wheelchair to a seat between him and Carol. Alan held Gene's hand as Carol put her arm around him and rested her head on his shoulder. When the lights went out and the movie began, Gene held tighter to Alan and Carol. The darkness seemed to frighten him.

"Carol, may I kiss you?" asked Gene shyly.

"Yes, you don't need to ask permission to kiss me," said Carol with so much love and tenderness in her voice for the kindest, most wonderful and yet the saddest, most tragic man she had ever known. The kiss was very gentle, honest, and loving. She knew that she had to be careful with Gene just as she did when they were sixteen. He was still as special to her as he had been so long ago. Gene felt safe and secure with Carol so close to him, but he still held on to Alan's hand. Occasionally, Alan would offer Gene a bite of popcorn, a small piece of candy, or he would hold his soda for him while he took a sip.

Gene and Carol kissed several times during the movie that day. At one time Gene even kissed Alan's hand, and then he took Alan's hand and put it on Carol's hand. He seemed almost happy, and he almost smiled.

At the restaurant that evening, Gene ordered a steak. His right hand was a little weak, so Alan cut it in small pieces for him.

"Gene, would you like for us to help you?" asked Carol.

"Yes, I feel very weak, and my hand is shaking. I'll probably drop everything," said Gene.

Alan and Carol took turns feeding Gene that night in one of the finest and most exclusive restaurants in the city. They did it out of love and necessity for the kindest, most wonderful man they had ever had the honor of knowing.

The next day they took Gene to a psychiatrist recommended by Dr. Wilson who accompanied them to the appointment. They all went with him and were planning to wait while Gene went into the doctor's office alone, but within about fifteen minutes, a nurse came out to the waiting room and asked Carol and Alan to be with Gene.

"The doctor doesn't usually have anyone else in the room when he is with a patient, but Gene has asked for the two of you to be with him, and Dr. Cassidy wants to talk to you in Gene's presence," said the nurse.

"I'm his personal physician. If he has any problems, please let me know," said Dr. Wilson.

"We will," said the nurse.

As they entered the room, the nurse told Dr. Cassidy what Dr. Wilson had said.

As Alan sat on one side of Gene and put his arm around him, Carol sat on the other side and held his hand.

Dr. Cassidy spoke in a very kind voice to them, "I will prescribe a mild medication for Gene to take. I don't want to give him anything strong because of all the medication he is already taking. Dr. Wilson gave me Gene's complete medical history. It was heartbreaking, and I am sorry that he has been through so much. But I might add that, in light of what he has been through, he is doing remarkably well. I think that what the two of you and his other friends are doing for him is the best medicine of all. Gene is very fragile right now," said Dr. Cassidy. "Hold him, love him, support him, and don't let him be hurt. He needs all of you more than anything else and more than you can ever realize."

"We know. We will take good care of him. Did Dr. Wilson tell you how much we all love Gene?" asked Carol.

"Yes, he told me," said Dr. Cassidy. "Everyone should be so lucky to have such good friends."

As Alan took Gene to the waiting room where his other friends were, Carol went back into Dr. Cassidy's office.

"May I ask you one question, Dr. Cassidy?" asked Carol.

"Yes, I hope I can answer it for you," said Dr. Cassidy.

"Gene's friend who had been staying with him was worried that he might attempt to take his own life. Do you see the signs?" asked Carol.

"Yes, and I know you do too," said Dr. Cassidy. "Love him. Always let him know how much you love him. Be sure that someone is always with him. He is afraid of being alone. He has been through so much, but you know all about that because you have been with him every step of the way. There is something very special about him. You are the one who will heal him, but you already know that too, don't you?"

"Yes, I know. The first time we met, we were only eight years old. Gene was so tiny. The first time he met my grandmother, he went to her and hugged her and told her his name. Everyone always thought that Gene learned a lot from me, but I was the one who learned from him. He taught me how to love and how to care. He made me a better person." Carol shook hands with Dr. Cassidy and went to join her friends.

The following day, they walked along the lake and went to Navy Pier. If it was possible, they kept Gene closer to them than ever before. They were like a protective shield around him that no outside forces could penetrate.

Mike got some blankets and pillows from the van. They gently helped Gene to lie on the blanket spread on the sand and rest his back against the pillows. Carol sat by him and held his hand and showed him how much she loved him, as did Alan.

John took the comb from his pocket. "I'll comb your hair a little for you, Gene. It's really windy here by the lake." John stood back and looked at Gene. "Your hair looks really good. I wish I had hair like yours."

Later, they went to Navy Pier. They got Gene an ice cream cone, and Alan fed it to him with a spoon. They asked him if he wanted to ride the Ferris wheel, but he didn't want to. He watched Carol and John do so reminiscent of Fairyland Park so long ago.

As they left Navy Pier that day, Mike couldn't resist a basketball game. He won a small brown teddy bear, just like John's. "Here, Gene. I won it for you," said Mike.

"Thanks, Mike," said Gene as he held it close to his chest.

"Do you remember how good we were that day at Fairyland Park when we made all those baskets and won so many stuffed toys for John's sisters?" asked Mike.

"I liked basketball. I didn't get hurt playing basketball like I did playing football," said Gene. "I can't make a basket anymore, Mike."

"I know, Gene. I know you can't," said Mike.

When they got home, Gene needed to rest. Carol walked with him to the bedroom and helped him put on his robe and lie down. She kissed him and told him she would be back later.

Carol went to the living room and sat by Alan on the sofa. Mike, Terry, and John were there also. "I have the feeling you guys were waiting for me," said Carol.

Alan put his arm around her. "We need to talk about Gene."

"I know," said Carol.

"Mike talked with Nathan. He is not sure when he will be back, but someone needs to stay with Gene until then and maybe even after," said Alan.

Gene was standing in the doorway. "May I come to the meeting?"

"Of course, Gene, it's all about you. We have no secrets. Sit between us," said Carol as she went to help him.

Gene's robe was open, and he only had his underwear on. He wasn't wearing shoes, socks, or his leg braces. He appeared to be on the brink of falling even though he did have his crutches. Mike and Alan also went to help him. Carol pulled his robe around him and tied the belt. Gene had always been somewhat modest, and Carol tried to protect him as much as possible.

Gene sat between Alan and Carol.

Alan set his crutches to the side for him and put his arm around him as he always did. "I'm going to stay here with you, Gene. We don't want you to be alone."

"But you all have lives of your own. You can't spend all of your time with me," said Gene. He was shivering. "I'm so cold." Carol got a blanket for him and covered up his legs.

"You are all that matters to us right now, Gene. Of all of us in this room, you are the most important," said Carol. "No one can equal you. You are the best man I have ever known."

"I don't hold a candle to any of you. I'm nothing compared to you guys," said Gene through tears as Alan held him in his arms. "I can't even speak without crying. I feel so completely useless. I don't know where my glasses are, and I can't see."

"We'll find them for you." Mike and Terry immediately went to Gene's room to look for his glasses.

John pushed the footstool to the sofa where Gene was sitting between Carol and Alan. "Gene, I'm going to help you put your feet up so your legs don't swell." John did so very gently and tucked the blanket in around his feet and, he took the comb from his pocket. "I'm going to comb your hair. It got a little messed up when you were resting."

Gene offered no resistance. "Thanks, John." Mike and Terry returned with Gene's glasses. "Where did you find them?"

"On the floor. They probably just got knocked off accidently," said Mike.

"I can't even keep track of my glasses," said Gene as he put them on.

"It's all right, Gene. Things will get better," said Alan as he spoke quietly and comforting to Gene. "Many years ago, Carol told me something her grandmother said about you and I have never forgotten it. She loved you very much, Gene, and she wanted you and Carol to be together forever because she felt there was something very special about you. My sweet Colleen felt the same way. You never partied or drank, and I have never heard you say a cuss word. You are never angry, and you are always so kind to everyone."

As John came to talk to Gene, Carol moved over so he could sit by him. "I would stay with you and help you, but I'm not as strong as the others. But I will always comb your hair and sleep with you to keep you warm because I know you get really cold." Gene embraced John as they both cried.

"You know, Gene, I'm not as good with words or as sentimental as everyone else, but I think you know I would do anything for you. You are a hero to me as you are to everyone else here today, and you always have been," said Mike.

"I love you, Gene," said Terry. "There has always been a special bond between us even before we both had a stroke. I remember in sophomore geometry class, Mr. Kirkland told me to sit by you, Mike, and Carol. He assured me that you three would never make fun of me or bully me. I'm sorry, I can't talk anymore."

Alan and Mike walked with Gene to the bedroom. "We will help you with a shower in the morning," said Alan. "It's been a long day for you. Never forget how much we all love you."

"Where's Carol?" asked Gene.

"She will be here in a minute. We will stay here with you until she is here," said Alan.

When Carol was with him, Alan gently kissed Gene, and Mike hugged him. As they left the room, they both had a concerned look on their face, and Mike touched Carol's hand, and Alan kissed her on the cheek. They all seemed to share the same uncertainty and worry for their friend.

"Gene, can I rub your back and legs to help you relax?" asked Carol.

"Not tonight. You always work so hard for me. Just lie by me and let's talk," said Gene.

This was not like Gene. He seemed to have so little to say lately. She lay by him and kissed him on the lips. Her long hair fell on his bare chest. "I've always thought you are so beautiful. Do you mind that I'm fat and have so many scars and am not good to look at anymore?" asked Gene.

"You are not fat, Gene, you are just a big man, and I love that about you. I don't mind your scars at all because they show that you are a fighter and a survivor," said Carol.

"When we made love, was I any good? Did I satisfy you? Was I the least bit sexy?" asked Gene.

"My dear Gene, sex with you was the best I ever had. No man has ever been able to equal you. You were tender and gentle and yet the sexiest man I have ever been with. And every time we were together, you satisfied me completely," said Carol.

"None of my girlfriends, or at least I considered them my girlfriends, ever seemed to think I was good at sex or even liked me for that matter," said Gene.

"Did you ever think that they might be the problem and not you?" asked Carol.

"I never thought about that," said Gene. "I always like the way you talk to me. I always have ever since I was a little boy."

"I have loved you, Gene, ever since we were small children playing in my grandmother's backyard. I love everything about you, your heart, your mind, your body, your face, your spirit, your kindness, your sweet infectious personality, and the way you have always treated me. I have learned so much from you. You have my respect and admiration for your high standards and the dignified fine man you are and always have been. You possess my heart, and you own it," Carol kissed Gene passionately, and he returned the kiss many times over.

They didn't make love that night, but they were very close to it. Physically, Gene was not quite ready yet, but he knew that if and when he was, Carol would be there for him.

Gene had an appointment with a heart specialist the following day. Carol, Mike, and Alan went with him. The waiting room was crowded. Carol sat by Gene and held his hand. Alan was on the other side of him, and Mike pulled up a chair in front of him. Gene had his little teddy bear on his lap.

A heart specialist once told Gene that he didn't have a very long life expectancy. Dr. Wilson did not approve of the heart doctor saying this to Gene. It definitely did not help his depression or anything else. For that reason, Mike knew this was the one appointment that Gene worried most about.

"Gene, I'll wait out here for you. I don't want to crowd the examining room. Carol and Alan will be with you."

"That's all right, Mike. I'm scared," said Gene.

Mike hugged Gene. "You'll do fine, Gene. It will be over soon."

Carol wiped the tears from Gene's cheeks. There was a small boy and his mother sitting next to Carol. They were with two older people, probably grandparents. When the little boy saw Gene was crying, without a word to his mother, he walked up to Gene and handed him a small brown stuffed dog.

"I want to give you this. It matches your teddy bear. It will make you feel better."

"Thank you," said Gene as he reached a shaking left hand out to accept the little boy's gift. "I'm Gene. What's your name?"

The little boy smiled. "My name's Connor."

When they called Gene's name, Alan pushed Gene's wheelchair through the door as Carol stayed behind for a moment. She went to the little boy and knelt down by him. "You are a very sweet little boy, Connor. That was very nice what you did for my friend. He will think about you and hold that little dog all the while he is being examined."

Connor smiled. "He seems nice, and I'm sorry he is so sad. I like him."

"He is very nice Connor, and I like him too. He has a little boy not much older than you and also a little girl." Carol waved and threw them all a kiss as a she went through the doors to the examining room to be with Gene and Alan.

As Connor went back to reading his book, his mother noticed that Mike was wiping his eyes too. She went to sit by him and put her arms around him and spoke quietly to him.

"Your friend seems very kind. My son sees that. He wouldn't do that for just anyone. Gene seems to be very ill, is he?"

"Yes. He had three strokes, the last one was a massive stroke, and then he had heart surgery, and he has many other problems. He's my best friend, and I love him. I'm worried about him," said Mike.

"I hope he will be all right soon. We will pray for Gene and for all of you," said Connor's mom.

Gene had many tests that day. He was in the doctor's office for over three hours. When they left, the waiting room was empty except for Mike. He knew Gene would be cold and his neck would be bothering him, so Mike got a blanket and pillow from the van. He gently covered Gene's legs with the blanket and put the pillow behind his neck. He noticed Gene was still holding tight to the teddy bear and the dog.

"You had a long wait. I'm sorry," said Gene.

"I'm the one who is sorry for all you had to go through in there. Let's go home," said Mike.

"Do you remember, not too long ago in my office, I told you I had a lot of the same problems as John except I wasn't childlike? As you can see, I'm there now." Gene was holding tight to the two stuffed toys.

Mike hugged his friend as Gene cried. "It's all right, Gene. Hold on to them as long as you need to. John always said it made him feel better."

In the van, Carol sat in the front with Mike, and Alan stayed close to Gene. He hardly ever left Gene's side. Mike stopped and got a takeout order for all of them as well as John and Terry. When they got home, they helped Gene eat a little, but he was so tired. They all helped him get ready for bed.

Carol took Gene's glasses off and cleaned them and dried his eyes and cheeks. She knew that always made him feel loved like it did when John combed his hair and Alan put his arms around him. The one thing that Carol knew for sure about her wonderful Gene was that he liked and needed to be close to her and touch her. Carol did something that night that she hadn't done for quite some time. She found her favorite spot and nestled in the bend of his arm with her head resting gently on the right side of his chest.

GENE AND STELLA SAY GOODBYE

On July 2, 1985, Carol's mother, Stella, entered St. John's Hospice in Springfield, Illinois. She had pancreatic cancer and only a few months or possibly weeks to live.

One evening Carol received an unexpected call from Leon, who had been visiting Gene in Chicago.

"Hello, Carol. It's Leon."

"Hello, Leon. Is Gene all right?" asked Carol.

"Yes, he's fine. He asked me to call you. He wants to come to Springfield to see your mother," said Leon.

"How soon can you come? I would suggest the sooner the better. She doesn't have much time left, and right now she is still conscious and coherent," said Carol.

"Would tomorrow be too soon?" asked Leon.

"She would love the company. You know, she always loved Gene so much. We'll see you tomorrow. Will Alan be with you?" asked Carol.

"Yes. He is very protective of Gene," said Leon. "Terry is also coming with us. Terry doesn't know your mother, but I think he wants to see you."

"It will be good to see all of you," said Carol.

When they arrived in Springfield, they went directly to St. John's Hospice and to Stella's room. Carol was there waiting for them.

"Mom, you have company. These are my friends from high school, Leon and Terry. This is my mom, Stella."

"I remember both of you. I didn't know you well, but I remember you from basketball," said Stella.

"We have brought a friend to see you. We will step out so there are not too many in your room," said Leon.

Leon and Terry both kissed Stella on the cheek.

Gene didn't want Stella to see him in a wheelchair or using crutches. He knew it would worry her. "Carol, if you hold my right arm, and Alan, if you walk on my left side, I think I can make it," said Gene.

"Are you sure you can do this?" asked Alan.

"I'm never sure of anything, but I'm going to try," said Gene. "Alan, please be certain there is a chair close to her bed."

Gene sat in the chair Alan placed by the bed, and Carol stood beside him and held his hand.

"Gene and Alan, it seems like such a long time since I've seen either one of you. How are you, Gene?" asked Stella.

"I'm improving, thanks to Carol and Alan and all those who have helped me," said Gene.

"You look good, Gene. It is so nice of you to come to see me. You were always such a kind boy and man. I always loved you so much," said Stella. "I'm glad to see you too, Alan. How have you been?"

"I'm fine, Stella," said Alan as he walked to the other side of the room and sat down. He would not leave Gene alone, especially with Stella. Even though she was very ill, Alan knew only too well how unpredictable Stella could be.

Gene was wearing a light-blue polo shirt and tan slacks. Stella noticed that his hair was very thick, dark, and so pretty with a sight curl to it. His face and arms looked very pale, not suntanned and ruddy as she remembered him looking. Gene had gained more weight than the last time she saw him. She could tell in his face, waist, and legs, but he was incredibly handsome even more so than when he was young. He even smiled at her, and she noticed the space between his teeth, and she realized that she had never seen him smile before. She noticed his pale-blue eyes behind the thick glasses, but she also noticed the dark circles around and under his eyes and how deep-set they appeared.

He picked up her hand with his slightly trembling left hand and kissed it gently. And his voice was so kind as he spoke to her. She had never heard such a kind voice.

"I just want you to know, Stella, how much your daughter has helped me through everything that has happened to me. She has saved my life more than once. She is a very special girl."

"Carol and I only became friends a few years ago. It took us a long time to get there," said Stella.

"I'm going out and wait with Leon and Terry so you two can talk more freely," said Carol as she kissed Gene on the cheek. "Be good to him, Mom. He came a long distance to see you."

"I would never be anything but good to Gene. He's a wonderful man," said Stella.

"Alan will be here if you get out of line," said Carol as she smiled slightly at Alan.

"Don't worry, I'll behave. Colleen is probably up there watching me too, isn't she, Alan?" asked Stella.

"Quite possibly. She loved both Gene and Carol very much," said Alan. "And you were her best friend."

"I'll tell you something, Gene, your mother, John's mother, Colleen, and Carol's grandmother, they all loved Carol. My mother loved Carol more than she did any of her daughters. She loved you too, Gene, long before I ever knew you," said Stella.

"She was so good to me when I was a sick little boy. Carol, Ethan, and Uncle Ray were all so kind to me. I will never forget their kindness," said Gene.

"You know something, Gene, I'll never forget that day you came to my house in 1975 right before Carol left Kansas City, to say goodbye to Carol and her little baby girl. There was so much I wanted to say and ask both you and Carol that day, but I couldn't. You held that little baby so sweetly, and she was so content and seemed to love you," said Stella.

"Do you want to ask me now? You can ask me anything," said Gene in the kindest, most understanding voice she had ever heard as he continued to hold her hand.

"No, I made a decision a long time ago. I didn't like Carol when she was young, and I didn't like her husband, Greg. And there was this beautiful, sweet little girl. She was nothing like either one of them. She didn't even look like them. I thought she was like you, so good and kind and tender, and she had such a sweet, pretty face. But then when I finally became friends with my daughter and loved her, I realized for the first time that she had all those qualities too," said Stella. "I had never noticed it before when others did. I wasted so much time."

"I've never known anyone quite like Carol. I've loved her since I was eight, and I think she has always loved me," said Gene.

"Then why in the world didn't the two of you end up together?" asked Stella. "You don't have to answer that. It doesn't matter, I didn't end up with my true love either. I guess that is something we have in common."

"Mike and John were my best friends and also Terry. They were all in love with Carol," said Gene. "Did Carol ever tell you how we used to always talk about the future and that I could never see mine? Everyone else could always see their future except me. It was as though I didn't have one. I felt a sense of doom like I didn't have much time left. I always thought I had to do everything in a hurry. Maybe it was the stroke, heart problems, depression, or the concussions. Maybe it's over, but for some reason, I don't think so."

Alan walked up behind Gene and put his arm around him. "Gene, that is getting really dark. Let's not go there," said Alan as he looked at Stella. "Gene had a severe problem with depression after his strokes, heart surgery, and other things we don't always talk about. We need to be careful with him."

"I'm sorry, Gene. You don't have to say anymore. I love you, and I'm glad you came to see me. We started out happy," said Stella.

"I go to dark places, Stella. I always have. I can't help it."

Stella could hear a deep sadness in his voice as well as see it in his eyes.

"I always tell Gene he is like a son to me." Alan hugged Gene and held him tight to him.

"He brings me back from the dark places. Alan and Carol are the only ones who can do that," said Gene.

"You have really nice, thick hair, Gene. It is so pretty." Stella ran her fingers through Gene's hair.

"John likes to comb my hair for me. He likes it too. I used to always smooth his hair down. He said it made him feel loved. I guess he is returning the love." Alan wiped tears from Gene's cheeks. "Thanks, Alan. Stella, did Carol tell you that I cry a lot? I have ever since the strokes."

"No, sweetie. She didn't tell me that," said Stella.

Alan bent down, and Gene put his head on Alan's shoulder. "Everything will be all right, Gene. Don't cry."

"It's fine, Gene. We all love you so much," said Stella.

"My dad died. I think Alan is my new dad," said Gene.

"And he is a very good one too. He takes very good care of you," said Stella.

"I'm embarrassed. You are the one who is sick, Stella. And you are both comforting me. I can't seem to stop crying," said Gene.

"Gene, my dear sweet Gene. It was so nice of you to come see me. I hope you have always known how much I loved you. I just hope you will be completely well soon. You are so young and honest and good, and you have your whole life ahead of you," said Stella.

At one time Carol had opened the door, but when she saw the three of them so close, she shut the door quietly. But she had heard a little, enough to make her sit by Terry and cry on his shoulder.

"What's wrong, Carol? What did they say?" asked Leon.

"I didn't hear much. Just a dying woman talking to a…" Carol paused, "…very kind man."

"You started to say something else, didn't you?" asked Leon.

"You both know what I started to say. I didn't want to say it or even think it," said Carol.

"John thinks Gene is going to die soon," said Terry quietly. "Do you think so too, Carol and Leon?

"No, he's getting better. He's a survivor. He will be well real soon, or at least I hope so."

Leon walked away from them and went to look out the window so no one would see his tears. Leon remembered when he first met Gene in high school. He was a sophomore and Gene was a junior on the basketball team. Some of the other guys were intimidated and jealous of him because he was better than they were, but not Gene, who supported and nurtured him and was always his friend.

Carol put her arms around Terry. "Don't cry, Terry. Leon's right. Gene's going to be fine. You're not going to lose your friend. I can't even imagine what life would be like without Gene a part of it. We all love him so much. That in itself will keep him with us."

Carol and Leon's eyes both met briefly. They knew they shared the same feelings and opinions, but they would keep them locked within their heart, and Carol and Leon, who were usually right, hoped for the love of God that this time they were wrong.

A few days after Gene's visit, Stella lapsed into a coma. She died in the early morning hours of July 29, 1985. Carol knew that Gene's visit had meant more to Stella than all the hours she had spent by her mother's side. But that was all right because it had always pleased Carol when others loved Gene as she did.

CHAPTER

A WINDOW OF TIME AND OPPORTUNITY

In the fall of 1985, Gene had recovered from the strokes and heart operation that nearly took his life. Also, he had almost, but not completely, overcome a heartbreaking bout with depression. Although his physical and mental health conditions were not perfect, the strides he had made were unprecedented. Gene had proved time and again that he was a survivor and a hero which had always been his title in the small group of friends. He was still working at the same advertising agency in Chicago. He had been divorced for several years, and he was the father of two young children who lived with their mother in another state.

Carol was also divorced and raising her daughter alone. Greg's two young sons, whom Carol had loved so much, now lived with their dad also in another state. Carol was still working for the lobbyist in Springfield and frequently traveled to Chicago for meetings and hearings either with her boss or alone.

At this stage in their lives, both Gene and Carol were somewhat jaded by the hand that had been dealt to them and the way their lives had turned out. Neither Gene nor Carol were particularly happy, and although Gene was much better, the hurtful face of depression still occasionally surfaced. He sometimes wondered if he would ever be able to escape it completely.

Mike and John were both married and still living in Kansas City. Mike and his wife had one daughter. John had recently married a woman who was the mother of two daughters and one son, so he was also a father. This had taken them all by surprise.

One warm autumn day in October, 1985, John received an invitation from Mike to fly to Chicago with him for three days. Carol would be there for two meetings but free the rest of the time. And Gene lived and worked there and would be able to take the time off. They would meet that evening at a restaurant they used to frequent on Chicago trips.

They all arrived at the restaurant early and were genuinely happy to see one another. It was rather strange, but even though they were all either married or divorced and had their own families, there was still an unbreakable bond between them that never seemed to change: Mike, always so strong and attempting to protect all his friends; John, always smiling and loving everyone and he didn't have an enemy in the world; Carol, always trying to heal her friends and even without professional training was successful; and Gene, their hero, who gave them courage and hope when he had none of his own.

When they were seated, Mike immediately led the conversation in a certain direction. "So, John, how is your marriage? Does your wife treat you good, or does she find fault with you, like mine does with me?"

"She's nice enough, but I know she doesn't like me being handicapped," said John.

"But she knew that when she married you," said Mike.

"I guess she thought I would get better. She just doesn't understand me," said John quietly.

Carol hugged John. "I'm sorry, John. I wish she understood you better."

"My wife has a lot of complaints about me," said Mike. "She thinks I work too much. She wants more kids, and I don't. And she doesn't like my red hair even though she has red hair too. Figure that one out." Carol hugged Mike as she had John. "You are very affectionate, and you have only had one drink. I've never seen you drink before," Mike paused. "How about you, Gene? Since you and Carol are both divorced, your stories are probably more interesting than mine and John's."

Gene's voice was quiet and reflective, and he sounded different from the Gene they used to know.

"I've had a lot of complaints, girlfriends in college and a girl I almost married. I guess none of them really liked me."

They ordered another round of drinks.

"One didn't like my glasses. She said they were too thick and I needed to get contacts. She thought my eyes were too light, and she talked me into getting brown contacts. They didn't work for me. I couldn't see anything, and they hurt my eyes. All of them hated the space between my teeth, and they said I needed braces. They told me I should smile more, but I was too self-conscious about my teeth, so I never smiled. I gained some weight, and two of them called me fat, and they always tried to make me diet. One thought my hair was to bushy and long and that my body was too hairy. They said my nose was too big, and I needed a nose job, and they didn't like the shape of my face. One didn't like the way I dressed, and she kept buying me clothes I hated. It was all so personal. I always wondered why they even went out with me if they hated everything about me." Gene paused and took a deep breath. "This is making me tired. Is that enough?"

Carol kissed Gene on the cheek. "You know something. All those things they didn't like about you are all the things I love about you."

"You are really nice, and I'm not just saying that because I've had two drinks," said Gene.

"So, Carol, how about you?" asked Mike.

"I'm not sure we have enough time, but you asked for it, so I'll tell you. It started right after we got married. He had three new young guys working for him. We took them out, and he told me to show them a good time and dance with them, so dance I did. We were at a convention in San Diego. When we got to the hotel room that night, he slapped me hard and not just once. He didn't like my clothes and hair. He wanted me to wear tailored suits and have short hair, probably so men wouldn't like me. I wouldn't change for him. He thought I was too friendly. He never wanted me to talk to anyone. He didn't even want me to have girlfriends." A single tear ran down Carol's cheek. John wiped it away and took hold of her hand. "I saw one of the guys I danced with the next day. My face was still red and scratched. He asked me what happened. I didn't answer him, but he knew. He held me in his arms and told me how sorry he was and asked if he could do anything for me. He talked to me and treated me nice like you guys always did."

Gene put his arm around Carol. "And I thought my story was bad. I'm so sorry that happened to you. I wish I could have been there for you."

Mike came over to Carol's side of the table. "I'm sorry too. I didn't know it was that bad."

"So who wins for the worst story this time?" asked Carol. "Who started this anyway?"

"It was me," said Mike. "I'm sorry. I guess it was a little depressing. Well, Carol, I guess you win for the worst story."

"No, not this time. There's another winner tonight," said Carol. "I need to summarize everything, and then I'll tell you who wins."

"Carol, you have had too much to drink. You probably don't remember what we said," John paused. "I wish I had a drink."

"I remember everything, John, and you do need a drink," said Carol as she motioned for the waitress. "Would you please bring him a Shirley Temple and another round of drinks for everyone, except him," said Carol as she hugged Gene. "You shouldn't have any more to drink, right?"

"You're right. That's all I can have with the medicine I take," said Gene.

"I personally feel that my story was not the worst," said Carol. "Now I will speak about each of you three wonderful men. I love you all very much. I'll start with Mike. It is very admirable that you work long hours, especially since I know many of those hours are volunteer work you do for the homeless veterans. It is wise to admit you don't want more children, and she should respect your feelings. And I think your hair is the prettiest color red I have ever seen. John, you will be next."

"This Shirley Temple is really good. Can I have another one, and I bet Gene would like one too," said John.

"It does look good. I'll try one," said Gene as the waitress took John's order.

"John, your handicaps make you the person you are today. Sure, I wish you were hundred-percent perfect, but no one is. If you hadn't been handicapped, we probably would never have met at the graduation rehearsal so long ago. Do you remember after the accident how Gene and I talked to you all the while you were in the coma and how I used to rub your head to make it feel better? You needed us, and we were there for you." Carol reached over and picked up John's bad hand. "It always made me feel special that you wanted me to hold your bad hand. I love your poor, scarred hand, John, just as I do Mike's red hair or the space between Gene's teeth, because it is part of you and always will be."

"You sure talk good, Carol. You make me feel better," said John.

Carol hugged John and took a sip of his drink. "That's good. Do you want a sip of mine?"

"No thanks. I better not," said John.

Then Carol turned to Gene. "You know how I used to say that I always leave you for last because you are the most difficult? You always took that wrong. I never meant you were difficult. I just meant that it is hard to say something about you because it is undoubtedly good, and you won't agree. As I told you, all the things they criticized about you are the very things I love. They make you the person you are today just as John's handicaps make him the person he is now. I've loved you for a very long time, and I have always thought you were the most handsome man I have ever seen." Carol gently touched Gene's cheek and kissed him. "I love the shape of your face and your nose, so strong and bold. Your hair is soft and thick and pretty, and your hairy body is so masculine. I love your mouth, and your lips are full and sexy, and I love to kiss them, and I think your teeth are perfect. I love your gentle, kind, light-blue eyes and your glasses. Don't ever let anyone make you stop wearing them because they are you. As far as them complaining because you have gained some weight, so what? I think you look great. I love everything about you. I always have, and I always will."

"So who is the winner, Carol?" asked Mike.

"The winner is John. You are helping her to raise her children. And there is nothing you can do to change the fact that you are handicapped. You are such a nice guy, John. I wish she was more understanding of you," said Carol.

"I wish she was like you," said John.

"No one is like Carol. She is the one and only," said Mike. "I always looked for reminders of Carol in every girl I met, but I couldn't find anybody like you."

"I love you three guys. You all look really cute tonight," said Carol.

"Carol, you really have had too much to drink. We're not cute anymore, but you're still cute," said John.

"Don't worry, John. I haven't had too much to drink. I'll remember everything about this night forever," said Carol.

"Well, maybe you haven't had too much to drink, but I have," said Mike. "We need to order some food."

When the waitress came, Mike ordered a steak. Gene and Carol ordered salmon.

"I haven't had a steak since the last time I was with you guys," said John.

"Why not?" asked Carol. "You always loved steak."

"I can't cut it, and nobody would ever help me," said John.

"Well, you have three of us to help you tonight," said Carol.

John ordered his first steak in a long time. He also ordered cheesecake, his favorite, for dessert that evening, as did Mike.

When they left the restaurant, Mike and John led the way, as Carol and Gene followed. Carol held tightly to Gene's arm. Earlier when he had asked her a question about something on the menu, she knew his eyes were bothering him, and he was having trouble seeing, as she also knew that the combination of the darkness and bright lights would make it difficult for him. She would not leave his side. There was a quiet look between them as Gene gently kissed Carol's cheek. There were no words spoken; they didn't need to say anything because they both knew each other's thoughts and feelings.

As they slowly walked toward the hotel, they passed an Irish pub.

"This place looks interesting. Let's go in," said Mike.

They all agreed. They sat in a half circle booth with Carol and Gene in the middle and John on the other side of Gene and Mike on the other side of Carol.

"What could I get you tonight?" asked the waitress.

Carol responded quickly, "A Manhattan, a bloody Mary, and two Shirley Temples."

"You know something. Just listening to the way you ordered those drinks makes me realize how much I've missed you," said Mike as he kissed Carol.

"I second that," said John. "You knew just what we wanted."

"Well, it may not be what Gene wants, but it is what he needs to have," said Carol.

"It's a good drink. I actually like it. I never could drink strong drinks or very much," said Gene.

Their waitress was a woman of about forty-five. When she brought the drinks, she said, "I have no idea who gets which drink. Let me see if I can guess." First, she looked at Carol, then John, and then she looked at Mike, then Gene. "You are definitely a bloody Mary girl, and you look really young so I would say you get a Shirley Temple. Because of your red hair, I'm guessing the Manhattan goes to you. That leaves the other Shirley Temple for you."

"That's perfect," said Mike. "You are really good."

"Well, I guess I haven't lost my knack," said the waitress as she walked away.

"She is good," said Gene. "I would never have guessed me as a Shirley Temple guy."

"It was probably just the process of elimination," said Carol.

"I have an idea for a fun game," said Mike. "Let's take turns telling secrets about ourselves. It can be either something serious or funny. I'll start. My first secret is that when we moved out of the house on Lansing Street, I became really depressed and saw a psychiatrist for over a year. All that doctor told me was that I loved you guys all too much and that I was too attached to the house."

"I missed you guys too and the house," said Carol as she hugged Mike. "Now it's my turn. I used to go to Studio 54 in Kansas City and not tell anyone. I liked the way they would motion for me to come to the front of the line. I don't remember its real name. We just called it Studio 54."

"Did you go alone?" asked Gene.

"No, girls from work went with me," said Carol. "They always liked to go with me because of the line, and everyone seemed to know me there."

"I guess I'm next. Carol, when you are with me, I feel secure and as though I can do anything. When we are apart, not so much so." Gene hugged Carol and kissed her gently on the cheek.

Then it was John's turn. "I have a really big secret. When we first met, Carol, I fell in love with you, and I stayed in love with you for a long time, but later it was Gene who I was in love with. What does that mean? Carol knew I was in love with her, but did you ever know I was in love with you, Gene?"

Gene embraced John as he noticed the tears in John's eyes.

"I always knew, John. I think we all did," said Gene quietly.

"Don't cry, John," Carol spoke very gently. "It's all right that you love Gene. I love him too, as does Mike. He deserves to be loved because he is the best man I have ever known." Carol paused. "Mike, it's your turn."

"I felt guilty for Danny's death, but I never admitted it," said Mike. "I thought it was my fault because I should have been able to stop him."

"I did too," said Carol. "My next secret, or maybe it's not a secret at all, is for you, Mike. I miss your mother something terrible. There are so many things I would like to talk to her about. I could confide in her, and I trusted her. She loved us all so much."

"I loved her too. She was a good woman," said Gene. "My next secret is that I was really scared of girls in high school. I didn't want to date because when I did the girl would always be mean to me and not like me, except you, Carol. You were always nice to me, and you never made fun of me. No girl would ever go out with me on a second date. What did I do wrong?"

"You were too serious about your studies and too focused on sports," said Mike.

"You were so much more mature than the girls in that class. You helped me so much," said Carol as she rested her head on Gene's shoulder. "You were my hero then, and you still are today."

"Remember when I told you guys that I haven't had a steak for a long time? Well, tonight was the first time I've had cheesecake in a long time too," said John.

"I hate being a lawyer. I enjoy my volunteer work with the homeless veterans," said Mike.

"I wish I would have accepted the job that Phillip York offered me at the advertising agency where you work, Gene," said Carol. "Big mistake on my part."

"I try hard to lose weight, and most of the time I feel like I'm starving but not tonight. I can be myself with you," said Gene as he took hold of Carol's hand.

"What I miss most, next to you three, is not being able to drive," said John.

"I wish I was back in high school," said Mike. "Things were easier and more fun then."

"Well, it's my turn," said Carol. "I would love to go on one of the white-water rafting trips that you go on, Gene. I think it would be fun and exciting."

"I don't like to swim," said Gene. "I'm a pretty good swimmer, but I'm afraid of water. I wish you could go on the trips in my place, Carol. I don't want to go. I feel as though I'm being forced to go, and to be honest the raft and rapids scare me. I don't see well in the water. I've never been able to."

"The three highlights of my high school years were walking in the graduation processional with Carol, when Gene helped me make a basket in an actual basketball game, and when Mike invited me to go to senior prom with the three of you," said John.

"Remember when I came home from Vietnam and called you guys and asked you to bring some jeans and a T-shirt to the airport so I could change from my uniform? I was more scared in that airport of the people screaming and calling us bad names and throwing rotten food at us than I was in Vietnam being shot at," said Mike.

"That's pretty powerful, Mike. You never talk about Vietnam," said Carol.

"I guess it's something I would just as soon forget," said Mike.

"My next secret is pretty serious too, and it's not actually a secret because Gene and Mike were there although I'm sure they both wished they hadn't been. But it is something I've never forgotten," said Carol. "Gene, I wish I hadn't told Sarah that it was all right to ask you to that dance in high school. She had changed since we were friends, and she was incredibly mean to you, and she hurt your feelings. I am so sorry that happened."

"That was before I knew you guys. What happened?" asked John.

"A week before the dance, Gene hurt his leg in a football game. He was in pain and using crutches. He also had a bad concussion. He had horrible headaches, and his eyes hurt, and he could barely hear. He just got new glasses that were quite strong, and he was having a hard time getting used to them, and he got hearing aids at the same time. Mike drove that night because Gene couldn't. We picked up Terry and David because they didn't have cars or dates. We drove to Sarah's house, and it was hard for Gene, but he walked to her door to get her, and when they came back to the car, and she saw the four of us in the car, she became so nasty. She started with me. She said my hair looked bad and I should wear it up like hers. She messed my hair up, and Gene tried to stop her from doing that. At the dance, she made fun of my clothes, where I lived, and everything about me. She even said she was richer than me, which was, of course, true. And then she said she had a car and I didn't, and she was going to a four-year college and I wasn't. I didn't care what she said about me, but then she started in on Gene. She made fun of his hearing aids, his glasses, and that he was using crutches. That was so much more damaging than any of the things she said to me. A couple of years earlier when we were friends, she was nice. I'm so sorry, Gene. Did you ever forgive me for that?" Carol was crying as Gene put his arms around her.

"I forgave you a long time ago," said Gene.

"I offered to take Sarah home early that night, and I came back for the rest of you," said Mike. "I didn't know what she was going to say next or who she was going to hurt. I had to stop her."

"That is all part of my next secret," said Gene. "I stayed at Mike's house for three days when I got hurt that time because my family was out of town. I didn't want to be alone. Carol, Mike, and Colleen were all worried about me. That concussion really scared me. Remember, Alan came to talk to me, and Colleen made you come with him because she didn't want him to be mean to me. I was so afraid and worried and deeply troubled. I was only sixteen. I knew Alan thought I was a coward and acting like a baby. He was nice because you were with him, Carol, but I knew how he really felt. I wish I had been braver then," said Gene.

"You are and always have been the bravest person I have ever known," said Carol. "Later, Alan loved you so much and took such good care of you."

"I know," said Gene. "He helped save me and cure me right along with you three."

"He treated you like a son as he did John, so I guess that makes us brothers," said Mike. "And my sweet Carol, you were more than a daughter to him. He loved you since you were twelve. He would have done anything for you, for all of us I guess."

"I'm sorry that happened to you, Gene. You always treated everyone so good," John paused. "My next secret is that I wish I lived with Jeremy in California. Do you guys think I could be gay?"

"No, John, you're not gay," said Carol. "You just love everybody, and they, in turn, love you."

"On that, I believe the game is over. I have really had too much to drink now," said Mike.

As they got up to leave, Carol took Gene's hand. She felt so protective of him and wanted to take care of him as she had when he was a little boy.

John was happy because he was with the three people he loved most in the whole world. He always had from the very beginning.

Mike put his arm around Carol, but he still held on to John's arm. Mike wanted so much to see Gene and Carol together forever.

He would do whatever he could for them to make that happen, but he knew it might not be enough. When they arrived at the hotel lobby, both Gene and John needed to sit down for a while. Mike went to get an extra key for their room. Their luggage was already in the room. As they entered their room on the twenty-second floor, they noticed the spectacular view of the Chicago skyline. Carol sat down by Gene on a sofa looking out the window.

"Are you all right, Gene?" asked Carol.

"I'm just tired. I tire easily anymore, and I have very little energy," said Gene.

Carol curled up beside Gene. She wanted to be close to him. He ran his fingers through her hair and kissed her gently and lovingly.

"The way you curl up by me reminds me of when we were sixteen. You haven't changed."

"Oh, but I have changed, so very much," said Carol.

"Maybe, but you still look the same, and you still talk to me kindly and with so much compassion. I miss that and you, so much," said Gene.

"I have to attend a meeting in the morning, but I won't be gone long," said Carol.

"I'll be patiently waiting for you," said Gene.

"Well, guys. I'm definitely tired. I drank more than anyone tonight. I'm going to bed. Good night," said Mike.

"Good night, Mike and John," said Carol.

John was already in bed. "Are you two going to stay up all night?"

"Probably not. I just want to sit here and look at Carol and look out the window for a while," said Gene.

Later in the night, Mike got up. He noticed that Carol and Gene were in the same position on the sofa that they had been earlier. He got a blanket and quietly covered them up. Carol opened her eyes and took Mike's hand. Her voice was almost a whisper as she spoke to him, "He has such a hard time relaxing and going to sleep. I don't want to wake him. I just want to be close to him."

Mike kissed Carol on the forehead and went back to bed. As he lay awake, he felt tears running down his cheeks. He cried silently and couldn't seem to stop. Evidently, John was awake too, because he reached over and took Mike's hand and patted it gently.

In a hotel room high above the streets of Chicago, one of the greatest tragedies of their lives was playing out right before their very eyes. The show was almost over. The curtain was almost drawn. Mike had wanted Gene and Carol to take advantage of the window of time and opportunity that was open to them, but he knew they were not going to be able to do what their hearts wanted.

As Ryan had told Carol over twenty years ago, "Always go with your heart." She hadn't been able to do it then, nor would she be able to do it now.

Together, Carol and Gene were so pure and good and perfect—apart, not so much so. It was as though they needed one another to survive. Gene brought out the good side of Carol, as she did him. Together they could have ruled the world, but alone they couldn't even control their own lives.

Everything had changed, and yet nothing had changed. Carol had always wanted what was best for Gene and to help him. That was all she had ever wanted. And Gene had always wanted to save Carol from the bad people who tried to be part of her life, especially Greg. In their hearts and souls, they both felt that they had failed but maybe not. There had always been something special, different, and beautiful about their relationship.

Mike, John, Mike's dad, and especially Mike's mother, Colleen, had all seen it. Never in all the years Carol and Gene had known one another had there ever been an unkind word between them or criticism or an argument or even a disagreement. They only loved and helped each other.

Gene had saved Carol's life twice, and Colleen had been very much a part of their lives at that time. And Carol, in turn, would save Gene's life, but Colleen was not alive to see that. It was as though she was their guardian angel. Carol had always had that belief ever since Colleen had requested that at her funeral, she wanted Carol to give her farewell speech, and if she was unable to do so, she wanted Gene to. And that was as it happened. Carol spoke until she could not continue, and then Gene stepped in and finished for her.

Love and Passion in the Afternoon

When Carol returned to the hotel from her morning meeting, she saw Mike and John having lunch at a small café in the hotel lobby.

"It looks like you two are having an early lunch. It's only eleven o'clock," said Carol.

"We just had a donut for breakfast. John and I have a few places to go while we are here in Chicago," said Mike.

"Where's Gene?" asked Carol.

"He's in the room," said Mike.

"Gene's waiting for you, Carol. He didn't want to leave. He was afraid he would miss you," said John. "You two look like you are about ready to cry. What's wrong?"

Mike put his arms around Carol, and she buried her face in his chest. "She's just worried. She will be fine." Mike paused and wiped Carol's eyes. "Go to him, Carol. As John said, he's waiting for you."

Without another word, Carol hugged John and waved to them as she headed toward the elevators.

When Carol entered the room, Gene was in the bed covered up. She couldn't tell if he was dressed or not, but it didn't really matter. She began undressing. She hung her clothes over a chair and walked toward Gene.

Gene opened his arms to her, and she eagerly went to him. She got under the covers with him, and their bodies became one.

"You are so beautiful. I've never forgotten your beauty," said Gene. "I imagined you coming to me like this during rough times. It gave me hope and made me want to live."

"You are just as I remember, my sweet, wonderful Gene," said Carol as they kissed passionately and lovingly.

"You don't mind that I've gained too much weight, do you?" asked Gene.

She put her fingers to his lips. "No, my love, a thousand times no. I love everything about you, and you have not gained too much weight. I actually think you look better if that is possible. You are incredibly sexy, and I want you so badly." Carol kissed and touched him everywhere she could. She moved slowly but deliberately. She knew this was his first time since his stroke. She was gentle, kind, and patient because she loved and wanted him so much only to be surpassed by how much he wanted her. They were both uninhibited, and they made love without reservations. Carol moved slowly with Gene. She knew that was the way it had to be. They held nothing back, but they were still careful and tender. They were afraid to let go of one another. They didn't want to stop.

Gene held Carol tight against his body. "You know something, I don't think anyone else could or would do what you have just done for me. I love you so much."

"This has been the best sex I have ever had. There is no one better than you," said Carol.

"I wasn't sure I could do it," said Gene.

"Well, now you know. I think that making love today was even better than when we were in California," said Carol.

"We were just a lot younger then, and we were a little reckless and wild. I was healthy then and in prime physical condition," said Gene.

"It doesn't matter. We are both more seasoned and experienced now. We just have to go a little easy because of your health, but I think that makes it all that much better," said Carol. "Nothing will ever change or diminish what happened in this room today. You are such a great person, Gene. You deserve so much happiness in life."

"Do you think Mike and John know what we are doing this afternoon?" asked Gene.

"I'm pretty sure they know," said Carol. "But it's all right that they know. They both love you so much, Gene."

"They love you too," said Gene.

"But not like they do you. You are their hero as you are mine," said Carol.

"They are both better men than I am. They are still married, and their children live with them. Mike is a lawyer and does so much volunteer work. John now owns the garage where he worked when he was sixteen, and he has several people working for him," said Gene.

"I wish you realized how great you are, but I don't think you ever will," said Carol. "Mike, John, and I have done some good things in our lives but not to the extent to which you have. Of the four of us, Gene, you are the only one who has never done anything wrong. Remember in high school how you graduated with no marks on your record against you. That has continued in life. You are still perfect."

"I am far from perfect," said Gene.

"We think you are perfect, and everyone loves you. They always have," said Carol.

"Do you think we should get dressed before Mike and John come back?" asked Gene.

"I suppose we should. Mike said they would be back about four o'clock," said Carol.

"What time is it now?" asked Gene.

"Four o'clock," answered Carol. "But I'm sure they will be later. Don't worry, Mike will give us plenty of time."

They showered together, and they also found that very stimulating for the passion they were feeling that afternoon. And then in the shower, Gene did something he had never done before. Gene and Carol made love again as they stood close with the water cascading down their bodies. As they left the shower, Carol held tight to Gene. He was doing fine, but she could tell that he was a little weak and needed her support.

They dressed and were sitting on the sofa as close together as they could be when Mike and John knocked on the door a little after five o'clock. Carol went to the door.

"Did you guys forget your key?" asked Carol.

"Oh, here it is in my pocket," said Mike as he smiled at Carol and looked at Gene.

Carol smiled back at Mike, but Gene seemed to be a little embarrassed. Carol sat back down close to Gene. Mike sat on the other side of him and put his arm around him. Mike knew they had to be careful with Gene just as Carol knew. He wasn't the same man he had been a few years ago.

"Are you feeling all right, Gene? Would you like to have some good Italian food tonight?"

"I'm fine. Italian sounds good," said Gene quietly.

John pulled a chair up close to his friends. He was busy telling them about what he had bought that afternoon. Carol and Gene couldn't keep their hands and eyes off one another. Mike knew their afternoon had been exactly what they had wanted and needed as well as what he had wanted for them.

They had decided to take a cab to the Italian restaurant that evening. It was three blocks from the hotel. They knew Gene couldn't walk that far yet. They ordered the same drinks as they had the night before. They all ordered lasagna and a salad. Gene and Carol stayed very close through dinner. The love and passion they felt for one another was very obvious.

"You know, I was thinking," said Mike.

They all looked at Mike. It always scared them when Mike said that he had been thinking. They never knew what to expect.

"Do you have an idea for another game?" asked John.

"No, but we learned a lot about one another last night playing those games," said Mike. "Why don't the four of us take a trip together, maybe next month?"

"And where do you want to go?" asked Gene.

"How about California? We can visit Jeremy in Carmel," said Mike.

"I would love that," said John.

"I thought you would like that," said Mike. "How about you two?"

"Do you think I will do all right on a trip that far? I'm still not hundred-percent, and I don't want to slow you down," said Gene.

"We will be by you every step of the way. I think this trip would be good for all of us but especially for you, Gene," said Mike.

"It would be fun, Mike, just like old times," said Gene, "or then again, maybe not exactly like 1964."

"It's a great idea, Mike," said Carol. "I love being with the three of you. Do you guys know why?

"I think it's because you love us," said John.

"You are right, John," said Carol. "Remember when we went to prom together, I told you I was so happy to be with the three nicest, most handsome guys in the class. I still feel that way. Everything has changed, and yet nothing has changed. We are a little tattered around the edges now, and our dreams have been somewhat disillusioned and damaged, but in our hearts, we are still those same four kids."

"All except me," said Gene. "My heart is pretty messed up right now."

"I'm sorry, Gene. It was a poor choice of words on my part," said Carol. "You know I would never say or do anything to hurt you."

"I know that, Carol," said Gene. "I just hope I am well enough to take a trip, but I don't want you guys to go without me."

That night Carol nestled in the bend of Gene's arm with her head resting gently on his chest.

BITTERSWEET JOURNEY

Exactly one month later they began what was to be their final journey together. It was somewhat bittersweet. They originally were going to make it a road trip reminiscent of 1964 but changed their plans to flying. No matter how careful Gene had tried to be, he had fallen and injured his legs. He was once again using crutches and had the braces on his legs. He was still somewhat weak. Carol would meet Gene in Chicago and fly to Kansas City with him. In Kansas City, Mike, John, Alan, and Terry would join them for the flight to California.

When Mike told Alan and Terry about the trip, especially when they heard Gene was injured, they both wanted to accompany their friends. Alan wanted and needed to be there for Gene. He knew without question that Gene would need them to be close to him.

And Terry wanted to see Carol, even though he knew that her heart belonged to Gene. Terry had no family, and he had loved Carol for a very long time. Terry really didn't have hope for a future with Carol, but that didn't change the love he felt for her. He couldn't change that even if he wanted to. She was the only girl he had ever loved.

Patrick had brought Gene to the airport. When Carol got off the plane from Springfield to board her connecting flight to Kansas City with Gene, she saw Patrick and Gene immediately. Carol bent over and kissed Gene.

"Thanks so much for bringing him, Patrick."

"I'll board with you so I can help him," said Patrick. He had his arm around Gene's shoulders. "He didn't want to use the wheelchair again, but I talked him into it."

Then Gene spoke for the first time. "I probably shouldn't go, but I want to be with you, Carol. I'm so tired of disappointing you and my friends and myself," said Gene.

"Gene, you're not disappointing anyone. Do you think this wheelchair matters to me or to your friends? You fell. It was an accident. It could happen to any one of us. They all just want to see you because they love you," said Carol.

As they announced it was time for the handicapped boarding, Patrick pushed Gene's wheelchair, and Gene held tightly to Carol's hand as they boarded the plane.

Patrick helped Gene get seated in a middle seat near the front of the plane. Carol sat in the window seat.

"Have a good time, you two."

"Thanks so much, Patrick. Thanks for helping Gene," said Carol.

Carol put Gene's seat belt around him as the plane took off. "Please talk to me, Gene. We've been through so much together. We will get through this too."

"Just hug me and hold my hand," said Gene. "That's the only time I feel normal."

"You aren't depressed, are you? Please tell me you're not," asked Carol.

"No, it's different this time. I'm glad I'm not depressed. I don't think I could live through that again. I liked what we had in Chicago. I thought it could be that way again in California, but then I fell," said Gene.

"It can be, and it will be. Don't worry, everything will be fine. I promise you that," said Carol as she kissed him. She comforted him and tried to soothe his nerves through the entire flight. When they arrived in Kansas City and their friends boarded the plane, Gene seemed to be a little better, but Alan noticed right away. He held Gene in his arms and loved him.

"I've missed you, Gene. I love you very much. We are going to have a good time in California," said Alan.

"Will you two stay with me? I will need your help while we are in California. Everything will be new and different, and my eyes are bothering me, and I can't see well. I'm really scared," said Gene quietly.

"I will not leave you. I promise," said Carol. "There's nothing for you to be afraid of. We'll take care of you."

"I'll always be with you when we are outside or in parts of the house you are not familiar with, but I also want you and Carol to have some time alone," said Alan. "Is that all right with you, Gene?"

"That's fine, Alan. I like that idea," said Gene.

Carol kissed Gene on the cheek and rested her head on his shoulder.

Alan talked so kindly and gently to Gene during the entire flight, as did Carol. Alan helped him with his soda and opened his peanuts for him, and Carol cleaned his glasses. It was these little things that seemed important to Gene and made him feel secure, safe, and loved.

At different times during the flight, Mike, John, and Terry all came to talk to Gene and show their love for him. He felt security also in having his five friends with him. They were the same five who had been with him through his bout with depression. They had seen him at his worst. None of them wanted to see him go back to that place again, and they would do all they could to keep him safe.

When the plane landed, they helped Gene to the wheelchair. As they went to get their luggage, the first people they saw were Jeremy and his driver, Marvin. Jeremy greeted Carol and Gene first and then everyone else. He was especially glad to see John as John was to see him.

Terry had never been to California before, and he was overwhelmed by the beauty of the ocean and even more so by the beautiful white house overlooking the ocean. It looked the same as it had over twenty years ago as did Jeremy. It was as though time had stood still. But there was no Ryan. Mike and Carol had loved Ryan so much, and they missed him terribly.

Carlos was still the cook for Jeremy and was thrilled to see all of them, especially Carol. After dinner, they all walked along the beach. Gene did fine, but Carol and Alan walked with him and they held tightly to him. There were places in the sand that made it difficult to walk, especially for Gene.

Everything in the house seemed to be frozen in time, and yet it was all more beautiful than they remembered. On this trip, unlike the first trip to California when they were just kids, there was no question as to who should have which bedroom.

"Gene and Carol, you will have the main floor suite," said Jeremy.

"Thank you," said Carol as she kissed Jeremy.

It had been a long flight, and Carol knew Gene was very tired. He had sat in the wheelchair when they returned from the walk on the beach. As Carol pushed Gene's wheelchair through the door to their suite, they remembered the beauty of it and the magnificent view.

She helped him sit on the edge of the bed and undress. And soon, she was also undressed.

"I'm so tired, but I want to make love to you," said Gene.

Carol sensed the underlying sadness in his voice, and she knew he was worried because of his recent injury.

"Just lie back and relax. I'll help you," said Carol.

She massaged every part of his body gently yet firmly. She pulled him close to her. He could feel her softness and warmth as she caressed him and engulfed him with love and the most fantastic sex he had ever experienced. As he became more relaxed, he was able to return the love and satisfy Carol with the same tenderness and outpouring of sexual gratification that she had given to him. They kissed, held one another tightly, and loved one another that night for a long time. Their love was so true and sincere, and they were so perfect together. They always had been.

The next day they went shopping in Carmel. They all wanted to buy gifts for their children. For lunch they went to a nice restaurant overlooking the ocean. That afternoon, they went out in the boat which put Gene slightly out of his comfort zone. The water was rough, and Gene was unsure of himself getting in and out of the boat. When they got off the boat, Gene was very unsteady on his feet.

That evening Jeremy asked Carol to join him on the balcony. Carol made sure Alan was with Gene before she left him.

"I just wanted to talk to you about Gene," said Jeremy. "Is there anything I can do to help him?"

"Thanks for caring about him, Jeremy. It's going to take time for him to be completely well. The doctors seem to think that time will heal him. They have more or less said that time heals all, but I don't feel that is true in Gene's case. So much has happened to him," said Carol.

"I remember Gene as being so athletic and handsome," said Jeremy. "Now he seems so weak and frail."

"He is," said Carol. "He is so fragile that I'm afraid he could break at any moment. I'm just not sure how much more he can take, especially the depression. That was very hard on him both mentally and physically."

"Alan seems to care a lot about Gene," said Jeremy. "He was always so hard on Ryan and Danny."

"Alan knows it was wrong the way he treated Ryan and Danny as well as Gene. He is trying to make amends for that. Unfortunately, it's too late for Ryan and Danny. Oh, Jeremy, I loved them both so much," said Carol.

"But he seems to be doing well by Gene," said Jeremy.

"Alan is very protective of Gene, some think a little too much so, but when Gene was so severely depressed, he needed Alan and me with him constantly. He was so afraid of falling, mostly because he didn't want to cause more injury, but also he is so tall, and he is such a big man that he knew it would be hard for us to get him up," said Carol. "Alan is so gentle and caring to Gene now, but he wasn't always that way. He was very cruel to Gene when he was just a boy. He was only sixteen. Gene had a bad concussion and injured his leg in a football game, and he was staying with Mike, and Alan didn't want him there. Gene was scared and alone and in extreme pain. Alan was so mean to him, and now he is dedicated to making up for past actions by being kind to Gene, John, and also Terry. Because Gene's problems have been so severe, Alan has tried to help him the most. Since the strokes, Gene has improved three times to where he was able to walk unassisted, but he always has a setback. He has just had a really hard time, and we all love him so much. He is an exceptionally good man."

"Always know that I would do anything for Gene and for you," said Jeremy. "You mentioned earlier that you and Mike loved Ryan very much. Ryan, of course, loved Mike. He was his little brother. But he also loved you and Gene. Maybe he had a premonition because he told me if Gene ever needed anything, he wanted me to help him. I only wish I could."

"I wish you could too, Jeremy, just as I wish I could," said Carol. "It is very kind of you to want to help Gene and me. I don't know what to say. You are wonderful man."

"I remember when I first met Gene over twenty years ago. He was only eighteen but so strong and quiet and dignified. He seemed older than you, John, and Mike. John seemed so young and immature, and Gene took such good care of him. Gene was so serious and such a gentleman. I could easily see why you loved him. You were so pretty, and you still are, and I could tell that he loved you," Jeremy paused. "Is he dying? Please tell me that I'm wrong."

Carol walked to the railing around the balcony and leaned against it as she looked out over the ocean. "Probably. With so many problems, I doubt that he will live to be very old or even to see his children grow up. His heart is not very strong. A cardiac specialist told Gene that he doesn't have a very long life expectancy. I think you see what I do."

"He just seems so sad and lost. I feel so bad for him," said Jeremy.

"I know what you mean. All his problems hide the real person that he is, but we know he is still that same wonderful man inside," said Carol.

Terry came out on the balcony and sat by Jeremy as Carol continued to look out over the ocean.

"So how do you like it here in California, Terry?" asked Jeremy.

"I love it. It would be nice to live here," said Terry.

"That's what I thought twenty years ago," said Carol. "Everything would have been so different if Gene and I had stayed here."

"But then I wouldn't have gotten to know you and Gene," said Terry.

She didn't turn to face them. She didn't want them to see her tears, but they knew she was crying. When Carol composed herself, she went to sit between Jeremy and Terry on the glider.

"Jeremy and Terry, I am so glad that you both are part of my life as well as Gene's. We love you both very much. I feel secure here in this beautiful house with all of you guys because you love and care about Gene as I do. You help me with Gene, and he needs each of you. Jeremy, you and Ryan were such a great couple. I wish the two of you could have had a longer time together and had a family like you wanted. Ryan was one of the best friends I have ever had. I loved him so much as did Mike. We think about him every day and talk about him often." Carol took hold of Terry's hand. "And my dear, sweet Terry, I fell in love with you in English class in high school. You were so kind and gentle. I loved you at the homeless camp in Kansas City when you were so protective of me. I loved you as John's companion after his surgery and how you took such good care of him. I loved you when you never left Gene's side during John's motivational speaking tour. I loved you when you and Leon brought Gene to see my dying mother, and I assure you, so did she. And I know how much you love both Gene and me," said Carol.

There was nothing left to say. Carol had said it all. Together they walked back into the house where the others were. Alan had his arm around Gene and was talking quietly to him. John was sitting on the other side of Gene, holding his hand.

"Carol, look at Gene's hair. Do you like it? I combed and styled it for him. I think it looks really nice," said John.

"You did a good job, John. It looks great. And, Gene, I think you have the best and thickest hair I have ever seen," said Carol as she kissed Gene.

"John, when I die will you comb my hair, so it doesn't look too bad when I'm in my casket?" asked Gene.

John hesitated for a moment. "Sure, Gene, I can do that for you." John moved over. "Sit here, Carol. You need to be by Gene."

"I'm sorry, everyone. I guess that was a little dark." Gene put his arm around Carol and kissed her on the cheek.

There was so much love in the room at that moment. If love alone could heal, Gene would have been completely well that very day.

Gene held tight to Alan's hand. Alan knew Gene had started to go to a dark place, and he needed to keep him from returning.

Carol gently touched Gene's cheek. "Are you feeling all right, Gene? You look a little pale," said Carol.

"My legs hurt, and I can't see well," said Gene.

Alan wiped the tears from Gene's cheeks as Carol took his glasses off and cleaned them.

"Don't cry, Gene. We all love you so much. Jeremy asked me if there is anything that he can do to help you. We all want you to be happy and well," said Carol.

Carlos prepared a delicious meal that evening. He had a particular fondness for both Carol and Gene. They were so polite and treated him so kindly. He was very attentive to them and to their needs. He always wanted to make sure that what he prepared was something Gene liked and would be able to eat. Alan and Carol helped Gene that evening as they always did by cutting his food and feeding him.

"Why is my right hand not working today? It's so weak," asked Gene.

"You just aren't completely well yet, Gene. You have a little more healing coming your way," said Carol.

"You're doing fine. We are all here to help you whenever you need us," said Alan.

"I was doing better a month ago," said Gene. "And then I fell."

Alan smoothed Gene's hair back. "Do you have any idea how proud we are of you and of how far you've come?"

"I love all of you, and I thank you for what you have done for me," said Gene.

"Excuse me. I'll be back in a minute," said Carol as she got up and went to the kitchen.

Mike could tell she was about ready to cry as he followed her.

Gene couldn't take his eyes off the door Carol had gone through. He became nervous and impatient when she left him if only for a few minutes.

"Don't worry, Gene. She will be right back," said Alan.

"She was going to cry. I made her cry. Mike doesn't like it when Carol cries," said Gene.

"That's why he went with her. He will take care of her. Don't worry, Gene," said Alan. "Carol will be fine. She just gets a little emotional where you are concerned because she loves you so much."

In the kitchen, Carlos brought Carol a glass of water.

Mike comforted her, "Don't cry, Carol. Gene isn't depressed. He is just confused. He can't understand why he keeps having setbacks. He will heal. He just needs time."

"But I'm not sure if he will have time, Mike. He might not have much time left," said Carol.

"Just love him, Carol. Whatever you do, don't stop loving him," said Mike.

"I couldn't stop loving him if I wanted to. He is very much a part of me," said Carol.

When they went back to where everyone else was, Gene seemed relieved to see Carol, and he greeted her as though she had been gone for a long time.

Carlos served dessert which was cheesecake, and John's eyes got very big. "I heard a rumor that someone here really likes cheesecake," said Carlos as he set a piece in front of John.

"That would be me," said John as he smiled at Carlos.

That night as Carol lay beside Gene in bed, she knew what she had to do as well as what she wanted to do. She knew he was in pain, and she had to be very careful. She began by kissing and touching Gene ever so gently. Each action on her part was done precisely and with the utmost care and love. Her goal was to make him feel loved, worthy, and satisfied, and she would accomplish that. She spoke quietly and kindly to him in the way he had always liked. She held nothing back; she was fully aware that tonight he was more sensitive and fragile than he had been the other times they had made love since his stroke. That night he loved everything she did to him, and as much as he was able, he also participated.

A few days later, they left the house overlooking the ocean and Jeremy. They would all return to their separate lives and try to live as normally as possible. Alan would go to Chicago and stay with Gene. He knew he was needed as was Carol. Although Carol had to return to her family and job, she wouldn't be able to stay away from Gene for very long. It had been a bittersweet journey for all of them, and it was their last journey together.

The love between Carol and Gene was real and beautiful, and it would last forever, but for them forever was not to be very long.

THE LETTER AND THE PHONE CALL

As Carol arrived home from work on Saturday, August 8, 1987, a date that would be embedded in her memory and heart forever, she grabbed a large stack of mail from the mailbox.

Her Aunt Martha was living with her at the time. As Carol walked into the living room, Aunt Martha said, "Mike McVary called about an hour ago. I wrote his number down this time. He called yesterday, but I forgot to tell you. I didn't get his number then. I'm sorry."

"I'll call him now. Here's the mail. You can go through it," said Carol.

Mike and Carol seldom talked on the phone. As she walked toward the phone, she could feel her heart beating fast. It was foolish to try to guess, but the first three times she dialed the phone, she hung up before she completed the number as if that would make any difference. Then she dialed the number again, this time completing it, but she already knew why he was calling.

Mike answered the phone on the first ring as though he was waiting for her call.

"Hello, Mike. It's Carol. My aunt forgot to tell me you called."

"There's no easy way to say this, but you probably already know. You always knew everything where Gene was concerned," said Mike as his voice broke, and she knew he was fighting back tears.

"Gene is dead, isn't he? What happened to him?" asked Carol.

"He was killed in a white-water rafting accident in British Columbia. A group of eleven were on a work-related trip. Five of them died when the raft overturned," said Mike.

For a moment Carol couldn't speak. She wasn't crying. She knew that would come later. "Gene was such a good man. He went through so much in his life. He shouldn't have been on a trip like that. He didn't even like to swim."

"I know, but he always liked adventure, and he was a risk-taker." Mike paused. "Two others from the same advertising agency where Gene worked also died in the accident, Patrick Monohan and Phillip York."

"They were good men too. I knew them both well. Patrick was always so helpful to Gene and Phillip was the one who interviewed me and wanted to hire me. He retired a few years ago. He was always so kind to Gene," said Carol.

"George Meyer was on the raft too. He survived," said Mike.

"Three good men died, and a bad man lived. Just for the record, I tried to forgive him for what he did to Gene, but I never could," said Carol.

"I never could either," said Mike. "The funeral was yesterday. We didn't know in time to attend. I feel really bad about that."

"I do too, Mike. We should have been there," said Carol. "How's John and your dad?"

"Everyone seems quiet and sad but not really shocked. It is almost as though they were expecting it, just not the way it happened," said Mike. "John is upset because he promised Gene that he would comb his hair when he died so it wouldn't look bad. I tried to explain to him that it would probably be a closed casket, but I don't think he understood."

"I remember when he made that promise to Gene. I thought at the time that it was the saddest thing I had ever heard, until today." Carol paused to compose herself as much as she could. "Oh, God, Mike, I wish I could have saved him."

"You did save him many times," said Mike.

"But not when it mattered," said Carol. "I'll always love him."

"I know. I love him too. It hurts me to know that I'm one of the reasons the two of you never ended up together," said Mike. "If you two had been together, he would still be alive."

"It was no one's fault, Mike. Remember, I'm the one who got married first. We had a window of time and opportunity open to us in 1985. You told me then what to do, and I didn't do it. I think we just loved one another too much, but it's all over now. I had better go now, Mike. I think I'm going to cry, and you know how you always hated it when I cried. It got so we used to laugh about that, but no one is laughing now. Call me once a week, for a while at least, if your wife doesn't mind," said Carol.

"She doesn't mind. I'll call you," said Mike.

And thus the conversation that they had never wanted to have ended. As Carol walked toward her bedroom, Aunt Martha handed her a stack of mail. The letter on top was from Janice, her friend from high school.

She hadn't talked to Janice since the last class reunion in 1984 when Gene was so sick. Inside the envelope there was another sealed envelope with a note written on it:

Dear Carol,

I am sorry to be sending this to you, but I knew you would want to know.

Love always,
Janice

Carol slowly opened the envelope. In it was a death notice and a newspaper article about the white-water rafting accident that had killed Gene.

Carol cried a lot that night and would many times in the future, quite possibly forever. She was crying for what was and for what never would be. She cried for Gene who had loved her so much and so passionately as she did him. She cried for herself and how much she missed Gene and would now miss him for eternity. She thought of Gene and of what life could have been with him even though she had always known they were not destined to be together.

She remembered how they could talk for hours about everything and nothing. She remembered her favorite spot nestled in the bend of his arm with her head resting on his chest. She remembered every moment she had spent with Gene as though it had happened yesterday.

THE REUNION
(TWENTY-FIVE YEARS)

When it was time for the next class reunion, which was twenty-five years, it was 1989. The four friends no longer existed, and any intrigue or interest they had once aroused and evoked in others had diminished. Gene had been dead for two years, which was still almost unbearable for the three remaining members of the elite group to even think about. There were still occasional, but somewhat limited, telephone conversations between Carol, Mike, and John.

Mike was still married to the girl from his law school class named Carol, and they had one daughter. His work as a lawyer provided less satisfaction to him than the work he did for the homeless veterans.

Carol had been divorced for several years and had not remarried. Her job working for the lobbyist in Springfield was an interesting, challenging job, but she no longer traveled to Chicago.

John was married and helping his wife raise her children. He still owned the garage where he had once worked as a mechanic, but he no longer kept in touch with them. This was strange, because of all of them, he was always the one who was interested in talking with them and knowing what was going on in their lives.

Carol received a call late one evening from Janice, her old friend from high school.

"I don't know how they talked me into being in charge of the reunion again, but I am. You are the very first person I've called," said Janice.

"And why do I get that honor?" asked Carol.

"The committee wants to do a tribute to Gene. They want you, Mike, and John to speak," said Janice.

Carol had no idea how to respond. "I actually wasn't planning to attend."

"Maybe the fact that the committee wants you to do it will change your mind. I think Gene would want you to do it. He would be proud of you. You were always such a great speaker," said Janice.

"The key word in that statement is *were*. I haven't spoken in public for years," said Carol.

"I haven't talked to Mike and John yet. I'll let you know if they agree to speak. The three of you knew him better than anyone else," said Janice.

"But what about his basketball and football teammates? There was a strong brotherhood between them. And the group of neighborhood boys that he basically went all through school with. They knew him really well," said Carol.

"Not as well as you, Carol. You knew him better than anyone," said Janice.

"We never even dated in high school. We were just friends. I stayed loyal to Richard even though he was in Vietnam. Richard wanted Gene, Mike, and me to go to school events together. He asked them to take care of me, and he didn't want us to miss out on everything," said Carol.

"Carol, you don't have to justify anything with me. It's been twenty-five years, but there was definitely a chemistry between you and Gene," said Janice. "Gene was a great guy. Everyone loved him."

As Carol hung up the phone, her emotions became overwhelming. She thought of the last reunion five years ago when Gene was so sick. And now he had been gone for two years. She didn't know if she would be able to do it or not. But if she did, the speech was already written. It had been written over and over again in her mind as well as in her heart. Carol knew that anything she said about Gene would come directly from her heart.

The following day at work, Carol received one of the calls she was expecting. It was Mike, but his voice lacked the joy and enthusiasm it used to have when he talked to her.

"I hadn't planned to go to the reunion, but since they want us to speak about Gene, I guess I will," said Mike hesitantly.

"I feel the same way. I just hope I can do it," said Carol.

"John called me last night. He feels pretty much the same way we do," said Mike.

"I haven't heard from John for a very long time. How is he doing?" asked Carol.

"You never really know for sure with John. He still goes by to see my dad occasionally." Mike's voice broke. "He said he would call you soon."

That evening, Carol's phone did ring, and it was John.

"I probably shouldn't be calling you at home. I didn't think," said John.

"It doesn't matter. You can call me here anytime. It's just me and Julie now. Do you remember Julie?" asked Carol.

"Yes, she was a very sweet, kind, beautiful little girl, just like her mother. How old is she now?" asked John.

"She's almost fourteen. She is a very good student and on the swim team. I'm very proud of her," said Carol.

"And rightly so," John paused. "So they want us to speak about Gene. I don't really speak publicly anymore since I did the motivational speaking. The only reason I was able to do that was because you, Gene, and Mike were with me and helped me. I wanted to be successful and make you three proud of me. And I was talking about my handicaps. That was easy for me. I don't know if I can speak in front of my former classmates. They never liked me very well. Remember, it was Gene who gave my graduation speech."

"Yes, and it was a very good speech. And, John, we have always been proud of you and everything you have accomplished and overcome." Carol had to stop to compose herself and wipe her tears. "I don't know if I will even be able to get the words out, speaking in front of that group, but I suppose I will try. What's wrong, John? Your voice sounds so different."

"We all know that Gene wasn't the one who should die first. It should have been me. I'm no good to anyone, and I never have been." John's voice was shaking.

"My dear John, we can't make the decision as to who dies first. We are alive, and we need to make Gene proud of us. Please never forget all that we have had together as well as all that we have been through," said Carol.

"I'll work on a speech tonight," said John. "I loved Gene a whole lot, and when I told him I would give him my heart, I was serious. I would have done that for him."

"I knew you were serious the minute you said it. And I loved him too, John. I think of him every day, and I always will. I still can see him sitting on my grandmother's lap when he only eight years old and everything that has happened since then, be it good or bad," said Carol.

"I have to go now, Carol, because I'm crying too much. I can't talk anymore right now," said John.

And with that, their conversation was over. Carol would work on her speech that night also. She knew what she wanted to say, speaking from her heart, but the piece of paper in front of her was blank and would remain so.

When Carol went to Kansas City for the reunion, there was no Gene sitting beside her on the plane, and there were no Mike and John picking her up at the airport. She took a cab to the hotel and realized she had never felt so alone in her whole life.

As Carol entered the conference room that evening where the reunion was being held, she didn't immediately recognize anyone. What she noticed first were the many pictures of Gene, and she could feel her heart breaking all over again. Then she saw Janice walking toward her.

"Hi, Janice. I don't feel like I know any of these people anymore," said Carol.

"There are a couple of guys over at the table near the podium that I think you will recognize," said Janice. "Thank you for agreeing to do this. I know it won't be easy."

Carol looked across the crowd and saw Mike and John. When she got to the table, Mike, his wife, and John stood up. There were no hugs and kisses in their greetings. They all seemed very unsure of themselves, and they needed the person with them who would never be with them again, and that person, of course, was Gene.

"Hello, Carol. This is my wife. Her name is also Carol," said Mike.

Mike's wife extended her hand. "I'm glad to meet you. I've heard so much about you."

"And that could be good or bad," said Carol.

"It's all good," said Mike's wife.

"Hello, John. It's good to see you," said Carol.

John's voice was very quiet, and he seemed nervous. "I don't think I'm going to be able to do this tonight."

"Don't feel bad. I speak in front of people all day, and I'm not sure I can do it either," said Mike.

"I don't have a speech prepared. It will just come from here." Carol put her hand to her heart. "John, just pretend like you are giving one of your motivational speeches."

"But Gene was always with me then, and he would help me if I forgot a word, and you would too. Now you won't be able to help me because you don't know what I'm going to say," said John.

The table of four tried to make small talk, but it wasn't working. Roy, who was MC of the reunion, stopped by their table.

"I hope you guys are ready for this. We'll show a short film, and then we would like for you to speak first, Carol."

"You know, Roy, this is kind of hard on us," said Mike.

"Just remember that what you are doing is for Gene," said Roy.

The lights were dimmed. The film began with a multitude of sports footage. Gene was spectacular on the football field and on the basketball court. He was a great quarterback. Then there was footage of Gene as class president and the passing of the robe to the junior class president. Carol was fine until it showed the alternative senior prom with Gene being crowned king and Carol his queen. It showed them dancing, and it showed Carol giving her crown to Bonnie and then Gene and Bonnie dancing.

"I didn't even know they filmed that. No one even acknowledged that prom." As the lights came on, Carol was wiping her eyes, but she got up and walked to the podium.

As she did so, she could hear Mike quietly saying, "You can do it."

"Good evening, everyone. I'm Carol Sullivan Martin. I'm sorry. I wasn't expecting this to be so difficult." All eyes were on her, especially those at her table. She began her unrehearsed speech. "The montage was very good. I remember everything as though it happened yesterday. Gene was my best friend, along with these two guys sitting right here, Mike and John." She nodded toward their table. "Gene was an exceptionally good person. He would do anything for you. He helped me so much, and he saved me many times. He was gentle and kind, and never in all the years I knew him did he ever hurt my feelings or say an unkind word to me. When I heard how Gene died, I was devastated but not completely surprised. He lived life fast and as though there was no tomorrow. He took many risks, and he was slightly wild and uninhibited. He tackled life, sports, and adventure with reckless abandonment, and this is part of what made him so great. Gene was always genuine and honest, and he never gave up. After graduation in 1964, Gene went through a lot of really bad times, and Mike, John, and I, as well as Mike's dad, Alan, were there for him." Carol's voice broke, and she wiped away a tear or two, but she continued, "If there is someone you love very much or someone who has helped you and cared for you, always tell them how much they mean to you and how grateful you are to them before they die. I am glad I was able to do this with Gene. I cannot think of Gene or say his name without crying. There's nothing I can do about this, and I wouldn't change it if I could. My tears are my tribute to him. I loved Gene with all my heart, and I miss him so much, and I think about him every day."

Carol sat down, and Mike approached the podium.

"I'm Mike McVary, and Gene was my best friend since we were fifteen. We went through a lot together. I miss him. I miss the four of us together." There was a long pause. Mike was crying, and he was dying up there alone. He looked at Carol, and she knew what she had to do. Carol stood up, she helped John up, and together they walked to the podium to stand by Mike. Carol stood in the middle of her two friends, holding their arms, as she motioned for John to speak.

John spoke in a clear, strong voice, "My name is John Kelley. Most of you here tonight probably don't remember me. Gene gave my speech at graduation. He told my story, and I will forever be grateful to him for that. After that, he didn't want to speak publicly again, but there were times when he had to. When I was twenty-three, a roof covered with ice and snow fell on me. I was in a coma for a long time." John stopped speaking.

Roy came to him and asked if he needed a chair. John said he would be all right. He just needed a minute. He continued talking very slowly as Carol held his hand tightly.

"Gene, Carol, and Mike brought me back from the brink of death. They talked to me while I was in the coma, and they taught me how to talk again and how to write with my left hand. Gene and Mike went to the garage where I was working when the accident happened. They hauled all the debris away and chopped at the ice and snow until all the blood was gone. Gene didn't want my mother and sisters to see it." That was all John could say. Carol put her arms around both of them, and they walked back to their seats.

The audience clapped, and as with Gene's graduation speech twenty-five years earlier, there wasn't a dry eye in the house. Carol remembered how she used to talk to Gene for hours about everything and nothing. Tonight it had taken everything she had to give a short speech about her dear friend. It was as though she had used all her words and she had nothing left to say.

It was Mike's wife who broke the awkward silence. "Why don't the three of you just stay here or go somewhere private. I'm going to leave. I know you have so much you want and need to talk about."

"That's not necessary," said Carol. "I thought I might take a red-eye flight back to Chicago tonight. We've done what we came here to do."

"I guess we could vote," said Mike. They all remembered that Mike always liked to vote. The vote was 2 to 1 to stay and talk. "I'm sorry, Carol. You lost, so I guess you'll be staying over."

As Mike's Carol got up to leave, she hugged Carol and said, "Thank you for taking such good care of three wonderful guys. I never met Gene. I wish I had known him, because I know he must have been a very special man. You are a wonderful woman. I understand why Mike still loves you so much." With this final statement, Mike's Carol left.

After a moment of silence, Mike stood up and took Carol's hand as Carol reached for John's arm. They stopped and looked at Gene's pictures one last time, and then they walked down the hall. Carol opened the door to her room. They walked in and shut the door behind them. As Carol sat down, Mike and John sat beside her. It was good to be alone with just themselves.

"Carol and John, I'm sure Gene would have been proud of you, but not so proud of me," said Mike. "I couldn't even give the speech I had planned."

"It's all right, Mike. You were with us. That's all that matters," said Carol.

"I didn't keep my promise to Gene. I didn't get to comb his hair for him when he was in his casket, and I promised him I would. Mike thinks that Gene's casket was closed. Do you know for sure, Carol? I really need to know," asked John.

"I'll find out for you, John. I'll let you know," said Carol. "I understand why you need to know. It's all a part of closure. I have no closure with Gene's death either. I miss him so much. I just wish I could have talked to him one more time."

"Was there something in particular that you wanted to say to him?" asked Mike.

"We shared so much and many of the same memories. I knew him almost all my life. It is as though I can't go on, because I can't let go of what we shared and my memories of him and my love for him. I don't know what to do," said Carol through her tears.

"Do you guys remember when we were telling our secrets when we were in that Irish pub in Chicago?" asked John. "I said my best memories of high school were when I walked in the graduation processional with Carol, when Mike invited me to go to senior prom with him, you, Carol, and Gene, and when Gene helped me make a basket in an actual basketball game. There's one more, and that was when Gene gave my speech at graduation. He did a really good job."

"Gene was a great speaker. There has never been anyone better than him. Everyone loved him whenever he spoke," said Carol. "I can still hear his voice. It is as though he is in this room with us and always will be. He lives in our hearts and souls and watches over us. I have always felt that knowing Gene made me a better person. We loved one another forever, but our forever was not long enough."

A New Job, Old Memories

In 1993, Carol was working in the Pathology Department of a large hospital in Springfield, the city that had become her home after leaving Kansas City. The pathologists would teach at the nearby medical school. The second-year medical students were required to take pathology. On the first day of their sophomore year, the students met in the auditorium at the school. Carol was there with handouts and books for the students.

One of the last students to leave the auditorium that day was a handsome, tall young man with curly blond hair. He had a pleasant, kind smile as he spoke to Carol.

"You probably don't remember me, do you?" asked the young man.

She studied him for a moment and then said, "I believe I do. You look just like your father, don't you?"

"People have told me that," said the young man.

"You're Billy Landis. You were only ten when I last saw you. Do you still go by Billy?" asked Carol.

Billy said, "Yes, my dad always called me Billy. I guess I'll always be Billy."

"And your mom and dad, how are they?" asked Carol.

"Mom is fine. She still lives in Chicago." Billy paused, and his smile faded somewhat. "Dad died of cancer three years ago. He didn't live to see me get into medical school."

"I'm so sorry. He was a fine man, a great doctor, and so kind," said Carol.

"I recognized you immediately. I have never forgotten that day on the plane or any of the people involved. I had so much respect for my dad that day. That was the day I decided to become a doctor just like him. And Gene was so brave and so kind to me. Dad told me how you worked with Gene. He credited you with saving his life," said Billy.

"No, it was your dad who saved him. I just loved him." Carol wiped a tear from her cheek. "Do you know what happened to Gene?"

"Yes, we were all devastated. There was an article about that accident in many newspapers in the United States as well as Canada," said Billy.

Carol spoke quietly. And Billy was acutely aware of the sadness in her voice.

"When I heard Gene had died such a horrible violent death, I was so sad and I cried so much, but as I thought about the way he died, I wasn't surprised. He died as he had lived, fast and as though there was no tomorrow. He was always willing to take a risk, and he did things that others were afraid to try. He always welcomed a challenge, and he had many of them."

"I thought you and Gene were so much in love," said Billy.

"We were, and we always had been. Someone told me once to go with my heart, but I never did that," said Carol. "I wish I had. Maybe life would have turned out differently for Gene and for me."

"Are you still married to Greg?" asked Billy.

"No. We were divorced years ago. I never remarried," said Carol.

"And John and Mike, where are they now?" asked Billy.

"As far as I know, they still live in Kansas City. You remember names really well," said Carol.

"I remember everything about that day in that plane and all the people involved. There was so much that impressed me. I was always glad that I told my dad how much that day meant to me before he died," said Billy. "My goal as a doctor is to work with stroke victims, mostly because of Gene."

Carol hugged Billy as they sat down in the empty auditorium.

"All the passengers waiting in that crowded boarding area could see and hear everything that was happening with you, Gene, Mike, and John that day. I saw Holly go to help you and then both Brian and Holly went to help John. They didn't want him to be alone," said Billy.

"They stayed with us through it all as did your dad and you too, Billy. Gene loved your visits when he was in the hospital." Carol paused. "Gene loved children. I'm sure he was a great father. He had two small children when he died."

"I didn't know Gene had ever been married," said Billy.

"He had been divorced for about five years," said Carol. "I remember that you were so considerate for a little boy of only ten. You picked up Gene's water bottle when he dropped it, and you told him you didn't mind if he reclined his seat as much as he wanted to because you wanted to help too. Your dad calmed him and treated him so good."

Carol and Billy talked for a long time that day about Billy's dad and about Gene and how much they had loved them and that they would miss then forever and that they would remember them always.

THE TRIBUTE

Carol could see the bright lights of Fairyland Park and the darkness of Grandview Beach. She could hear the cheers as Gene entered the football stadium or the basketball court. She remembered everything as though it had happened yesterday when in all reality it had happened more than fifty years ago.

"It is so strange, but I see faces from the past. I see them all the time. It is not disturbing but kind of wonderful," said Carol.

"You know, I don't see well anymore even in my memory. Will you tell me about them?" asked John.

"I'm not quite sure how to explain it. Even though they seem so real, I know they are not actually there. It is always good people, those I've loved," said Carol.

John put his arm around Carol. "You know I've always loved to hear your voice. I've missed it for so long. Paint me a picture that I can visualize in my mind. Would you do that for me?"

"I'll try," said Carol. "The first person I ever saw was Danny, Mike's little brother. I saw him as a little boy holding his mother's hand at the Christmas party in 1958, and then I saw him sitting on the corner of my desk in the little office Mr. Chambers let us use at the high school. I saw him playing the trombone in the school band, and I could see him always looking up to Mike, not just because he was small and Mike was tall, but because he worshipped Mike. And then in a flash, he is gone. I never see the ending, the really bad part."

"But you remember the ending, right?" asked John.

"Yes, every second of it. But it's not with the other visions of him. It is as though it is in a separate compartment that I don't have to always open," said Carol.

"What about someone I know?" asked John.

"That would be Alan McVary. I see him dressed as Santa Claus giving me my first Christmas gift. I see all the things he did for us, all of us, but especially you and Gene. I think you two replaced the sons he lost, and he loved both of you so much. I see him sitting by you in the hospital after the accident. He was so worried about you. And after you went home to our house on Lansing Street, he would come there and stay with you after Gene and I returned to work. Do you remember?" Carol paused.

"I remember," said John. "I never understood why he loved me so much, but I knew he did."

"And when Gene was so sick, he never left his side," said Carol. "He took such good care of him, and he was so kind, gentle, and patient with him. He wanted to make it up to Gene for treating him badly when he was just a boy."

"I believe he succeeded," said John.

"I see Ryan and Jeremy in that beautiful house in California. They both loved you also, John, especially Jeremy. I think he would have done anything for you," said Carol. "They always tried to make things so good for all of us, and they certainly did so."

"I think some of my fondest memories are of California and Ryan and Jeremy and you in California. I think you really liked it there," said John.

"I would have stayed if anyone would have asked me to. I loved it that much." Carol paused to wipe a tear. "I see Colleen McVary and my mom going to the movies, shopping downtown, and taking trips together. They looked pretty, and they would have their arms around one another, and they were always smiling and laughing. That is the only time I remember seeing my mother laugh. I felt glad that she was happy." Carol paused again. "I see your mother smiling whenever she looked at you. She loved you so much. I see your sisters at Fairyland Park. They had fun that day."

"I think we all did," said John.

"Gene and I knew how hard that day was for you, but you never complained." Carol wiped a tear from John's cheek.

"The girls had so much fun. Mike was like one of the kids that day," said John. "You, Gene, and Mike never left my side when I started feeling bad. I've missed that and the three of you every day of my life."

"So have I, John, rest assured, so have I," said Carol. "I remember the good teachers in that meeting and how they came to our defense. I don't remember the bad part of the meeting. We both got to speak, and we had one small victory. Do you remember those wonderful teachers: Mr. Chambers, senior class sponsor and journalism; Mr. Grant, auto mechanics; Mr. Olson, football coach and social studies; Ms. Dombrowski and Mr. Dalton, physical education and swimming; Mr. Eliason, speech and debate; Mr. Kirkland geometry and math; and Mrs. Anders, English?"

"I remember all of them, whether I had them or not," said John.

"I can see my beautiful, kind grandmother holding Gene in her rocking chair when he was so small. And years later we went to see her before we went to senior prom together. She loved you, Gene, and Mike. She thought you were all such nice boys and so handsome," said Carol.

"She was a kind lady, and she loved you too," said John.

"And my dear, sweet Mike, always taking care of me and looking out for me. He was so hurt by the way they treated us by not giving us any awards and taking National Honor Society away from us. He wanted it more for me than he did for himself. He invited you into our group, and it was his idea for you guys to move into the house on Lansing Street with me," said Carol. "Mike did so much for all of us. He was different after Vietnam. He had a head wound, and for a long time, he couldn't seem to think right or study properly when he went to college. He had a hard struggle, but in the end he was successful. Mike didn't like being rich. He would have traded places with any one of us if he could. That is part of the reason why he worked so hard for the homeless veterans. I can see us going to the homeless camp in Kansas City looking for Rodger. I see Nathan,

Terry, and Rodger taking care of you and Gene. They were all so kind and loving to you and Gene."

"Mike had a good heart, and he did love you so very much," said John.

"I know, but there was someone who loved me even more," said Carol. "I always knew since graduation rehearsal. I knew that very night."

"You were right. Mike said he fell in love with you the first time he met you when you were twelve. It was the same for me, but we were both eighteen," said John.

"I can see Dr. Wilson, that great doctor, and Alan's friend, in Dallas. I have never seen a doctor take such a personal interest in a patient as he did in you, and he really helped you. I think more than we realized at the time," said Carol. "And then after the strokes and heart surgery, he helped Gene and became his personal physician."

"And he fell in love with you. I think I knew that long before you did," said John.

"And all those wonderful, caring people we met on that flight from Kansas City to Chicago that fateful day when Gene was so sick. I will never forget how kind Brian and Holly were to you and all of us for that matter. Dr. Landis was so good to Gene, and Captain Robinson was so considerate. And little Billy, do you remember him? He became a doctor just like his dad," said Carol. "Flight 721, I will never forget it. I can still see the plane just as it looked in 1984."

"They were all fine people, and they took such good care of Gene," said John.

"All the suffering Gene went through after his strokes, heart surgery, and depression, what you went through after the accident at the garage and later after that terrible fall, Grandview Beach, my cousin Ethan's death, and Cathy—poor, sweet Cathy—are all locked away. I remember every minute of them, but they don't come to me like the other memories do," said Carol.

"There is someone you have only mentioned in passing. You have said very little about him," said John.

"It has been over thirty-one years, and I still can't think about Gene without crying. He breaks my heart," said Carol as she wiped her eyes. "There are many times that both you and Gene come to me. My first memory of Gene is when he was only eight. He was so tiny and so sick, and he loved to sit on my grandma's lap and hug her. The firemen sent him on a trip to Chicago. His mother, Ethan, my grandma, and I went with him. What those firemen did for Gene in 1954 would now be called make-a-wish, then it didn't have a name. I see you, John, holding my little Julie when she was only three and the basketball team coming to see you in the hospital led by Leon. I see Gene giving your speech at graduation and us walking together in the graduation processional. And the house on Lansing Street, Gene told me once how much he loved that house and those years, and so did I," said Carol.

"I loved it too even though that is where I lived when the accident happened. I still think those were some of the best years we had together," said John.

"I think that was the closest we ever were to one another," said Carol.

John put his arm tighter around Carol and pulled her as close to him as he could.

"Do you remember how Gene always said, if there was any chance that we would ever be together, he wouldn't stand in the way, and he never did," said John. He knew this would be the hardest part for her to talk about, so he continued to hold her close.

"I loved Gene so much. A day doesn't go by that I don't think of him. I remember the good things about him. He was a wonderful, kind man, but he had a dark sense of humor. I never wanted to say it or even think it, but I believe Gene felt his time was limited on this earth. He wanted to do everything in a hurry. I wanted to help him, and I didn't know how." Carol was crying, but she always cried when she spoke or thought of Gene. She knew there was nothing she could do about this, and she wouldn't change it if she could. Her tears were her tribute to him.

"Gene always knew how much you loved him, and he loved you too," said John.

EPILOGUE

Carol would see her beautiful daughter grow into a lovely young woman with a successful career, and she would have a precious daughter of her own. She was very proud of both her daughter and her granddaughter. Greg's two sons whom she had loved and cared for so much would disappear from her life.

Gene would not live to see his two beautiful children grow up. They were seven and eleven when he died. Gene would have been so proud of his son and daughter and the wonderful adults they became. He would have also been proud of Carol's daughter.

All who came in contact with Carol and Gene and those who loved them could feel the genuine caring in their relationship. The kindness, compassion, and sensitive feelings were so strong. If their children would have seen them together, what they felt for one another would have been evident. But it never happened, as was true with so many things in their lives. Carol often wished they could have raised their children together so they would have seen the gentle, tender love she shared with Gene.

They had loved one another for a very long time.

Unfortunately, neither Carol nor Gene had a good marriage. The greatest tragedies of their lives were that they were not together for eternity, and in Gene's case, that he died so young. He was forty-one years old when he died. The love they shared lasted forever, but their forever was not long enough.

Mike once told Carol that if she had been with Gene, he would not have died the way he did or when he did. That may be true, but it didn't happen, so they would never know for sure.

There was a strange guilt that Mike would carry with him to his grave. He always thought he was responsible for Carol and Gene not being together. The only person he ever mentioned this to was Carol, and she tried to assure him that he was not to blame, but he still felt guilty because he had loved them both so much.

ABOUT THE AUTHOR

Carol Brannin (Johanson) was born and raised in Kansas City, Kansas. She now lives in Springfield, Illinois, and has called that city her home after leaving Kansas City, although in the 1980s, she spent a considerable amount of time in Chicago. She has one daughter, Julie, and one granddaughter, Chloe.

In Kansas City, Carol worked for ten years at an insurance company. In Springfield, she worked for a lobbyist for eleven years and in the Pathology Department of Memorial Medical Center for twenty-two years. She has also been a caregiver for seven family members and friends all on a voluntary basis. She feels that being a caregiver is the most rewarding work she has ever done.

This is Carol's first novel, and it was her wonderful friends from long ago who encouraged her to write a book based on their lives and experiences and suggested the title.